I0460315

THE SAGA OF GÖSTA BERLING

By SELMA LAGERLÖF

Translated by PAULINE BANCROFT FLACH

A Digireads.com Book
Digireads.com Publishing

The Saga of Gösta Berling
By Selma Lagerlöf
Translated by Pauline Bancroft Flach
ISBN 10: 1-4209-4809-1
ISBN 13: 978-1-4209-4809-7

This edition copyright © 2013

Please visit *www.digireads.com*

CONTENTS

TRANSLATOR'S PREFACE

"The Story of Gösta Berling" was published in Sweden in 1894 and immediately brought its author into prominence.

The tales are founded on actual occurrences and depict the life in the province of Värmland at the beginning of this century. Värmland is a lonely tract in the southern part of Sweden, and has retained many of its old customs, while mining is the principal industry of its sparse population. It consists of great stretches of forest, sloping down to long, narrow lakes, connected by rivers.

Miss Lagerlöf has grown up in the midst of the wild legends of her country, and, deeply imbued with their spirit, interprets them with a living force all her own.

Her efforts have been materially encouraged by the Crown Prince of Sweden, and there is every reason to expect that her genius has not reached its fullest development.

STOCKHOLM, May, 1898.

INTRODUCTION

I. THE PRIEST

AT last the minister stood in the pulpit. The heads of the congregation were lifted. Well, there he finally was. There would be no default this Sunday, as on the last and on many other Sundays before.

The minister was young, tall, slender, and strikingly handsome. With a helmet on his head, and girt with sword and shirt of mail, he could have been cut in marble and taken for an ideal of Grecian beauty.

He had a poet's deep eyes, and a general's firm, rounded chin; everything about him was beautiful, noble, full of feeling, glowing with genius and spiritual life.

The people in the church felt themselves strangely subdued to see him so. They were more used to see him come reeling out of the public house with his good friends, Beerencreutz, the Colonel with the thick, white moustaches, and the stalwart Captain Christian Bergh.

He had drunk so deeply that he had not been able to attend to his duties for many weeks, and the congregation had been obliged to complain, first to the dean, and then to the bishop and the chapters. Now the bishop had come to the parish to make a strict inquiry. He sat in the choir with the gold cross on his breast; the clergymen of the neighboring parishes sat round about him.

There was no doubt that the minister's conduct had gone beyond the permissible limit. At that time, in the twenties, much in the matter of drinking was overlooked, but this man had deserted his post for the sake of drink, and now must lose it.

He stood in the pulpit and waited while the last verse of the psalm was sung.

A feeling came over him as he stood there, that he had only enemies in the church, enemies in all the seats. Among the gentry in the pews, among the peasants in the farther seats, among the little boys in the choir, he had enemies, none but enemies. It was an enemy who worked the organ-bellows, an enemy who played. In the churchwardens' pews he had enemies. They all hated him, every one,—from the children in arms, who were carried into the church, to the sexton, a formal and stiff old soldier, who had been at Leipsic.

He longed to throw himself on his knees and to beg for mercy.

But a moment after, a dull rage came over him. He remembered well what he had been when, a year ago, he first stood in this pulpit. He was then a blameless man, and now he stood there and looked down on the man with the gold cross on his breast, who had come to pass sentence on him.

While he read the introduction, wave after wave of blood surged up in his face,—it was rage.

It was true enough that he had drunk, but who had a right to blame him for that? Had they seen the vicarage where he had to live? Pine forests grew dark and gloomy close up to his windows. The dampness dripped from the black roofs and ran down the mouldy walls. Was not brandy needed to keep the spirits up when rain and driving snow streamed in through the broken panes, when the neglected earth would not give bread enough to keep hunger away?

He thought that he was just such a minister as they deserved. For they all drank. Why should he alone control himself? The man who had buried his wife got drunk at the funeral feast; the father who had baptized his child had a carouse afterwards. The congregation drank on the way back from church, so that most of them were drunk when they reached home. A drunken priest was good enough for them.

It was on his pastoral visits, when he drove in his thin cloak over miles of frozen seas, where all the icy winds met, it was when his boat was tossed about on these same seas in storm and pouring rain, it was when he must climb out of his sledge in blinding snow to clear the way for his horse through drifts high as houses, or when he waded through the forest swamps,—it was then that he learned to love brandy.

The year had dragged itself out in heavy gloom. Peasant and master had passed their days with their thoughts on the soil, but at evening their spirits cast off their yokes, freed by brandy. Inspiration came, the heart grew warm, life became glowing, the song rang out, roses shed their perfume. The public-house bar-room seemed to him a tropical garden: grapes and olives hung down over his head, marble statues shone among dark leaves, songsters and poets wandered under the palms and plane-trees.

No, he, the priest, up there in the pulpit, knew that without brandy life could not be borne in this end of the world; all his congregation knew that, and yet they wished to judge him.

They wished to tear his vestments from him, because he had come drunken into God's house. Oh, all these people, had they believed, did they want to believe, that they had any other God than brandy?

He had finished the exordium, and he knelt to say the Lord's Prayer.

There was a breathless silence in the church during the prayer. But suddenly the minister with both hands caught hold of the ribbons which held his surplice. It seemed to him as if the whole congregation, with the bishop at the head, were stealing up the pulpit steps to take his bands from him. He was kneeling and his head was turned away, but he could feel how they were dragging, and he saw them so plainly, the bishop and the deans, the clergymen, the churchwardens, the sexton, and the whole assemblage in a long line, tearing and straining to get his surplice off. And he could picture to himself how all these people who were dragging so eagerly would fall over one another down the steps when the bands gave way, and the whole row of them below, who had not got up as far as his cape, but only to the skirts of his coat, would also fall.

He saw it all so plainly that he had to smile as he knelt, but at the same time a cold sweat broke out on his forehead. The whole thing was too horrible.

That he should now become a dishonored man for the sake of brandy. A clergyman, dismissed! Was there anything on God's earth more wretched?

He should be one of the beggars at the roadside, lie drunk at the edge of a ditch, go dressed in rags, with vagrants for companions.

The prayer was ended. He should read his sermon. Then a thought came to him and checked the words on his lips. He thought that it was the last time he should stand in the pulpit and proclaim the glory of God.

For the last time—that took hold of him. He forgot the brandy and the bishop. He thought that he must use the chance, and testify to the glory of God.

He thought that the floor of the church with all his hearers sank deep, deep down, and the roof was lifted off, so that he saw far into the sky. He stood alone, quite alone in his pulpit; his spirit took its flight to the heavens opened above him; his voice became strong and powerful, and he proclaimed the glory of God.

He was inspired. He left what he had written; thoughts came to him like a flock of tame doves. He felt, as if it were not he who spoke, but he felt too that it was the best earth had to give, and that no one could reach a greater height of brilliancy and splendor than he who stood there and proclaimed the glory of God.

As long as the flame of inspiration burned in him he continued to speak, but when it died out, and the roof sank down over the church, and the floor came up again from far, far below, he bowed his head and wept, for he thought that the best of life, for him, was now over.

After the service came the inspection and the vestry meeting. The bishop asked if the congregation had any complaints to make against their clergyman.

The minister was no longer angry and defiant as before the sermon. Now he was ashamed and hung his head. Oh, all the miserable brandy stories, which were coming now!

But none came. There was a deep silence about the long table in the parish-hall.

The minister looked first at the sexton,—no, he was silent; then at the churchwardens, then at the powerful peasants and mine-owners; they were all silent. They sat with their lips pressed close together and looked embarrassed down on the table.

"They are waiting for somebody to begin, "thought the minister.

One of the churchwardens cleared his throat.

"I think we 've got a fine minister," he said.

"Your Reverence has heard how he preaches," interrupted the sexton.

The bishop spoke of repeated absences.

"The minister has the right to be ill, as well as another," was the peasants' opinion.

The bishop hinted at their dissatisfaction with the minister's mode of life.

They defended him with one voice. He was so young, their minister; there was nothing wrong with him. No; if he would only always preach as he had done to-day they would not exchange him for the bishop himself.

There were no accusers; there could be no judge.

The minister felt how his heart swelled and how swiftly the blood flew through his veins. Could it be that he was no longer among enemies; that he had won them over when he had least thought of it; that he should still be their priest?

After the inspection the bishop and the clergymen of the neighborhood and the deans and the chief men of the parish dined at the vicarage. The wife of one of the neighbors had taken charge of the dinner; for the minister was not married. She had arranged it all so well that it made him open his eyes, for the vicarage was not so dreadful. The long dining-table was spread out under the pines and shone with its white cloth, with its blue and white china, its glittering glass and folded napkins. Two birches bent over the door, the floor of the entry was strewn with rushes, a wreath of flowers hung from the rafters, there were flowers in all the rooms; the mouldy smell was gone, and the green window-panes shone bravely in the sunshine.

He was glad to the bottom of his heart, the minister; he thought that he would never drink again.

There was not one who was not glad at that dinner-table. Those who had been generous and had forgiven were glad, and the priests in authority were glad because they had escaped a scandal.

The good bishop raised his glass and said that he had started on this journey with a heavy heart, for he had heard many evil rumors. He had gone forth to meet Saul, but lo, Saul was already changed to a Paul, who should accomplish more than any of them. And the worthy man spoke of the rich gifts which their young brother possessed, and praised them. Not that he should be proud, but that he should strain every nerve and keep a close watch over himself, as he must do who bears an exceedingly heavy and costly burden on his shoulders.

The minister was not drunk at that dinner, but he was intoxicated. All this great unlooked-for happiness went to his head. Heaven had let the flame of inspiration burn in him, and these people had given him their love. His blood was at fever heat, and at raging speed rushed through his veins still when the evening came and his guests departed. Far into the night he sat awake in his room, and let the night air stream in through the open window to cool this fever of happiness, this pleasant restlessness which would not let him sleep.

He heard a voice.

"Are you awake?"

A man came over the lawn up to the window. The minister looked out and recognized Captain Christian Bergh, one of his trusty boon-companions. He was a wayfarer without house or land, this Captain Bergh, and a giant in stature and strength; big was he as Goliath, malicious and stupid as a mountain goblin.

"Of course I am up, Captain Christian," answered the minister. "Do you think I could sleep to-night?"

And hear now what this Captain Bergh says to him! The giant had guessed, he had understood, that the minister would now be afraid to drink. He would never have any peace, thought Captain Christian; for those priests from Karlstad, who had been here once, could come again and take his surplice from him if he drank.

But now Captain Christian had put his heavy hand to the good work; now he had arranged that those priests never should come again, neither they nor the bishop. Henceforth the minister and his friends could drink as much as they liked at the vicarage.

Hear what a deed he had done, he, Christian Bergh, the mighty Captain. When the bishop and the two deans had climbed into their closed carriage, and the doors had been shut tight on them, then he had mounted on the box and driven them ten miles or so in the light summer night.

And then had Christian Bergh taught the reverend gentlemen how loose life sits in the human body. He had let the horses run at the maddest pace. That was because they would not let an honorable man get drunk in peace.

Do you suppose he followed the road with them; do you believe he saved them from jolts? He drove over ditches and ploughed fields; he drove in a dizzy gallop down the hills; he drove along the water's edge, till the waves covered the wheels; he almost stuck in a bog; he drove down over bare rocks, where the horses slid with legs held stiff.

And all the time the bishop and the priests sat with blanched faces behind the leather curtains and murmured prayers. It was the worst journey they had ever made.

And think how they must have looked when they came to Rissäter's inn, living, but shaken like shot in a leather pouch.

"What does this mean, Captain Christian?" says the bishop, as he opens the door for them.

"It means that you shall think twice, bishop, before you make a new journey of inspection to Gösta Berling," says Captain Christian; and he had thought that sentence well out beforehand, so as not to get it wrong.

"Tell Gösta Berling," says the bishop, "that to him neither I nor any other bishop will ever come again."

This exploit the mighty Captain Christian stands and relates at the open window in the summer night. For Captain Christian has only just left the horses at the inn, and has come directly to the minister with his news.

"Now you can be at rest, comrade," he says.

Ah, Captain Christian, the clergymen sat with pale faces behind the leather curtains, but the priest at the window looks in the bright summer night far, far paler. Ah, Captain Christian!

The minister raised his arm and measured a terrible blow at the giant's coarse, stupid face, but checked himself. He shut the window with a bang, and stood in the middle of the room, shaking his clenched fist on high.

He in whom the fire of inspiration had flamed, he who had been able to proclaim the glory of God, stood there and thought that God had made a fool of him.

Would not the bishop believe that Captain Christian had been sent by the minister? Would he not believe that he had dissembled and lied the whole day? Now he would investigate everything about him in earnest; now he would suspend him and dismiss him.

When the dawn broke the minister was far from his home. He did not care to stay and defend himself. God had mocked at him. God would not help him. He knew that he would be dismissed. God would have it. He might as well go at once.

All this happened in the beginning of the twenties in a far-a-way parish in Western Värmland.

It was the first misfortune which befell Gösta Berling; it was not the last.

For colts who cannot bear spur or whips find life hard. For every pain which comes to them they bolt down wild ways to yawning chasms. As soon as the road is stony and the way hard they know no other remedy than to cast off their load and rush away in frenzy.

II. THE BEGGAR

ONE cold December day a beggar came wandering up the slopes of Broby. He was dressed in the most miserable rags, and his shoes were so worn that the cold snow wet his feet.

Löfven is a long, narrow lake in Värmland, intersected in several places by long narrow sounds. In the north it stretches up to the Finn forests, in the south down to the lake Väner. There are many parishes along its shores, but the parish of Bro is the largest and richest. It takes up a large part of the lake's shores both on the east and west sides, but on the west side are the largest estates, such as Ekeby and Björne, known far and wide for wealth and beauty, and Broby, with its large village and inn, court-house, sheriff-quarters, vicarage, and market-place.

Broby lies on a steep slope. The beggar had come past the inn, which lies at the foot of the hill, and was struggling up towards the parsonage, which lies at the top.

A little girl went in front of him up the hill; she dragged a sledge laden with a bag of meal. The beggar caught up with the child and began to talk to her.

"A little horse for such a heavy load," he said.

The child turned and looked at him. She was a little creature about twelve years old, with sharp, suspicious eyes, and lips pressed together.

"Would to God the horse was smaller and the load larger; it might last longer," answered the girl.

"Is it then your own food you are dragging home?"

"By God's grace it is; I have to get my own food, although I am so little."

The beggar seized the sled rope to drag it up.

The girl turned and looked at him.

"You needn't think that you will get anything for this," she said.

The beggar laughed.

"You must be the daughter of the Broby clergyman."

"Yes, yes, I am indeed. Many have poorer fathers, but none have worse. That's the Lord's truth, although it's a shame that his own child should have to say it."

"I hear he is mean and ill-natured, your father."

"Mean he is, and ill-natured he is, but they say his daughter will be worse if she lives so long; that's what people say."

"I fancy people are right. What I would like to know is, where you found this meal-bag."

"It makes no difference if I tell you. I took the grain out of father's store-house this morning, and now I have been to the mill."

"May he not see you when you come dragging it behind you?"

"You have left school too early. Father is away on his parish visits, can't you see?"

"Somebody is driving up the hill behind us; I hear the creaking of the runners. Think if it were he who is coming!"

The girl listened and peered down, then she burst into tears.

"It is father," she sobbed. "He will kill me! He will kill me!"

"Yes, good advice is now precious, and prompt advice better than silver and gold," said the beggar.

"Look here," said the child, "you can help me. Take the rope and drag the sledge; then father will believe it is yours."

"What shall I do with it afterwards?" asked the beggar, and put the rope round his shoulders.

"Take it where you like for the moment, but come up to the parsonage with it when it is dark. I shall be looking out for you. You are to come with the bag and the sledge, you understand."

"I shall try."

"God help you if you don't come!" called the girl, while she ran, hurrying to get home before her father.

The beggar turned the sledge with a heavy heart and dragged it down to the inn.

The poor fellow had had his dream, as he went in the snow with half-naked feet. He had thought of the great woods north of lake Löfven, of the great Finn forests.

Here in the parish of Bro, where he was now wandering along the sound which connects the upper and lower Löfven,—in this rich and smiling country, where one estate joins another, factory lies near factory,—here all the roads seemed to him too heavy, the rooms too small, the beds too hard. Here he longed for the peace of the great, eternal forests.

Here he heard the blows echoing in all the barns as they threshed out the grain. Loads of timber and charcoal-vans kept coming down from the inexhaustible forests. Endless loads of metal followed the deep ruts which the hundreds gone before had cut. Here he saw sleighs filled with travellers speed from house to house, and it seemed to him as if pleasure held the reins, and beauty and love stood on the runners. Oh, how he longed for the peace of the forest.

There the trees rise straight and pillar-like from the even ground, there the snow rests in heavy layers on the motionless pines, there the wind is powerless and only plays softly in the topmost leaves, there he would wander deeper and still farther in, until at last his strength would fail him, and he would drop under the great trees, dying of hunger and cold.

He longed for the great murmuring grave above the Löfven, where he would be overcome by the powers of annihilation, where at last hunger, cold, fatigue, and brandy should succeed in destroying his poor body, which had endured everything.

He came down to the inn to await the evening. He went into the bar-room and threw himself down on a bench by the door, dreaming of the eternal forests.

The innkeeper's wife felt sorry for him and gave him a glass of brandy. She even gave him another, he implored her so eagerly.

But more she would not give him, and the beggar was in despair. He must have more of the strong, sweet brandy. He must once again feel his heart dance in his body and his thoughts flame up in intoxication. Oh, that sweet spirit of the corn!

The summer sun, the song of the birds, perfume and beauty floated in its white wave. Once more, before he disappears into the night and the darkness, let him drink sunshine and happiness.

So he bartered first the meal, then the meal-sack, and last the sledge, for brandy. On it he got thoroughly drunk, and slept the greater part of the afternoon on a bench in the bar-room.

When he awoke he understood that there was left for him only one thing to do. Since his miserable body had taken possession of his soul, since he had been capable of drinking up what a child had confided to him, since he was a disgrace to the earth, he must free it of the burden of such wretchedness. He must give his soul its liberty, let it go to its God.

He lay on the bench in the bar-room and passed sentence on himself: "Gösta Berling, dismissed priest, accused of having drunk up the food of a hungry child, is condemned to death. What death? Death in the snow-drifts."

He seized his cap and reeled out. He was neither quite awake nor quite sober. He wept in pity for himself, for his poor, soiled soul, which he must set free.

He did not go far, and did not turn from the road. At the very roadside lay a deep drift, and there he threw himself down to die. He closed his eyes and tried to sleep.

No one knows how long he lay there; but there was still life in him when the daughter of the minister of Broby came running along the road with a lantern in her hand, and found him in the drift by the roadside. She had stood for hours and waited for him; now she had run down Broby hill to look for him.

She recognized him instantly, and she began to shake him and to scream with all her might to get him awake.

She must know what he had done with her meal-bag.

She must call him back to life, at least for so long a time that he could tell her what had become of her sledge and her meal-bag. Her father would kill her if she had lost his sledge. She bit the beggar's finger and scratched his face, and at the same time she screamed madly.

Then some one came driving along the road.

"Who the devil is screaming so?" asked a harsh voice.

"I want to know what this fellow has done with my meal-bag and my sledge," sobbed the child, and beat with clenched fists on the beggar's breast.

"Are you clawing a frozen man? Away with you, wild-cat!"

The traveller was a large and coarse woman. She got out of the sleigh and came over to the drift. She took the child by the back of the neck and threw her on one side. Then she leaned over, thrust her arms under the beggar's body, and lifted him up. Then she carried him to the sleigh and laid him in it.

"Come with me to the inn, wild-cat," she called to the child, "that we may hear what you know of all this."

An hour later the beggar sat on a chair by the door in the best room of the inn, and in front of him stood the powerful woman who had rescued him from the drift.

Just as Gösta Berling now saw her, on her way home from the charcoal kilns, with sooty hands, and a clay-pipe in her mouth, dressed in a short, unlined sheepskin jacket and striped homespun skirt, with tarred shoes on her feet and a sheath-knife in her bosom, as he saw her with gray hair combed back from an old, beautiful face, so had he heard her described a thousand times, and he knew that he had come across the far-famed major's wife of Ekeby.

She was the most influential woman in all Värmland, mistress of seven iron-works, accustomed to command and to be obeyed; and he was only a poor, condemned man, stripped of everything, knowing that every road was too heavy for him, every room too crowded. His body shook with terror, while her glance rested on him.

She stood silent and looked at the human wretchedness before her, the red, swollen hands, the emaciated form, and the splendid head, which even in its ruin and neglect shone in wild beauty.

"You are Gösta Berling, the mad priest?" she said, peering at him.

The beggar sat motionless.

"I am the mistress of Ekeby."

A shudder passed over the beggar's body. He clasped his hands and raised his eyes with a longing glance. What would she do with him? Would she force him to live? He shook before her strength. And yet he had so nearly reached the peace of the eternal forests.

She began the struggle by telling him the minister's daughter had got her sledge and her meal-sack again, and that she, the major's wife, had a shelter for him as for so many other homeless wretches in the bachelor's wing at Ekeby.

She offered him a life of idleness and pleasure, but he answered he must die.

Then she struck the table with her clenched fist and let him hear what she thought of him.

"So you want to die, that's what you want. That would not surprise me, if you were alive. Look, such a wasted body and such powerless limbs and such dull eyes, and you think that there is something left of you to die. Do you think that you have to lie stiff and stark with a coffin-lid nailed down over you to be dead? Don't you believe that I stand here and see how dead you are, Gösta Berling?

"I see that you have a skull for a head, and it seems to me as if the worms were creeping out of the sockets of your eyes. Do you not feel that your mouth is full of dust? Do you not hear how your bones rattle when you move?

"You have drowned yourself in brandy, Gösta Berling, and you are dead.

"That which now moves in you is only death spasms, and you will not allow them to live, if you call that life. It is just as if you grudged the dead a dance over the graves in the star-light.

"Are you ashamed that you were dismissed, since you wish to die now? It would have been more to your honor had you made use of your gifts and been of some use on God's green earth, I tell you. Why did you not come directly to me? I should have arranged everything for you. Yes, now you expect much glory from being wrapped in a winding-sheet and laid on saw-dust and called a beautiful corpse."

The beggar sat calm, almost smiling, while she thundered out her angry words. There was no danger, he rejoiced, no danger. The eternal forests wait, and she has no power to turn thy soul from them.

But the major's wife was silent and walked a couple of times up and down the room; then she took a seat before the fire, put her feet on the fender, and leaned her elbows on her knees.

"Thousand devils!" she said, and laughed softly to herself. "It is truer, what I am saying, than I myself thought. Don't you believe, Gösta Berling, that most of the people in this world are dead or half-dead? Do you think that I am alive? No! No, indeed!

"Yes, look at me! I am the mistress of Ekeby, and I am the most powerful in Värmland. If I wave one finger the governor comes, if I wave with two the bishop comes, and if I wave with three all the chapter and the aldermen and mine-owners in Värmland dance to my music in Karlstad's market-place. A thousand devils! Boy, I tell you that I am only a dressed-up corpse. God knows how little life there is in me."

The beggar leaned forward on his chair and listened with strained attention. The old woman sat and rocked before the fire. She did not look at him while she talked.

"Don't you know," she continued, "that if I were a living being, and saw you sitting there, wretched and deplorable with suicidal thoughts, don't you believe that I should take them out of you in a second? I should have tears for you and prayers, which would turn you upside down, and I should save your soul; but now I am dead.

"Have you heard that I once was the beautiful Margareta Celsing? That was not yesterday, but I can still sit and weep my old eyes red for her. Why shall Margareta Celsing be dead, and Margareta Samzelius live? Why shall the major's wife at Ekeby live?—tell me that, Gösta Berling.

"Do you know what Margareta Celsing was like? She was slender and delicate and modest and innocent, Gösta Berling. She was one over whose grave angels weep.

"She knew nothing of evil, no one had ever given her pain, she was good to all. And she was beautiful, really beautiful.

"There was a man, his name was Altringer. God knows how he happened to be travelling up there in Älfdal wildernesses, where her parents had their ironworks. Margareta Celsing saw him, he was a handsome man, and she loved him.

"But he was poor, and they agreed to wait for one another five years, as it is in the legend. When three years had passed another suitor came. He was ugly and bad, but her parents believed that he was rich, and they forced Margareta Celsing, by fair means and foul, by blows and hard words, to take him for her husband. And that day, you see, Margareta Celsing died.

"After that there was no Margareta Celsing, only Major Samzelius's wife, and she was not good nor modest; she believed in much evil and never thought of the good.

"You know well enough what happened afterwards. We lived at Sjö by the Lake Löfven, the major and I. But he was not rich, as people had said. I often had hard days.

"Then Altringer came again, and now he was rich. He became master of Ekeby, which lies next to Sjö; he made himself master of six other estates by Lake Löfven. He was able, thrifty; he was a man of mark.

"He helped us in our poverty; we drove in his carriages; he sent food to our kitchen, wine to our cellar. He filled my life with feasting and pleasure. The major went off to the wars, but what did we care for that? One day I was a guest at Ekeby, the next he came to Sjö. Oh, it was like a long dance of delight on Löfven's shores.

"But there was evil talk of Altringer and me. If Margareta Celsing had been living, it would have given her much pain, but it made no difference to me. But as yet I did not understand that it was because I was dead that I had no feeling.

"At last the tales of us reached my father and mother, as they went among the charcoal kilns up in Älfdal's forest. My mother did not stop to think; she travelled hither to talk to me.

"One day, when the major was away and I sat dining with Altringer and several others, she arrived. I saw her come into the room, but I could not feel that she was my mother, Gösta Berling. I greeted her as a stranger, and invited her to sit down at my table and take part in the meal.

"She wished to talk with me, as if I had been her daughter, but I said to her that she was mistaken, that my parents were dead, they had both died on my wedding day.

"Then she agreed to the comedy. She was sixty years old; a hundred and twenty miles had she driven in three days. Now she sat without ceremony at the dinner-table and ate her food; she was a strong and capable woman.

"She said that it was very sad that I had had such a loss just on that day.

"'The saddest thing was,' I said, 'that my parents did not die a day sooner; then the wedding would never have taken place.'

"'Is not the gracious lady pleased with her marriage?' she then asked.

"'Oh, yes,' said I, 'I am pleased. I shall always be pleased to obey my dear parents' wish!'

"She asked if it had been my parents' wish that I should heap shame upon myself and them and deceive my husband. I did my parents little honor by making myself a byword in every man's mouth.

"'They must lie as they have made their bed,' I answered her. And moreover I wished her to understand, that I did not intend to allow any one to calumniate my parents' daughter.

"We ate, we two. The men about us sat silent and could not lift knife nor fork.

"She stayed a day to rest, then she went. But all the time I saw her, I could not understand that she was my mother. I only knew that my mother was dead.

"When she was ready to leave, Gösta Berling, and I stood beside her on the steps, and the carriage was before the door, she said to me:—

"'Twenty-four hours have I been here, without your greeting me as your mother. By lonely roads I came here, a hundred and twenty miles in three days. And for shame for you my body is trembling, as if it had been beaten with rods. May you be disowned, as I have been disowned, repudiated as I have been repudiated! May the highway be your home, the haystack your bed, the charcoal-kiln your stove! May shame and dishonor be your reward; may others strike you, as I strike you!'

"And she gave me a heavy blow on the cheek.

"But I lifted her up, carried her down the steps, and put her in her carriage.

"'Who are you, that you curse me?' I asked; 'who are you that you strike me? That I will suffer from no one.'

"And I gave her the blow again.

"The carriage drove away, but then, at that moment, Gösta Berling, I knew that Margareta Celsing was dead.

"She was good and innocent; she knew no evil. Angels had wept at her grave. If she had lived, she would not have struck her mother."

The beggar by the door had listened, and the words for a moment had drowned the sound of the eternal forests' alluring murmur. For see, this great lady, she made herself his equal in sin, his sister in perdition, to give him courage to live. For he should learn that sorrow and wrong-doing weighed down other heads than his. He rose and went over to the major's wife.

"Will you live now? Gösta Berling?" she asked with a voice which broke with tears. "Why should you die? You could have been such a good priest, but it was never Gösta Berling whom you drowned in brandy, he as gleamingly innocent-white as that Margareta Celsing I suffocated in hate. Will you live?"

Gösta fell on his knees before her.

"Forgive me," he said, "I cannot."

"I am an old woman, hardened by much sorrow," answered the major's wife, "and I sit here and give myself as a prize to a beggar, whom I have found half-frozen in a snow-drift by the roadside. It serves me right. Let him go and kill himself; then at least he won't be able to tell of my folly."

"I am no suicide, I am condemned to die. Do not make the struggle too hard for me! I may not live. My body has taken possession of my soul, therefore I must let it escape and go to God."

"And so you believe you will get there?"

"Farewell, and thank you!"

"Farewell, Gösta Berling."

The beggar rose and walked with hanging head and dragging step to the door. This woman made the way up to the great forests heavy for him.

When he came to the door, he had to look back. Then he met her glance, as she sat still and looked after him. He had never seen such a change in any face, and he stood and stared at her. She, who had just been angry and threatening, sat transfigured, and her eyes shone with a pitying, compassionate love.

There was something in him, in his own wild heart, which burst before that glance; he leaned his forehead against the door-post, stretched his arms up over his head, and wept as if his heart would break.

The major's wife tossed her clay pipe into the fire and came over to Gösta. Her movements were as tender as a mother's.

"There, there, my boy!"

And she got him down beside her on the bench by the door, so that he wept with his head on her knees.

"Will you still die?"

Then he wished to rush away. She had to hold him back by force.

"Now I tell you that you may do as you please. But I promise you that, if you will live, I will take to me the daughter of the Broby minister and make a human being of her, so that she can thank her God that you stole her meal. Now will you?"

He raised his head and looked her right in the eyes.

"Do you mean it?"

"I do, Gösta Berling."

Then he wrung his hands in anguish. He saw before him the peering eyes, the compressed lips, the wasted little hands. This young creature would get protection and care, and the marks of degradation be effaced from her body, anger from her soul. Now the way up to the eternal forests was closed to him.

"I shall not kill myself as long as she is under your care," he said. "I knew well enough that you would force me to live. I felt that you were stronger than I."

"Gösta Berling," she said solemnly, "I have fought for you as for myself. I said to God: 'If there is anything of Margareta Celsing living in me, let her come forward and show herself, so that this man may not go and kill himself.' And He granted it, and you saw her, and therefore you could not go. And she whispered to me that for that poor child's sake you would give up your plan of dying. Ah, you fly, you wild birds, but our Lord knows the net which will catch you."

"He is a great and wonderful God," said Gösta Berling. "He has mocked me and cast me out, but He will not let me die. May His will be done!"

From that day Gösta Berling became a guest at Ekeby. Twice he tried to leave and make himself a way to live by his own work. The first time the major's wife gave him a cottage near Ekeby; he moved thither and meant to live as a laborer. This succeeded for a while, but he soon wearied of the loneliness and the daily labor, and again returned as a guest. There was another time, when he became tutor at Borg for Count Henry Dohna. During this time he fell in love with the young Ebba Dohna, the count's sister; but when she died, just as thought he had nearly won her, he gave up every thought of being anything but guest at Ekeby. It seemed to him that for dismissed priest all ways to make amends were closed.

PART I

CHAPTER I. THE LANDSCAPE

I MUST now describe the long lake, the rich plains and the blue mountains, since they were the scene where Gösta Berling and the other knights of Ekeby passed their joyous existence.

The lake has its sources far up in the north, and it is a perfect country for a lake. The forest and the mountains never cease to collect water for it; rivulets and brooks stream into it the whole year round. It has fine white sand to stretch itself over, headlands and islands to mirror and to look at, river sprites and sea nymphs have free play room there, and it quickly grows large and beautiful. There, in the north, it is smiling and friendly; one needs but to see it on a summer morning, when it lies half awake under a veil of mist, to perceive how gay it is. It plays first for a while, creeps softly, softly, out of its light covering, so magically beautiful that one can hardly recognize it; but then it casts from it, suddenly, the whole covering, and lies there bare and uncovered and rosy, shining in the morning light.

But the lake is not content with this life of play; it draws itself together to a narrow strait, breaks its way out through the sand-hills to the south, and seeks out a new kingdom for itself. And such a one it also finds; it gets larger and more powerful, has bottomless depths to fill, and a busy landscape to adorn. And now its water is darker, its shores less varying, its winds sharper, its whole character more severe. It has become a stately and magnificent lake. Many are the ships and the rafts of timber which pass there; late in the year it finds time to take its winter rest, rarely before Christmas. Often is it in peevish mood, when it grows white with wrath and drags down sailing-boats; but it can also lie in a dreamy calm and reflect the heavens.

But still farther out into the world will the lake go, although the mountains become bolder and space narrower; still farther down it comes, so that it once again must creep as a narrow strait between sand-bound shores. Then it broadens out for the third time, but no longer with the same beauty and might.

The shores sink down and become tame, gentler winds blow, the lake takes its winter rest early. It is still beautiful, but it has lost youth's giddiness and manhood's strength—it is now a lake like any other. With two arms it gropes after a way to Lake Vänern, and when that is found it throws itself with the feebleness of old age over the slopes and goes with a last thundering leap to rest.

The plain is as long as the lake; but it has no easy time to find a place between sea and mountain, all the way from the valley of the basin at the lake's northern end, where it first dares to spread itself out, till it lays itself to easy rest by the Vänern's shore. There is no doubt that the plain would rather follow the shore of the lake, long as it is, but the mountains give it no peace. The mountains are mighty granite walls, covered with woods, full of cliffs difficult to cross, rich in moss and lichen,—in those old days the home of many wild things.

On the far-stretching ridges one often comes upon a wet swamp or a pool with dark water. Here and there is a charcoal kiln or an open patch where timber and wood have been cut, or a burnt clearing, and these all bear witness that there is work going on on the mountains; but as a rule they lie in careless peace and amuse themselves with watching the lights and shadows play over their slopes.

And with these mountains the plain, which is peaceful and rich, and loves work, wages a perpetual war, in a friendly spirit, however.

"It is quite enough," says the plain to the mountains; "if you set up your walls about me, that is safety enough for me."

But the mountains will not listen. They send out long rows of hills and barren table-lands way down to the lake. They raise great look-out towers on every promontory, and leave the shores of the lake so seldom that the plain can but rarely stretch itself out by the soft, broad sands. But it does not help to complain.

"You ought to be glad that we stand here," the mountains say. "Think of that time before Christmas, when the icy fogs, day after day, rolled up from the Löfven. We do you good service."

The plain complains that it has no space and an ugly view.

"You are so stupid," answer, the mountains; "if you could only feel how it is blowing down here by the lake. One needs at least a granite back and a fir-tree jacket to withstand it. And, besides, you can be glad to have us to look at."

Yes, looking at the mountains, that is just what the plain is doing. It knows so well all the wonderful shiftings of light and shade, which pass over them. It knows how they sink down in the noonday heat towards the horizon, low and a dim light-blue, and in the morning or evening light raise their venerable heights, clear blue as the sky at noon.

Sometimes the light falls so sharply over them that they look green or dark-blue, and every separate fir-tree, each path and cleft, is visible miles away.

There are places where the mountains draw back and allow the plain to come forward and gaze at the lake. But when it sees the lake in its anger, hissing and spitting like a wildcat, or sees it covered with that cold mist which happens when the sea-sprite is busy with brewing or washing, then it agrees that the mountains were right, and draws back to its narrow prison again.

Men have cultivated the beautiful plain time out of mind, and have built much there. Wherever a stream in white foaming falls throws itself down the slope, rose up factories and mills. On the bright, open places, where the plain came down to the lake, churches and vicarages were built; but on the edges of the valley, half-way up the slope, on stony grounds, where grain would not grow, lie farmhouses and officers' quarters, and here and there a manor.

Still, in the twenties, this district was not nearly so much cultivated as now. Many were the woods and lakes and swamps which now can be tilled. There were not so many people either, and they earned their living partly by carting and day labor at the many factories, partly by working at neighboring places; agriculture could not feed them. At that time they went dressed in homespun, ate oatcakes, and were satisfied with a wage of ten cents a day. Many were in great want; but life was often made easier for them by a light and glad temper, and by an inborn handiness and capability.

And all those three, the long lake, the rich plain, and the blue mountains, made the most beautiful scenery, and still do, just as the people are still to this day, strong, brave and intelligent. Great progress has been made, however, in prosperity and culture.

May everything go well with those who live far away by the long lake and the blue mountains! I shall now recall some of their memories.

CHAPTER II. CHRISTMAS EVE

SINTRAM is the name of the wicked master of the works at Fors, with his clumsy ape-body, and his long arms, with his bald head and ugly, grinning face,—he whose delight is to make mischief.

Sintram it is who takes only vagrants and bullies for workmen, and has only quarrelsome, lying maids in his service; he who excites dogs to madness by sticking pins in their noses, and lives happiest among evil people and fierce beasts.

It is Sintram whose greatest pleasure is to dress himself up in the foul fiend's likeness, with horns, and tail, and cloven hoof, and hairy body, and suddenly appearing from dark corners, from behind the stove or the wood-pile, to frighten timid children and superstitious women.

It is Sintram who delights to change old friendship to new hate, and to poison the heart with lies.

Sintram is his name—and one day he came to Ekeby.

Drag the great wood-sledge into the smithy, put it in the middle of the floor, and lay a cart-bottom on the frame! There we have a table. Hurrah for the table; the table is ready!

Come now with chairs, with everything which will serve for a seat! Come with three-legged stools and empty boxes! Come with ragged old arm-chairs without any backs, and push up the runnerless sleigh and the old coach! Ha, ha, ha, up with the old coach; it shall be the speaker's chair!

Just look; one wheel gone, and the whole bottom out! Only the coach-box is left. The cushion is thin and worn, its moss stuffing coming through, the leather is red with age. High as a house is the old wreck. Prop it up, prop it up, or down it will come!

Hurrah! Hurrah! It is Christmas eve at Ekeby.

Behind the broad bed's silken curtains sleep the major and the major's wife, sleep and believe that the bachelors' wing sleeps. The men-servants and maids can sleep, heavy with feasting and the bitter Christmas ale; but not their masters in the bachelors' wing. How can any one think that the bachelors' wing sleeps?

Sleeps, sleeps (oh, child of man, sleeps!), when the pensioners are awake. The long tongs stand upright on the floor, with tallow candles in their claws. From the mammoth kettle of shining copper flames the blue fire of the burning brandy, high up to the dark roof. Beerencreutz's horn-lantern hangs on the forge-hammer. The yellow punch glows in the bowl like a bright sun. The pensioners are celebrating Christmas eve in the smithy.

There is mirth and bustle. Fancy, if the major's wife should see them!

What then? Probably she would sit down with them and empty a bumper. She is a doughty woman; she's not afraid of a thundering drinking-song or to take a hand at *kille*.[1] The richest woman in Värmland, as bold as a man, proud as a queen. Songs she loves, and sounding fiddles, and the hunting-horn. She likes wine and games of cards, and tables surrounded by merry guests are her delight. She likes to see the larder emptied, to have dancing and merry-making in chamber and hall, and the bachelors' wing full of pensioners.

See them round about the bowl! Twelve are they, twelve men. Not butterflies nor dandies, but men whose fame will not soon die out in Värmland; brave men and strong.

---

[1] A Swedish game of cards.

Not dried-up parchment, nor close-fisted moneybags; poor men, without a care, gentlemen the whole day long.

No mother's darlings, no sleepy masters on their own estates. Wayfaring men, cheerful men, knights of a hundred adventures.

Now for many years the bachelors' wing has stood empty. Ekeby is no longer the chosen refuge of homeless gentlemen. Pensioned officers and impoverished noblemen no longer drive about Värmland in shaky one-horse vehicles. But let the dead live, Jet them rise up in their glad, careless, eternal youth!

All these notorious men could play on one or several instruments. All were as full of wit and humor and conceits and songs as an ant-hill is full of ants; but each one had his particular great quality, his much esteemed merit which distinguished him from the others.

First of all who sit about the bowl will I name Beerencreutz, the colonel with the great white moustaches, player of cards, singer of songs; and next to him, his friend and brother in arms, the silent major, the great bear-hunter, Anders Fuchs; and, as the third in order, little Ruster, the drummer, who had been for many years the coloners servant, but had won the rank of pensioner through his skill in brewing punch and his knowledge of thoroughbass. Then may be mentioned the old ensign, Rutger von Örneclou, lady-killer, dressed in stock and wig and ruffles, and painted like a woman,—he was one of the most important pensioners; also Christian Bergh, the mighty captain, who was a stalwart hero, but as easy to outwit as a giant in the fairy story. In these two men's company one often saw the little, round Master Julius, witty, merry, and gifted, speaker, painter, songster, and storyteller. He often had his joke with the gout-crippled ensign and the dull giant.

There was also the big German Kevenhüller, inventor of the automatic carriage and the flying-machine, he whose name still echoes in the murmuring forests,—a nobleman by birth and in appearance, with great curled moustaches, a pointed beard, aquiline nose, and narrow, squinting eyes in a net of intersecting wrinkles. There sat the great warrior cousin, Christopher, who never went outside the walls of the bachelors' wing unless there was to be a bear-hunt or some foolhardy adventure; and beside him Uncle Eberhard, the philosopher, who had not come to Ekeby for pleasure and play, but in order to be able, undisturbed by concern for daily bread, to complete his great work in the science of sciences.

Last of all, and the best, the gentle Lövenborg, who sought the good in the world, and understood little of its ways, and Lilliecrona, the great musician, who had a good home, and was always longing to be there, but still remained at Ekeby, for his soul needed riches and variety to be able to bear life.

These eleven men had all left youth behind them, and several were in old age; but in the midst of them was one who was not more than thirty years old, and still possessed the full, undiminished strength of his mind and body. It was Gösta Berling, the Knight of Knights, who alone in himself was a better speaker, singer, musician, hunter, drinking companion and card-player than all of the others together. He possessed all gifts. What a man the major's wife had made of him!

Look at him now in the speaker's chair! The darkness sinks from the black roof in great festoons over him. His blond head shines through it like a young god's. Slender, beautiful, eager for adventure, he stands there.

But he is speaking very seriously.

"Gentlemen and brothers, the time passes, the feast is far advanced, it is time to drink a toast to the thirteenth at the table!"

"Little brother Gösta," cries Master Julius, "there is no thirteenth; we are only twelve."

"At Ekeby a man dies every year," continues Gösta with a more and more gloomy voice. "One of the guests of the bachelors' wing dies, one of the glad, the careless, the eternal youth dies. What of that? Gentlemen should never be old. Could our trembling hands not lift a glass, could our quenched eyes not distinguish the cards, what has life for us, and what are we for life? One must die of the thirteen who celebrate Christmas eve in the smithy at Ekeby; but every year a new one comes to complete our number; a man, experienced in pleasure, one who can handle violin and card, must come and make our company complete. Old butterflies should know how to die while the summer sun is shining. A toast to the thirteenth!"

"But, Gösta, we are only twelve," remonstrate the pensioners, and do not touch their glasses.

Gösta Berling, whom they called the poet, although he never wrote verses, continues with unaltered calmness: "Gentlemen and brothers! Have you forgotten who you are? You are they who hold pleasure by force in Värmland. You are they who set the fiddle-bows going, keep up the dance, make song and music resound through the land. You know how to keep your hearts from the love of gold, your hands from work. If you did not exist the dance would die, summer die, the roses die, card-playing die, song die, and in this whole blessed land there would be nothing but iron and owners of iron-works. Pleasure lives while you live. For six years have I celebrated Christmas eve in the Ekeby smithy, and never before has any one refused to drink to the thirteenth."

"But, Gösta," cry they all, "when we are only twelve how can we drink to the thirteenth?"

"Are we only twelve?" he says. "Why must we die out from the earth? Shall we be but eleven next year, but ten the year after. Shall our name become a legend, our company destroyed? I call upon him, the thirteenth, for I have stood up to drink his toast. From the ocean's depths, from the bowels of the earth, from heaven, from hell I call him who shall complete our number."

Then it rattled in the chimney, then the furnace-door opened, then the thirteenth came.

He was hairy, with tail and cloven-hoof, with horns and a pointed beard, and at the sight of him the pensioners start up with a cry.

But in uncontrollable joy Gösta Berling cries, "The thirteenth has come—a toast to the thirteenth!"

Yes, he has come, the old enemy of mankind, come to these foolhardy men who trouble the peace of the Holy Night. The friend of witches on their way to hell, who signs his bargains in blood on coal-black paper, he who danced with the countess at Ivarsnäs for seven days, and could not be exorcized by seven priests,—he has come.

In stormy haste thoughts fly through the heads of the old adventurers at the sight of him. They wonder for whose sake he is out this night.

Many of them were ready to hurry away in terror, but they soon saw that the horned one had not come to carry them down to his dark kingdom, but that the ring of the cups and their songs had attracted him. He wished to enjoy a little human pleasure in this holy night, and cast aside his burden during this glad time.

Oh, pensioners, pensioners, who of you now remembers it is the night before Christmas; that even now angels are singing for the shepherds in the fields? Children are lying anxious lest they sleep too soundly, that they may not wake in time for the beautiful morning worship. Soon it will be time to light the Christmas candles in the church at Bro, and far away in the forest homes the young man in the evening has prepared a resin torch to light his girl to church. In all the houses the mistress has placed dip-lights in the windows, ready to light as the people go by to church. The sexton takes up the Christmas psalm in his sleep, and the old minister lies and tries if he has enough voice left to sing: "Glory be to God on high, on earth peace, good-will towards men!"

Oh, pensioners, better had it been for you if you had spent this peaceful night quietly in your beds than to trouble the company with the Prince of Darkness.

But they greet him with cries of welcome, as Gösta had done. A goblet filled with burning brandy is placed in his hand. They give him the place of honor at the table, and they look upon him with gladness, as if his ugly satyr face wore the delicate features of their youth's first love.

Beerencreutz invites him to a game of cards, Master Julius sings his best songs for him, and Örneclou talks to him of lovely women, those beautiful creatures who make life sweet.

He enjoys everything, the devil, as with princely bearing he leans back on the old coach-box, and with clawed hand lifts the brimming goblet to his smiling mouth.

But Gösta Berling of course must make a speech in his honor.

"Your Grace," he says, "we have long awaited you here at Ekeby, for you have little access, we suppose, to any other paradise. Here one can live without toiling or spinning, as your Grace perhaps knows. Here roasted ortolans fly into one's mouth, and the bitter ale and the sweet brandy flow in brooks and rivulets. This is a good place, your Grace! We pensioners have waited for you, I tell you, for we have never been complete before. See, we are something finer than we seem; we are the mighty twelve of the poet, who are of all time. We were twelve when we steered the world, up there on Olympus's cloud-veiled top, and twelve when we lived like birds in Ygdrasil's green crown. Wherever there has been poetry there have we followed. Did we not sit twelve men strong about King Arthur's Round Table, and were there not twelve paladins at Charlemagne's court? One of us has been a Thor, a Jupiter; any one can see that in us now. They can perceive the divine splendor under our rags, the lion's mane under the ass's head. Times are bad with us, but if we are there a smithy becomes Olympus and the bachelors' wing Valhalla.

"But, your Grace, our number has not been complete. Every one knows that in the poet's twelve there must always be a Loki, a Prometheus. Him have we been without.

"Your Grace, I wish you welcome!"

"Hear, hear, hear!" says the evil one; "such a fine speech, a fine speech indeed! And I, who have no time to answer. Business, boys, business. I must be off, otherwise I should so gladly be at your service in any rôle you like. Thanks for a pleasant evening, old gossips. We shall meet again."

Then the pensioners demand where he is going; and he answers that the noble major's wife, mistress of Ekeby, is waiting for him to get her contract renewed.

Great wonder seizes upon the pensioners.

A harsh and capable woman is she, the major's wife at Ekeby. She can lift a barrel of flour on her broad shoulders. She follows the loads of ore from the Bergslagen mines, on the long road to Ekeby. She sleeps like a waggoner on the stable floor, with a meal-bag under her head. In the winter she will watch by a charcoal kiln, in the summer follow a timber-raft down to the Löfven. She is a powerful woman. She swears like a trooper, and rules over her seven estates like a king; rules her own parish and all the neighboring parishes; yes, the whole of lovely Värmland. But for the homeless gentlemen she had been like a mother, and therefore they had closed their ears when slander had whispered to them that she was in league with the devil.

So they ask him with wonder what kind of a contract she has made with him.

And he answers them, the black one, that he had given the major's wife her seven estates on the condition that she should send him every year a human soul.

Oh, the horror which compresses the pensioners' hearts!

Of course they knew it, but they had not understood before.

At Ekeby every year, a man dies, one of the guests in the bachelors' wing dies, one of the glad, the careless, the ever young dies. What of that?—gentlemen may not be old! If their trembling fingers cannot lift the glass, if their dulled eyes cannot see the cards, what has life for them, and what are they to life? Butterflies should know how to die while the sun is shining.

But now, now for the first time, they grasp its real meaning.

Woe to that woman! That is why she had given them so many good meals, why she had let them drink her bitter ale and her sweet brandy, that they might reel from the drinking-halls and the card-tables at Ekeby down to the king of hell,—one a year, one for each passing year.

Woe to the woman, the witch! Strong men had come to this Ekeby, had come hither to perish. For she had destroyed them here. Their brains were as sponges, dry ashes their lungs, and darkness their spirit, as they sank back on their death-beds and were ready for their long journey, hopeless, soulless, virtueless.

Woe to the woman! So had those died who had been better men than they, and so should they die.

But not long are they paralyzed by weight of terror.

"You king of perdition!" they cry, "never again shall you make a blood-signed contract with that witch; she shall die! Christian Bergh, the mighty captain, has thrown over his shoulder the heaviest sledge-hammer in the smithy. He will bury it to the handle in the hag's head. No more souls shall she sacrifice to you.

"And you, you horned thing, we shall lay you on the anvil and let the forge-hammer loose. We shall hold you quiet with tongs under the hammer's blows and teach you to go a-hunting for gentlemen's souls."

He is a coward, the devil, as every one knows of old, and all this talk of the forge-hammer does not please him at all. He calls Christian Bergh back and begins to bargain with the pensioners.

"Take the seven estates; take them yourselves, gentlemen, and give me the major's wife!"

"Do you think we are as base as she?" cries Master Julius. "We will have Ekeby and all the rest, but you must look after the majors wife yourself."

"What does Gösta say? what does Gösta say?" asks the gentle Löwenborg. "Gösta Berling must speak. We must hear what he thinks of this important matter."

"It is madness," says Gösta Berling. "Gentlemen, don't let him make fools of you! What are you all against the major's wife? It may fare as it will with our souls, but with my consent we will not be such ungrateful wretches as to act like rascals and traitors. I have eaten her food for too many years to deceive her now."

"Yes, you can go to hell, Gösta, if you wish! We would rather rule at Ekeby."

"But are you all raving, or have you drunk away your wits? Do you believe it is true? Do you believe that that thing is the devil? Don't you see that it's all a confounded lie?"

"Tut, tut, tut," says the black one; "he does not see that he will soon be ready, and yet he has been seven years at Ekeby. He does not see how far advanced he is."

"Begone, man! I myself have helped to shove you into the oven there."

"As if that made any difference; as if I were not as good a devil as another. Yes, yes, Gösta Berling, you are in for it. You have improved, indeed, under her treatment."

"It was she who saved me," says Gösta. "What had I been without her?"

"As if she did not know what she was about when she kept you here at Ekeby. You can lure others to the trap; you have great gifts. Once you tried to get away from her; you let her give you a cottage, and you became a laborer; you wished to earn your bread. Every day she passed your cottage, and she had lovely young girls with her. Once it was Marianne Sinclair; then you threw aside your spade and apron, Gösta Berling, and came back as pensioner."

"It lay on the highway, you fool."

"Yes, yes, of course; it lay on the highway. Then you came to Borg, were tutor there to Henrik Dohna, and might have been Countess Märta's son-in-law. Who was it who managed that the young Ebba Dohna should hear that you were only a dismissed priest, so that she refused you? It was the major's wife, Gösta Berling. She wanted you back again."

"Great matter!" says Gösta. "Ebba Dohna died soon afterwards. I would never have got her anyway."

Then the devil came close up to him and hissed right in his face: "Died! yes, of course she died. Killed herself for your sake, did she? But they never told you that."

"You are not such a bad devil," says Gösta.

"It was the major's wife who arranged it all, I tell you. She wanted to have you back in the bachelors' wing."

Gösta burst out laughing.

"You are not such a bad devil," he cried wildly. "Why should we not make a contract with you? I'm sure you can get us the seven estates if you like."

"It is well that you do not longer withstand your fate."

The pensioners drew a sigh of relief. It had gone so far with them that they could do nothing without Gösta. If he had not agreed to the arrangement it could never have come to anything. And it was no small matter for destitute gentlemen to get seven estates for their own.

"Remember, now," says Gösta, "that we take the seven estates in order to save our souls, but not to be iron-work owners who count their money and weigh their iron. No dried-up parchments, no purse-proud money-bags will we become, but gentlemen will we be and remain."

"The very words of wisdom," murmurs the black one.

"If you, therefore, will give us the seven estates for one year we will accept them; but remember that if we do anything during that time which is not worthy of a gentleman, if we do anything which is sensible, or useful, or effeminate, then you may take the whole twelve of us when the year is out, and give the estates to whom you will."

The devil rubbed his hands with delight.

"But if we always behave like true gentlemen," continues Gösta, "then you may never again make any contract about Ekeby, and no pay do you get for this year either from us or from the major's wife."

"That is hard," says the devil. "Oh, dear Gösta, I must have one soul, just one little, poor soul. Couldn't I have the major's wife? Why should you spare the major's wife?"

"I do not drive any bargains with such wares," roars Gösta; "but if you must have some one, you can take old Sintram at Fors; he is ready, I can answer for that."

"Well, well, that will do," says the devil, with-out blinking. "The pensioners or Sintram, they can balance one another. This will be a good year."

And so the contract was written, with blood from Gösta's little finger, on the devil's black paper and with his quill-pen.

And when it was done the pensioners rejoiced. Now the world should belong to them for a whole year, and afterwards there would always be some way.

They push aside the chairs, make a ring about the kettle, which stands in the middle of the black floor, and whirl in a wild dance. Innermost in the circle dances the devil, with wild bounds; and at last he falls flat beside the kettle, rolls it over, and drinks.

Then Beerencreutz throws himself down beside him, and also Gösta Berling; and after them all the others lay themselves in a circle round the kettle, which is rolled from mouth to mouth. At last it is tipped over by a push, and the hot, sticky drink pours over them.

When they rise up, swearing, the devil is gone; but his golden promises float like shining crowns over the pensioners' heads.

CHAPTER III. CHRISTMAS DAY

ON Christmas day the major's wife gives a great dinner at Ekeby.

She sits as hostess at a table laid for fifty guests. She sits there in splendor and magnificence; here her short sheepskin jacket, her striped woollen skirt, and clay-pipe do not follow her. She rustles in silk, gold weighs on her bare arms, pearls cool her white neck.

Where are the pensioners? Where are they who on the black floor of the smithy, out of the polished copper kettle, drank a toast to the new masters of Ekeby?

In the corner by the stove the pensioners are sitting at a separate table; to-day there is no room for them at the big table. To them the food comes late, the wine sparingly; to them are sent no glances from beautiful women, no one listens to Gösta's jokes.

But the pensioners are like tamed birds, like satiated wild beasts. They had had scarcely an hour's sleep that night; then they had driven to morning worship, lighted by torches and the stars. They saw the Christmas candles, they heard the Christmas hymns, their faces were like smiling children's. They forgot the night in the smithy as one forgets an evil dream.

Great and powerful is the major's wife at Ekeby. Who dares lift his arm to strike her; who his voice to give evidence against her? Certainly not poor gentlemen who for many years have eaten her bread and slept under her roof. She can put them where she will, she can shut her door to them when she will, and they have not the power to fly from her might. God be merciful to their souls! Far from Ekeby they cannot live.

At the big table there was rejoicing: there shone Marianne Sinclair's beautiful eyes; there rang the gay Countess Dohna's low laugh.

But the pensioners are gloomy. Was it not just as easy to have put them at the same table with the other guests? What a lowering position there in the corner by the stove. As if pensioners were not fit to associate with fine people!

The major's wife is proud to sit between the Count at Borg and the Bro clergyman. The pensioners hang their heads like shame-faced children, and by degrees awake in them thoughts of the night.

Like shy guests the gay sallies, the merry stories come to the table in the corner by the stove. There the rage of the night and its promises enter into their minds. Master Julius makes the mighty captain, Christian Bergh, believe that the roasted grouse, which are being served at the big table, will not go round for all the guests; but it amuses no one.

"They won't go round," he says. "I know how many there are. But they'll manage in spite of it, Captain Christian; they have some roasted crows for us here at the little table."

But Colonel Beerencreutz's lips are curved by only a very feeble smile, under the fierce moustaches, and Gösta has looked the whole day as if he was meditating somebody's death.

"Any food is good enough for pensioners," he says.

At last the dish heaped up with magnificent grouse reaches the little table.

But Captain Christian is angry. Has he not had a life-long hate of crows,—those odious, cawing, winged things?

He hated them so bitterly that last autumn he had put on a woman's trailing dress, and had fastened a cloth on his head and made himself a laughing-stock for all men, only to get in range when they ate the grain in the fields.

He sought them out at their caucuses on the bare fields in the spring and killed them. He looked for their nests in the summer, and threw out the screaming, featherless young ones, or smashed the half-hatched eggs.

Now he seizes the dish of grouse.

"Do you think I don't know them?" he cries to the servant. "Do I need to hear them caw to recognize them? Shame on you, to offer Christian Bergh crows! Shame on you!"

Thereupon he takes the grouse, one by one, and throws them against the wall.

"Shame, shame!" he reiterates, so that the whole room rings,—"to offer Christian Bergh crows! Shame!"

And just as he used to hurl the helpless young crows against the cliffs, so now he sends grouse after grouse whizzing against the wall.

Sauce and grease spatter about him, the crushed birds rebound to the floor.

And the bachelors' wing rejoices.

Then the angry voice of the major's wife penetrates to the pensioners' ears.

"Turn him out!" she calls to the servants.

But they do not dare to touch him. He is still Christian Bergh, the mighty captain.

"Turn him out!"

He hears the command, and, terrible in his rage, he now turns upon the major's wife as a bear turns from a fallen enemy to meet a new attack. He marches up to the horse-shoe table. His heavy tread resounds through the hall. He stands opposite her, with the table between them.

"Turn him out!" cries the major's wife again.

But he is raging; none dare to face his frowning brow and great clenched hand. He is big as a giant, and as strong. The guests and servants tremble, and dare not approach him. Who would dare to touch him now, when rage has taken away his reason?

He stands opposite the major's wife and threatens her.

"I took the crow and threw it against the wall. And I did right."

"Out with you, captain!"

"Shame, woman! Offer Christian Bergh crows! If I did right I would take you and your seven hell's—"

"Thousand devils, Christian Bergh! don't swear. Nobody but I swears here."

"Do you think I am afraid of you, hag? Don't you think I know how you got your seven estates?"

"Silence, captain!"

"When Altringer died he gave them to your husband because you had been his mistress."

"Will you be silent?"

"Because you had been such a faithful wife, Margareta Samzelius. And the major took the seven estates and let you manage them and pretended not to know. And the devil arranged it all; but now comes the end for you."

The major's wife sits down; she is pale and trembling. She assents in a strange, low voice.

"Yes, now it is the end for me, and it is your doing, Christian Bergh."

At her voice Captain Christian trembles, his face works, and his eyes are filled with tears of anguish.

"I am drunk," he cries. "I don't know what I am saying; I have n't said anything. Dog and slave, dog and slave, and nothing more have I been for her for forty years. She is Margareta Celsing, whom I have served my whole life. I say nothing against her. What should I have to say against the beautiful Margareta Celsing! I am the dog which guards her door, the slave who bears her burdens. She may strike me, she may kick me! You see how I hold my tongue and bear it. I have loved her for forty years. How could I say anything against her?"

And a wonderful sight it is to see how he kneels and begs for forgiveness. And as she is sitting on the other side of the table, he goes on his knees round the table till he comes to her; then he bends down and kisses the hem of her dress, and the floor is wet with his tears.

But not far from the major's wife sits a small, strong man. He has shaggy hair, small, squinting eyes, and a protruding under-jaw. He looks like a bear. He is a man of few words, who likes to go his own quiet way and let the world take care of itself. He is Major Samzelius.

He rises when he hears Captain Christian's accusing words, and the major's wife rises, and all the fifty guests. The women are weeping in terror of what is coming, the men stand dejected, and at the feet of the major's wife lies Captain Christian, kissing the hem of her dress, wetting the floor with his tears.

The major slowly clenches his broad, hairy hands, and lifts his arm.

But the woman speaks first. Her voice sounds hollow and unfamiliar.

"You stole me," she cried. "You came like a thief and took me. They forced me, in my home, by blows, by hunger, and hard words to be your wife. I have treated you as you deserved."

The major's broad fist is clenched. His wife gives way a couple of steps. Then she speaks again.

"Living eels twist under the knife; an unwilling wife takes a lover. Will you strike me now for what happened twenty years ago? Do you not remember how he lived at Ekeby, we at Sjö? Do you not remember how he helped us in our poverty? We drove in his carriages, we drank his wine. Did we hide anything from you? Were not his servants your servants? Did not his gold weigh heavy in your pocket? Did you not accept the seven estates? You held your tongue and took them; then you should have struck, Berndt Samzelius,—then you should have struck."

The man turns from her and looks on all those present. He reads in their faces that they think she is right, that they all believe he took the estates in return for his silence.

"I never knew it!" he says, and stamps on the floor.

"It is well that you know it now!" she cries, in a shrill, ringing voice. "Was I not afraid lest you should die without knowing it? It is well that you know it now, so that I can speak out to you who have been my master and jailer. You know now that I, in spite of all, was his from whom you stole me. I tell you all now, you who have slandered me!"

It is the old love which exults in her voice and shines from her eyes. Her husband stands before her with lifted hand. She reads horror and scorn on the fifty faces about her. She feels that it is the last hour of her power. But she cannot help rejoicing that she may speak openly of the tenderest memory of her life.

"He was a man, a man indeed. Who were you, to come between us? I have never seen his equal. He gave me happiness, he gave me riches. Blessed be his memory!"

Then the major lets his lifted arm fall without striking her; now he knows how he shall punish her.

"Away!" he cries; "out of my house!"

She stands motionless.

But the pensioners stand with pale faces and stare at one another. Everything was going as the devil had prophesied. They now saw the consequences of the non-renewal of the contract. If that is true, so is it also true that she for more than twenty years had sent pensioners to perdition, and that they too were destined for the journey. Oh, the witch!

"Out with you!" continues the major. "Beg your bread on the highway! You shall have no pleasure of his money, you shall not live on his lands. There is no more a mistress of Ekeby. The day you set your foot in my house I will kill you."

"Do you drive me from my home?"

"You have no home. Ekeby is mine."

A feeling of despair comes over the major's wife. She retreats to the door, he following close after her.

"You who have been my life's curse," she laments, "shall you also now have power to do this to me?"

"Out, out!"

She leans against the door-post, clasps her hands, and holds them before her face. She thinks of her mother and murmurs to herself:—

"'May you be disowned, as I have been disowned; may the highway be your home, the hay-stack your bed!' It is all coming true."

The good old clergyman from Bro and the judge from Munkerud came forward now to Major Samzelius and tried to calm him. They said to him that it would be best to let all those old stories rest, to let everything be as it was, to forget and forgive.

He shakes the mild old hands from his shoulder. He is terrible to approach, just as Christian Bergh had been.

"It is no old story," he cries. "I never knew anything till to-day. I have never been able before to punish the adulteress."

At that word the major's wife lifts her head and regains her old courage.

"You shall go out before I do. Do you think that I shall give in to you?" she says. And she comes forward from the door.

The major does not answer, but he watches her every movement, ready to strike if he finds no better way to revenge himself.

"Help me, good gentlemen," she cries, "to get this man bound and carried out, until he gets back the use of his senses. Remember who I am and who he is! Think of it, before I must give in to him! I arrange all the work at Ekeby, and he sits the whole day long and feeds his bears. Help me, good friends and neighbors! There will be a boundless misery if I am no longer here. The peasant gets his living by cutting my wood and carting my iron. The charcoal burner lives by getting me charcoal, the lumber man by bringing down my timber. It is I who give out the work which brings prosperity. Smiths, mechanics, and carpenters live by serving me. Do you think that man can keep my work going? I tell you that if you drive me away you let famine in."

Again are many hands lifted to help the major's wife; again mild, persuading hands are laid on the major's shoulders.

"No," he says, "away with you. Who will defend an adulteress? I tell you that if she does not go of her own will I shall take her in my arms and carry her down to my bears."

At these words the raised hands are lowered.

Then, as a last resource, she turns to the pensioners.

"Will you also allow me to be driven from my home? Have I let you freeze out in the snow in winter? Have I denied you bitter ale and sweet brandy? Did I take any pay or any work from you because I gave you food and clothes? Have you not played at my feet, safe as children at their mother's side? Has not the dance gone through my halls? Have not merriment and laughter been your daily bread? Do not let this man, who has been my life's misfortune, drive me from my home, gentlemen! Do not let me become a beggar on the highway!"

At these words Gösta Berling had stolen away to a beautiful dark-haired girl who sat at the big table.

"You were much at Borg five years ago, Anna," he says. "Do you know if it was the major's wife who told Ebba Dohna that I was a dismissed priest?"

"Help her, Gösta!" is the girl's only answer.

"You must know that I will first hear if she has made me a murderer."

"Oh, Gösta, what a thought! Help her, Gösta!"

"You won't answer, I see. Then Sintram told the truth."And Gösta goes back to the other pensioners. He does not lift a finger to help the major's wife.

Oh, if only she had not put the pensioners at a separate table off there in the corner by the stove! Now the thoughts of the night awake in their minds, and a rage burns in their faces which is not less than the major's own.

In pitiless hardness they stand, unmoved by her prayers.

Did not everything they saw confirm the events of the night?

"One can see that she did not get her contract renewed," murmurs one.

"Go to hell, hag!" screams another. "By rights we ought to hunt you from the door."

"Fools," cries the gentle old Uncle Eberhard to the pensioners. "Don't you understand it was Sintram?"

"Of course we understand; of course we know it," answers Julius; "but what of that? May it not be true, at any rate? Does not Sintram go on the devil's errands? Don't they understand one another?"

"Go yourself, Eberhard; go and help her!" they mock. "You don't believe in hell. You can go!"

And Gösta Berling stands, without a word, motion less.

No, from the threatening, murmuring, struggling bachelors' wing she will get no help.

Then once again she retreats to the door and raises her clasped hands to her eyes.

"'May you be disowned, as I have been disowned,'" she cries to herself in her bitter sorrow. "'May the highway be your home, the hay-stack your bed!'"

Then she lays one hand on the door latch, but the other she stretches on high.

"Know you all, who now let me fall, know that your hour is soon coming! You shall be scattered, and your place shall stand empty. How can you stand when I do not hold you up? You, Melchior Sinclair, who have a heavy hand and let your wife feel it, beware! You, minister at Broby, your pun-ishment is coming! Madame Uggla, look after your house; poverty is coming! You young, beautiful women—Elizabeth Dohna, Marianne Sinclair, Anna Stjärnhök—do not think that I am the only one who must flee from her home. And beware, pensioners, a storm is coming over the land. You will be swept away from the earth; your day is over, it is verily over! I do not lament for myself, but for you; for the storm shall pass over your heads, and who shall stand when I have fallen? And my heart bleeds for my poor people. Who will give them work when I am gone?"

She opens the door; but then Captain Christian lifts his head and says:—

"How long must I lie here at your feet, Margareta Celsing? Will you not forgive me, so that I may stand up and fight for you?"

Then the major's wife fights a hard battle with herself; but she sees that if she forgives him he will rise up and attack her husband; and this man, who has loved her faithfully for forty years will become a murderer.

"Must I forgive, too?" she says. "Are you not the cause of all my misfortune, Christian Bergh? Go to the pensioners and rejoice over your work."

So she went. She went calmly, leaving terror and dismay behind her. She fell, but she was not without greatness in her fall.

She did not lower herself to grieving weakly, but in her old age she still exulted over the love of her youth. She did not lower herself to lamenting and pitiable weeping when she left everything; she did not shrink from wandering about the land with beggar's bag and crutch. She pitied only the poor peasants and the happy, careless people on the shores of the Löfven, the penniless pensioners,—all those whom she had taken in and cared for.

She was abandoned by all, and yet she had strength to turn away her last friend that he should not be a murderer.

She was a woman great in strength and love of action. We shall not soon see her like again.

The next day Major Samzelius moved from Ekeby to his own farm of Sjö, which lies next to the large estate.

In Altringer's will, by which the major had got the estates, it was clearly stated that none of them should be sold or given away, but that after the death of the major his wife and her heirs should inherit them all. So, as he could not dissipate the hated inheritance, he placed the pensioners to reign over it, thinking that he, by so doing, most injured Ekeby and the other six estates.

As no one in all the country round now doubted that the wicked Sintram went on the devil's errands, and as everything he had promised had been so brilliantly fulfilled the pensioners were quite sure that the contract would be carried out in every point, and they were entirely decided not to do, during the year, anything sensible, or useful, or effeminate, convinced that the major's wife was an abominable witch who sought their ruin.

The old philosopher, Eberhard, ridiculed their belief. But who paid any attention to such a man, who was so obstinate in his unbelief that if he had lain in the midst of the fires of hell and had seen all the devils standing and grinning at him, would still have insisted that they did not exist, because they could not exist?—for Uncle Eberhard was a great philosopher.

Gösta Berling told no one what he thought. It is certain that he considered he owed the major's wife little thanks because she had made him a pensioner at Ekeby; it seemed better to him to be dead than to have on his conscience the guilt of Ebba Dohna's suicide.

He did not lift his hand to be revenged on the major's wife, but neither did he to help her. He could not. But the pensioners had attained great power and magnificence. Christmas was at hand, with its feasts and pleasures. The hearts of the pensioners were filled with rejoicing; and whatever sorrow weighed on Gösta Berling's heart he did not show in face or speech.

CHAPTER IV. GÖSTA BERLING, POET

IT was Christmas, and there was to be a ball at Borg.

At that time, and it is soon sixty years ago, a young Count Dohna lived at Borg; he was newly married, and he had a young, beautiful countess. It was sure to be gay at the old castle.

An invitation had come to Ekeby, but it so happened that of them all who were there that year, Gösta Berling, whom they called "the poet," was the only one who wished to go.

Borg and Ekeby both lie by the Löfven, but on opposite shores. Borg is in Svartsjö parish, Ekeby in Bro. When the lake is impassable it is a ten or twelve miles' journey from Ekeby to Borg.

The pauper, Gösta Berling, was fitted out for the festival by the old men, as if he had been a king's son, and had the honor of a kingdom to keep up.

His coat with the glittering buttons was new, his ruffles were stiff, and his buckled shoes shining. He wore a cloak of the finest beaver, and a cap of sable on his yellow, curling hair. They spread a bear-skin with silver claws over his sledge, and gave him black Don Juan, the pride of the stable, to drive.

He whistled to his white Tancred, and seized the braided reins. He started rejoicing, surrounded by the glitter of riches and splendor, he who shone so by his own beauty and by the playful brilliancy of his genius.

He left early in the forenoon. It was Sunday, and he heard the organ in the church at Bro as he drove by. He followed the lonely forest road which led to Berga, where Captain Uggla then lived. There he meant to stop for dinner.

Berga was no rich man's home. Hunger knew the way to that turf-roofed house; but he was met with jests, charmed with song and games like other guests, and went as unwillingly as they.

The old Mamselle Ulrika Dillner, who looked after everything at Berga, stood on the steps and wished Gösta Berling welcome. She courtesied to him, and the false curls, which hung down over her brown face with its thousand wrinkles, danced with joy. She led him into the dining-room, and then she began to tell him about the family, and their changing fortunes.

Distress stood at the door, she said; it was hard times at Berga. They would not even have had any horse-radish for dinner, with their corned beef, if Ferdinand and the girls had not put Disa before a sledge and driven down to Munkerud to borrow some.

The captain was off in the woods again, and would of course come home with a tough old hare, on which one had to use more butter in cooking it than it was worth itself. That's what he called getting food for the house. Still, it would do, if only he did not come with a miserable fox, the worst beast our Lord ever made; no use, whether dead or alive.

And the captain's wife, yes, she was not up yet. She lay abed and read novels, just as she had always done. She was not made for work, that God's angel.

No, that could be done by some one who was old and gray like Ulrika Dillner, working night and day to keep the whole miserable affair together. And it was n't always so easy; for it was the truth that for one whole winter they had not had in that house any other meat than bear-hams. And big wages she did not expect; so far she had never seen any; but they would not turn her out on the roadside either, when she could n't work any longer in return for her food. They treated a house-maid like a human being in that house, and they would one of these days give old Ulrika a good burial if they had anything to buy the coffin with.

"For who knows how it will be?" she bursts out, and wipes her eyes, which are always so quick to tears. "We have debts to the wicked Sintram, and he can take everything from us. Of course Ferdinand is engaged to the rich Anna Stjärnhök; but she is tired,—she is tired of him. And what will become of us, of our three cows, and our nine horses, of our gay young ladies who want to go from one ball to another, of our dry fields where nothing grows, of our mild Ferdinand, who will never be a real man? What will become of the whole blessed house, where everything thrives except work?"

But dinner-time came, and the family gathered. The good Ferdinand, the gentle son of the house, and the lively daughters came home with the borrowed horse-radish. The captain came, fortified by a bath in a hole in the ice and a tramp through the woods. He threw up the window to get more air, and shook Gösta's hand with a strong grip. And his wife came, dressed in silk, with wide laces hanging over her white hands, which Gösta was allowed to kiss.

They all greeted Gösta with joy; jests flew about the circle; gayly they asked him:—

"How are you all at Ekeby; how is it in that promised land?"

"Milk and honey flow there," he answered. "We empty the mountains of iron and fill our cellar with wine. The fields bear gold, with which we gild life's misery, and we cut down our woods to build bowling-alleys and summer houses."

The captain's wife sighed and smiled at his answer, and her lips murmured the word,—

"Poet!"

"Many sins have I on my conscience," answered Gösta, "but I have never written a line of poetry."

"You are nevertheless a poet, Gösta; that name you must put up with. You have lived through more poems than all our poets have written."

Then she spoke, tenderly as a mother, of his wasted life. "I shall live to see you become a man," she said. And he felt it sweet to be urged on by this gentle woman, who was such a faithful friend, and whose romantic heart burned with the love of great deeds.

But just as they had finished the gay meal and had enjoyed the corned beef and horse-radish and cabbage and apple fritters and Christmas ale, and Gösta had made them laugh and cry by telling them of the major and his wife and the Broby clergyman, they heard sleigh-bells outside, and immediately afterward the wicked Sintram walked in.

He beamed with satisfaction, from the top of his bald head down to his long, flat feet. He swung his long arms, and his face was twisted. It was easy to see that he brought bad news.

"Have you heard," he asked,—"have you heard that the banns have been called to-day for Anna Stjärnhök and the rich Dahlberg in the Svartsjö church? She must have forgotten that she was engaged to Ferdinand."

They had not heard a word of it. They were amazed and grieved.

Already they fancied the home pillaged to pay the debt to this wicked man; the beloved horses sold, as well as the worn furniture which had come from the home of the captain's wife. They saw an end to the gay life with feasts and journeyings from ball to ball. Bear-hams would again adorn the board, and the young people must go out into the world and work for strangers.

The captain's wife caressed her son, and let him feel the comfort of a never-failing love.

But—there sat Gösta Berling in the midst of them, and, unconquerable, turned over a thousand plans in his head.

"Listen," he cried, "it is not yet time to think of grieving. It is the minister's wife at Svartsjö who has arranged all this. She has got a hold on Anna, since she has been living with her at the vicarage. It is she who has persuaded her to forsake Ferdinand and take old Dahlberg; but they 're not married yet, and will never be either. I am on my way to Borg, and shall meet Anna there. I shall talk to her; I shall get her away from the clergyman's, from her fiancé,—I shall bring her with me here to-night And afterwards old Dahlberg shall never get any good of her."

And so it was arranged. Gösta started for Borg alone, without taking any of the gay young ladies, but with warm good wishes for his return. And Sintram, who rejoiced that old Dahlberg should be cheated, decided to stop at Berga to see Gösta come back with the faithless girl. In a burst of good-will he even wrapt round him his green plaid, a present from Mamselle Ulrika.

The captain's wife came out on the steps with three little books, bound in red leather, in her hand.

"Take them," she said to Gösta, who already sat in the sledge; "take them, if you fail! It is 'Corinne,' Madame de Staël's 'Corinne.' I do not want them to go by auction."

"I shall not fail."

"Ah, Gösta, Gösta," she said, and passed her hand over his bared head, "strongest and weakest of men! How long will you remember that a few poor people's happiness lies in your hand?"

Once more Gösta flew along the road, drawn by the black Don Juan, followed by the white Tancred, and the joy of adventure filled his soul. He felt like a young conqueror, the spirit was in him.

His way took him past the vicarage at Svartsjö. He turned in there and asked if he might drive Anna Stjärnhök to the ball. And that he was permitted.

A beautiful, self-willed girl it was who sat in his sledge. Who would not want to drive behind the black Don Juan?

The young people were silent at first, but then she began the conversation, audaciousness itself.

"Have you heard what the minister read out in church to-day?"

"Did he say that you were the prettiest girl between the Löfven and the Klar River?"

"How stupid you are! but every one knows that. He called the banns for me and old Dahlberg."

"Never would I have let you sit in my sledge nor sat here myself, if I had known that. Never would I have wished to drive you at all."

And the proud heiress answered:—

"I could have got there well enough without you, Gösta Berling."

"It is a pity for you, Anna," said Gösta, thoughtfully, "that your father and mother are not alive. You are your own mistress, and no one can hold you to account."

"It is a much greater pity that you had not said that before, so that I might have driven with some one else."

"The minister's wife thinks as I do, that you need some one to take your father's place; else she had never put you to pull in harness with such an old nag."

"It is not she who has decided it."

"Ah, Heaven preserve us!—have you yourself chosen such a fine man?"

"He does not take me for my money."

"No, the old ones, they only run after blue eyes and red cheeks; and awfully nice they are, when they do that."

"Oh, Gösta, are you not ashamed?"

"But remember that you are not to play with young men any longer. No more dancing and games. Your place is in the corner of the sofa—or perhaps you mean to play cribbage with old Dahlberg?"

They were silent, till they drove up the steep hill to Borg.

"Thanks for the drive! It will be long before I drive again with you, Gösta Berling."

"Thanks for the promise! I know many who will be sorry to-day they ever drove you to a party."

Little pleased was the haughty beauty when she entered the ball-room and looked over the guests gathered there.

First of all she saw the little, bald Dahlberg beside the tall, slender, golden-haired Gösta Berling. She wished she could have driven them both out of the room.

Her fiancé came to ask her to dance, but she received him with crushing astonishment.

"Are you going to dance? You never do!"

And the girls came to wish her joy.

"Don't give yourselves the trouble, girls. You don't suppose that any one could be in love with old Dahlberg. But he is rich, and I am rich, therefore we go well together."

The old ladies went up to her, pressed her white hand, and spoke of life's greatest happiness.

"Congratulate the minister's wife," she said. "She is gladder about it than I."

But there stood Gösta Berling, the gay cavalier, greeted with joy for his cheerful smile and his pleasant words, which sifted gold-dust over life's gray web. Never before had she seen him as he was that night. He was no outcast, no homeless jester; no, a king among men, a born king.

He and the other young men conspired against her. She should think over how badly she had behaved when she gave herself with her lovely face and her great fortune to an old man. And they let her sit out ten dances.

She was boiling with rage.

At the eleventh dance came a man, the most insignificant of all, a poor thing, whom nobody would dance with, and asked her for a turn.

"There is no more bread, bring on the crusts," she said.

They played a game of forfeits. The fair-haired girls put their heads together and condemned her to kiss the one she loved best. And with smiling lips they waited to see the proud beauty kiss old Dahlberg.

But she rose, stately in her anger, and said:—

"May I not just as well give a blow to the one I like the least!"

The moment after Gösta's cheek burned under her firm hand. He flushed a flaming red, but he conquered himself, seized her hand, held it fast a second, and whispered:—

"Meet me in half an hour in the red drawing-room on the lower floor!"

His blue eyes flashed on her, and encompassed her with magical waves. She felt that she must obey.

She met him with proud and angry words.

"How does it concern you whom I marry?"

He was not ready to speak gently to her, nor did it seem to him best to speak yet of Ferdinand.

"I thought it was not too severe a punishment for you to sit out ten dances. But you want to be allowed unpunished to break vows and promises. If a better man than I had taken your sentence in his hand, he could have made it harder."

"What have I done to you and all the others, that I may not be in peace? It is for my money's sake you persecute me. I shall throw it into the Löfven, and any one who wants it can fish it up."

She put her hands before her eyes and wept from anger.

That moved the poet's heart. He was ashamed of his harshness. He spoke in caressing tones.

"Ah, child, child, forgive me! Forgive poor Gösta Berling! Nobody cares what such a poor wretch says or does, you know that. Nobody weeps for his anger, one might just as well weep over a mosquito's bite. It was madness in me to hope that I could prevent our loveliest and richest girl marrying that old man. And now I have only distressed you."

He sat down on the sofa beside her. Gently he put his arm about her waist, with caressing tenderness, to support and raise her.

She did not move away. She pressed closer to him, threw her arms round his neck, and wept with her beautiful head on his shoulder.

O poet, strongest and weakest of men, it was not about your neck those white arms should rest.

"If I had known that," she whispered, "never would I have taken the old man. I have watched you this evening; there is no one like you."

From between pale lips Gösta forced out,—

"Ferdinand."

She silenced him with a kiss.

"He is nothing; no one but you is anything. To you will I be faithful."

"I am Gösta Berling," he said gloomily; "you cannot marry me."

"You are the man I love, the noblest of men. You need do nothing, be nothing. You are born a king."

Then the poet's blood seethed. She was beautiful and tender in her love. He took her in his arms.

"If you will be mine, you cannot remain at the vicarage. Let me drive you to Ekeby to-night; there I shall know how to defend you till we can be married."

That was a wild drive through the night Absorbed in their love, they let Don Juan take his own pace. The noise of the runners was like the lamentations of those they had deceived. What did they care for that? She hung on his neck, and he leaned forward and whispered in her ear.

"Can any happiness be compared in sweetness to stolen pleasures?"

What did the banns matter? They had love. And the anger of men! Gösta Berling believed in fate; fate had mastered them: no one can resist fate.

If the stars had been the candles which had been lighted for her wedding, if Don Juan's bells had been the church chimes, calling the people to witness her marriage to old Dahlberg, still she must have fled with Gösta Berling. So powerful is fate.

They had passed the vicarage and Munkerud. They had three miles to Berga and three miles more to Ekeby. The road skirted the edge of the wood; on their right lay dark hills, on their left a long, white valley.

Tancred came rushing. He ran so fast that he seemed to lie along the ground. Howling with fright, he sprang up in the sledge and crept under Anna's feet.

Don Juan shied and bolted.

"Wolves!" said Gösta Berling.

They saw a long, gray line running by the fence. There were at least a dozen of them.

Anna was not afraid. The day had been richly blessed with adventure, and the night promised to be equally so. It was life,—to speed over the sparkling snow, defying wild beasts and men.

Gösta uttered an oath, leaned forward, and struck Don Juan a heavy blow with the whip.

"Are you afraid?" he asked. "They mean to cut us off there, where the road turns."

Don Juan ran, racing with the wild beasts of the forest, and Tancred howled in rage and terror. They reached the turn of the road at the same time as the wolves, and Gösta drove back the foremost with the whip.

"Ah, Don Juan, my boy, how easily you could get away from twelve wolves, if you did not have us to drag."

They tied the green plaid behind them. The wolves were afraid of it, and fell back for a while. But when they had overcome their fright, one of them ran, panting, with hanging tongue and open mouth up to the sledge. Then Gösta took Madame de Staël's "Corinne" and threw it into his mouth.

Once more they had breathing-space for a time, while the brutes tore their booty to pieces, and then again they felt the dragging as the wolves seized the green plaid, and heard their panting breath. They knew that they should not pass any human dwelling before Berga, but worse than death it seemed to Gösta to see those he had deceived. But he knew that the horse would tire, and what should become of them then?

They saw the house at Berga at the edge of the forest. Candles burned in the windows. Gösta knew too well for whose sake.

But now the wolves drew back, fearing the neighborhood of man, and Gösta drove past Berga. He came no further than to the place where the road once again buried itself in the wood; there he saw a dark group before him,—the wolves were waiting for him.

"Let us turn back to the vicarage and say that we took a little pleasure trip in the starlight. We can't go on."

They turned, but in the next moment the sledge was surrounded by wolves. Gray forms brushed by them, their white teeth glittered in gaping mouths, and their glowing eyes shone. They howled with hunger and thirst for blood. The glittering teeth were ready to seize the soft human flesh. The wolves leaped up on Don Juan, and hung on the saddlecloth. Anna sat and wondered if they would eat them entirely up, or if there would be something left, so that people the next morning would find their mangled limbs on the trampled, bloody snow.

"It's a question of our lives," she said, and leaned down and seized Tancred by the nape of the neck.

"Don't,—that will not help! It is not for the dog's sake the wolves are out to-night."

Thereupon Gösta drove into the yard at Berga, but the wolves hunted him up to the very steps. He had to beat them off with the whip.

"Anna," he said, as they drew up, "God would not have it. Keep a good countenance; if you are the woman I take you for, keep a good countenance!"

They had heard the sleigh-bells in the house, and came out.

"He has her!" they cried, "he has her! Long live Gösta Berling!" and the new-comers were embraced by one after another.

Few questions were asked. The night was far advanced, the travellers were agitated by their terrible drive and needed rest. It was enough that Anna had come.

All was well. Only "Corinne" and the green plaid, Mamselle Ulrika's prized gift, were destroyed.

The whole house slept. But Gösta rose, dressed himself, and stole out. Unnoticed he led Don Juan out of the stable, harnessed him to the sledge, and meant to set out. But Anna Stjärnhök came out from the house.

"I heard you go out," she said. "So I got up, too. I am ready to go with you."

He went up to her and took her hand.

"Don't you understand it yet? It cannot be. God does not wish it. Listen now and try to understand. I was here to dinner and saw their grief over your faithlessness. I went to Borg to bring you back to Ferdinand. But I have always been a good-for-nothing, and will never be anything else. I betrayed him, and kept you for myself. There is an old woman here who believes that I shall become a man. I betrayed her. And another poor old thing will freeze and starve here for the sake of dying among friends, but I was ready to let the wicked Sintram take her home. You were beautiful, and sin is sweet. It is so easy to tempt Gösta Berling. Oh, what a miserable wretch I am! I know how they love their home, all those in there, but I was ready just now to leave it to be pillaged. I forgot everything for your sake, you were so sweet in your love. But now, Anna, now since I have seen their joy, I will not keep you; no, I will not. You could have made a man of me, but I may not keep you. Oh, my beloved! He there above mocks at our desires. We must bow under His chastising hand. Tell me that you from this day will take up your burden! All of them rely upon you. Say that you will stay with them and be their prop and help! If you love me, if you will lighten my deep sorrow, promise me this! My beloved, is your heart so great that you can conquer yourself, and smile in doing it?"

She accepted the renunciation in a sort of ecstasy.

"I shall do as you wish,—sacrifice myself and smile."

"And not hate my poor friends?"

She smiled sadly.

"As long as I love you, I shall love them."

"Now for the first time I know what you are. It is hard to leave you."

"Farewell, Gösta! Go, and God be with you! My love shall not tempt you to sin."

She turned to go in. He followed her.

"Will you soon forget me?"

"Go, Gösta! We are only human."

He threw himself down in the sledge, but then she came back again.

"Do you not think of the wolves?"

"Just of them I am thinking, but they have done
their work. From me they have nothing more to get this night."

Once more he stretched his arms towards her, but Don Juan became impatient and set off. He did not take the reins. He sat backwards and looked after her. Then he leaned against the seat and wept despairingly.

"I have possessed happiness and driven her from me; I myself drove her from me. Why did I not keep her?"

Ah, Gösta Berling, strongest and weakest of men!

CHAPTER V. LA CACHUCHA

WAR-HORSE! war-horse! Old friend, who now stand tethered in the pasture, do you remember your youth?

Do you remember the day of the battle? You sprang forward, as if you had been borne on wings, your mane fluttered about you like waving flames, on your black haunches shone drops of blood and frothy foam. In harness of gold you bounded forward; the ground thundered under you. You trembled with joy. Ah, how beautiful you were!

It is the gray hour of twilight in the pensioners' wing. In the big room the pensioners' red-painted chests stand against the walls, and their holiday clothes hang on hooks in the corner. The firelight plays on the white-washed walls and on the yellow-striped curtains which conceal the beds. The pensioners' wing is not a kingly dwelling,—no seraglio with cushioned divans and soft pillows.

But there Lilliecrona's violin is heard. He is playing the cachucha in the dusk of the evening. And he plays it over and over again.

Cut the strings, break his bow! Why does he play that cursed dance? Why does he play it, when Örneclou, the ensign, is lying sick with the pains of gout, so severe that he cannot move in his bed? No; snatch the violin away and throw it against the wall if he will not stop.

La cachucha, is it for us, master? Shall it be danced over the shaking floor of the pensioners' wing, between the narrow walls, black with smoke and greasy with dirt, under that low ceiling? Woe to you, to play so.

La cachucha, is it for us,—for us pensioners? Without the snow-storm howls. Do you think to teach the snow-flakes to dance in time? Are you playing for the light-footed children of the storm?

Maiden forms, which tremble with the throbbing of hot blood, small sooty hands, which have thrown aside the pot to seize the castanets, bare feet under tucked-up skirts, courts paved with marble slabs, crouching gypsies with bagpipe and tambourine, Moorish arcades, moonlight, and black eyes,—have you these, master? If not, let the violin rest.

The pensioners are drying their wet clothes by the fire. Shall they swing in high boots with iron-shod heels and inch-thick soles? Through snow yards deep they have waded the whole day to reach the bear's lair. Do you think they will dance in wet, reeking homespun clothes, with shaggy bruin as a partner?

An evening sky glittering with stars, red roses in dark hair, troublous tenderness in the air, untutored grace in their movements, love rising from the ground, raining from the sky, floating in the air,—have you all that, master? If not, why do you force us to long for such things?

Most cruel of men, are you summoning the tethered war-horse to the combat? Rutger von Örneclou is lying in his bed, a prisoner to the gout. Spare him the pain of tender memories, master! He too has worn sombrero and bright-colored hair-net; he too has owned velvet jacket and belted poniard. Spare old Örneclou, master!

But Lilliecrona plays the cachucha, always the cachucha, and Örneclou is tortured like the lover when he sees the swallow fly away to his beloved's distant dwelling, like the hart when he is driven by the hurrying chase past the cooling spring.

Lilliecrona takes the violin for a second from his chin.

"Ensign, do you remember Rosalie von Berger?"

Örneclou swears a solemn oath.

"She was light as a candle-flame. She sparkled and danced like the diamond in the end of the fiddle-bow. You must remember her in the theatre at Karlstad. We saw her when we were young; do you remember?"

And the ensign remembered. She was small and ardent. She was like a sparkling flame. She could dance la cachucha. She taught all the young men in Karlstad to dance cachucha and to play the castanets. At the governor's ball a *pas de deux* was danced by the ensign and Mlle. von Berger, dressed as Spaniards.

And he had danced as one dances under fig-trees and magnolias, like a Spaniard,—a real Spaniard.

No one in the whole of Värmland could dance cachucha like him. No one could dance it so that it was worth speaking of it, but he.

What a cavalier Värmland lost when the gout stiffened his legs and great lumps grew out on his joints! What a cavalier he had been, so slender, so handsome, so courtly! "The handsome Örneclou" he was called by those young girls, who were ready to come to blows over a dance with him.

Then Lilliecrona begins the cachucha again, always the cachucha, and Örneclou is taken back to old times.

There he stands, and there she stands, Rosalie von Berger. Just now they were alone in the dressing-room. She was a Spaniard, he too. He was allowed to kiss her, but carefully, for she was afraid of his blackened moustache. Now they dance. Ah, as one dances under fig-trees and magnolias! She draws away, he follows; he is bold, she proud; he wounded, she conciliatory. When he at the end falls on his knees and receives her in his outstretched arms, a sigh goes through the ball-room, a sigh of rapture.

He had been like a Spaniard, a real Spaniard.

Just at that stroke had he bent so, stretched his arms so, and put out his foot to glide forward. What grace! He might have been hewn in marble.

He does not know how it happened, but he has got his foot over the edge of the bed, he stands upright, he bends, he raises his arms, snaps his fingers, and wishes to glide forward over the floor in the same way as long ago, when he wore so tight patent leather shoes the stocking feet had to be cut away.

"Bravo, Örneclou! Bravo, Lilliecrona, play life into him!"

His foot gives way; he cannot rise on his toe. He kicks a couple of times with one leg; he can do no more, he falls back on the bed.

Handsome señor, you have grown old.

Perhaps the señorita has too.

It is only under the plane-trees of Granada that the cachucha is danced by eternally young gitanas. Eternally young, because, like the roses, each spring brings new ones.

So now the time has come to cut the strings.

No, play on, Lilliecrona, play the cachucha, always the cachucha!

Teach us that, although we have got slow bodies and stiff joints, in our feelings we are always the same, always Spaniards.

War-horse, war-horse!

Say that you love the trumpet-blast, which decoys you into a gallop, even if you also cut your foot to the bone on the steel-link of the tether.

CHAPTER VI. THE BALL AT EKEBY

AH, women of the olden times!

To speak of you is to speak of the kingdom of heaven; you were all beauties, ever bright, ever young, ever lovely and gentle as a mother's eyes when she looks down on her child. Soft as young squirrels you hung on your husband's neck. Your voice never trembled with anger, no frowns ruffled your brow, your white hand was never harsh and hard. You, sweet saints, like adored images stood in the temple of home. Incense and prayers were offered you, through you love worked its wonders, and round your temples poetry wreathed its gold, gleaming glory.

Ah, women of the past, this is the story of how one of you gave Gösta Berling her love.

Two weeks after the ball at Borg there was one at Ekeby.

What a feast it was! Old men and women become young again, smile and rejoice, only in speaking of it.

The pensioners were masters at Ekeby at that time. The major's wife went about the country with beggar's wallet and crutch, and the major lived at Sjö. He could not even be present at the ball, for at Sjö small-pox had broken out, and he was afraid to spread the infection.

What pleasures those twelve hours contained, from the pop of the first cork at the dinner-table to the last wail of the violins, long after midnight.

They have sunk into the background of time, those crowned hours, made magical by the most fiery wines, by the most delicate food, by the most inspiring music, by the wittiest of theatricals, by the most beautiful tableaux. They have sunk away, dizzy with the dizziest dance. Where are to be found such polished floors, such courtly knights, such lovely women?

Ah, women of the olden days, you knew well how to adorn a ball. Streams of fire, of genius, and youthful vigor thrilled each and all who approached you. It was worth wasting one's gold on wax-candles to light up your loveliness, on wine to instil gayety into your hearts; it was worth dancing soles to dust and rubbing stiff arms which had drawn the fiddle-bow, for your sakes.

Ah, women of the olden days, it was you who owned the key to the door of Paradise.

The halls of Ekeby are crowded with the loveliest of your lovely throng. There is the young Countess Dohna, sparklingly gay and eager for game and dance, as befits her twenty years; there are the lovely daughters of the judge of Munkerud, and the lively young ladies from Berga; there is Anna Stjärnhök, a thousand times more beautiful than ever before, with that gentle dreaminess which had come over her ever since the night she had been hunted by wolves; there are many more, who are not yet forgotten but soon will be; and there is the beautiful Marianne Sinclair.

She, the famed queen of beauty, who had shone at royal courts, who had travelled the land over and received homage everywhere, she who lighted the spark of love wherever she showed herself,—she had deigned to come to the pensioners' ball.

At that time Varmland's glory was at its height, borne up by many proud names. Much had the beautiful land's happy children to be proud of, but when they named their glories they never neglected to speak of Marianne Sinclair.

The tales of her conquests filled the land.

They spoke of the coronets which had floated over her head, of the millions which had been laid at her feet, of the warriors' swords and poets' wreaths whose splendor had tempted her.

And she possessed not only beauty. She was witty and learned. The cleverest men of the day were glad to talk with her. She was not an author herself, but many of her ideas, which she had put into the souls of her poet-friends, lived again in song.

In Värmland, in the land of the bear, she seldom stayed. Her life was spent in perpetual journeyings. Her father, the rich Melchior Sinclair, remained at home at Björne and let Marianne go to her noble friends in the large towns or at the great country-seats. He had his pleasure in telling of all the money she wasted, and both the old people lived happy in the splendor of Marianne's glowing existence.

Her life was a life of pleasures and homage. The air about her was love—love her light and lamp, love her daily bread.

She, too, had often loved, often, often; but never had that fire lasted long enough to forge the chains which bind for life.

"I wait for him, the irresistible," she used to say of love. "Hitherto he has not climbed over several ramparts, nor swum through several trenches. He has come tamely, without wildness in his eye and madness in his heart. I wait for the conqueror, who shall take me out of myself. I will feel love so strong within me that I must tremble before him; now I know only the love at which my good sense laughs."

Her presence gave fire to talk, life to the wine. Her glowing spirit set the fiddle-bows going, and the dance floated in sweeter giddiness than before over the floor which she had touched with her feet. She was radiant in the tableaux, she gave genius to the comedy, her lovely lips—

Ah, hush, it was not her fault, she never meant to do it! It was the balcony, it was the moonlight, the lace veil, the knightly dress, the song, which were to blame. The poor young creatures were innocent.

All that which led to so much unhappiness was with the best intentions. Master Julius, who could do anything, had arranged a tableau especially that Marianne might shine in full glory.

In the theatre, which was set up in the great drawing-room at Ekeby, sat the hundred guests and looked at the picture, Spain's yellow moon wandering through a dark night sky. A Don Juan came stealing along Sevilla's street and stopped under an ivy-clad balcony. He was disguised as a monk, but one could see an embroidered cuff under the sleeve, and a gleaming sword-point under the mantle's hem.

He raised his voice in song:—

"I kiss the lips of no fair maid,
Nor wet mine with the foaming wine
  Within the beaker's gold.
A cheek upon whose rose-leaf shade
Mine eyes have lit a glow divine,
A look which shyly seeketh mine,—
  These leave me still and cold.

"Ah, come not in thy beauty's glow,
Señora, through yon terrace-door;
  I fear when thou art nigh!
Cope and stole my shoulders know,
The Virgin only I adore,
And water-jugs hold comfort's store;
  For ease to them I fly."

As he finished, Marianne came out on the balcony, dressed in black velvet and lace veil. She leaned over the balustrade and sang slowly and ironically:

"Why tarry thus, thou holy man
Beneath my window late or long?
Dost pray for my soul's weal?"

Then suddenly, warmly and eagerly:—

"Ah, flee, begone while yet you can!
Your gleaming sword sticks forth so long,
And plainly, spite your holy song,
The spurs clank on your heel."

At these words the monk cast off his disguise, and Gösta Berling stood under the balcony in a knight's dress of silk and gold. He heeded not the beauty's warning, but climbed up one of the balcony supports, swung himself over the balustrade, and, just as Master Julius had arranged it, fell on his knees at the lovely Marianne's feet.

Graciously she smiled on him, and gave him her hand to kiss, and while the two young people gazed at one another, absorbed in their love, the curtain fell.

And before her knelt Gösta Berling, with a face tender as a poet's and bold as a soldier's, with deep eyes, which glowed with wit and genius, which implored and constrained. Supple and full of strength was he, fiery and captivating.

While the curtain went up and down, the two stood always in the same position. Gösta's eyes held the lovely Marianne fast; they implored; they constrained.

Then the applause ceased; the curtain hung quiet; no one saw them.

Then the beautiful Marianne bent down and kissed Gösta Berling. She did not know why,—she had to. He stretched up his arms about her head and held her fast. She kissed him again and again.

But it was the balcony, it was the moonlight, it was the lace veil, the knightly dress, the song, the applause, which were to blame. They had not wished it. She had not thrust aside the crowns which had hovered over her head, and spurned the millions which lay at her feet, out of love for Gösta Berling; nor had he already forgotten Anna Stjärnhök. No; they were blameless; neither of them had wished it.

It was the gentle Löwenborg,—he with the fear in his eye and the smile on his lips,—who that day was curtain-raiser. Distracted by the memory of many sorrows, he noticed little of the things of this world, and had never learned to look after them rightly. When he now saw that Gösta and Marianne had taken a new position, he thought that it also belonged to the tableau, and so he began to drag on the curtain string.

The two on the balcony observed nothing until a thunder of applause greeted them.

Marianne started back and wished to flee, but Gösta held her fast, whispering:—

"Stand still; they think it belongs to the tableau."

He felt how her body shook with shuddering, and how the fire of her kisses died out on her lips.

"Do not be afraid," he whispered; "lovely lips have a right to kiss."

They had to stand while the curtain went up and went down, and each time the hundreds of eyes saw them, hundreds of hands thundered out a stormy applause.

For it was beautiful to see two fair young people represent love's happiness. No one could think that those kisses were anything but stage delusion. No one guessed that the señora shook with embarrassment and the knight with uneasiness. No one could think that it did not all belong to the tableau.

At last Marianne and Gösta stood behind the scenes.

She pushed her hair back from her forehead.

"I don't understand myself," she said.

"Fie! for shame, Miss Marianne," said he, grimacing, and stretched out his hands. "To kiss Gösta Berling; shame on you!"

Marianne had to laugh.

"Every one knows that Gösta Berling is irresistible. My fault is no greater than others'."

And they agreed to put a good face on it, so that no one should suspect the truth.

"Can I be sure that the truth will never come out *Herr* Gösta?" she asked, before they went out among the guests.

"That you can. Gentlemen can hold their tongues. I promise you that."

She dropped her eyes. A strange smile curved her lips.

"If the truth should come out, what would people think of me, Herr Gösta?"

"They would not think anything. They would know that it meant nothing. They would think that we entered into our parts and were going on with the play."

Yet another question, with lowered lids and with the same forced smile,—

"But you yourself? What do you think about it, Herr Gösta?"

"I think that you are in love with me," he jested.

"Think no such thing," she smiled, "for then I must run you through with my stiletto to show you that you are wrong."

"Women's kisses are precious," said Gösta. "Does it cost one's life to be kissed by Marianne Sinclair?"

A glance flashed on him from Marianne's eyes, so sharp that it felt like a blow.

"I could wish to see you dead, Gösta Berling! dead! dead!"

These words revived the old longing in the poet's blood.

"Ah," he said, "would that those words were more than words!—that they were arrows which came whistling from some dark ambush; that they were daggers or poison, and had the power to destroy this wretched body and set my soul free!"

She was calm and smiling now.

"Childishness!" she said, and took his arm to join the guests.

They kept their costumes, and their triumphs were renewed when they showed themselves in front of the scenes. Every one complimented them. No one suspected anything.

The ball began again, but Gösta escaped from the ballroom.

His heart ached from Marianne's glance, as if it had been wounded by sharp steel. He understood too well the meaning of her words. It was a disgrace to love him; it was a disgrace to be loved by him, a shame worse than death.

He would never dance again. He wished never to see them again, those lovely women.

He knew it too well. Those beautiful eyes, those red cheeks burned not for him. Not for him floated those light feet, nor rung that low laugh.

Yes, dance with him, flirt with him, that they could do, but not one of them would be his in earnest.

The poet went into the smoking-room to the old men, and sat down by one of the card-tables. He happened to throw himself down by the same table where the powerful master of Björne sat and played "baccarat" holding the bank with a great pile of silver in front of him.

The play was already high. Gösta gave it an even greater impulse. Green bank-notes appeared, and always the pile of money grew in front of the powerful Melchior Sinclair.

But before Gösta also gathered both coins and notes, and soon he was the only one who held out in the struggle against the great land-owner at Björne,

Soon the great pile of money changed over from Melchior Sinclair to Gösta Berling.

"Gösta, my boy," cried the land-owner, laughing, when he had played away everything he had in his pocket-book and purse, "what shall we do now? I am bankrupt, and I never play with borrowed money. I promised my wife that."

He discovered a way. He played away his watch and his beaver coat, and was just going to stake his horse and sledge when Sintram checked him.

"Stake something to win on," he advised him. "Stake something to turn the luck."

"What the devil have I got?"

"Play your reddest heart's blood, brother Melchior. Stake your daughter!"

"You would never venture that," said Gösta, laughing. "That prize I would never get under my roof."

Melchior could not help laughing also. He could not endure that Marianne's name should be mentioned at the card-tables, but this was so insanely ridiculous that he could not be angry. To play away Marianne to Gösta, yes, that he certainly could venture.

"That is to say," he explained, "that if you can win her consent, Gösta, I will stake my blessing to the marriage on this card."

Gösta staked all his winnings and the play began. He won, and Sinclair stopped playing. He could not fight against such bad luck; he saw that.

The night slipped by; it was past midnight. The lovely women's cheeks began to grow pale; curls hung straight, ruffles were crumpled. The old ladies rose up from the sofa-corners and said that as they had been there twelve hours, it was about time for them to be thinking of home.

And the beautiful ball should be over, but then Lilliecrona himself seized the fiddle and struck up the last polka. The horses stood at the door; the old ladies were dressed in their cloaks and shawls; the old men wound their plaids about them and buckled their galoshes.

But the young people could not tear themselves from the dance. They danced in their out-door wraps, and a mad dance it was. As soon as a girl stopped dancing with one partner, another came and dragged her away with him.

And even the sorrowful Gösta was dragged into the whirl. He hoped to dance away grief and humiliation; he wished to have the love of life in his blood again; he longed to be gay, he as well as the others. And he danced till the walls went round, and he no longer knew what he was doing.

Who was it he had got hold of in the crowd? She was light and supple, and he felt that streams of fire went from one to the other. Ah, Marianne!

While Gösta danced with Marianne, Sintram sat in his sledge before the door, and beside him stood Melchior Sinclair.

The great land-owner was impatient at being forced to wait for Marianne. He stamped in the snow with his great snow-boots and beat with his arms, for it was bitter cold.

"Perhaps you ought not to have played Marianne away to Gösta," said Sintram.

"What do you mean?"

Sintram arranged his reins and lifted his whip, before he answered:—

"It did not belong to the tableau, that kissing."

The powerful land-owner raised his arm for a death-blow, but Sintram was already gone. He drove away, whipping the horse to a wild gallop without daring to look back, for Melchior Sinclair had a heavy hand and short patience.

He went now into the dancing-room to look for his daughter, and saw how Gösta and Marianne were dancing.

Wild and giddy was that last polka.

Some of the couples were pale, others glowing red, dust lay like smoke over the hall, the wax-candles gleamed, burned down to the sockets, and in the midst of all the ghostly ruin, they flew on, Gösta and Marianne, royal in their tireless strength, no blemish on their beauty, happy in the glorious motion.

Melchior Sinclair watched them for a while; but then he went and left Marianne to dance. He slammed the door, tramped down the stairs, and placed himself in the sledge, where his wife already waited, and drove home.

When Marianne stopped dancing and asked after her parents, they were gone.

When she was certain of this she showed no surprise. She dressed herself quietly and went out in the yard. The ladies in the dressing-room thought that she drove in her own sledge.

She hurried in her thin satin shoes along the road without telling any one of her distress.

In the darkness no one recognized her, as she went by the edge of the road; no one could think that this late wanderer, who was driven up into the high drifts by the passing sledges, was the beautiful Marianne.

When she could go in the middle of the road she began to run. She ran as long as she was able, then walked for a while, then ran again. A hideous, torturing fear drove her on.

From Ekeby to Björne it cannot be farther than at most two miles. Marianne was soon at home, but she thought almost that she had come the wrong way. When she reached the house all the doors were closed, all the lights out; she wondered if her parents had not come home.

She went forward and twice knocked loudly on the front door. She seized the door-handle and shook it till the noise resounded through the whole house. No one came and opened, but when she let the iron go, which she had grasped with her bare hands, the fast-frozen skin was torn from them.

Melchior Sinclair had driven home in order to shut his door on his only child.

He was drunk with much drinking, wild with rage. He hated his daughter, because she liked Gösta Berling. He had shut the servants into the kitchen, and his wife in the bedroom. With solemn oaths be told them that the one who let Marianne in, he would beat to a jelly. And they knew that he would keep his word.

No one had ever seen him so angry. Such a grief had never come to him before. Had his daughter come into his presence, he would perhaps have killed her.

Golden ornaments, silken dresses had he given her, wit and learning had been instilled in her. She had been his pride, his glory. He had been as proud of her as if she had worn a crown. Oh, his queen, his goddess, his honored, beautiful, proud Marianne! Had he ever denied her anything? Had he not always considered himself too common to be her father? Oh, Marianne, Marianne!

Ought he not to hate her, when she is in love with Gösta Berling and kisses him? Should he not cast her out, shut his door against her, when she will disgrace her greatness by loving such a man? Let her stay at Ekeby, let her run to the neighbors for shelter, let her sleep in the snow-drifts; it's all the same, she has already been dragged in the dirt, the lovely Marianne. The bloom is gone. The lustre of her life is gone.

He lies there in his bed, and hears how she beats on the door. What does that matter to him? He is asleep. Outside stands one who will marry a dismissed priest; he has no home for such a one. If he had loved her less, if he had been less proud of her, he could have let her come in.

Yes, his blessing he could not refuse them. He had played it away. But to open the door for her, that he would not do. Ah, Marianne!

The beautiful young woman still stood outside the door of her home. One minute she shook the lock in powerless rage, the next she fell on her knees, clasped her mangled hands, and begged for forgiveness.

But no one heard her, no one answered, no one opened to her.

Oh! was it not terrible? I am filled with horror as I tell of it. She came from a ball whose queen she had been! She had been proud, rich, happy; and in one minute she was cast into such an endless misery. Shut out from her home, exposed to the cold,—not scorned, not beaten, not cursed, but shut out with cold, immovable lovelessness.

Think of the cold, starlit night, which spread its arch above her, the great wide night with the empty, desolate snow-fields, with the silent woods. Everything slept, everything was sunk in painless sleep; only one living point in all that sleeping whiteness. All sorrow and pain and horror, which otherwise had been spread over the world, crept forward towards that one lonely point. O God, to suffer alone in the midst of this sleeping, ice-bound world!

For the first time in her life she met with unmercifulness and hardness. Her mother would not take the trouble to leave her bed to save her. The old servants, who had guided her first steps, heard her and did not move a finger for her sake. For what crime was she punished?

Where should she find compassion, if not at this door? If she had been a murderess, she would still have knocked on it, knowing that they would forgive her. If she had sunk to being the most miserable of creatures, come wasted and in rags, she would still confidently have gone up to that door, and expected a loving welcome. That door was the entrance to her home; behind it she could only meet with love.

Had not her father tried her enough? Would they not soon open to her?

"Father, father!" she called. "Let me come in! I freeze, I tremble. It is terrible out here!

"Mother, mother! You who have gone so many steps to serve me, you who have watched so many nights over me, why do you sleep now? Mother, mother, wake just this one night, and I will never give you pain again!"

She calls, and falls into breathless silence to listen for an answer. But no one heard her, no one obeyed her, no one answered.

Then she wrings her hands in despair, but there are no tears in her eyes.

The long, dark house with its closed doors and darkened windows lay awful and motionless in the night. What would become of her, who was home-less? Branded and dishonored was she, as long as she encumbered the earth. And her father himself pressed the red-hot iron deeper into her shoulders.

"Father," she called once more, "what will become of me? People will believe the worst of me."

She wept and suffered; her body was stiff with cold.

Alas, that such misery can reach one, who but lately stood so high! It is so easy to be plunged into the deepest suffering! Should we not fear life? Who sails in a safe craft? Round about us swell sorrows like a heaving ocean; see how the hungry waves lick the ship's sides, see how they rage up over her. Ah, no safe anchorage, no solid ground, no steady ship, as far as the eye can see; only an unknown sky over an ocean of sorrow!

But hush! At last, at last! A light step comes through the hall.

"Is it mother?" asked Marianne.

"Yes, my child."

"May I come in now?"

"Father will not let you come in."

"I have run in the snow-drifts in my thin shoes all the way from Ekeby. I have stood here an hour and knocked and called. I am freezing to death out here. Why did you drive away and leave me?"

"My child, my child, why did you kiss Gösta Berling?"

"But father must have seen that I do not like him
for that. It was in fun. Does he think that I will marry Gösta?"

"Go to the gardener's house, Marianne, and beg that you pass the night there. Your father is drunk. He will not listen to reason. He has kept me a prisoner up there. I crept out when I thought he was asleep. He will kill me, if you come in."

"Mother, mother, shall I go to strangers when I have a home? Are you as hard as father? How can you allow me to be shut out? I will lay myself in the drift out here, if you do not let me in."

Then Marianne's mother laid her hand on the lock to open the door, but at the same moment a heavy step was heard on the stair, and a harsh voice called her.

Marianne listened: her mother hurried away, the harsh voice cursed her and then—
Marianne heard something terrible,—she could hear every sound in the silent house.

She heard the thud of a blow, a blow with a stick or a box on the ear; then she heard a faint noise, and then again a blow.

He struck her mother, the terrible brutal Melchior Sinclair struck his wife!

And in pale horror Marianne threw herself down on the threshold and writhed in anguish. Now she wept, and her tears froze to ice on the threshold of her home.

Grace! pity! Open, open, that she might bend her own back under the blows! Oh, that he could strike her mother, strike her, because she did not wish to see her daughter the next day lying dead in the snow-drift, because she had wished to comfort her child!

Great humiliation had come to Marianne that night She had fancied herself a queen, and she lay there little better than a whipped slave.

But she rose up in cold rage. Once more she struck the door with her bloody hand and called:—

"Hear what I say to you,—you, who beat my mother. You shall weep for this, Melchior Sinclair, weep!"

Then she went and laid herself to rest in the snowdrift. She threw off her cloak and lay in her black velvet dress, easily distinguishable against the white snow. She lay and thought how her father would come out the next day on his early morning tour of inspection and find her there. She only hoped that he himself might find her.

O Death, pale friend, is it as true as it is consoling, that I never can escape meeting you? Even to me, the lowliest of earth's workers, will you come, to loosen the torn leather shoes from my feet, to take the spade and the barrow from my hand, to take the working-dress from my body. With gentle force you lay me out on a lace-trimmed bed; you adorn me with draped linen sheets. My feet need no more shoes, my hands are clad in snow-white gloves, which no more work shall soil. Consecrated by thee to the sweetness of rest, I shall sleep a sleep of a thousand years. Oh deliverer! The lowliest of earth's laborers am I, and I dream with a thrill of pleasure of the hour when I shall be received into your kingdom.

Pale friend, on me you can easily try your strength, but I tell you that the fight was harder against those women of the olden days. Life's strength was mighty in their slender bodies, no cold could cool their hot blood. You had laid Marianne on your bed, O Death, and you sat by her side, as an old nurse sits by the cradle to lull the child to sleep. You faithful old nurse, who know what is good for the children of men, how angry you must be when playmates come, who with noise and romping wake your sleeping child. How vexed you must have been when the pensioners lifted the lovely Marianne out of the bed, when a man laid her against his breast, and warm tears fell from his eyes on to her face.

At Ekeby all lights were out, and all the guests had gone. The pensioners stood alone in the bachelors' wing, about the last half-emptied punch bowl.

Then Gösta rung on the edge of the bowl and made a speech for you, women of the olden days. To speak of you, he said, was to speak of the kingdom of heaven: you were all beauties, ever bright, ever young, ever lovely and gentle as a mother's eyes when she looks down on her child. Soft as young squirrels you hung on your husband's neck, your voice never trembled with anger, no frowns ruffled your brow, your white hands were never harsh and hard. Sweet saints, you were adored images in the temple of home. Men lay at your feet, offering you incense and prayers. Through you love worked its wonders, and round your temples poetry wreathed its gold, gleaming glory.

And the pensioners sprang up, wild with wine, wild with his words, with their blood raging. Old Eberhard and the lazy Christopher drew back from the sport. In the wildest haste the pensioners harnessed horses to sledges and hurried out in the cold night to pay homage to those who never could be honored enough, to sing a serenade to each and all of them who possessed the rosy cheeks and bright eyes which had just lighted up Ekeby halls.

But the pensioners did not go far on their happy way, for when they came to Björne, they found Marianne lying in the snow-drift, just by the door of her home.

They trembled and raged to see her there. It was like finding a worshipped saint lying mangled and stripped outside the church-door.

Gösta shook his clenched hand at the dark house. "You children of hate," he cried, "you hail-storms, you ravagers of God's pleasure-house!"

Beerencreutz lighted his horn lantern and let it shine down on the livid face. Then the pensioners saw Marianne's mangled hands, and the tears which had frozen to ice on her eyelashes, and they wailed like women, for she was not merely a saintly image, but a beautiful woman, who had been a joy to their old hearts.

Gösta Berling threw himself on his knees beside her.

"She is lying here, my bride," he said. "She gave me the betrothal kiss a few hours ago, and her father has promised me his blessing. She lies and waits for me to come and share her white bed."

And Gösta lifted up the lifeless form in his strong arms.

"Home to Ekeby with her!" he cried. "Now she is mine. In the snow-drift I have found her; no one shall take her from me. We will not wake them in there. What has she to do behind those doors, against which she has beaten her hand into blood?"

He was allowed to do as he wished. He laid Marianne in the foremost sledge and sat down at her side. Beerencreutz sat behind and took the reins.

"Take snow and rub her, Gösta!" he commanded.

The cold had paralyzed her limbs, nothing more. The wildly agitated heart still beat. She had not even lost consciousness; she knew all about the pensioners, and how they had found her, but she could not move. So she lay stiff and stark in the sledge, while Gösta Berling rubbed her with snow and alternately wept and kissed, and she felt an infinite longing to be able only to lift a hand, that she might give a caress in return.

She remembered everything. She lay there stiff and motionless and thought more clearly than ever before. Was she in love with Gösta Berling? Yes, she was. Was it merely a whim of the moment? No, it had been for many years. She compared herself with him and the other people in Värmland. They were all just like children. They followed whatever impulse came to them.. They only lived the outer life, had never looked deep into their souls. But she had become what one grows to be by living in the world; she could never really lose herself in anything. If she loved, yes, whatever she did, one half of her stood and looked on with a cold scorn. She had longed for a passion which should carry her away in wild heedlessness, and now it had come. When she kissed Gösta Berling on the balcony, for the first time she had forgotten herself.

And now the passion came over her again, her heart throbbed so that she heard it beat. Should she not soon be mistress of her limbs? She felt a wild joy that she had been thrust out from her home. Now she could be Gösta's without hesitation. How stupid she had been, to have subdued her love so many years. Ah, it is so sweet to yield to love.

But shall she never, never be free from these icy chains? She has been ice within and fire on the surface; now it is the opposite, a soul of fire in a body of ice.

Then Gösta feels how two arms gently are raised about his neck in a weak, feeble pressure.

He could only just feel them, but Marianne thought that she gave expression to the suppressed passion in her by a suffocating embrace.

But when Beerencreutz saw it he let the horse go as it would along the familiar road. He raised his eyes and looked obstinately and unceasingly at the Pleiades.

CHAPTER VII. THE OLD VEHICLES

IF it should happen to you that you are sitting or lying and reading this at night, as I am writing it during the silent hours, then do not draw a sigh of relief here and think that the good pensioners were allowed to have an undisturbed sleep, after they had come back with Marianne and made her a good bed in the best guest-room beyond the big drawing-room.

They went to bed, and went to sleep, but it was not their lot to sleep in peace and quiet till noon, as you and I, dear reader, might have done, if we had been awake till four in the morning and our limbs ached with fatigue.

It must not be forgotten that the old major's wife went about the country with beggar's wallet and stick, and that it never was her way, when she had anything to do, to think of a poor tired sinner's convenience. And now she would do it even less, as she had decided to drive the pensioners that very night from Ekeby.

Gone was the day when she sat in splendor and magnificence at Ekeby and sowed happiness over the earth, as God sows stars over the skies. And while she wandered homeless about the land, the authority and honor of the great estate was left in the pensioners' hands to be guarded by them, as the wind guards ashes, as the spring sun guards the snow-drift.

It sometimes happened that the pensioners drove out, six or eight of them, in a long sledge drawn by four horses, with chiming bells and braided reins. If they met the major's wife, as she went as a beggar, they did not turn away their heads.

Clenched fists were stretched against her. By a violent swing of the sledge, she was forced up into the drifts by the roadside, and Major Fuchs, the bear-killer, always took pains to spit three times to take away the evil effect of meeting the old woman.

They had no pity on her. She was as odious as a witch to them as she went along the road. If any mishap had befallen her, they would no more have grieved than he who shoots off his gun on Easter Eve, loaded with brass hooks, grieves that he has hit a witch flying by.

It was to secure their salvation that these unhappy pensioners persecuted the major's wife. People have often been cruel and tortured one another with the greatest hardness, when they have trembled for their souls.

When the pensioners late at night reeled from the drinking-tables to the window to see if the night was calm and clear, they often noticed a dark shadow, which glided over the grass, and knew that the major's wife had come to see her beloved home; then the bachelors' wing rang with the pensioners' scornful laughter, and gibes flew from the open windows down to her.

Verily, lovelessness and arrogance began to take possession of the penniless adventurers' hearts. Sin-tram had planted hate. Their souls could not have been in greater danger if the major's wife had remained at Ekeby. More die in flight than in battle.

The major's wife cherished no great anger against the pensioners.

If she had had the power, she would have whipped them like naughty boys and then granted them he grace and favor again.

But now she feared for her beloved lands, which were in the pensioners' hands to be guarded by them, as wolves guard the sheep, as crows guard the spring grain.

There are many who have suffered the same sorrow. She is not the only one who has seen ruin come to a beloved home and well-kept fields fall into decay. They have seen their childhood's home look at them like a wounded animal. Many feel like culprits when they see the trees there wither away, and the paths covered with tufts of grass. They wish to throw themselves on their knees in those fields, which once boasted of rich harvests, and beg them not to blame them for the disgrace which befalls them. And they turn away from the poor old horses; they have not courage to meet their glance. And they dare not stand by the gate and see the cattle come home from pasture. There is no spot on earth so sad to visit as an old home in ruin.

When I think what that proud Ekeby must have suffered under the pensioners' rule, I wish that the plan of the major's wife had been fulfilled, and that Ekeby had been taken from them.

It was not her thought to take back her dominion again.

She had only one object,—to rid her home of these madmen, these locusts, these wild brigands, in whose path no grass grew.

While she went begging about the land and lived on alms, she continually thought of her mother; and the thought bit deep into her heart, that there could be no bettering for her till her mother lifted the curse from her shoulders.

No one had ever mentioned the old woman's death, so she must be still living up there by the iron-works in the forest. Ninety years old, she still lived in unceasing labor, watching over her milk-pans in the summer, her charcoal-kilns in the winter, working till death, longing for the day when she would have completed her life's duties.

And the major's wife thought that her mother had lived so long in order to be able to lift the curse from her life. That mother could not die who had called down such misery on her child.

So the major's wife wanted to go to the old woman, that they might both get rest. She wished to struggle up through the dark woods by the long river to the home of her childhood.

Till then she could not rest There were many who offered her a warm home and all the comforts of a faithful friendship, but she would not stop anywhere. Grim and fierce, she went from house to house, for she was weighed down by the curse.

She was going to struggle up to her mother, but first she wanted to provide for her beloved home. She would not go and leave it in the hands of light-minded spendthrifts, of worthless drunkards, of good-for-nothing dispersers of God's gifts.

Should she go to find on her return her inheritance gone to waste, her hammers silent, her horses starving, her servants scattered? Ah, no, once more she will rise in her might and drive out the pensioners.

She well understood that her husband saw with joy how her inheritance was squandered. But she knew him enough to understand, also, that if she drove away his devouring locusts, he would be too lazy to get new ones. Were the pensioners removed, then her old bailiff and overseer could carry on the work at Ekeby in the old grooves.

And so, many nights her dark shadow had glided along the black lanes. She had stolen in and out of the cottagers' houses, she had whispered with the miller and the mill-hands in the lower floor of the great mill, she had conferred with the smith in the dark coal-house.

And they had all sworn to help her. The honor of the great estate should no longer be left in the hands of careless pensioners, to be guarded as the wind guards the ashes, as the wolf guards the flock of sheep.

And this night, when the merry gentlemen had danced, played, and drunk until they had sunk down on their beds in a dead sleep, this very night they must go. She has let them have their good time. She has sat in the smithy and awaited the end of the ball. She has waited still longer, until the pensioners should return from their nocturnal drive. She has sat in silent waiting, until the message was brought her that the last light was out in the bachelors' wing and that the great house slept. Then she rose and went out.

The major's wife ordered that all the workmen on the estate should be gathered together up by the bachelors' wing; she herself went to the house. There she went to the main building, knocked, and was let in. The young daughter of the minister at Broby, whom she had trained to be a capable maidservant, was there to meet her.

"You are so welcome, madame," said the maid, and kissed her hand.

"Put out the light!" said the major's wife. "Do you think I cannot find my way without a candle?"

And then she began a wandering through the silent house. She went from the cellar to the attic, and said farewell. With stealthy step they went from room to room.

The major's wife was filled with old memories. The maid neither sighed nor sobbed, but tear after tear flowed unchecked from her eyes, while she followed her mistress. The major's wife had her open the linen-closet and silver-chest, and passed her hand over the fine damask table-cloths and the magnificent silver service. She felt caressingly the mighty pile of pillows in the store-closet She touched all the implements, the looms, the spinning-wheels, and winding-bobbins. She thrust her hand into the spice-box, and felt the rows of tallow candles which hung from the rafters.

"The candles are dry," she said. "They can be taken down and put away."

She was down in the cellar, carefully lifted the beer-casks, and groped over the rows of wine bottles.

She went into the pantry and kitchen; she felt everything, examined everything. She stretched out her hand and said farewell to everything in her house.

Last she went through the rooms. She found the long broad sofas in their places; she laid her hand on the cool slabs of the marble tables, and on the mirrors with their frames of gilded dancing nymphs.

"This is a rich house," she said. "A noble man was he who gave me all this for my own."

In the great drawing-room, where the dance had lately whirled, the stiff-backed arm-chairs already stood in prim order against the walls.

She went over to the piano, and very gently struck a chord.

"Joy and gladness were no strangers here in my time, either," she said.

She went also to the guest-room beyond. It was pitch-dark. The major's wife groped with her hands and came against the maid's face.

"Are you weeping?" she said, for she felt her hands were wet with tears.

Then the young girl burst out sobbing.

"Madame," she cried, "madame, they will destroy everything. Why do you leave us and let the pensioners ruin your house?"

The major's wife drew back the curtain and pointed out into the yard.

"Is it I who have taught you to weep and lament?" she cried. "Look out! the place is full of people; to-morrow there will not be one pensioner left at Ekeby."

"Are you coming back?" asked the maid.

"My time has not yet come," said the major's wife. "The highway is my home, and the haystack my bed. But you shall watch over Ekeby for me, child, while I am away."

And they went on. Neither of them knew or thought that Marianne slept in that very room. But she did not sleep. She was wide awake, heard everything, and understood it all. She had lain there in bed and sung a hymn to Love.

"You conqueror, who have taken me out of myself," she said, "I lay in fathomless misery and you have changed it to a paradise. My hands stuck fast to the iron latch of the closed door and were torn and wounded; on the threshold of my home my tears lie frozen to pearls of ice. Anger froze my heart when I heard the blows on my mother's back. In the cold snow-drift I hoped to sleep away my anger, but you came. O Love, child of fire, to one who was frozen by much cold you came. When I compare my sufferings to the glory won by them, they seem to me as nothing. I am free of all ties. I have no father nor mother, no home. People will believe all evil of me and turn away from me. It has pleased you to do this, O Love, for why should I stand higher than my beloved? Hand in hand we will wander out into the world. Gösta Berling's bride is penniless; he found her in a snow-drift. We shall not live in lofty halls, but in a cottage at the edge of the wood. I shall help him to watch the kiln, I shall help him to set snares for partridges and hares, I shall cook his food and mend his clothes. Oh, my beloved, how I shall long and mourn, while I sit there alone by the edge of the wood and wait for you! But not for the days of riches, only for you; only you shall I look for and miss,—your footstep on the forest path, your joyous song, as you come with your axe on your shoulder. Oh, my beloved, my beloved! As long as my life lasts, I could sit and wait for you."

So she lay and sang hymns to the heart-conquering god, and never once had closed her eyes in sleep when the major's wife came in.

When she had gone, Marianne got up and dressed herself. Once more must she put on the black velvet dress and the thin satin slippers. She wrapped a blanket about her like a shawl, and hurried out once again into the terrible night.

Calm, starlit, and bitingly cold the February night lay over the earth; it was as if it would never end. And the darkness and the cold of that long night lasted on the earth long, long after the sun had risen, long after the snow-drifts through which Marianne wandered had been changed to water. Marianne hurried away from Ekeby to get help. She could not let those men who had rescued her from the snow-drift and opened their hearts and home to her be hunted away. She went down to Sjö to Major Samzelius. It would be an hour before she could be back.

When the major's wife had said farewell to her home, she went out into the yard, where her people were waiting, and the struggle began.

She placed them round about the high, narrow house, the upper story of which was the pensioners' far-famed home,—the great room with the whitewashed walls, the red-painted chests, and the great folding-table, where playing-cards swim in the spilled brandy, where the broad beds are hidden by yellow striped curtains where the pensioners sleep.

And in the stable before full mangers the pensioners' horses sleep and dream of the journeys of their youth. It is sweet to dream when they know that they never again shall leave the filled cribs, the warm stalls of Ekeby.

In a musty old carriage-house, where all the broken-down coaches and worn-out sledges were stored, was a wonderful collection of old vehicles.

Many are the pensioners who have lived and died at Ekeby. Their names are forgotten on the earth, and they have no longer a place in men's hearts; but the major's wife has kept the vehicles in which they came to Ekeby, she has collected them all in the old carriage-house.

And there they stand and sleep, and dust falls thick, thick over them.

But now in this February night the major's wife has the door opened to the carriage-house, and with lanterns and torches she seeks out the vehicles which belong to Ekeby's present pensioners,—Beerencreutz's old gig, and Örneclou's coach, painted with coat of arms, and the narrow cutter which had brought Cousin Christopher.

She does not care if the vehicles are for summer or winter, she only sees that each one gets his own.

And in the stable they are now awake, all the pensioners' old horses, who had so lately been dreaming before full mangers. The dream shall be true.

You shall again try the steep hills, and the musty hay in the sheds of wayside inns, and drunken horse-dealers' sharp whips, and the mad races on ice so slippery that you tremble only to walk on it.

The old beasts mouth and snort when the bit is put into their toothless jaws; the old vehicles creak and crack. Pitiful infirmity, which should have been allowed to sleep in peace till the end of the world, was now dragged out before all eyes; stiff joints, halting forelegs, spavin, and broken-wind are shown up.

The stable grooms succeed, however, in getting the horses harnessed; then they go and ask the major's wife in what Gösta Berling shall be put, for, as every one knows, he came to Ekeby in the coal-sledge of the major's wife.

"Put Don Juan in our best sledge," she says, "and spread over it the bear-skin with the silver claws!" And when the grooms grumble, she continues: "There is not a horse in my stable which I would not give to be rid of that man, remember that!"

Well, now the vehicles are waked and the horses too, but the pensioners still sleep. It is now their time to be brought out in the winter night; but it is a more perilous deed to seize them in their beds than to lead out stiff-legged horses and shaky old carriages. They are bold, strong men, tried in a hundred adventures; they are ready to defend themselves till death; it is no easy thing to take them against their will from out their beds and down to the carriages which shall carry them away.

The major's wife has them set fire to a hay-stack, which stands so near the house that the flames must shine in to where the pensioners are sleeping.

"The hay-stack is mine, all Ekeby is mine," she says.

And when the stack is in flames, she cries: "Wake them now!"

But the pensioners sleep behind well-closed doors. The whole mass of people begin to cry out that terrible "Fire, fire!" but the pensioners sleep on.

The master-smith's heavy sledge-hammer thunders against the door, but the pensioners sleep.

A hard snowball breaks the window-pane and flies into the room, rebounding against the bed-curtains, but the pensioners sleep.

They dream that a lovely girl throws a handkerchief at them, they dream of applause from behind fallen curtains, they dream of gay laughter and the deafening noise of midnight feasts.

The noise of cannon at their ears, an ocean of ice-cold water were needed to awake them.

They have bowed, danced, played, acted, and sung. They are heavy with wine, exhausted, and sleep a sleep as deep as death's.

This blessed sleep almost saves them.

The people begin to think that this quiet conceals a danger. What if it means that the pensioners are already out to get help? What if it means that they stand awake, with finger on the trigger, on guard behind windows or door, ready to fall upon the first who enters?

These men are crafty, ready to fight; they must mean something by their silence. Who can think it of them, that they would let themselves be surprised in their lairs like bears?

The people bawl their "Fire, fire!" time after time, but nothing avails.

Then when all are trembling, the major's wife herself takes an axe and bursts open the outer door.

Then she rushes alone up the stairs, throws open the door to the bachelors' wing, and calls into the room: "Fire!"

Hers is a voice which finds a better echo in the pensioners' ears than the people's outcry. Accustomed to obey that voice, twelve men at the same moment spring from their beds, see the flames, throw on their clothes, and rush down the stairs out into the yard.

But at the door stands the great master-smith and two stout mill-hands, and deep disgrace then befalls the pensioners. Each, as he comes down, is seized, thrown to the ground, and his feet bound; thereupon he is carried without ceremony to the vehicle prepared for him.

None escaped; they were all caught. Beerencreutz, the grim colonel, was bound and carried away; also Christian Bergh, the mighty captain, and Eberhard, the philosopher.

Even the invincible, the terrible Gösta Berling was caught. The major's wife had succeeded.

She was still greater than the pensioners.

They are pitiful to see, as they sit with bound limbs in the mouldy old vehicles. There are hanging heads and angry glances, and the yard rings with oaths and wild bursts of powerless rage.

The major's wife goes from one to the other.

"You shall swear," she says, "never to come back to Ekeby."

"Begone, hag!"

"You shall swear," she says, "otherwise I will throw you into the bachelors' wing, bound as you are, and you shall burn up in there, for tonight I am going to burn down the bachelors' wing."

"You dare not do that."

"Dare not! Is not Ekeby mine? Ah, you villain! Do you think I do not remember how you spit at me on the highway? Did I not long to set fire here just now and let you all burn up? Did you lift a finger to defend me when I was driven from my home? No, swear now!"

And she stands there so terrible, although she pretends perhaps to be more angry than she is, and so many men armed with axes stand about her, that they are obliged to swear, that no worse misfortune may happen.

The major's wife has their clothes and boxes brought down and has their hand-fetters loosened; then the reins are laid in their hands.

But much time has been consumed, and Marianne has reached Sjö.

The major was no late-riser; he was dressed when she came. She met him in the yard; he had been out with his bears' breakfast.

He did not say anything when he heard her story. He only went in to the bears, put muzzles on them, led them out, and hurried away to Ekeby.

Marianne followed him at a distance. She was dropping with fatigue, but then she saw a bright light of fire in the sky and was frightened nearly to death.

What a night it was! A man beats his wife and leaves his child to freeze to death outside his door. Did a woman now mean to burn up her enemies; did the old major mean to let loose the bears on his own people?

She conquered her weariness, hurried past the major, and ran madly up to Ekeby.

She had a good start. When she reached the yard, she made her way through the crowd. When she stood in the middle of the ring, face to face with the major's wife, she cried as loud as she could,—

"The major, the major is coming with the bears!"

There was consternation among the people; all eyes turned to the major's wife.

"You have gone for him;" she said to Marianne.

"Run!" cried the latter, more earnestly. "Away, for God's sake! I do not know what the major is thinking of, but he has the bears with him."

All stood still and looked at the major's wife.

"I thank you for your help, children," she said quietly to the people. "Everything which has happened to-night has been so arranged that no one of you can be prosecuted by the law or get into trouble

for it. Go home now! I do not want to see any of my people murder or be murdered. Go now!"

Still the people waited.

The major's wife turned to Marianne.

"I know that you are in love," she said. "You act in love's madness. May the day never come when you must look on powerless at the ruin of your home! May you always be mistress over your tongue and your hand when anger fills the soul!"

"Dear children, come now, come!" she continued, turning to the people. "May God protect Ekeby! I must go to my mother. Oh, Marianne, when you have got back your senses, when Ekeby is ravaged, and the land sighs in want, think on what you have done this night, and look after the people!"

Thereupon she went, followed by her people.

When the major reached the yard, he found there no living thing but Marianne and a long line of horses with sledges and carriages,—a long dismal line, where the horses were not worse than the vehicles, nor the vehicles worse than their owners. Ill-used in the struggle of life were they all.

Marianne went forward and freed them.

She noticed how they bit their lips and looked away. They were ashamed as never before. A great disgrace had befallen them.

"I was not better off when I lay on my knees on the steps at Björne a couple of hours ago," said Marianne.

And so, dear reader, what happened afterwards that night—how the old vehicles were put into the carriage-house, the horses in the stable, and the pensioners in their house—I shall not try to relate. The dawn began to appear over the eastern hills, and

the day came clear and calm."How much quieter the bright, sunny days are than the dark nights, under whose protecting wings beasts of prey hunt and owls hoot!

I will only say that when the pensioners had gone in again and had found a few drops in the last punchbowl to fill their glasses, a sudden ecstasy came over them.

"A toast for the major's wife!" they cried.

Ah, she is a matchless woman! What better could they wish for than to serve her, to worship her?

Was it not sad that the devil had got her in his power, and that all her endeavors were to send poor gentlemen's souls to hell?

CHAPTER VIII. THE GREAT BEAR IN GURLITTA CLIFF

IN the darkness of the forests dwell unholy creatures, whose jaws are armed with horrible, glittering teeth or sharp beaks, whose feet have pointed claws, which long to sink themselves in a blood-filled throat, and whose eyes shine with murderous desires.

There the wolves live, who come out at night and hunt the peasant's sledge until the wife must take her little child, which sits upon her knee, and throw it to them, to save her own and her husband's life.

There the lynx lives, which the people call "göpa," for in the woods at least it is dangerous to call it by its right name. He who speaks of it during the day had best see that the doors and windows of the sheep-house are well closed towards night, for otherwise it will come. It climbs right up the walls, for its claws are strong as steel nails, glides in through the smallest hole, and throws itself on the sheep. And "göpa "hangs on their throats, and drinks their blood, and kills and tears, till every sheep is dead. He does not cease his wild death-dance among the terrified animals as long as any of them show a sign of life.

And in the morning the peasant finds all the sheep lying dead with torn throats, for "göpa" leaves nothing living where he ravages.

There the great owl lives, which hoots at dusk. If one mimics him, he comes whizzing down with outspread wings and strikes out one's eyes, for he is no real bird, but an evil spirit.

And there lives the most terrible of them all, the bear, who has the strength of twelve men, and who, when he becomes a devil, can be killed only with a silver bullet.

And if one should chance to meet him in the wood, big and high as a wandering cliff, one must not run, nor defend one's self; one must throw one's self down on the ground and pretend to be dead. Many small children have imagined themselves lying on the ground with the bear over them. He has rolled them over with his paw, and they have felt his hot breath on their faces, but they have lain quiet, until he has gone away to dig a hole to bury them in. Then they have softly raised themselves up and stolen away, slowly at first, then in mad haste.

But think, think if the bear had not thought them really dead, but had taken a bite, or if he had been very hungry and wanted to eat them right up, or if he had seen them when they moved and had run after them. O God!

Terror is a witch. She sits in the dimness of the forest, sings magic songs to people, and fills their hearts with frightful thoughts. From her comes that deadly fear which weighs down life and darkens the beauty of smiling landscapes. Nature is malignant, treacherous as a sleeping snake; one can believe nothing. There lies Lofven's lake in brilliant beauty; but trust it not, it lures to destruction. Every year it must gather its tribute of the drowned. There lies the wood temptingly peaceful; but trust it not! The wood is full of unholy things, beset with evil spirits and bloodthirsty vagrants' souls.

Trust not the brook with its gliding waters. It is sudden sickness and death to wade in it after sunset. Trust not the cuckoo, who sings so gayly in the spring. In the autumn he becomes a hawk with fierce eyes and terrible claws. Trust not the moss, nor the heather, nor the rock. Nature is evil, full of invisible powers, who hate man. There is no spot where you can set your foot in safety; it is wonderful that your weak race can escape so much persecution.

Terror is a witch. Does she still sit in the darkness of the woods of Värmland? Does she still darken the beauty of smiling places, does she still dampen the joy of living? Great her power has been. I know it well, who have put steel in the cradle and a red-hot coal in the bath; I know it, who have felt her iron hand around my heart.

But no one shall think that I now am going to relate anything terrible or dreadful. It is only an old story of the great bear in Gurlitta Cliff which I must tell; and any one can believe it or not, as it always is with hunting stories.

The great bear has its home on the beautiful mountain summit which is called Gurlitta Cliff, and which raises itself precipitously from the shores of the Löfven.

The roots of a fallen pine between which tufts of moss are hanging make the walls and roof of his dwelling, branches and twigs protect it, the snow makes it warm. He can lie there and sleep a good quiet sleep from summer to summer.

Is he, then, a poet, a dreamer, this hairy monarch of the forest? Will he sleep away the cold winter's chill nights and colorless days to be waked by purling brooks and the song of birds? Will he lie there and dream of blushing cranberry bogs, and of ant-hills filled with brown delicious creatures, and of the white lambs which graze on the green slopes? Does he want, happy one! to escape the winter of life?

Outside the snow-storm rages; wolves and foxes wander about, mad with hunger. Why shall the bear alone sleep? Let him get up and feel how the cold bites, how heavy it is to wade in deep snow.

He has bedded himself in so well. He is like the sleeping princess in the fairy tale; and as she was waked by love, so will he be waked by the spring. By a ray of sunlight which penetrates through the twigs and warms his nose, by the drops of melting snow which wet his fur, will he be waked. Woe to him who untimely disturbs him!

He hears, suddenly, shouts, noise, and shots. He shakes the sleep out of his joints, and pushes aside the branches to see what it is. It is not spring, which rattles and roars outside his lair, nor the wind, which overthrows pine-trees and casts up the driving snow, but it is the pensioners, the pensioners from Ekeby, old acquaintances of the forest monarch. He remembered well the night when Fuchs and Beerencreutz sat and dozed in a Nygård peasant's barn, where they awaited a visit from him. They had just fallen asleep over their brandy-bottle, when he swung himself in through the peat-roof; but they awoke, when he was trying to lift the cow he had killed out of the stall, and fell upon him with gun and knife. They took the cow from him and one of his eyes, but he saved his life.

Yes, verily the pensioners and he are old acquaintances. He remembered how they had come on him another time, when he and his queen consort had just laid themselves down for their winter sleep in the old lair here on Gurlitta Cliff and had young ones in the hole. He remembered well how they came on them unawares. He got away all right, throwing to either side everything that stood in his path; but he must limp for life from a bullet in his thigh, and when he came back at night to the royal lair, the snow was red with his queen consort's blood, and the royal children had been carried away to the plain, to grow up there and be man's servants and friends.

Yes, now the ground trembles; now the snow-drift which hides his lair shakes; now he bursts out, the great bear, the pensioners' old enemy. Look out, Fuchs, old bear-killer; look out now, Beerencreutz; look out, Gösta Berling, hero of a hundred adventures!

Woe to all poets, all dreamers, all heroes of romance! There stands Gösta Berling with finger on trigger, and the bear comes straight towards him. Why does he not shoot? What is he thinking of?

Why does he not send a bullet straight into the broad breast? He stands in just the place to do it. The others are not placed right to shoot. Does he think he is on parade before the forest monarch?

Gösta of course stood and dreamed of the lovely Marianne, who is lying at Ekeby dangerously ill, from the chill of that night when she slept in the snow-drift.

He thinks of her, who also is a sacrifice to the curse of hatred which overlies the earth, and he shudders at himself, who has come out to pursue and to kill.

And there comes the great bear right towards him, blind in one eye from the blow of a pensioner's knife, lame in one leg from a bullet from a pensioner's gun, fierce and shaggy, alone, since they had killed his wife and carried away his children. And Gösta sees him as he is,—a poor, persecuted beast, whom he will not deprive of life, all he has left, since people have taken from him everything else.

"Let him kill me," thinks Gösta, "but I will not shoot."

And while the bear breaks his way towards him, he stands quite still as if on parade, and when the forest monarch stands directly in front of him, he presents arms and takes a step to one side.

The bear continues on his way, knowing too well that he has no time to waste, breaks into the wood, ploughs his way through drifts the height of a man, rolls down the steep slopes, and escapes, while all of them, who had stood with cocked guns and waited for Gösta's shot, shoot off their guns after him.

But it is of no avail; the ring is broken, and the bear gone. Fuchs scolds, and Beerencreutz swears, but Gösta only laughs.

How could they ask that any one so happy as he should harm one of God's creatures?

The great bear of Gurlitta Cliff got away thus with his life, and he is waked from his winter sleep, as the peasants will find. No bear has greater skill than he to tear apart the roofs of their low, cellar-like cow-barns; none can better avoid a concealed ambush.

The people about the upper Löfven soon were at their wits' end about him. Message after message was sent down to the pensioners, that they should come and kill the bear.

Day after day, night after night, during the whole of February, the pensioners scour the upper Löfven to find the bear, but he always escapes them. Has he learned cunning from the fox, and swiftness from the wolf? If they lie in wait at one place, he is ravaging the neighboring farmyard; if they seek him in the wood, he is pursuing the peasant, who comes driving over the ice. He has become the boldest of marauders: he creeps into the garret and empties the housewife's honey-jar; he kills the horse in the peasant's sledge.

But gradually they begin to understand what kind of a bear he is and why Gösta could not shoot him. Terrible to say, dreadful to believe, this is no ordinary-bear. No one can hope to kill him if he does not have a silver bullet in his gun. A bullet of silver and bell-metal cast on a Thursday evening at new moon in the church-tower without the priest or the sexton or anybody knowing it would certainly kill him, but such a one is not so easy to get.

There is one man at Ekeby who, more than all the rest, would grieve over all this. It is, as one can easily guess, Anders Fuchs, the bear-killer. He loses both his appetite and his sleep in his anger at not being able to kill the great bear in Gurlitta Cliff. At last even he understands that the bear can only be kilted with a silver bullet.

The grim Major Anders Fuchs was not handsome. He had a heavy, clumsy body, and a broad, red face, with hanging bags under his cheeks and several double chins. His small black moustache sat stiff as a brush above his thick lips, and his black hair stood out rough and thick from his head. Moreover, he was

a man of few words and a glutton. He was not a person whom women meet with sunny smile and open arms, nor did he give them tender glances back again. One could not believe that he ever would see a woman whom he could tolerate, and everything which concerned love and enthusiasm was foreign to him.

One Thursday evening, when the moon, just two fingers wide, lingers above the horizon an hour or two after the sun has gone down, Major Fuchs betakes himself from Ekeby without telling any one where he means to go. He has flint and steel and a bullet-mould in his hunting-bag, and his gun on his back, and goes up towards the church at Bro to see what luck there may be for an honest man.

The church lies on the eastern shore of the narrow sound between the upper and lower Löfven, and Major Fuchs must go over a bridge to get there. He wends his way towards it, deep in his thoughts, without looking up towards Broby hill, where the houses cut sharply against the clear evening sky; he only looks on the ground, and wonders how he shall get hold of the key of the church without anybody's knowing it.

When he comes down to the bridge, he hears some one screaming so despairingly that he has to look up.

At that time the little German, Faber, was organist at Bro. He was a slender man, small in body and mind. And the sexton was Jan Larsson, an energetic peasant, but poor, for the Broby clergyman had cheated him out of his patrimony, five hundred rix-dollars.

The sexton wanted to marry the organist's sister, the little, delicate maiden Faber, but the organist would not let him have her, and therefore the two were not good friends. That evening the sexton has met the organist as he crossed the bridge and has fallen upon him. He seizes him by the shoulder, and holding him at arm's length out over the railing tells him solemnly that he shall drop him into the sound if he does not give him the little maiden. The little German will not give in; he struggles and screams, and reiterates "No," although far below him he sees the black water rushing between the white banks.

"No, no," he screams; "no, no!"

And it is uncertain if the sexton in his rage would have let him down into the cold black water if Major Fuchs had not just then come over the bridge. The sexton is afraid, puts Faber down on solid ground, and runs away as fast as he can.

Little Faber falls on the major's neck to thank him for his life, but the major pushes him away, and says that there is nothing to thank him for. The major has no love for Germans, ever since he had his quarters at Putbus on the Rügen during the Pomeranian war. He had never so nearly starved to death as in those days.

Then little Faber wants to run up to the bailiff Scharling and accuse the sexton of an attempt at murder, but the major lets him know that it is of no use here in the country, for it does not count for anything to kill a German.

Little Faber grows calmer and asks the major to come home with him to eat a bit of sausage and to taste his home-brewed ale.

The major follows him, for he thinks that the organist must have a key to the church-door; and so they go up the hill, where the Bro church stands, with the vicarage, the sexton's cottage and the organist's house round about it.

"You must excuse us," says little Faber, as he and the major enter the house. "It is not really in order to-day. We have had a little to do, my sister and I. We have killed a cock."

"The devil!" cries the major.

The little maid Faber has just come in with the ale in great earthen mugs. Now, every one knows that the major did not look upon women with a tender glance, but this little maiden he had to gaze upon with delight, as she came in so neat in lace and cap. Her light hair lay combed so smooth above her forehead, the home-woven dress was so pretty and so dazzlingly clean, her little hands were so busy and eager, and her little face so rosy and round, that he could not help thinking that if he had seen such a little woman twenty-five years ago, he must have come forward and offered himself.

She is so pretty and rosy and nimble, but her eyes are quite red with weeping. It is that which suggests such tender thoughts.

While the men eat and drink, she goes in and out of the room. Once she comes to her brother, courtesies, and says,—

"How do you wish me to place the cows in the stable?"

"Put twelve on the left and eleven on the right, then they can't gore one another."

"Have you so many cows, Faber?" bursts out the major.

The fact was that the organist had only two cows, but he called one eleven and the other twelve, that it might sound fine, when he spoke of them.

And then the major hears that Faber's barn is being altered, so that the cows are out all day and at night are put into the woodshed.

The little maiden comes again to her brother, courtesies to him, and says that the carpenter had asked how high the barn should be made.

"Measure by the cows," says the organist," measure by the cows!"

Major Fuchs thinks that is such a good answer. However it comes to pass, the major asks the organist why his sister's eyes are so red, and learns that she weeps because he will not let her marry the penniless sexton, in debt and without inheritance as he is.

Major Fuchs grows more and more thoughtful. He empties tankard after tankard, and eats sausage after sausage, without noticing it. Little Faber is appalled at such an appetite and thirst; but the more the major eats and drinks, the clearer and more determined his mind grows. The more decided becomes his resolution to do something for the little maiden Faber.

He has kept his eyes fixed on the great key which hangs on a knob by the door, and as soon as little Faber, who has had to keep up with the major in drinking the home-brewed ale, lays his head on the table and snores, Major Fuchs has seized the key, put on his cap, and hurried away.

A minute later he is groping his way up the tower stairs, lighted by his little horn lantern, and comes at last to the bell-room, where the bells open their wide throats over him. He scrapes off a little of the bell-metal with a file, and is just going to take the bullet-mould and melting-ladle out of his hunting-bag, when he finds that he has forgotten what is most important of all: he has no silver with him. If there shall be any power in the bullet, it must be cast there in the tower. Everything is right; it is Thursday evening and a new moon, and no one has any idea he is there, and now he cannot do anything. He sends forth into the silence of the night an oath with such a ring in it that the bells hum.

Then he hears a slight noise down in the church and thinks he hears steps on the stairs. Yes, it is true, heavy steps are coming up the stairs.

Major Fuchs, who stands there and swears so that the bells vibrate, is a little thoughtful at that. He wonders who it can be who is coming to help him with the bullet-casting. The steps come nearer and nearer. Whoever it is, is coming all the way up to the bell-room.

The major creeps far in among the beams and rafters, and puts out his lantern. He is not exactly afraid, but the whole thing would be spoiled if any one should see him there. He has scarcely had time to hide before the new-comer's head appears above the floor.

The major knows him well; it is the miserly Broby minister. He, who is nearly mad with greed, has the habit of hiding his treasures in the strangest places. He comes now with a roll of bank-notes which he is going to hide in the tower-room. He does not know that any one sees him. He lifts up a board in the floor and puts in the money and takes himself off again.

The major is not slow; he lifts up the same board. Oh, so much money! Package after package of bank-notes, and among them brown leather bags, full of silver. The major takes just enough silver to make a bullet; the rest he leaves.

When he comes down to the earth again, he has the silver bullet in his gun. He wonders what luck has in store for him that night. It is marvellous on Thursday nights, as every one knows. He goes up towards the organist's house. Fancy if the bear knew that Faber's cows are in a miserable shed, no better than under the bare sky.

What! surely he sees something black and big coming over the field towards the woodshed; it must be the bear. He puts the gun to his cheek and is just going to shoot, but then he changes his mind.

The little maid's red eyes come before him in the darkness; he thinks that he will help her and the sexton a little, but it is hard not to kill the great bear himself. He said afterwards that nothing in the world had ever been so hard, but as the little maiden was so dear and sweet, it had to be done.

He goes up to the sexton's house, wakes him, drags him out, half dressed and half naked, and says that he shall shoot the bear which is creeping about outside of Faber's woodshed.

"If you shoot the bear, he will surely give you his sister," he says, "for then you will be a famous man. That is no ordinary bear, and the best men in the country would consider it an honor to kill it."

And he puts into his hand his own gun, loaded with a bullet of silver and bell-metal cast in a church tower on a Thursday evening at the new moon, and he cannot help trembling with envy that another than he shall shoot the great forest monarch, the old bear of Gurlitta Cliff.

The sexton aims,—God help us! aims, as if he meant to hit the Great Bear, which high up in the sky wanders about the North Star, and not a bear wandering on the plain,— and the gun goes off with a bang which can be heard all the way to Gurlitta Cliff.

But however he has aimed, the bear falls. So it is when one shoots with a silver bullet. One shoots the bear through the heart, even if one aims at the Dipper.

People come rushing out from all the neighboring farmyards and wonder what is going on, for never had a shot sounded so loud nor waked so many sleeping echoes as this one, and the sexton wins much praise, for the bear had been a real pest.

Little Faber comes out too, but now is Major Fuchs sadly disappointed. There stands the sexton covered with glory, besides having saved Faber's cows, but the little organist is neither touched nor grateful. He does not open his arms to him and greet him as brother-in-law and hero.

The major stands and frowns and stamps his foot in rage over such smallness. He wants to explain to the covetous, narrow-minded little fellow what a deed it is, but he begins to stammer, so that he cannot get out a word. And he gets angry and more angry at the thought that he has given up the glory of killing the great bear in vain.

Oh, it is quite impossible for him to comprehend that he who had done such a deed should not be worthy to win the proudest of brides.

The sexton and some of the young men are going to skin the bear; they go to the grindstone and sharpen the knives. Others go in and go to bed Major Fuchs stands alone by the dead bear.

Then he goes to the church once more, puts the key again in the lock, climbs up the narrow stairs and the twisted ladder, wakes the sleeping pigeons, and once more comes up to the tower-room.

Afterwards, when the bear is skinned under the major's inspection, they find between his jaws a package of notes of five hundred rix-dollars. It is impossible to say how it came there, but of course it was a marvellous bear; and as the sexton had killed him, the money is his, that is very plain.

When it is made known, little Faber too understands what a glorious deed the sexton has done, and he declares that he would be proud to be his brother-in-law.

On Friday evening Major Anders Fuchs returns to Ekeby, after having been at a feast, in honor of the lucky shot, at the sexton's and an engagement dinner at the organist's. He follows the road with a heavy heart; he feels no joy that his enemy is dead, and no pleasure in the magnificent bear-skin which the sexton has given him.

Many perhaps will believe that he is grieving that the sweet little maiden shall be another's. Oh no, that causes him no sorrow. But what goes to his very heart is that the old, one-eyed forest king is dead, and it was not he who shot the silver bullet at him.

So he comes into the pensioners' wing, where the pensioners are sitting round the fire, and without a word throws the bear-skin down among them. Let no one think that he told about that expedition; it was not until long, long after that any one could get out of him the truth of it. Nor did he betray the Broby clergyman's hiding-place, who perhaps never noticed the theft.

The pensioners examine the skin.

"It is a fine skin," says Beerencreutz. "I would like to know why this fellow has come out of his winter sleep, or perhaps you shot him in his hole?"

"He was shot at Bro."

"Yes, as big as the Gurlitta bear he never was," says Gösta, "but he has been a fine beast."

"If he had had one eye," says Kevenhüller," I would have thought that you had killed the old one himself, he is so big; but this one has no wound or inflammation about his eyes, so it cannot be the same."

Fuchs swears over his stupidity, but then his face lights up so that he is really handsome. The great bear has not been killed by another man's bullet.

"Lord God, how good thou art!" he says, and folds his hands.

CHAPTER IX. THE AUCTION AT BJÖRNE

WE young people often had to wonder at the old people's tales. "Was there a ball every day, as long as your radiant youth lasted?" we asked them. "Was life then one long adventure?"

"Were all young women beautiful and lovely in those days, and did every feast end by Gösta Berling carrying off one of them?"

Then the old people shook their worthy heads, and began to tell of the whirring of the spinning-wheel and the clatter of the loom, of work in the kitchen, of the thud of the flail and the path of the axe through the forest; but it was not long before they harked back to the old theme. Then sledges drove up to the door, horses speeded away through the dark woods with the joyous young people; then the dance whirled and the violin-strings snapped. Adventure's wild chase roared about Löfven's long lake with thunder and crash. Far away could its noise be heard. The forest tottered and fell, all the powers of destruction were let loose; fire flamed out, floods laid waste the land, wild beasts roamed starving about the farmyards. Under the light-footed horses' hoofs all quiet happiness was trampled to dust. Wherever the hunt rushed by, men's hearts flamed up in madness, and the women in pale terror had to flee from their homes.

And we young ones sat wondering, silent, troubled, but blissful. "What people!" we thought. "We shall never see their like."

"Did the people of those days never *think* of what they were doing?" we asked.

"Of course they thought, children," answered the old people.

"But not as we think," we insisted.

But the old people did not understand what we meant.

But we thought of the strange spirit of self-consciousness which had already taken possession of us. We thought of him, with his eyes of ice and his long, bent fingers,—he who sits there in the soul's darkest corner and picks to pieces our being, just as old women pick to pieces bits of silk and wool.

Bit by bit had the long, hard, crooked fingers picked, until our whole self lay there like a pile of rags, and our best impulses, our most original thoughts, everything which we had done and said, had been examined, investigated, picked to pieces, and the icy eyes had looked on, and the toothless mouth had laughed in derision and whispered,—

"See, it is rags, only rags."

There was also one of the people of that time who had opened her soul to the spirit with the icy eyes. In one of them he sat, watching the causes of all actions, sneering at both evil and good, understanding everything, condemning nothing, examining, seeking out, picking to pieces, paralyzing the emotions of the heart and the power of the mind by sneering unceasingly.

The beautiful Marianne bore the spirit of introspection within her. She felt his icy eyes and sneers follow every step, every word. Her life had become a drama where she was the only spectator. She had ceased to be a human being, she did not suffer, she was not glad, nor did she love; she carried out the beautiful Marianne Sinclair's rôle, and self-consciousness sat with staring, icy eyes and busy, picking fingers, and watched her performance.

She was divided into two halves. Pale, unsympathetic, and sneering, one half sat and watched what the other half was doing; and the strange spirit who picked to pieces her being never had a word of feeling or sympathy.

But where had he been, the pale watcher of the source of deeds, that night, when she had learned to know the fulness of life? Where was he when she, the sensible Marianne, kissed Gösta Berling before a hundred pairs of eyes, and when in a gust of passion she threw herself down in the snow-drift to die? Then the icy eyes were blinded, then the sneer was weakened, for passion had raged through her soul. The roar of adventure's wild hunt had thundered in her ears. She had been a whole person during that one terrible night.

Oh, you god of self-mockery, when Marianne with infinite difficulty succeeded in lifting her stiffened arms and putting them about Gösta's neck, you too, like old Beerencreutz, had to turn away your eyes from the earth and look at the stars.

That night you had no power. You were dead while she sang her love-song, dead while she hurried down to Sjö after the major, dead when she saw the flames redden the sky over the tops of the trees.

For they had come, the mighty storm-birds, the griffins of demoniac passions. With wings of fire and claws of steel they had come swooping down over you, you icy-eyed spirit; they had struck their claws into your neck and flung you far into the unknown. You have been dead and crushed.

But now they had rushed on,—they whose course no sage can predict, no observer can follow; and out of the depths of the unknown had the strange spirit of self-consciousness again raised itself and had once again taken possession of Marianne's soul.

During the whole of February Marianne lay ill at Ekeby. When she sought out the major at Sjö she had been infected with small-pox. The terrible illness had taken a great hold on her, who had been so chilled and exhausted. Death had come very near to her, but at the end of the month she had recovered. She was still very weak and much disfigured. She would never again be called the beautiful Marianne.

This, however, was as yet only known to Marianne and her nurse. The pensioners themselves did not know it. The sick-room where small-pox raged was not open to any one.

But when is the introspective power greater than during the long hours of convalescence? Then the fiend sits and stares and stares with his icy eyes, and picks and picks with his bony, hard fingers. And if one looks carefully, behind him sits a still paler creature, who stares and sneers, and behind him another and still another, sneering at one another and at the whole world.

And while Marianne lay and looked at herself with all these staring icy eyes, all natural feelings died within her.

She lay there and played she was ill; she lay there and played she was unhappy, in love, longing for revenge.

She was it all, and still it was only a play. Everything became a play and unreality under those icy eyes, which watched her while they were watched by a pair behind them, which were watched by other pairs in infinite perspective.

All the energy of life had died within her. She had found strength for glowing hate and tender love for one single night, not more.

She did not even know if she loved Gösta Berling. She longed to see him to know if he could take her out of herself.

While under the dominion of her illness, she had had only one clear thought: she had worried lest her illness should be known. She did not wish to see her parents; she wished no reconciliation with her father, and she knew that he would repent if he should know how ill she was. Therefore she ordered that her parents and every one else should only know that the troublesome irritation of the eyes, which she always had when she visited her native country, forced her to sit in a darkened room. She forbade her nurse to say how ill she was; she forbade the pensioners to go after the doctor at Karlstad. She had of course small-pox, but only very lightly; in the medicine-chest at Ekeby there were remedies enough to save her life.

She never thought of death; she only lay and waited for health, to be able to go to the clergyman with Gösta and have the banns published.

But now the sickness and the fever were gone. She was once more cold and sensible. It seemed to her as if she alone was sensible in this world of fools.

She neither hated nor loved. She understood her father; she understood them all. He who understands does not hate.

She had heard that Melchior Sinclair meant to have an auction at Björne and make way with all his wealth, that she might inherit nothing after him. People said that he would make the devastation as thorough as possible; first he would sell the furniture and utensils, then the cattle and implements, and then the house itself with all its lands, and would put the money in a bag and sink it to the bottom of the Löfven. Dissipation, confusion, and devastation should be her inheritance. Marianne smiled approvingly when she heard it: such was his character, and so he must act.

It seemed strange to her that she had sung that great hymn to love. She had dreamed of love in a cottage, as others have done. Now it seemed odd to her that she had ever had a dream.

She sighed for naturalness. She was tired of this continual play. She never had a strong emotion. She only grieved for her beauty, but she shuddered at the compassion of strangers.

Oh, one second of forgetfulness of herself! One gesture, one word, one act which was not calculated!

One day, when the rooms had been disinfected and she lay dressed on a sofa, she had Gösta Berling called. They answered her that he had gone to the auction at Björne.

At Björne there was in truth a big auction. It was an old, rich home. People had come long distances to be present at the sale.

Melchior Sinclair had flung all the property in the house together in the great drawing-room. There lay thousands of articles, collected in piles, which reached from floor to ceiling.

He had himself gone about the house like an angel of destruction on the day of judgment, and dragged together what he wanted to sell. Everything in the kitchen,—the black pots, the wooden chairs, the pewter dishes, the copper kettles, all were left in peace, for among them there was nothing which recalled Marianne; but they were the only things which escaped his anger.

He burst into Marianne's room, turning everything out. Her doll-house stood there, and her book-case, the little chair he had had made for her, her trinkets and clothes, her sofa and bed, everything must go.

And then he went from room to room. He tore down everything he found unpleasant, and carried great loads down to the auction-room. He panted under the weight of sofas and marble slabs; but he went on. He had thrown open the sideboards and taken out the magnificent family silver. Away with it! Marianne had touched it He filled his arms with snow-white damask and with shining linen sheets with hemstitching as wide as one's hand,—honest home-made work, the fruit of many years of labor,—and flung them down together on the piles. Away with them! Marianne was not worthy to own them. He stormed through the rooms with piles of china, not caring if he broke the plates by the dozen, and he seized the hand-painted cups on which the family arms were burned. Away with them! Let any one who will use them! He staggered under mountains of bedding from the attic: bolsters and pillows so soft that one sunk down in them as in a wave. Away with them! Marianne had slept on them.

He cast fierce glances on the old, well-known furniture. Was there a chair where she had not sat, or a sofa which she had not used, or a picture which she had not looked at, a candlestick which had not lighted her, a mirror which had not reflected her features? Gloomily he shook his fist at this world of memories. He would have liked to have rushed on them with swinging club and to have crushed everything to small bits and splinters.

But it seemed to him a more famous revenge to sell them all at auction. They should go to strangers! Away to be soiled in the cottagers' huts, to be in the care of indifferent strangers. Did he not know them, the dented pieces of auction furniture in the peasants' houses, fallen into dishonor like his beautiful daughter? Away with them! May they stand with torn-out stuffing and worn-off gilding, with cracked legs and stained leaves, and long for their former home! Away with them to the ends of the earth, so that no eye can find them, no hand gather them together!

When the auction began, he had filled half the hall with an incredible confusion of piled-up articles.

Right across the room he had placed a long counter. Behind it stood the auctioneer and put up the things; there the clerks sat and kept the record, and there Melchior Sinclair had a keg of brandy standing. In the other half of the room, in the hall, and in the yard were the buyers. There were many people, and much noise and gayety. The bids followed close on one another, and the auction was lively. But by the keg of brandy, with all his possessions in endless confusion behind him, sat Melchior Sinclair, half drunk and half mad. His hair stood up in rough tufts above his red face; his eyes were rolling, fierce, and bloodshot. He shouted and laughed, as if he had been in the best of moods; and every one who had made a good bid he called up to him and offered a dram.

Among those who saw him there was Gösta Ber-ling, who had stolen in with the crowd of buyers, but who avoided coming under Melchior Sinclair's eyes. He became thoughtful at the sight, and his heart stood still, as at a presentiment of a misfortune.

He wondered much where Marianne's mother could be during all this. And he went out, against his will, but driven by fate, to find Madame Gustava Sinclair.

He had to go through many doors before he found her. Her husband had short patience and little fondness for wailing and women's complaints. He had wearied of seeing her tears flow over the fate which had befallen her household treasures. He was furious that she could weep over table and bed linen, when, what was worse, his beautiful daughter was lost; and so he had hunted her, with clenched fists, before him, through the house, out into the kitchen, and all the way to the pantry.

She could not go any farther, and he had rejoiced at seeing her there, cowering behind the step-ladder, awaiting heavy blows, perhaps death. He let her stay there, but he locked the door and stuffed the key in his pocket. She could sit there as long as the auction lasted. She did not need to starve, and his ears had rest from her laments.

There she still sat, imprisoned in her own pantry, when Gösta came through the corridor between the kitchen and the dining-room. He saw her face at a little window high up in the wall. She had climbed up on the step-ladder, and stood staring out of her prison.

"What are you doing up there?" asked Gösta.

"He has shut me in," she whispered.

"Your husband?"

"Yes. I thought he was going to kill me. But listen, Gösta, take the key of the dining-room door, and go into the kitchen and unlock the pantry door with it, so that I can come out. That key fits here."

Gösta obeyed, and in a couple of minutes the little woman stood in the kitchen, which was quite deserted.

"You should have let one of the maids open the door with the dining-room key," said Gösta.

"Do you think I want to teach them that trick? Then I should never have any peace in the pantry. And, besides, I took this chance to put the upper shelves in order. They needed it, indeed. I cannot understand how I could have let so much rubbish collect there."

"You have so much to attend to," said Gösta.

"Yes, that you may believe. If I were not everywhere, neither the loom nor the spinning-wheel would be going right. And if—"

Here she stopped and wiped away a tear from the corner of her eye.

"God help me, how I do talk!" she said; "they say that I won't have anything more to look after. He is selling everything we have."

"Yes, it is a wretched business," said Gösta.

"You know that big mirror in the drawing-room, Gösta. It was such a beauty, for the glass was whole in it, without a flaw, and there was no blemish at all on the gilding. I got it from my mother, and now he wants to sell it."

"He is mad."

"You may well say so. He is not much better. He won't stop until we shall have to go and beg on the highway, we as well as the major's wife."

"It will never be so bad as that," answered Gösta.

"Yes, Gösta. When the major's wife went away from Ekeby, she foretold misfortune for us, and now it is coming. She would never have allowed him to sell Björne. And think, his own china, the old Canton cups from his own home, are to be sold. The major's wife would never have let it happen."

"But what is the matter with him?" asked Gösta.

"Oh, it is only because Marianne has not come back again. He has waited and waited. He has gone up and down the avenue the whole day and waited for her. He is longing himself mad, but I do not dare to say anything."

"Marianne believes that he is angry with her."

"She does not believe that. She knows him well enough; but she is proud and will not take the first step. They are stiff and hard, both of them, and I have to stand between them."

"You must know that Marianne is going to marry me?"

"Alas, Gösta, she will never do that. She says that only to make him angry. She is too spoiled to marry a poor man, and too proud, too. Go home and tell her that if she does not come home soon, all her inheritance will have gone to destruction. Oh, he will throw everything away, I know, without getting anything for it."

Gösta was really angry with her. There she sat on a big kitchen table, and had no thought for anything but her mirrors and her china.

"You ought to be ashamed!" he burst out. "You throw your daughter out into a snow-drift, and then you think that it is only temper that she does not come back. And you think that she is no better than to forsake him whom she cares for, lest she should lose her inheritance."

"Dear Gösta, don't be angry, you too. I don't know what I am saying. I tried my best to open the door for Marianne, but he took me and dragged me away. They all say here that I don't understand anything. I shall not grudge you Marianne, Gösta, if you can make her happy. It is not so easy to make a woman happy, Gösta."

Gösta looked at her. How could he too have raised his voice in anger against such a person as she,—terrified and cowed, but with such a good heart!

"You do not ask how Marianne is," he said gently.

She burst into tears.

"Will you not be angry with me if I ask you?" she said. "I have longed to ask you the whole time. Think that I know no more of her than that she is living. Not one greeting have I had from her the whole time, not once when I sent clothes to her, and so I thought that you and she did not want to have me know anything about her."

Gösta could bear it no longer. He was wild, he was out of his head,—sometimes God had to send his wolves after him to force him to obedience,—but this old woman's tears, this old woman's laments were harder for him to bear than the howling of the wolves He let her know the truth.

"Marianne has been ill the whole time," he said. "She has had small-pox. She was to get up to-day and lie on the sofa. I have not seen her since the first night."

Madame Gustava leaped with one bound to the ground. She left Gösta standing there, and rushed away without another word to her husband.

The people in the auction-room saw her come up to him and eagerly whisper something in his ear. They saw how his face grew still more flushed, and his hand, which rested on the cock, turned it round so that the brandy streamed over the floor.

It seemed to all as if Madame Gustava had come with such important news that the auction must end immediately. The auctioneer's hammer no longer fell, the clerks' pens stopped, there were no new bids.

Melchior Sinclair roused himself from his thoughts.

"Well," he cried, "what is the matter?"

And the auction was in full swing once more.

Gösta still sat in the kitchen, and Madame Gustava came weeping out to him.

"It's no use," she said. "I thought he would stop when he heard that Marianne had been ill; but he is letting them go on. He would like to, but now he is ashamed."

Gösta shrugged his shoulders and bade her farewell.

In the hall he met Sintram.

"This is a funny show," exclaimed Sintram, and rubbed his hands. "You are a master, Gösta. Lord, what you have brought to pass!"

"It will be funnier in ä little while," whispered Gösta. "The Broby clergyman is here with a sledge full of money. They say that he wants to buy the whole of Björne and pay in cash. Then I would like to see Melchior Sinclair, Sintram."

Sintram drew his head down between his shoulders and laughed internally a long time. And then he made his way into the auction-room and up to Melchior Sinclair.

"If you want a drink, Sintram, you must make a bid first."

Sintram came close up to him.

"You are in luck to-day as always," he said. "A fellow has come to the house with a sledge full of money. He is going to buy Björne and every-thing both inside and out. He has told a lot of people to bid for him. He does not want to show himself yet for a while."

"You might say who he is; then I suppose I must give you a drink for your pains."

Sintram took the dram and moved a couple of steps backwards, before he answered,—

"They say it is the Broby clergyman, Melchior."

Melchior Sinclair had many better friends than the Broby clergyman. It had been a life-long feud between them. There were legends of how he had lain in wait on dark nights on the roads where the minister should pass, and how he had given him many an honest drubbing, the old fawning oppressor of the peasants.

It was well for Sintram that he had drawn back a step or two, but he did not entirely escape the big man's anger. He got a brandy glass between his eyes and the whole brandy keg on his feet. But then followed a scene which for a long time rejoiced his heart.

"Does the Broby clergyman want my house?" roared Melchior Sinclair. "Do you stand there and bid on my things for the Broby clergyman? Oh, you ought to be ashamed! You ought to know better!"

He seized a candlestick, and an inkstand, and slung them into the crowd of people.

All the bitterness of his poor heart at last found expression. Roaring like a wild beast, he clenched his fist at those standing about, and slung at them whatever missile he could lay his hand on. Brandy glasses and bottles flew across the room. He did not know what he was doing in his rage.

"It's the end of the auction," he cried. "Out with you! Never while I live shall the Broby clergyman have Björne. Out! I will teach you to bid for the Broby clergyman!"

He rushed on the auctioneer and the clerks. They hurried away. In the confusion they overturned the desk, and Sinclair with unspeakable fury burst into the crowd of peaceful people.

There was a flight and wildest confusion. A couple of hundred people were crowding towards the door, fleeing before a single man. And he stood, roaring his "Out with you!" He sent curses after them, and now and again he swept about him with a chair, which he brandished like a club.

He pursued them out into the hall, but no farther. When the last stranger had left the house, he went back into the drawing-room and bolted the door after him. Then he dragged together a mattress and a couple of pillows, laid himself down on them, went to sleep in the midst of all the havoc, and never woke till the next day.

When Gösta got home, he heard that Marianne wished to speak to him. That was just what he wanted. He had been wondering how he could get a word with her.

When he came into the dim room where she lay, he had to stand a moment at the door. He could not see where she was.

"Stay where you are, Gösta," Marianne said to him. "It may be dangerous to come near me."

But Gösta had come up the stairs in two bounds, trembling with eagerness and longing. What did he care for the contagion? He wished to have the bliss of seeing her.

For she was so beautiful, his beloved! No one had such soft hair, such an open, radiant brow. Her whole face was a symphony of exquisite lines.

He thought of her eyebrows, sharply and clearly drawn like the honey-markings on a lily, and of the bold curve of her nose, and of her lips, as softly turned as rolling waves, and of her cheek's long oval and her chin's perfect shape.

And he thought of the rosy hue of her skin, of the magical effect of her coal-black eyebrows with her light hair, and of her blue irises swimming in clear white, and of the light in her eyes.

She was beautiful, his beloved! He thought of the warm heart which she hid under a proud exterior. She had strength for devotion and self-sacrifice concealed under that fine skin and her proud words. It was bliss to see her.

He had rushed up the stairs in two bounds, and she thought that he would stop at the door. He stormed through the room and fell on his knees at the head of her bed.

But he meant to see her, to kiss her, and to bid her farewell.

He loved her. He would certainly never cease to love her, but his heart was used to being trampled on. Oh, where should he find her, that rose without support or roots, which he could take and call his own? He might not keep even her whom he had found disowned and half dead at the roadside.

When should his love raise its voice in a song so loud and clear that he should hear no dissonance through it? When should his palace of happiness be built on a ground for which no other heart longed restlessly and with regret?

He thought how he would bid her farewell.

"There is great sorrow in your home," he would say. "My heart is torn at the thought of it. You must go home and give your father his reason again. Your mother lives in continual danger of death. You must go home, my beloved."

These were the words he had on his lips, but they were never spoken.

He fell on his knees at the head of her bed, and he took her face between his hands and kissed her; but then he could not speak. His heart began to beat so fiercely, as if it would burst his breast.

Small-pox had passed over that lovely face. Her skin had become coarse and scarred. Never again should the red blood glow in her cheeks, or the fine blue veins show on her temples. Her eyebrows had fallen out, and the shining white of her eyes had changed to yellow.

Everything was laid waste. The bold lines had become coarse and heavy.

They were not few who mourned over Marianne Sinclair's lost beauty. In the whole of Värmland, people lamented the change in her bright color, her sparkling eyes, and blond hair. There beauty was prized as nowhere else. The joyous people grieved, as if the country had lost a precious stone from the crown of its honor, as if their life had received a blot on its glory.

But the first man who saw her after she had lost her beauty did not indulge in sorrow.

Unutterable emotion filled his soul. The more he looked at her, the warmer it grew within him. Love grew and grew, like a river in the spring. In waves of fire it welled up in his heart, it filled his whole being, it rose to his eyes as tears; it sighed on his lips, trembled in his hands, in his whole body.

Oh, to love her, to protect her, to keep her from all harm!

To be her slave, her guide!

Love is strong when it has gone through the baptismal fire of pain. He could not speak to Marianne of parting and renunciation. He could not leave her—he owed her his life. He could commit the unpardonable sin for her sake.

He could not speak a coherent word, he only wept and kissed, until at last the old nurse thought it was time to lead him out.

When he had gone, Marianne lay and thought of him and his emotion. "It is good to be so loved," she thought.

Yes, it was good to be loved, but how was it with herself? What did she feel? Oh, nothing, less than nothing!

Was it dead, her love, or where had it taken flight? Where had it hidden itself, her heart's child?

Did it still live? Had it crept into her heart's darkest corner and sat there freezing under the icy eyes, frightened by the pale sneer, half suffocated under the bony fingers?

"Ah, my love," she sighed, "child of my heart! Are you alive, or are you dead, dead as my beauty?"

The next day Melchior Sinclair went in early to his wife.

"See to it that there is order in the house again, Gustava!" he said. "I am going to bring Marianne home."

"Yes, dear Melchior, here there will of course be order," she answered.

Thereupon there was peace between them.

An hour afterwards he was on his way to Ekeby.

It was impossible to find a more noble and kindly old gentleman than Melchior Sinclair, as he sat in the open sledge in his best fur cloak and his best rug. His hair lay smooth on his head, but his face was pale and his eyes were sunken in their sockets.

There was no limit to the brilliancy of the clear sky on that February day. The snow sparkled like a young girl's eyes when she hears the music of the first waltz. The birches stretched the fine lace-work of their reddish-brown twigs against the sky, and on some of them hung a fringe of little icicles.

There was a splendor and a festive glow in the day. The horses prancing threw up their forelegs, and the coachman cracked his whip in sheer pleasure of living.

After a short drive the sledge drew up before the great steps at Ekeby.

The footman came out.

"Where are your masters?" asked Melchior.

"They are hunting the great bear in Gurlitta Cliff."

"All of them?"

"All of them, sir. Those who do not go for the sake of the bear go for the sake of the luncheon."

Melchior laughed so that it echoed through the silent yard. He gave the man a crown for his answer.

"Go say to my daughter that I am here to take her home. She need not be afraid of the cold. I have the big sledge and a wolfskin cloak to wrap her in."

"Will you not come in, sir?"

"Thank you! I sit very well where I am."

The man disappeared, and Melchior began his waiting.

He was in such a genial mood that day that nothing could irritate him. He had expected to have to wait a little for Marianne; perhaps she was not even up. He would have to amuse himself by looking about him for a while.

From the cornice hung a long icicle, with which the sun had terrible trouble. It began at the upper end, melted a drop, and wanted to have it run down along the icicle and fall to the earth. But before it had gone half the way, it had frozen again. And the sun made continual new attempts, which always failed. But at last a regular freebooter of a ray hung itself on the icicle's point, a little one, which shone and sparkled; and however it was, it accomplished its object,—a drop fell tinkling to the ground.

Melchior looked on and laughed. "You were not such a fool," he said to the ray of sunlight.

The yard was quiet and deserted. Not a sound was heard in the big house. But he was not impatient. He knew that women needed plenty of time to make themselves ready.

He sat and looked at the dove-cote. The birds had a grating before the door. They were shut in, as long as the winter lasted, lest hawks should exterminate them. Time after time a pigeon came and stuck out its white head through the meshes.

"She is waiting for the spring," said Melchior Sinclair, "but she must have patience for a while."

The pigeon came so regularly that he took out his watch and followed her, with it in his hand. Exactly every third minute she stuck out her head.

"No, my little friend," he said, "do you think spring will be ready in three minutes? You must learn to wait."

And he had to wait himself; but he had plenty of time.

The horses first pawed impatiently in the snow, but then they grew sleepy from standing and blinking in the sun. They laid their heads together and slept.

The coachman sat straight on his box, with whip and reins in his hand and his face turned directly towards the sun, and slept, slept so that he snored.

But Melchior did not sleep. He had never felt less like sleeping. He had seldom passed pleasanter hours than during this glad waiting. Marianne had been ill. She had not been able to come before, but now she would come. Oh, of course she would. And everything would be well again.

She must understand that he was not angry with her. He had come himself with two horses and the big sledge.

It is nothing to have to wait when one is sure of one's self, and when there is so much to distract one's mind.

There comes the great watch-dog. He creeps forward on the tips of his toes, keeps his eyes on the ground, and wags his tail gently, as if he meant to set out on the most indifferent errand. All at once he begins to burrow eagerly in the snow. The old rascal must have hidden there some stolen goods. But just as he lifts his head to see if he can eat it now undisturbed, he is quite out of countenance to see two magpies right in front of him.

"You old thief!" say the magpies, and look like conscience itself. "We are police officers. Give up your stolen goods!"

"Oh, be quiet with your noise! I am the steward—"

"Just the right one," they sneer.

The dog throws himself on them, and they fly away with slow flaps. The dog rushes after them, jumps, and barks. But while he is chasing one, the other is already back. She flies down into the hole, tears at the piece of meat, but cannot lift it. The dog snatches away the meat, holds it between his paws, and bites in it. The magpies place themselves close in front of him, and make disagreeable remarks. He glares fiercely at them, while he eats, and when they get too impertinent, he jumps up and drives them away.

The sun began to sink down towards the western hills. Melchior looked at his watch. It is three o'clock. And his wife, who had had dinner ready at twelve!

At the same moment the footman came out and announced that Miss Marianne wished to speak to him.

Melchior laid the wolfskin cloak over his arm and went beaming up the steps.

When Marianne heard his heavy tread on the stairs, she did not even then know if she should go home with him or not. She only knew that she must put an end to this long waiting.

She had hoped that the pensioners would come home; but they did not come. So she had to do something to put an end to it all. She could bear it no longer.

She had thought that he in a burst of anger would have driven away after he had waited five minutes, or that he would break the door in or try to set the house on fire.

But there he sat calm and smiling, and only waited. She cherished neither hatred nor love for him. But there was a voice in her which seemed to warn her against putting herself in his power again, and moreover she wished to keep her promise to Gösta.

If he had slept, if he had spoken, if he had been restless, if he had shown any sign of doubt, if he had had the carriage driven into the shade! But he was only patience and certainty.

Certain, so infectiously certain, that she would come if he only waited!

Her head ached. Every nerve quivered. She could get no rest as long as she knew that he sat there. It was as if his will dragged her bound down the stairs.

So she thought she would at least talk with him.

Before he came, she had all the curtains drawn up, and she placed herself so that her face came in the full light.

For it was her intention to put him to a sort of test; but Melchior Sinclair was a wonderful man that day.

When he saw her, he did not make a sign, nor did he exclaim. It was as if he had not seen any change in her. She knew how highly he prized her beauty. But he showed no sorrow. He controlled himself not to wound her. That touched her. She began to understand why her mother had loved him through everything.

He showed no hesitation. He came with neither reproaches nor excuses.

"I will wrap the wolf-skin about you, Marianne; it is not cold. It has been on my knees the whole time."

To make sure, he went up to the fire and warmed it.

Then he helped her to raise herself from the sofa, wrapped the cloak about her, put a shawl over her head, drew it down under her arms, and knotted it behind her back.

She let him do it. She was helpless. It was good to have everything arranged, it was good not to have to decide anything, especially good for one who was so picked to pieces as she, for one who did not possess one thought or one feeling which was her own.

Melchior lifted her up, carried her down to the sleigh, closed the top, tucked the furs in about her, and drove away from Ekeby.

She shut her eyes and sighed, partly from pleasure, partly from regret. She was leaving life, the real life; but it did not make so much difference to her,—she who could not live but only act.

A few days later her mother arranged that she should meet Gösta. She sent for him while her husband was off on his long walk to see after his timber, and took him in to Marianne.

Gösta came in; but he neither bowed nor spoke. He stood at the door and looked on the ground like an obstinate boy.

"But, Gösta!" cried Marianne. She sat in her armchair and looked at him half amused.

"Yes, that is my name."

"Come here, come to me, Gösta!"

He went slowly forward to her, but did not raise his eyes.

"Come nearer! Kneel down here!"

"Lord God, what is the use of all that?" he cried; but he obeyed.

"Gösta, I want to tell you that I think it was best that I came home."

"Let us hope that they will not throw you out in the snow-drift again."

"Oh, Gösta, do you not care for me any longer? Do you think that I am too ugly?"

He drew her head down and kissed her, but he looked as cold as ever.

She was almost amused. If he was pleased to be jealous of her parents, what then? It would pass. It amused her to try and win him back. She did not know why she wished to keep him, but she did. She thought that it was he who had succeeded for once in freeing her from herself. He was the only one who would be able to do it again.

And now she began to speak, eager to win him back. She said that it had not been her meaning to desert him for good, but for a time they must for appearance's sake break off their connection. He must have seen, himself, that her father was on the

verge of going mad, that her mother was in continual danger of her life. He must understand that she had been forced to come home.

Then his anger burst out in words. She need not give herself so much trouble. He would be her plaything no longer. She had given him up when she had gone home, and he could not love her any more. When he came home the day before yesterday from his hunting-trip and found her gone without a message, without a word, his blood ran cold in his veins, he had nearly died of grief. He could not love any one who had given him such pain. She had, besides, never loved him. She was a coquette, who wanted to have some one to kiss her and caress her when she was here in the country, that was all.

Did he think that she was in the habit of allowing young men to caress her?

Oh yes, he was sure of it. Women were not so saintly as they seemed. Selfishness and coquetry from beginning to end! No, if she could know how he had felt when he came home from the hunt. It was as though he had waded in ice-water. He should never get over that pain. It would follow him through the whole of his life. He would never be the same person again.

She tried to explain to him how it had all happened. She tried to convince him that she was still faithful. Well, it did not matter, for now he did not love her any more. He had seen through her. She was selfish. She did not love him. She had gone without leaving him a message.

He came continually back to that She really enjoyed the performance. She could not be angry, she understood his wrath so well. She did not fear any real break between them. But at last she became uneasy. Had there really been such a change in him that he could no longer care for her?

"Gösta," she said, "was I selfish when I went to Sjö after the major; I knew that they had small-pox there. Nor is it pleasant to go out in satin slippers in the cold and snow."

"Love lives on love, and not on services and deeds," said Gösta.

"You wish, then, that we shall be as strangers from now on, Gösta?"

"That is what I wish."

"You are very changeable, Gösta Berling."

"People often charge me with it."

He was cold, impossible to warm, and she was still colder. Self-consciousness sat and sneered at her attempt to act love.

"Gösta," she said, making a last effort, "I have never intentionally wronged you, even if it may seem so. I beg of you, forgive me!"

"I cannot forgive you."

She knew that if she had possessed a real feeling she could have won him back. And she tried to play the impassioned. The icy eyes sneered at her, but she tried nevertheless. She did not want to lose him.

"Do not go, Gösta! Do not go in anger! Think how ugly I have become! No one will ever love me again."

"Nor I, either," he said. "You must accustom yourself to see your heart trampled upon as well as another."

"Gösta, I have never loved any one but you. Forgive me. Do not forsake me! You are the only one who can save me from myself."

He thrust her from him.

"You do not speak the truth," he said with icy calmness. "I do not know what you want of me, but I see that you are lying. Why do you want to keep me? You are so rich that you will never lack suitors."

And so he went.

And not until he had closed the door, did regret and pain in all their strength take possession of Marianne's heart.

It was love, her heart's own child, who came out of the corner where the cold eyes had banished him. He came, he for whom she had so longed when it was too late.

When Marianne could with real certainty say to herself that Gösta Berling had forsaken her, she felt a purely physical pain so terrible that she almost fainted. She pressed her hands against her heart, and sat for hours in the same place, struggling with a tearless grief.

And it was she herself who was suffering, not a stranger, nor an actress. It was she herself. Why had her father come and separated them? Her love had never been dead. It was only that in her weak condition after her illness she could not appreciate his power.

O God, O God, that she had lost him! O God, that she had waked so late!

Ah, he was the only one, he was her heart's conqueror! From him she could bear anything. Hardness and angry words from him bent her only to humble love. If he had beaten her, she would have crept like a dog to him and kissed his hand.

She did not know what she would do to get relief from this dull pain.

She seized pen and paper and wrote with terrible eagerness. First she wrote of her love and regret. Then she begged, if not for his love, only for his pity. It was a kind of poem she wrote.

When she had finished she thought that if he should see it he must believe that she had loved him. Well, why should she not send what she had written to him? She would send it the next day, and she was sure that it would bring him back to her.

The next day she spent in agony and in struggling with herself. What she had written seemed to her paltry and so stupid. It had neither rhyme nor metre. It was only prose. He would only laugh at such verses.

Her pride was roused too. If he no longer cared for her, it was such a terrible humiliation to beg for his love.

Sometimes her good sense told her that she ought to be glad to escape from the connection with Gösta, and all the deplorable circumstances which it had brought with it.

Her heart's pain was still so terrible that her emotions finally conquered. Three days after she had become conscious of her love, she enclosed the verses and wrote Gösta Berling's name on the cover. But they were never sent. Before she could find a suitable messenger she heard such things of Gösta Berling that she understood it was too late to win him back.

But it was the sorrow of her life that she had not sent the verses in time, while she could have won him.

All her pain fastened itself on that point: "If I only had not waited so long, if I had not waited so many days!"

The happiness of life, or at any rate the reality of life, would have been won to her through those written words. She was sure they would have brought him back to her.

Grief, however, did her the same service as love. It made her a whole being, potent to devote herself to good as well as evil. Passionate feelings filled her soul, unrestrained by self-consciousness's icy chill. And she was, in spite of her plainness, much loved.

But they say that she never forgot Gösta Berling. She mourned for him as one mourns for a wasted life.

And her poor verses, which at one time were much read, are forgotten long ago. I beg of you to read them and to think of them. Who knows what power they might have had, if they had been sent? They are impassioned enough to bear witness of a real feeling. Perhaps they could have brought him back to her.

They are touching enough, tender enough in their awkward formlessness. No one can wish them different. No one can want to see them imprisoned in the chains of rhyme and metre, and yet it is so sad to think that it was perhaps just this imperfection which prevented her from sending them in time.

I beg you to read them and to love them. It is a person in great trouble who has written them.

> "Child, thou hast loved once, but nevermore
> Shalt thou taste of the joys of love!
> A passionate storm has raged through thy soul
> Rejoice thou hast gone to thy rest!
>
> No more in wild joy shalt thou soar up on high
> Rejoice, thou hast gone to thy rest!
> No more shalt thou sink in abysses of pain,
> Oh, nevermore.
>
> "Child, thou hast loved once, but nevermore
> Shall your soul burn and scorch in the flames.
> Thou wert as a field of brown, sun-dried grass
> Flaming with fire for a moment's space;
> From the whirling smoke-clouds the fiery sparks
> Drove the birds of heaven with piercing cries.
> Let them return! Thou burnest no more!—
> Wilt burn nevermore.
>
> "Child, thou hast loved, but now nevermore
> Shalt thou hear love's murmuring voice.
> Thy young heart's strength, like a weary child
> That sits still and tired on the hard school-bench,
> Yearns for freedom and pleasure.
> But no man calleth it more like a forgotten song;
> No one sings it more,—nevermore.

"Child, the end has now come!
And with it gone love and love's joy.
He whom thou lovedst as if he had taught thee
With wings to hover through space,
He whom thou lovedst as if he had given thee
Safety and home when the village was flooded,
Is gone, who alone understood
The key to the door of thy heart.

"I ask but one thing of thee, O my beloved:
'Lay not upon me the load of thy hate!'
That weakest of all things, the poor human heart,
How can it live with the pang and the thought
That it gave pain to another?

"O my beloved, if thou wilt kill me,
Use neither dagger nor poison nor rope!
Say only you wish me to vanish
From the green earth and the kingdom of life,
And I shall sink to my grave.

"From thee came life of life; thou gavest me love,
And now thou recallest thy gift, I know it too well.
But do not give me thy hate!
I still have love of living! Oh, remember that;
But under a load of hate I have but to die."

CHAPTER X. THE YOUNG COUNTESS

THE young countess sleeps till ten o'clock in the morning, and wants fresh bread on the breakfast-table every day. The young countess embroiders, and reads poetry. She knows nothing of weaving and cooking. The young countess is spoiled.

But the young countess is gay, and lets her joyousness shine on all and everything. One is so glad to forgive her the long morning sleep and the fresh bread, for she squanders kindness on the poor and is friendly to every one.

The young countess's father is a Swedish nobleman, who has lived in Italy all his life, retained there by the loveliness of the land and by one of that lovely land's beautiful daughters. When Count Henrik Dohna travelled in Italy he had been received in this nobleman's house, made the acquaintance of his daughters, married one of them, and brought her with him to Sweden.

She, who had always spoken Swedish and had been brought up to love everything Swedish, is happy in the land of the bear. She whirls so merrily in the long dance of pleasure, on Löfven's shores, that one could well believe she had always lived there. Little she understands what it means to be a countess. There is no state, no stiffness, no condescending dignity in that young, joyous creature.

It was the old men who liked the young countess best. It was wonderful, what a success she had with old men. When they had seen her at a ball, one could be sure that all of them, the judge at Munkerud and the clergyman at Bro and Melchior Sinclair and the captain at Berga, would tell their wives in the greatest confidence that if they had met the young countess thirty or forty years ago—

"Yes, then she was not born," say the old ladies.

And the next time they meet, they joke with the young countess, because she wins the old men's hearts from them.

The old ladies look at her with a certain anxiety. They remember so well Countess Märta. She had been just as joyous and good and beloved when she first came to Borg. And she had become a vain and pleasure-seeking coquette, who never could think of anything but her amusements. "If she only had a husband who could keep her at work!" say the old ladies. "If she only could learn to weave!" For weaving was a consolation for everything; it swallowed up all other interests, and had been the saving of many a woman.

The young countess wants to be a good housekeeper. She knows nothing better than as a happy wife to live in a comfortable home, and she often comes at balls, and sits down beside the old people.

"Henrik wants me to learn to be a capable housekeeper," she says, "just as his mother is. Teach me how to weave!"

Then the old people heave a sigh: first, over Count Henrik, who can think that his mother was a good house-keeper; and then over the difficulty of initiating this young, ignorant creature in such a complicated thing. It was enough to speak to her of heddles, and harnesses, and warps, and woofs,[2] to make her head spin.

No one who sees the young countess can help wondering why she married stupid Count Henrik. It is a pity for him who is stupid, wherever he may be. And it is the greatest pity for him who is stupid and lives in Värmland.

There are already many stories of Count Henrik's stupidity, and he is only a little over twenty years old. They tell how he entertained Anna Stjärnhök on a sleighing party a few years ago.

"You are very pretty, Anna," he said.

"How you talk, Henrik!"

"You are the prettiest girl in the whole of Värmland."

"That I certainly am not."

"The prettiest in this sleighing party at any rate."

"Alas, Henrik, I am not that either."

"Well, you are the prettiest in this sledge, that you can't deny."

No, that she could not.

For Count Henrik is no beauty. He is as ugly as he is stupid. They say of him that that head on the top of his thin neck has descended in the family for a couple of hundred years. That is why the brain is so worn out in the last heir.

"It is perfectly plain that he has no head of his own," they say. "He has borrowed his father's. He does not dare to bend it; he is afraid of losing it,—he is already yellow and wrinkled. The head has been in use with both his father and grandfather. Why should the hair otherwise be so thin and the lips so bloodless and the chin so pointed?"

He always has scoffers about him, who encourage him to say stupid things, which they save up, circulate, and add to.

---

[2] Terms used in weaving.

It is lucky for him that he does not notice it. He is solemn and dignified in everything he does. He moves formally, he holds himself straight, he never turns his head without turning his whole body.

He had been at Munkerud on a visit to the judge a few years ago. He had come riding with high hat, yellow breeches, and polished boots, and had sat stiff and proud in the saddle. When he arrived everything went well, but when he was to ride away again it so happened that one of the low-hanging branches of a birch-tree knocked off his hat. He got off, put on his hat, and rode again under the same branch. His hat was again knocked off; this was repeated four times.

The judge at last went out to him and said: "If you should ride on one side of the branch the next time?"

The fifth time he got safely by.

But still the young countess cared for him in spite of his old-man's head. She of course did not know that he was crowned with such a halo of stupidity in his own country, when she saw him in Rome. There, there had been something of the glory of youth about him, and they had come together under such romantic circumstances. You ought to hear the countess tell how Count Henrik had to carry her off. The priests and the cardinals had been wild with rage that she wished to give up her mother's religion and become a Protestant. The whole people had been in uproar. Her father's palace was besieged. Henrik was pursued by bandits. Her mother and sisters implored her to give up the marriage. But her father was furious that that Italian rabble should prevent him from giving his daughter to whomsoever he might wish. He commanded Count Henrik to carry her off. And so, as it was impossible for them to be married at home without its being discovered, Henrik and she stole out by side streets and all sorts of dark alleys to the Swedish consulate. And when she had abjured the Catholic faith and become a Protestant, they were immediately married and sent north in a swift travelling-carriage. "There was no time for banns, you see. It was quite impossible," the young countess used to say. "And of course it was gloomy to be married at a consulate, and not in one of the beautiful churches, but if we had not Henrik would have had to do without me. Every one is so impetuous down there, both papa and mamma and the cardinals and the priests, all are so impetuous. That was why everything had to be done so secretly, and if the people had seen us steal out of the house, they would certainly have killed us both—only to save my soul; Henrik was of course already lost."

The young countess loves her husband, ever since they have come home to Borg and live a quieter life. She loves in him the glory of the old name and the famous ancestors. She likes to see how her presence softens the stiffness of his manner, and to hear how his voice grows tender when he speaks to her. And besides, he cares for her and spoils her, and she is married to him. The young countess cannot imagine that a married woman should not care for her husband.

In a certain way he corresponds to her ideal of manliness. He is honest and loves the truth. He had never broken his word. She considers him a true nobleman.

On the 18th of March Bailiff Scharling celebrates his birthday, and many then drive up Broby Hill. People from the east and the west, known and unknown, invited and uninvited, come to the bailiffs on that day. All are welcome, all find plenty of food and drink, and in the ballroom there is room for dancers from seven parishes.

The young countess is coming too, as she always does where there is to be dancing and merry-making.

But she is not happy as she comes. It is as if she has a presentiment that it is now her turn to be dragged-in in adventure's wild chase.

On the way she sat and watched the sinking sun. It set in a cloudless sky and left no gold edges on the light clouds. A pale, gray, twilight, swept by cold squalls, settled down over the country.

The young countess saw how day and night struggled, and how fear seized all living things at the mighty contest. The horses quickened their pace with the last load to come under shelter. The woodcutters hurried home from the woods, the maids from the farmyard. Wild creatures howled at the edge of the wood. The day, beloved of man, was conquered.

The light grew dim, the colors faded. She only saw chillness and ugliness. What she had hoped, what she had loved, what she had done, seemed to her to be also wrapped in the twilight's gray light It was the hour of weariness, of depression, of impotence for her as for all nature.

She thought that her own heart, which now in its playful gladness clothed existence with purple and gold, she thought that this heart perhaps sometime would lose its power to light up her world.

"Oh, impotence, my own heart's impotence!" she said to herself. "Goddess of the stifling, gray twilight. You will one day be mistress of my soul. Then I shall see life ugly and gray, as it perhaps is, then my hair will grow white, my back be bent, my brain be paralyzed."

At the same moment the sledge turned in at the bailiffs gate, and as the young countess looked up, her eyes fell on a grated window in the wing, and on a fierce, staring face behind.

That face belonged to the major's wife at Ekeby, and the young woman knew that her pleasure for the evening was now spoiled.

One can be glad when one does not see sorrow, only hears it spoken of. But it is harder to keep a joyous heart when one stands face to face with black, fierce, staring trouble.

The countess knows of course that Bailiff Scharling had put the major's wife in prison, and that she shall be tried for the assault she made on Ekeby the night of the great ball. But she never thought that she should be kept in custody there at the bailiff's house, so near the ballroom that one could look into her room, so near that she must hear the dance music and the noise of merry-making. And the thought takes away all her pleasure.

The young countess dances both waltz and quadrille. She takes part in both minuet and contra-dance; but after each dance she steals to the window in the wing. There is a light there and she can see how the major's wife walks up and down in her room. She never seems to rest, but walks and walks.

The countess takes no pleasure in the dance She only thinks of the major's wife going backwards and forwards in her prison like a caged wild beast. She wonders how all the others can dance. She is sure there are many there who are as much moved as she to know that the major's wife is so near, and still there is no one who shows it.

But every time she has looked out her feet grow heavier in the dance, and the laugh sticks in her throat.

The bailiffs wife notices her as she wipes the moisture from the window-pane to see out, and comes to her.

"Such misery! Oh, it is such suffering!" she whispers to the countess.

"I think it is almost impossible to dance to-night," whispers the countess back again.

"It is not with my consent that we dance here, while she is sitting shut up there," answers Madame Scharling. "She has been in Karlstad since she was arrested. But there is soon to be a trial now, and that is why she was brought here to-day. We could not put her in that miserable cell in the court-house, so she was allowed to stay in the weaving-room in the wing. She should have had my drawing-room, countess, if all these people had not come to-day. You hardly know her, but she has been like a mother and queen to us all. What will she think of us, who are dancing here, while she is in such great trouble. It is as well that most of them do not know that she is sitting there."

"She ought never to have been arrested," says the young countess, sternly.

"No, that is a true word, countess, but there was nothing else to do, if there should not be a worse misfortune. No one blamed her for setting fire to her own hay-stack and driving out the pensioners, but the major was scouring the country for her. God knows what he would have done if she had not been put in prison. Scharling has given much offence because he arrested the major's wife, countess. Even in Karlstad they were much displeased with him, because he did not shut his eyes to everything which happened at Ekeby; but he did what he thought was best."

"But now I suppose she will be sentenced?" says the countess.

"Oh, no, countess, she will not be sentenced. She will be acquitted, but all that she has to bear these days is being too much for her. She is going mad. You can understand, such a proud woman, how can she bear to be treated like a criminal! I think that it would have been best if she had been allowed to go free. She might have been able to escape by herself."

"Let her go," says the countess.

"Any one can do that but the bailiff and his wife," whispers Madame Scharling. "We have to guard her. Especially to-night, when so many of her friends are here, two men sit on guard outside her door, and it is locked and barred so that no one can come in. But if any one got her out, countess, we should be so glad, both Scharling and I."

"Can I not go to her?" says the young countess. Madame Scharling seizes her eagerly by the wrist and leads her out with her. In the hall they throw a couple of shawls about them, and hurry across the yard.

"It is not certain that she will even speak to us," says the bailiff's wife. "But she will see that we have not forgotten her."

They come into the first room in the wing, where the two men sit and guard the barred door, and go in without being stopped to the major's wife. She was in a large room crowded with looms and other implements. It was used mostly for a weaving-room, but it had bars in the window and a strong lock on the door, so that it could be used, in case of need, for a cell.

The major's wife continues to walk without paying any attention to them.

She is on a long wandering these days. She cannot remember anything except that she is going the hundred and twenty miles to her mother, who is up in the Älfdal woods, and is waiting for her. She never has time to rest She must go. A never-resting haste is on her. Her mother is over ninety years old. She would soon be dead.

She has measured off the floor by yards, and she is now adding up the yards to furlongs and the furlongs to half-miles and miles.

Her way seems heavy and long, but she dares not rest She wades through deep drifts. She hears the forests murmur over her as she goes. She rests in Finn huts and in the charcoal-burner's log cabin. Sometimes, when there is nobody for many miles, she has to break branches for a bed and rest under the roots of a fallen pine.

And at last she has reached her journey's end, the hundred and twenty miles are over, the wood opens out, and the red house stands in a snow-covered yard. The Klar River rushes foaming by in a succession of little waterfalls, and by that well-known sound she hears that she is at home. And her mother, who must have seen her coming begging, just as she had wished, comes to meet her.

When the major's wife has got so far she always looks up, glances about her, sees the closed door, and knows where she is.

Then she wonders if she is going mad, and sits down to think and to rest. But after a time she sets out again, calculates the yards and the furlongs, the half-miles and the miles, rests for a short time in Finn huts, and sleeps neither night nor day until she has again accomplished the hundred and twenty miles.

During all the time she has been in prison she has almost never slept.

And the two women who had come to see her looked at her with anguish.

The young countess will ever afterwards remember her, as she walked there. She sees her often in her dreams, and wakes with eyes full of tears and a moan on her lips.

The old woman is so pitifully changed, her hair is so thin, and loose ends stick out from the narrow braid. Her face is relaxed and sunken, her dress is disordered and ragged. But with it all she has so much still of her lofty bearing that she inspires not only sympathy, but also respect.

But what the countess remembered most distinctly were her eyes, sunken, turned inward, not yet deprived of all the light of reason, but almost ready to be extinguished, and with a spark of wildness lurking in their depths, so that one had to shudder and fear to have the old woman in the next moment upon one, with teeth ready to bite, fingers to tear.

They have been there quite a while when the major's wife suddenly stops before the young woman and looks at her with a stern glance. The countess takes a step backwards and seizes Madame Scharling's arm.

The features of the major's wife have life and expression, her eyes look out into the world with full intelligence.

"Oh, no; oh, no," she says and smiles; "as yet it is not so bad, my dear young lady."

She asks them to sit down, and sits down herself. She has an air of old-time stateliness, known since days of feasting at Ekeby and at the royal balls at the governor's house at Karlstad. They forget the rags and the prison and only see the proudest and richest woman in Värmland.

"My dear countess," she says, "what possessed you to leave the dance to visit a lonely old woman? You must be very good."

Countess Elizabeth cannot answer. Her voice is choking with emotion. Madame Scharling answers for her, that she had not been able to dance for thinking of the major's wife.

"Dear Madame Scharling," answers the major's wife, "has it gone so far with me that I disturb the young people in their pleasure? You must not weep for me, my dear young countess," she continued. "I am a wicked old woman, who deserves all I get. You do not think it right to strike one's mother?"

"No, but—"

The major's wife interrupts her and strokes the curly, light hair back from her forehead.

"Child, child," she says, "how could you marry that stupid Henrik Dohna?"

"But I love him."

"I see how it is, I see how it is," says the major's wife. "A kind child and nothing more; weeps with those in sorrow, and laughs with those who are glad. And obliged to say 'yes' to the first man who says, 'I love you.' Yes, of course. Go back now and dance, my dear young countess. Dance and be happy! There is nothing bad in you."

"But I want to do something for you."

"Child," says the major's wife, solemnly, "an old woman lived at Ekeby who held the winds of heaven prisoners. Now she is caught and the winds are free. Is it strange that a storm goes over the land?

"I, who am old, have seen it before, countess. I know it. I know that the storm of the thundering God is coming. Sometimes it rushes over great kingdoms, sometimes over small out-of-the-way communities. God's storm forgets no one. It comes over the great as well as the small. It is grand to see God's storm coming.

"Anguish shall spread itself over the land. The small birds' nests shall fall from the branches. The hawk's nest in the pine-tree's top shall be shaken down to the earth with a great noise, and even the eagle's nest in the mountain cleft shall the wind drag out with its dragon tongue.

"We thought that all was well with us; but it was not so. God's storm is needed. I understand that, and I do not complain. I only wish that I might go to my mother."

She suddenly sinks back.

"Go now, young woman," she says. "I have no more time. I must go. Go now, and look out for them who ride on the storm-cloud!"

Thereupon she renews her wandering. Her features relax, her glance turns inward. The countess and Madame Scharling have to leave her.

As soon as they are back again among the dancers the young countess goes straight to Gösta Berling.

"I can greet you from the major's wife," she says. "She is waiting for you to get her out of prison."

"Then she must go on waiting, countess."

"Oh, help her, Herr Berling!"

Gösta stares gloomily before him. "No," he says, "why should I help her? What thanks do I owe her? Everything she has done for me has been to my ruin."

"But Herr Berling—"

"If she had not existed," he says angrily, "I would now be sleeping up there in the forest. Is it my duty to risk my life for her, because she has made me a pensioner at Ekeby? Do you think much credit goes with that profession?"

The young countess turns away from him without answering. She is angry.

She goes back to her place thinking bitter thoughts of the pensioners. They have come to-night with horns and fiddles, and mean to let the bows scrape the strings until the horse-hair is worn through, without thinking that the merry tunes ring in the prisoner's miserable room. They come here to dance until their shoes fall to pieces, and do not remember that their old benefactress can see their shadows whirling by the misty window-panes. Alas, how gray and ugly the world was! Alas, what a shadow trouble and hardness had cast over the young countess's soul!

After a while Gösta comes to ask her to dance.

She refuses shortly.

"Will you not dance with me, countess?" he asks, and grows very red.

"Neither with you nor with any other of the Ekeby pensioners," she says.

"We are not worthy of such an honor."

"It is no honor, Herr Berling. But it gives me no pleasure to dance with those who forget the precepts of gratitude."

Gösta has already turned on his heel.

This scene is heard and seen by many. All think the countess is right The pensioners' ingratitude and heartlessness had waked general indignation.

But in these days Gösta Berling is more dangerous than a wild beast in the forest. Ever since he came home from the hunt and found Marianne gone, his heart has been like an aching wound. He longs to do some one a bloody wrong and to spread sorrow and pain far around.

If she wishes it so, he says to himself, it shall be as she wishes. But she shall not save her own skin. The young countess likes abductions. She shall get her fill. He has nothing against adventure. For eight days he has mourned for a woman's sake. It is long enough. He calls Beerencreutz the colonel, and Christian Bergh the great captain, and the slow Cousin Christopher, who never hesitates at any mad adventure, and consults with them how he shall avenge the pensioners' injured honor.

It is the end of the party. A long line of sledges drive up into the yard. The men are putting on their fur cloaks. The ladies look for their wraps in the dreadful confusion of the dressing-room.

The young countess has been in great haste to leave this hateful ball. She is ready first of all the ladies. She stands smiling in the middle of the room and looks at the confusion, when the door is thrown open, and Gösta Berling shows himself on the threshold.

No man has a right to enter this room. The old ladies stand there with their thin hair no longer adorned with becoming caps; and the young ones have turned up their skirts under their cloaks, that the stiff ruffles may not be crushed on the way home.

But without paying any attention to the warning cries, Gösta Berling rushes up to the countess and seizes her.

He lifts her in his arms and rushes from the room out into the hall and then on to the steps with her.

The astonished women's screams could not check him. When they hurry after, they only see how he throws himself into a sledge with the countess in his arms.

They hear the driver crack his whip and see the horse set off. They know the driver: it is Beerencreutz. They know the horse: it is Don Juan. And in deep distress over the countess's fate they call their husbands.

And these waste no time in questions, but hasten to their sledges. And with the count at their head they chase after the ravisher.

But he lies in the sledge, holding the young countess fast. He has forgotten all grief, and mad with adventure's intoxicating joy, he sings at the top of his voice a song of love and roses.

Close to him he presses her; but she makes no attempt to escape. Her face lies, white and stiffened, against his breast.

Ah, what shall a man do when he has a pale, helpless face so near his own, when he sees the fair hair which usually shades the white, gleaming forehead, pushed to one side, and when the eyelids have closed heavily over the gray eyes' roguish glance?

What shall a man do when red lips grow pale beneath his eyes?

Kiss, of course, kiss the fading lips, the closed eyes, the white forehead.

But then the young woman awakes. She throws herself back. She is like a bent spring. And he has to struggle with her with his whole strength to keep her from throwing herself from the sledge, until finally he forces her, subdued and trembling, down in the corner of the sledge.

"See," says Gösta quite calmly to Beerencreutz, "the countess is the third whom Don Juan and I have carried off this winter. But the others hung about my neck with kisses, and she will neither be kissed by me nor dance with me. Can you understand these women, Beerencreutz?"

But when Gösta drove away from the house, when the women screamed and the men swore, when the sleigh-bells rang and the whips cracked, and there was nothing but cries and confusion, the men who guarded the major's wife were wondering.

"What is going on?" they thought. "Why are they screaming?"

Suddenly the door is thrown open, and a voice calls to them.

"She is gone. He is driving away with her."

They rush out, running like mad, without waiting to see if it was the major's wife or who it was who was gone. Luck was with them, and they came up with a hurrying sledge, and they drove both far and fast, before they discovered whom they were pursuing.

But Berg and Cousin Christopher went quietly to the door, burst the lock, and opened it for the major's wife.

"You are free," they said.

She came out. They stood straight as ramrods on either side of the door and did not look at her.

"You have a horse and sledge outside."

She went out, placed herself in the sledge, and drove away. No one followed her. No one knew whither she went.

Down Broby hill Don Juan speeds towards the Löfven's ice-covered surface. The proud courser flies on. Strong, ice-cold breezes whistle by their cheeks. The bells jingle. The stars and the moon are shining. The snow lies blue-white and glitters from its own brightness.

Gösta feels poetical thoughts wake in him.

"Beerencreutz," he says, "this is life. Just as Don Juan hurries away with this young woman, so time hurries away with man. You are necessity, who steers the journey. I am desire, who fetters the will, and she is dragged helpless, always deeper and deeper down."

"Don't talk!" cries Beerencreutz. "They are coming after us."

And with a whistling cut of the whip he urges Don Juan to still wilder speed.

"Once it was wolves, now it is spoils," cries Gösta. "Don Juan, my boy, fancy that you are a young elk. Rush through the brushwood, wade through the swamps, leap from the mountain top down into the clear lake, swim across it with bravely lifted head, and vanish, vanish in the thick pine-woods' rescuing darkness! Spring, Don Juan! Spring like a young elk!"

Joy fills his wild heart at the mad race. The cries of the pursuers are to him a song of victory. Joy fills his wild heart when he feels the countess's body shake with fright, when he hears her teeth chatter.

Suddenly he loosens the grip of iron with which he has held her. He stands up in the sledge and waves his cap.

"I am Gösta Berling," he cries, "lord of ten thousand kisses and thirteen thousand love-letters! Hurra for Gösta Berling! Take him who can!"

And in the next minute he whispers in the countess's ear:—

"Is not the pace good? Is not the course kingly? Beyond Löfven lies Lake Vaner. Beyond Vaner lies the sea, everywhere endless stretches of clear blue-black ice, and beyond all a glowing world. Rolling thunders in the freezing ice, shrill cries behind us, shooting stars above us, and jingling bells before us! Forward! Always forward! Have you a mind to try the journey, young, beautiful lady?"

He had let her go. She pushes him roughly away. The next instant finds him on his knees at her feet.

"I am a wretch, a wretch. You ought not to have angered me, countess. You stood there so proud and fair, and never thought that a pensioner's hand could reach you. Heaven and earth love you. You ought not to add to the burden of those whom heaven and earth scorn."

He draws her hands to him and lifts them to his face.

"If you only knew," he says, "what it means to be an outcast. One does not stop to think what one does. No, one does not."

At the same moment he notices that she has nothing on her hands. He draws a pair of great fur gloves from his pocket and puts them on her.

And he has become all at once quite quiet. He places himself in the sledge, as far from the young countess as possible.

"You need not be afraid," he says. "Do you not see where we are driving? You must understand that we do not dare to do you any harm."

She, who has been almost out of her mind with fright, sees that they have driven across the lake and that Don Juan is struggling up the steep hill to Borg.

They stop the horse before the steps of the castle, and let the young countess get out of the sledge at the door of her own home.

When she is surrounded by attentive servants, she regains her courage and presence of mind.

"Take care of the horse, Andersson!" she says to the coachman. "These gentlemen who have driven me home will be kind enough to come in for a while. The count will soon be here."

"As you wish, countess," says Gösta, and instantly gets out of the sledge. Beerencreutz throws the reins to the groom without a moment's hesitation. And the young countess goes before them and ushers them into the hall with ill-concealed malicious joy.

The countess had expected that the pensioners would hesitate at the proposition to await her husband.

They did not know perhaps what a stern and upright man he was. They were not afraid of the inquiry he should make of them, who had seized her by force and compelled her to drive with them. She longed to hear him forbid them ever again to set their foot in her house.

She wished to see him call in the servants to point out the pensioners to them as men who thereafter never should be admitted within the doors of Borg. She wished to hear him express his scorn not only of what they had done to her, but also of their conduct toward the old major's wife, their benefactress.

He, who showed her only tenderness and consideration, would rise in just wrath against her persecutors. Love would give fire to his speech. He, who guarded and looked after her as a creature of finer stuff than any other, would not bear that rough men had fallen upon her like birds of prey upon a sparrow. She glowed with thirst of revenge.

Beerencreutz, however, walked undaunted into the dining-room, and up to the fire, which was always lighted when the countess came home from a ball.

Gösta remained in the darkness by the door and silently watched the countess, while the servant removed her outer wraps. As he sat and looked at the young woman, he rejoiced as he had not done for many years. He saw so clearly it was like a revelation, although he did not understand how he had discovered it, that she had in her one of the most beautiful of souls.

As yet it lay bound and sleeping; but it would some day show itself. He rejoiced at having discovered all the purity and gentleness and innocence which was hidden in her. He was almost ready to laugh at her, because she looked so angry and stood with flushed cheeks and frowning brows.

"You do not know how gentle and good you are," he thought.

The side of her being which was turned towards the outside world would never do her inner personality justice, he thought. But Gösta Berling from that hour must be her servant, as one must serve everything beautiful and godlike. Yes, there was nothing to be sorry for that he had just been so violent with her. If she had not been so afraid, if she had not thrust him from her so angrily, if he had not felt how her whole being was shaken by his roughness, he would never have known what a fine and noble soul dwelt within her.

He had not thought it before. She had only cared for pleasure-seeking and amusement. And she had married that stupid Count Henrik.

Yes, now he would be her slave till death; dog and slave as Captain Bergh used to say, and nothing more.

He sat by the door, Gösta Berling, and held with clasped hands a sort of service. Since the day when he for the first time felt the flame of inspiration burn in him, he had not known such a holiness in his soul. He did not move, even when Count Dohna came in with a crowd of people, who swore and lamented over the pensioners' mad performance.

He let Beerencreutz receive the storm. With indolent calm, tried by many adventures, the latter stood by the fireplace. He had put one foot up on the fender, rested his elbow on his knee, and his chin on his hand, and looked at the excited company.

"What is the meaning of all this?" roared the little count at him.

"The meaning is," he said, "that as long as there are women on earth, there will be fools to dance after their piping."

The young count's face grew red.

"I ask what that means!" he repeated.

"I ask that too," sneered Beerencreutz. "I ask what it means when Henrik Dohna's countess will not dance with Gösta Berling."

The count turned questioning to his wife.

"I could not, Henrik," she cried. "I could not dance with him or any of them. I thought of the major's wife, whom they allowed to languish in prison."

The little count straightened his stiff body and stretched up his old-man's head.

"We pensioners," said Beerencreutz, "permit no one to insult us. She who will not dance with us must drive with us. No harm has come to the countess, and there can be an end of the matter."

"No," said the count. "It cannot be the end. It is I who am responsible for my wife's acts. Now I ask why Gösta Berling did not turn to me to get satisfaction when my wife had insulted him."

Beerencreutz smiled.

"I ask that," repeated the count.

"One does not ask leave of the fox to take his skin from him," said Beerencreutz.

The count laid his hand on his narrow chest.

"I am known to be a just man," he cried. "I can pass sentence on my servants. Why should I not be able to pass sentence on my wife? The pensioners have no right to judge her. The punishment they have given her, I wipe out. It has never been, do you understand, gentlemen. It has never existed."

The count screamed out the words in a high falsetto. Beerencreutz cast a swift glance about the assembly. There was not one of those present—Sintram and Daniel Bendix and Dahlberg and all the others who had followed in—who did not stand and smile at the way he outwitted stupid Henrik Dohna.

The young countess did not understand at first. What was it which should not be considered? Her anguish, the pensioner's hard grip on her tender body, the wild song, the wild words, the wild kisses, did they not exist? Had that evening never been, over which the goddess of the gray twilight had reigned?

"But, Henrik—"

"Silence!" he said. And he drew himself up to chide her. "Woe to you, that you, who are a woman, have wished to set yourself up as a judge of men," he says. "Woe to you, that you, who are my wife, dare to insult one whose hand I gladly press. What is it to you if the pensioners have put the major's wife in prison? Were they not right? You can never know how angry a man is to the bottom of his soul when he hears of a woman's infidelity. Do you also mean to go that evil way, that you take such a woman's part?"

"But, Henrik—"

She wailed like a child, and stretched out her arms to ward off the angry words. She had never before heard such hard words addressed to her. She was so helpless among these hard men, and now her only defender turned against her. Never again would her heart have power to light up the world.

"But, Henrik, it is you who ought to protect me."

Gösta Berling was observant now, when it was too late. He did not know what to do. He wished her so well. But he did not dare to thrust himself between man and wife.

"Where is Gösta Berling?" asked the count.

"Here," said Gösta. And he made a pitiable attempt to make a jest of the matter. "You were making a speech, I think, count, and I fell asleep. What do you say to letting us go home and letting you all go to bed?"

"Gösta Berling, since my countess has refused to dance with you, I command her to kiss your hand and to ask you for forgiveness."

"My dear Count Henrik," says Gösta, smiling, "it is not a fit hand for a young woman to kiss. Yesterday it was red with blood from killing an elk, to-day black with soot from a fight with a charcoal-burner. You have given a noble and high-minded sentence. That is satisfaction enough. Come, Beerencreutz!."

The count placed himself in his way.

"Do not go," he said. "My wife must obey me, I wish that my countess shall know whither it leads to be self-willed."

Gösta stood helpless. The countess was quite white; but she did not move.

"Go," said the count.

"Henrik, I cannot."

"You can," said the count, harshly. "You can. But I know what you want. You will force me to fight with this man, because your whim is not to like him. Well, if you will not make him amends, I shall do so. You women love to have a man killed for your sake. You have done wrong, but will not atone for it. Therefore I must do it. I shall fight the duel, countess. In a few hours I shall be a bloody corpse."

She gave him a long look. And she saw him as he was,—stupid, cowardly, puffed up with pride and vanity, the most pitiful of men.

"Be calm," she said. And she became as cold as ice. "I will do it."

But now Gösta Berling became quite beside himself,

"You shall not, countess! No, you shall not! You are only a child, a poor, innocent child, and you would kiss my hand. You have such a white, beautiful soul. I will never again come near you. Oh, never again! I bring death and destruction to everything good and blameless. You shall not touch me. I shudder for you like fire for water. You shall not!"

He put his hands behind his back.

"It is all the same to me, Herr Berling. Nothing makes any difference to me any more. I ask you for forgiveness. I ask you to let me kiss your hand!"

Gösta kept his hands behind his back. He approached the door.

"If you do not accept the amends my wife offers, I must fight with you, Gösta Berling, and moreover must impose upon her another, severer, punishment."

The countess shrugged her shoulders. "He is mad from cowardice," she whispered. "Let me do it! It does not matter if I am humbled. It is after all what you wanted the whole time."

"Did I want that? Do you think I wanted that? Well, if I have no hands to kiss, you must see that I did not want it," he cried.

He ran to the fire and stretched out his hands into it. The flames closed over them, the skin shrivelled up, the nails crackled. But in the same second Beerencreutz seized him by the neck and threw him across the floor. He tripped against a chair and sat down. He sat and almost blushed for such a foolish performance. Would she think that he only did it by way of boast? To do such a thing in the crowded room must seem like a foolish vaunt. There had not been a vestige of danger.

Before he could raise himself, the countess was kneeling beside him. She seized his red, sooty hands and looked at them.

"I will kiss them, kiss them," she cried, "as soon as they are not too painful and sore!" And the tears streamed from her eyes as she saw the blisters rising under the scorched skin.

For he had been like a revelation to her of an unknown glory. That such things could happen here on earth, that they could be done for her! What a man this was, ready for everything, mighty in good as in evil, a man of great deeds, of strong words, of splendid actions! A hero, a hero, made of different stuff from others! Slave of a whim, of the desire of the moment, wild and terrible, but possessor of a tremendous power, fearless of everything.

She had been so depressed the whole evening she had not seen anything but pain and cruelty and cowardice. Now everything was forgotten. The young countess was glad once more to be alive. The goddess of the twilight was conquered. The young countess saw light and color brighten the world.

It was the same night in the pensioners' wing.

There they scolded and swore at Gösta Berling.

The old men wanted to sleep; but it was impossible. He let them get no rest. It was in vain that they drew the bed-curtains and put out the light. He only talked.

He let them know what an angel the young countess was, and how he adored her. He would serve her, worship her. He was glad that every one had forsaken him. He could devote his life to her service. She despised him of course. But he would be satisfied to lie at her feet like a dog.

Had they ever noticed an island out in the Löfven? Had they seen it from the south side, where the rugged cliff rises precipitously from the water? Had they seen it from the north, where it sinks down to the sea in a gentle slope, and where the narrow shoals, covered with great pines wind out into the water, and make the most wonderful little lakes? There on the steep cliff, where the ruins of an old viking fortress still remain, he would build a palace for the young countess, a palace of marble. Broad steps, at which boats decked with flags should land, should be hewn in the cliff down to the sea. There should be glowing halls and lofty towers with gilded pinnacles. It should be a suitable dwelling for the young countess. That old wooden house at Borg was not worthy for her to enter.

When he had gone on so for a while, first one snore and then another began to sound behind the yellow-striped curtains. But most of them swore and bewailed themselves over him and his foolishness.

"Friends," he then says solemnly, "I see the green earth covered with the works of man or with the ruins of men's work. The pyramids weigh down the earth, the tower of Babel has bored through the sky, the beautiful temples and the gray castles have fallen into ruins. But of all which hands have built, what is it which has not fallen, nor shall fall? Ah, friends, throw away the trowel and the mortar! Spread your mason's aprons over your heads and lay you down to build bright palaces of dreams! What has the soul to do with temples of stone and clay? Learn to build everlasting palaces of dreams and visions!"

Thereupon he went laughing to bed.

When, shortly after, the countess heard that the major's wife had been set free, she gave a dinner for the pensioners.

And then began hers and Gösta Berling's long friendship.

CHAPTER XI. GHOST-STORIES

OH, children of the present day!

I have nothing new to tell you, only what is old and almost forgotten. I have legends from the nursery, where the little ones sat on low stools about the old nurse with her white hair, or from the log-fire in the cottage, where the laborers sat and chatted, while the steam reeked from their wet clothes, and they drew knives from leather sheaths at their necks to spread the butter on thick, soft bread, or from the hall where old men sat in their rocking-chairs, and, cheered by the steaming toddy, talked of old times.

When a child, who had listened to the old nurse, to the laborers, to the old men, stood at the window on a winter's evening, it saw no clouds on the horizon without their being the pensioners; the stars were wax-candles, which were lighted at the old house at Borg; and the spinning-wheel which hummed in the next room was driven by old Ulrika Dillner. For the child's head was filled with the people of those old days; it lived for and adored them.

But if such a child, whose whole soul was filled with stones, should be sent through the dark attic to the store-room for flax or biscuits, then the small feet scurried; then it came flying down the stairs, through the passage to the kitchen. For up there in the dark it could not help thinking of the wicked mill-owner at Fors,—of him who was in league with the devil.

Sintram's ashes have been resting long in Svartsjö churchyard, but no one believes that his soul has been called to God, as it reads on his tombstone.

While he was alive he was one of those to whose home, on long, rainy Sunday afternoons, a heavy coach, drawn by black horses, used to come. A gentleman richly but plainly dressed gets out of the carriage, and helps with cards and dice to while away the long hours which with their monotony have driven the master of the house to despair. The game is carried on far into the night; and when the stranger departs at dawn he always leaves behind some baleful parting-gift.

As long as Sintram was here on earth he was one of those whose coming is made known by spirits. They are heralded by visions. Their carriages roll into the yard, their whip cracks, their voices sound on the stairs, the door of the entry is opened and shut. The dogs and people are awakened by the noise, it is so loud; but there is no one who has come, it is only an hallucination which goes before them.

Ugh, those horrible people, whom evil spirits seek out! What kind of a big black dog was it which showed itself at Fors in Sintram's time? He had terrible, shining eyes, and a long tongue which dripped blood and hung far out of his panting throat. One day, when the men-servants had been in the kitchen and eaten their dinner, he had scratched at the kitchen door, and all the maids had screamed with fright; but the biggest and strongest of the men had taken a burning log from the fire, thrown open the door, and hurled it into the dog's gaping mouth.

Then he had fled with terrible howls, flames and smoke had burst from his throat, sparks whirled about him, and his foot-prints on the path shone like fire.

And was it not dreadful that every time Sintram came home from a journey he had changed the animals which drew him? He left with horses, but when he came home at night he had always black bulls before his carriage. The people who lived near the road saw their great black horns against the sky when he drove by, and heard the creatures' bellowing, and were terrified by the line of sparks which the hoofs and wheels drew out of the dry gravel.

Yes, the little feet needed to hurry, indeed, to come across the big, dark attic. Think if something awful, if he, whose name one may not say, should come out of a dark corner! Who can be sure? It was not only to wicked people that he showed himself. Had not Ulrika Dillner seen him? Both she and Anna Stjärnhök could say that they had seen him.

Friends, children, you who dance, you who laugh! I beg you so earnestly to dance carefully, laugh gently, for there can be so much unhappiness if your thin slippers tread on sensitive hearts instead of on hard boards; and your glad, silvery laughter can drive a soul to despair.

It was surely so; the young people's feet had trodden too hard on old Ulrika Dillner, and the young people's laughter had rung too arrogantly in her ears; for there came over her suddenly an irresistible longing for a married woman's titles and dignities. At last she said "yes" to the evil Sintram's long courtship, followed him to Fors as his wife, and was parted from the old friends at Berga, the dear old work, and the old cares for daily bread.

It was a match which went quickly and gayly. Sintram offered himself at Christmas, and in February they were married. That year Anna Stjärnhök was living in Captain Uggla's home. She was a good substitute for old Ulrika, and the latter could draw back without compunction, and take to herself married honors.

Without compunction, but not without regret. It was not a pleasant place she had come to; the big, empty rooms were filled with dreadful terrors. As soon as it was dark she began to tremble and to be afraid. She almost died of homesickness.

The long Sunday afternoons were the hardest of all. They never came to an end, neither they nor the long succession of torturing thoughts which travelled through her brain.

So it happened one day in March, when Sintram had not come home from church to dinner, that she went into the drawing-room, on the second floor, and placed herself at the piano. It was her last consolation. The old piano, with a flute-player and shepherdess painted on the white cover, was her own, come to her from her parents' home. To it she could tell her troubles; it understood her.

But is it not both pitiful and ridiculous? Do you know what she is playing? Only a polka, and she who is so heart-broken!

She does not know anything else. Before her fingers stiffened round broom and carving-knife she had learned this one polka. It sticks in her fingers; but she does not know any other piece,—no funeral march, no impassioned sonata, not even a wailing ballad,—only the polka.

She plays it whenever she has anything to confide to the old piano. She plays it both when she feels like weeping and like smiling. When she was married she played it, and when for the first time she had come to her own home, and also now.

The old strings understand her: she is unhappy, unhappy.

A traveller passing by and hearing the polka ring could well believe that Sintram was having a ball for neighbors and friends, it sounds so gay. It is such a brave and glad melody. With it, in the old days, she has played carelessness in and hunger out at Berga; when they heard it every one must up and dance. It burst the fetters of rheumatism about the joints, and lured pensioners of eighty years on to the floor. The whole world would gladly dance to that polka, it sounds so gay—but old Ulrika weeps. Sintram has sulky, morose servants about him, and savage animals. She longs for friendly faces and smiling mouths. It is this despairing longing which the lively polka shall interpret.

People find it hard to remember that she is Madame Sintram. Everybody calls her Mamselle Dillner. She wants the polka tune to express her sorrow for the vanity which tempted her to seek for married honors.

Old Ulrika plays as if she would break the strings. There is so much to drown: the lamentations of the poor peasants, the curses of over-worked cottagers, the sneers of insolent servants, and, first and last, the shame,—the shame of being the wife of a bad man.

To those notes Gösta Berling has led young Countess Dohna to the dance. Marianne Sinclair and her many admirers have danced to them, and the major's wife at Ekeby has moved to their measure when Altringer was still alive. She can see them, couple after couple, in their youth and beauty, whirl by. There was a stream of gayety from them to her, from her to them. It was her polka which made their cheeks glow, their eyes shine. She is parted from all that now. Let the polka resound,—so many memories, so many tender memories to drown!

She plays to deaden her anguish. Her heart is ready to burst with terror when she sees the black dog, when she hears the servants whispering of the black bulls. She plays the polka over and over again to deaden her anguish.

Then she perceives that her husband has come home. She hears that he comes into the room and sits down in the rocking-chair. She knows so well the sound as the rockers creak on the deal floor that she does not even look round.

All the time she is playing the rocking continues; she soon hears the music no longer, only the rocking.

Poor old Ulrika, so tortured, so lonely, so helpless, astray in a hostile country, without a friend to complain to, without any consoler but a cracked piano, which answers her with a polka.

It is like loud laughter at a funeral, a drinking song in a church.

While the rocking-chair is still rocking she hears suddenly how the piano is laughing at her sorrows, and she stops in the middle of a bar. She rises and turns to the rocking-chair.

But the next instant she is lying in a swoon on the floor. It was not her husband who sat in the rocking-chair, but another,—he to whom little children do not dare to give a name, he who would frighten them to death if they should meet him in the deserted attic.

Can any one whose soul has been filled with legends ever free himself from their dominion? The night wind howls outside, the trees whip the pillars of the balcony with their stiff branches, the sky arches darkly over the far-stretching hills, and I, who sit alone in the night and write, with the lamp lighted and the curtain drawn, I, who am old and ought to be sensible, feel the same shudder creeping up my back as when I first heard this story, and I have to keep lifting my eyes from my work to be certain that no one has come in and hidden himself in that further corner; I have to look out on the balcony to see if there is not a black head looking over the railing. This fright never leaves me when the night is dark and solitude deep; and it becomes at last so dreadful that I must throw aside my pen, creep down in my bed and draw the blanket up over my eyes.

It was the great, secret wonder of my childhood that Ulrika Dillner survived that afternoon. I should never have done so.

I hope, dear friends, that you may never see the tears of old eyes. And that you may not have to stand helpless when a gray head leans against your breast for support, or when old hands are clasped about yours in a silent prayer. May you never see the old sunk in a sorrow which you cannot comfort.

What is the grief of the young? They have strength, they have hope. But what suffering it is when the old weep; what despair when they, who have always been the support of your young days, sink into helpless wailing.

There sat Anna Stjärnhök and listened to old Ulrika, and she saw no way out for her.

The old woman wept and trembled. Her eyes were wild. She talked and talked, sometimes quite incoherently, as if she did not know where she was. The thousand wrinkles which crossed her face were twice as deep as usual, the false curls, which hung down over her eyes, were straightened by her tears, and her whole long, thin body was shaken with sobs.

At last Anna had to put an end to the wailings. She had made up her mind. She was going to take her back with her to Berga. Of course, she was Sintram's wife, but she could not remain at Fors. He would drive her mad if she stayed with him. Anna Stjärnhök had decided to take old Ulrika away.

Ah, how the poor thing rejoiced, and yet trembled at this decision! But she never would dare to leave her husband and her home. He would perhaps send the big black dog after her.

But Anna Stjärnhök conquered her resistance, partly by jests, partly by threats, and in half an hour she had her beside her in the sledge. Anna was driving herself, and old Disa was in the shafts. The road was wretched, for it was late in March; but it did old Ulrika good to drive once more in the well-known sledge, behind the old horse who had been a faithful servant at Berga almost as long as she.

As she had naturally a cheerful spirit, she stopped crying by the time they passed Arvidstorp; at Högberg she was already laughing, and when they passed Munkeby she was telling how it used to be in her youth, when she lived with the countess at Svaneholm.

They drove up a steep and stony road in the lonely and deserted region north of Munkeby. The road sought out all the hills it possibly could find; it crept up to their tops by slow windings, rushed down them in a steep descent, hurried across the even valley to find a new hill to climb over.

They were just driving down Vestratorp's hill, when old Ulrika stopped short in what she was saying, and seized Anna by the arm. She was staring at a big black dog at the roadside.

"Look!" she said.

The dog set off into the wood. Anna did not see much of him.

"Drive on," said Ulrika; "drive as fast as you can! Now Sintram will hear that I have gone."

Anna tried to laugh at her terror, but she insisted.

"We shall soon hear his sleigh-bells, you will see. We shall hear them before we reach the top of the next hill."

And when Disa drew breath for a second at the top of Elofs hill sleigh-bells could be heard behind them.

Old Ulrika became quite mad with fright. She trembled, sobbed, and wailed as she had done in the drawing-room at Fors. Anna tried to urge Disa on, but she only turned her head and gave her a glance of unspeakable surprise. Did she think that Disa had forgotten when it was time to trot and when it was time to walk? Did she want to teach her how to drag a sledge, to teach her who had known every stone, every bridge, every gate, every hill for more than twenty years?

All this while the sleigh-bells were coming nearer.

"It is he, it is he! I know his bells," wails old Ulrika.

The sound comes ever nearer. Sometimes it seems so unnaturally loud that Anna turns to see if Sintram's horse has not got his head in her sledge; sometimes it dies away. They hear it now on the right, now on the left of the road, but they see no one. It is as if the jingling of the bells alone pursues them.

Just as it is at night, on the way home from a party, is it also now. These bells ring out a tune; they sing, speak, answer. The woods echo with their sound.

Anna Stjärnhök almost wishes that their pursuer would come near enough for her to see Sin t ram himself and his red horse. The dreadful sleigh-bells anger her.

"Those bells torture me," she says.

The word is taken up by the bells. "Torture me," they ring. "Torture me, torture, torture, torture me," they sing to all possible tunes.

It was not so long ago that she had driven this same way, hunted by wolves. She had seen their white teeth, in the darkness, gleam in their gaping mouths; she had thought that her body would soon be torn to pieces by the wild beasts of the forest; but then she had not been afraid. She had never lived through a more glorious night. Strong and beautiful had the horse been which drew her, strong and beautiful was the man who had shared the joy of the adventure with her.

Ah, this old horse, this old, helpless, trembling companion. She feels so helpless that she longs to cry. She cannot escape from those terrible, irritating bells.

So she stops and gets out of the sledge. There must be an end to it all. Why should she run away as if she were afraid of that wicked, contemptible wretch?

At last she sees a horse's head come out of the advancing twilight, and after the head a whole horse, a whole sledge, and in the sledge sits Sintram himself.

She notices, however, that it is not as if they had come along the road—this sledge, and this horse, and their driver—but more as if they had been created just there before her eyes, and had come forward out of the twilight as soon as they were made ready.

Anna threw the reins to Ulrika and went to meet Sintram.

He stops the horse.

"Well, well," he says; "what a piece of luck! Dear Miss Stjärnhök, let me move my companion over to your sledge. He is going to Berga to-night, and I am in a hurry to get home."

"Where is your companion?"

Sintram lifts his blanket, and shows Anna a man who is lying asleep on the bottom of the sledge. "He is a little drunk," he says; "but what does that matter? He will sleep. It's an old acquaintance, moreover; it is Gösta Berling."

Anna shudders,

"Well, I will tell you," continues Sintram, "that she who forsakes the man she loves sells him to the devil. That was the way I got into his claws. People think they do so well, of course; to renounce is good, and to love is evil."

"What do you mean? What are you talking about?" asks Anna, quite disturbed.

"I mean that you should not have let Gösta Berling go from you, Miss Anna."

"It was God's will."

"Yes, yes, that's the way it is; to renounce is good, and to love is evil. The good God does not like to see people happy. He sends wolves after them. But if it was not God who did it, Miss Anna? Could it not just as well have been I who called my little gray lambs from the Dovre mountains to hunt the young man and the young girl? Think, if it was I who sent the wolves, because I did not wish to lose one of my own! Think, if it was not God who did it!"

"You must not tempt me to doubt that," says Anna, in a weak voice, "for then I am lost."

"Look here," says Sintram, and bends down over the sleeping Gösta Berling; "look at his little finger. That little sore never heals. We took the blood there when he signed the contract. He is mine. There is a peculiar power in blood. He is mine, and it is only love which can free him; but if I am allowed to keep him he will be a fine thing."

Anna Stjärnhök struggles and struggles to shake off the fascination which has seized her. It is all madness, madness. No one can swear away his soul to the odious tempter. But she has no power over her thoughts; the twilight lies so heavy over her, the woods stand so dark and silent. She cannot escape the dreadful terror of the moment.

"You think, perhaps," continues Sintram, "that there is not much left in him to ruin. But don't think that! Has he ground down the peasants, has he deceived poor friends, has he cheated at cards? Has he, Miss Anna, has he been a married woman's lover?"

"I think you are the devil himself!"

"Let us exchange. You take Gösta Berling, take him and marry him. Keep him, and give them at Berga the money. I yield him up to you, and you know that he is mine. Think that it was not God who sent the wolves after you the other night, and let us exchange!"

"What do you want as compensation?"

Sintram grinned.

"I—what do I want? Oh, I am satisfied with little. I only want that old woman there in your sledge, Miss Anna."

"Satan, tempter," cries Anna, "leave me! Shall I betray an old friend who relies on me? Shall I leave her to you, that you may torture her to madness?"

"There, there, there; quietly, Miss Anna! Think what you are doing! Here is a fine young man, and there an old, worn-out woman. One of them I must have. Which of them will you let me keep?"

Anna Stjärnhök laughed wildly.

"Do you think that we can stand here and exchange souls as they exchange horses at the market at Broby?"

"Just so, yes. But if you will, we shall put it on another basis. We shall think of the honor of the Stjärnhöks."

Thereupon he begins to call in a loud voice to his wife, who is sitting in Anna's sledge; and, to the girl's unspeakable horror, she obeys the summons instantly, gets out of the sledge, and comes, trembling and shaking, to them.

"See, see, see!—such an obedient wife," says Sintram. "You cannot prevent her coming when her husband calls. Now, I shall lift Gösta out of my sledge and leave him here,—leave him for *good*, Miss Anna. Whoever may want to can pick him up."

He bends down to lift Gösta up; but Anna leans forward, fixes him with her eyes, and hisses like an angry animal:—

"In God's name, go home! Do you not know who is sitting in the rocking-chair in the drawing-room and waiting for you? Do you dare to let him wait?"

It was for Anna almost the climax of the horrors of the day to see how these words affect him. He drags on the reins, turns, and drives homewards, urging the horse to a gallop with blows and wild cries down the dreadful hill, while a long line of sparks crackle under the runners and hoofs in the thin March snow.

Anna Stjärnhök and Ulrika Dillner stand alone in the road, but they do not say a word. Ulrika trembles before Anna's wild eyes, and Anna has nothing to say to the poor old thing, for whose sake she has sacrificed her beloved.

She would have liked to weep, to rave, to roll on the ground and strew snow and sand on her head.

Before, she had known the sweetness of renunciation, now she knew its bitterness. What was it to sacrifice her love compared to sacrificing her beloved's soul? They drove on to Berga in the same silence; but when they arrived, and the hall-door was opened, Anna Stjärnhök fainted for the first and only time in her life. There sat both Sintram and Gösta Berling, and chatted quietly. The tray with toddy had been brought in; they had been there at least an hour.

Anna Stjärnhök fainted, but old Ulrika stood calm. She had noticed that everything was not right with him who had followed them on the road.

Afterwards the captain and his wife arranged the matter so with Sintram that old Ulrika was allowed to stay at Berga. He agreed good-naturedly.

"He did not want to drive her mad," he said.

I do not ask any one to believe these old stories. They cannot be anything but lies and fiction. But the anguish which passes over the heart, until it wails as the floor boards in Sintram's room wailed under the swaying rockers; but the questions which ring in the ears, as the sleigh-bells rang for Anna Stjärnhök in the lonely forest,—when will they be as lies and fiction?

Oh, that they could be!

CHAPTER XII. EBBA DOHNA'S STORY

THE beautiful point on Löfven's eastern shore, about which the bay glides with lapping waves, the proud point where the manor of Borg lies, beware of approaching.

Löfven never looks more glorious than from its summit.

No one can know how lovely it is, the lake of my dreams, until he has seen from Borg's point the morning mist glide away from its smooth surface; until he, from the windows of the little blue cabinet, where so many memories dwell, has seen it reflect a pink sunset.

But I still say, go not thither!

For perhaps you will be seized with a desire to remain in that old manor's sorrowful halls; perhaps you will make yourself the owner of those fair lands; and if you are young, rich, and happy, you will make your home there with a young wife.

No, it is better never to see the beautiful point, for at Borg no one can live and be happy. No matter how rich, how happy you may be, who move in there, those old tear-drenched floors would soon drink *your* tears as well, and those walls, which could give back so many moans, would also glean *your* sighs.

An implacable fate is on this lovely spot. It is as if misfortune were buried there, but found no rest in its grave, and perpetually rose from it to terrify the living. If I were lord of Borg I would search through the ground, both in the park and under the cellar floor in the house, and in the fertile mould out in the meadows, until I had found the witch's worm-eaten corpse, and then I would give her a grave in consecrated earth in the Svartsjö churchyard. And at the burial I would not spare on the ringer's pay, but let the bells sound long and loud over her; and to the clergyman and sexton I should send rich gifts, that they with redoubled strength might with speech and song consecrate her to everlasting rest.

Or, if that did not help, some stormy night I would set fire to the wooden walls, and let it destroy everything, so that no one more might be tempted to live in the home of misfortune. Afterwards no one should be allowed to approach that doomed spot; only the church-tower's black jackdaws should build in the great chimney, which, blackened and dreadful, would raise itself over the deserted foundations.

Still, I should certainly mourn when I saw the flames close over the roof, when thick smoke, reddened by the fire and flecked with sparks, should roll out from the old manor-house. In the crackling and the roaring I should fancy I heard the wails of homeless memories; on the blue points of the flames I should see disturbed spirits floating. I should think how sorrow beautifies, how misfortune adorns, and weep as if a temple to the old gods had been condemned to destruction.

But why croak of unhappiness? As yet Borg lies and shines on its point, shaded by its park of mighty pines, and the snow-covered fields glitter in March's burning sun; as yet is heard within those walls the young Countess Elizabeth's gay laughter.

Every Sunday she goes to church at Svartsjö, which lies near Borg, and gathers together a few friends for dinner. The judge and his family from Munkerud used to come, and the Ugglas from Berga, and even Sintram. If Gösta Berling happens to be in Svartsjö, wandering over Löfven's ice, she invites him too. Why should she not invite Gösta Berling?

She probably does not know that the gossips are beginning to whisper that Gösta comes very often over to the east shore to see her. Perhaps he also comes to drink and play cards with Sintram; but no one thinks so much of that; every one knows that his body is of steel; but it is another matter with his heart. No one believes that he can see a pair of shining eyes, and fair hair which curls about a white brow, without love.

The young countess is good to him. But there is nothing strange in that; she is good to all. She takes ragged beggar children on her knee, and when she drives by some poor old creature on the highroad she has the coachman stop, and takes the poor wanderer up into her sledge.

Gösta used to sit in the little blue cabinet, where there is such a glorious view over the lake, and read poetry to her. There can be no harm in that. He does not forget that she is a countess, and he a homeless adventurer; and it is good for him to be with some one whom he holds high and holy. He could just as well be in love with the Queen of Sheba as with her.

He only asks to be allowed to wait on her as a page waits on his noble mistress: to fasten her skates, to hold her skeins, to steer her sled. There cannot be any question of love between them; he is just the man to find his happiness in a romantic, innocent adoration.

The young count is silent and serious, and Gösta is playfully gay. He is just such a companion as the young countess likes. No one who sees her fancies that she is hiding a forbidden love. She thinks of dancing,—of dancing and merrymaking. She would like the earth to be quite flat, without stones, without hills or seas, so that she could dance everywhere. From the cradle to the grave she would like to dance in her small, thin-soled, satin slippers.

But rumor is not very merciful to young women.

When the guests come to dinner at Borg, the men generally, after the meal, go into the count's room to sleep and smoke; the old ladies sink down in the easy-chairs in the drawing-room, and lean their venerable heads against the high backs; but the countess and Anna Stjärnhök go into the blue cabinet and exchange endless confidences.

The Sunday after the one when Anna Stjärnhök took Ulrika Dillner back to Berga they are sitting there again.

No one on earth is so unhappy as the young girl. All her gayety is departed, and gone is the glad defiance which she showed to everything and everybody who wished to come too near her.

Everything which had happened to her that day has sunk back into the twilight from which it was charmed; she has only one distinct impression left,—yes, one, which is poisoning her soul.

"If it really was not God who did it," she used to whisper to herself. "If it was not God, who sent the wolves?"

She asks for a sign, she longs for a miracle. She searches heaven and earth. But she sees no finger stretched from the sky to point out her way.

As she sits now opposite the countess in the blue cabinet, her eyes fall on a little bunch of hepaticas which the countess holds in her white hand. Like a bolt it strikes her that she knows where the flowers have grown, that she knows who has picked them.

She does not need to ask. Where else in the whole countryside do hepaticas bloom in the begin-ning of April, except in the birch grove which lies on the slopes of Ekeby?

She stares and stares at the little blue stars; those happy ones who possess all hearts; those little prophets who, beautiful in themselves, are also glorified by the splendor of all the beauty which they herald, of all the beauty which is coming. And as she watches them a storm of wrath rises in her soul, rumbling like the thunder, deadening like the lightning.

"By what right," she thinks, "does Countess Dohna hold this bunch of hepaticas, picked by the shore at Ekeby?"

They were all tempters: Sintram, the countess, everybody wanted to allure Gösta Berling to what was evil. But she would protect him; against all would she protect him. Even if it should cost her heart's blood, she would do it.

She thinks that she must see those flowers torn out of the countess's hand, and thrown aside, trampled, crushed, before she leaves the little blue cabinet.

She thinks that, and she begins a struggle with the little blue stars. Out in the drawing-room the old ladies lean their venerable heads against the chair-backs and suspect nothing; the men smoke their pipes in calm and quiet in the count's room; peace is everywhere; only in the little blue cabinet rages a terrible struggle.

Ah, how well they do who keep their hands from the sword, who understand how to wait quietly, to lay their hearts to rest and let God direct! The restless heart always goes astray. Ill-will makes the pain worse.

But Anna Stjärnhök believes that at last she has seen a finger in the sky.

"Anna," says the countess, "tell me a story!"

"About what?"

"Oh," says the countess, and caresses the flowers with her white hand. "Do not you know something about love, something about loving?"

"No, I know nothing of love."

"How you talk! Is there not a place here which is called Ekeby,—a place full of pensioners?"

"Yes," says Anna, "there is a place which is called Ekeby, and there are men there who suck the marrow of the land, who make us incapable of serious work, who ruin growing youth, and lead astray our geniuses. Do you want to hear of them? Do you want to hear love-stories of them?"

"Yes. I like the pensioners."

So Anna Stjärnhök speaks,—speaks in short sentences, like an old hymn-book, for she is nearly choking with stormy emotions. Suppressed suffering trembles in each word, and the countess was both frightened and interested to hear her.

"What is a pensioner's love, what is a pensioner's faith?—one sweetheart to-day, another to-morrow, one in the east, another in the west. Nothing is too high for him, nothing too low; one day a count's daughter, the next day a beggar girl. Nothing on earth is so capacious as his heart. But alas, alas for her who loves a pensioner. She must seek him out where he lies drunk at the wayside. She must silently look on while he at the card-table plays away the home of her childhood. She must bear to have him hang about other women. Oh, Elizabeth, if a pensioner asks an honorable woman for a dance she ought to refuse it to him; if he gives her a bunch of flowers she ought to throw the flowers on the ground and trample on them; if she loves him she ought rather to die than to marry him. There was one among the pensioners who was a dismissed priest; he had lost his vestments for drunkenness. He was drunk in the church. He drank up the communion wine. Have you ever heard of him?"

"No."

"After he had been dismissed he wandered about the country as a beggar. He drank like a madman. He would steal to get brandy."

"What is his name?"

"He is no longer at Ekeby. The major's wife got hold of him, gave him clothes, and persuaded your mother-in-law, Countess Dohna, to make him tutor to your husband, young Count Henrik."

"A dismissed priest!"

"Oh, he was a young, powerful man, of good intelligence. There was no harm in him, if he only did not drink. Countess Märta was not particular. It amused her to quarrel with the neighboring clergymen. Still, she ordered him to say nothing of his past life to her children. For then her son would have lost respect for him, and her daughter would not have endured him, for she was a saint.

"So he came here to Borg. He always sat just inside the door, on the very edge of his chair, never said a word at the table, and fled out into the park when any visitors came.

"But there in the lonely walks he used to meet young Ebba Dohna. She was not one who loved the noisy feasts which resounded in the halls at Borg after the countess became a widow. She was so gentle, so shy. She was still, although she was seventeen, nothing but a tender child; but she was very lovely, with her brown eyes, and the faint, delicate color in her cheeks. Her thin, slender body bent forward. Her little hand would creep into yours with a shy pressure. Her little mouth was the most silent of mouths and the most serious. Ah, her voice, her sweet little voice, which pronounced the words so slowly and so well, but never rang with the freshness and warmth of youth,—its feeble tones were like a weary musician's last chord.

"She was not as others. Her foot trod so lightly, so softly, as if she were a frightened fugitive. She kept her eyelids lowered in order not to be disturbed in her contemplation of the visions of her soul. It had turned from the earth when she was but a child.

"When she was little her grandmother used to tell her stories; and one evening they both sat by the fire; but the stories had come to an end. But still the little girl's hand lay on the old woman's dress, and she gently stroked the silk,—that funny stuff which sounded like a little bird. And this stroking was her prayer, for she was one of those children who never beg in words.

"Then the old lady began to tell her of a little child in the land of Judah; of a little child who was born to become a great King. The angels had filled the earth with songs of praise when he was born. The kings of the East came, guided by the star of heaven, and gave him gold and incense; and old men and women foretold his glory. This child grew up to greater beauty and wisdom than all other children. Already, when he was twelve years old, his wisdom was greater than that of the chief-priests and the scribes.

"Then the old woman told her of the most beautiful thing the earth has ever seen: of that child's life while he remained among men, those wicked men who would not acknowledge him their King.

"She told her how the child became a man, but that the glory surrounded him still.

"Everything on the earth served him and loved him, except mankind. The fishes let themselves be caught in his net, bread filled his baskets, water changed itself to wine when he wished it.

"But the people gave the great King no golden crown, no shining throne. He had no bowing courtiers about him. They let him go among them like a beggar.

"Still, he was so good to them, the great King! He cured their sicknesses, gave back to the blind their sight, and waked the dead.

"'But,' said the grandmother, 'the people would not have the great King for their lord.

"'They sent their soldiers against him, and took him prisoner; they dressed him, by way of mockery, in crown and sceptre, and in a silken cloak, and made him go out to the place of execution, bearing a heavy cross. Oh, my child, the good King loved the high mountains. At night he used to climb them to talk with those who dwelt in heaven, and he liked by day to sit on the mountain-side and talk to the listening people. But now they led him up on a mountain to crucify him. They drove nails through his hands and feet, and hung the good King on a cross, as if he had been a robber or a malefactor.

"'And the people mocked at him. Only his mother and his friends wept, that he should die before he had been a King.

"'Oh, how the dead things mourned his death!

"'The sun lost its light, and the mountains trembled; the curtain in the temple was rent asunder, and the graves opened, that the dead might rise up and show their grief.'

"The little one lay with her head on her grandmother's knee, and sobbed as if her heart would break.

"'Do not weep, little one; the good King rose from his grave and went up to his Father in heaven.'

"'Grandmother,' sobbed the poor little thing, 'did he ever get any kingdom?'

"'He sits on God's right hand in heaven.'

"But that did not comfort her. She wept helplessly and unrestrainedly, as only a child can weep.

"'Why were they so cruel to him? Why were they allowed to be so cruel to him?'

"Her grandmother was almost frightened at her overwhelming sorrow.

"'Say, grandmother, say that you have not told it right! Say that it did not end so! Say that they were not so cruel to the good King! Say that he got a kingdom on earth!'

"She threw her arms around the old woman and beseeched her with streaming tears.

"'Child, child,' said her grandmother, to console her. There are some who believe that he will come again. Then he will put the earth under his power and direct it. The beautiful earth will be a glorious kingdom. It shall last a thousand years. Then the fierce animals will be gentle; little children will play by the viper's nest, and bears and cows will eat together. No one shall injure or destroy the other; the lance shall be bent into scythes, and the sword forged into ploughs. And everything shall be play and happiness, for the good will possess the earth.'

"Then the little one's face brightened behind her tears.

"'Will the good King then get a throne, grandmother?'

"'A throne of gold.'

"'And servants, and courtiers, and a golden crown?'

"'Yes.'

"'Will he come soon, grandmother?'

"'No one knows when he will come.'

"'May I sit on a stool at his feet?'

"'You may.'

"'Grandmother, I am so happy,' says the little one.

"Evening after evening, through many winters, they both sat by the fire and talked of the good

King and his kingdom. The little one dreamed of the kingdom which should last a thousand years, both by night and by day. She never wearied of adorning it with everything beautiful which she could think of.

"Ebba Dohna never dared to speak of it to any one; but from that evening she only lived for the Lord's kingdom, and to await his coming.

"When the evening sun crimsoned the western sky, she wondered if he would ever appear there, glowing with a mild splendor, followed by a host of millions of angels, and march by her, allowing her to touch the hem of his garment.

"She often thought, too, of those pious women who had hung a veil over their heads, and never lifted their eyes from the ground, but shut themselves in in the gray cloister's calm, in the darkness of little cells, to always contemplate the glowing visions which appear from the night of the soul.

"Such had she grown up; such she was when she and the new tutor met in the lonely paths of the park.

"I will not speak more harshly of him than I must. I will believe that he loved that child, who soon chose him for companion in her lonely wanderings. I think that his soul got back its wings when he walked by the side of that quiet girl, who had never confided in any other. I think that he felt himself a child again, good, gentle, virtuous.

"But if he really loved her, why did he not remember that he could not give her a worse gift than his love? He, one of the world's outcasts, what did he want, what did he think of when he walked at the side of the count's daughter? What did the dismissed clergyman think when she confided to him her gentle dreams? What did he want, who had been a drunkard, and would be again when he got the chance, at the side of her who dreamed of a bridegroom in heaven? Why did he not fly far, far away from her? Would it not have been better for him to wander begging and stealing about the land than to walk under the silent pines and again be good, gentle, virtuous, when it could not change the life he had led, nor make it right that Ebba Dohna should love him?

"Do not think that he looked like a drunkard, with livid cheeks and red eyes. He was always a splendid man, handsome and unbroken in soul and body. He had the bearing of a king and a body of steel, which was not hurt by the wildest life."

"Is he still living?" asks the countess.

"Oh, no, he must be dead now. All that happened so long ago."

There is something in Anna Stjärnhök which begins to tremble at what she is doing. She begins to think that she will never tell the countess who the man is of whom she speaks; that she will let her believe that he is dead.

"At that time he was still young;" and she begins her story again. "The joy of living was kindled in him. He had the gift of eloquence, and a fiery, impulsive heart.

"One evening he spoke to Ebba Dohna of love. She did not answer; she only told him what her grandmother had told her that winter evening, and described to him the land of her dreams. Then she exacted a promise from him. She made him swear that he would be a proclaimer of the word of God; one of those who would prepare the way for the Lord, so that his coming might be hastened.

"What could he do? He was a dismissed clergyman, and no way was so closed to him as that on which she wanted him to enter. But he did not dare to tell her the truth. He did not have the heart to grieve that gentle child whom he loved. He promised everything she wished.

"After that few words were needed. It went without saying that some day she should be his wife. It was not a love of kisses and caresses. He hardly dared come near her. She was as sensitive as a fragile flower. But her brown eyes were sometimes raised from the ground to seek his. On moonlit evenings, when they sat on the veranda, she would creep close to him, and then he would kiss her hair without her noticing it.

"But you understand that his sin was in his for getting both the past and the future. That he was poor and humble he could forget; but he ought always to have remembered that a day must come when in her soul love would rise against love, earth against heaven, when she would be obliged to choose between him and the glorious Lord of the kingdom of the thousand years. And she was not one who could endure such a struggle.

"A summer went by, an autumn, a winter. When the spring came, and the ice melted, Ebba Dohna fell ill. It was thawing in the valleys; there were streams down all the hills, the ice was unsafe, the roads almost impassable both for sledge and cart.

"Countess Dohna wanted to get a doctor from Karlstad; there was none nearer. But she commanded in vain. She could not, either with prayers or threats, induce a servant to go. She threw herself on her knees before the coachman, but he refused. She went into hysterics of grief over her daughter—she was always immoderate, in sorrow as in joy, Countess Märta.

"Ebba Dohna lay ill with pneumonia, and her life was in danger; but no doctor could be got.

"Then the tutor drove to Karlstad. To take that journey in the condition the roads were in was to play with his life; but he did it. It took him over bending ice and break-neck freshets. Sometimes he had to cut steps for the horse in the ice, sometimes drag him out of the deep clay in the road. It was said that the doctor refused to go with him, and that he, with pistol in hand, forced him to set out.

"When he came back the countess was ready to throw herself at his feet. 'Take everything!' she said. 'Say what you want, what you desire,—my daughter, my lands, my money!'

"'Your daughter,' answered the tutor."

Anna Stjärnhök suddenly stops.

"Well, what then, what then?" asks Countess Elizabeth.

"That can be enough for now," answers Anna, for she is one of those unhappy people who live in the anguish of doubt. She has felt it a whole week. She does not know what she wants. What one moment seems right to her the next is wrong. Now she wishes that she had never begun this story.

"I begin to think that you want to deceive me, Anna. Do you not understand that I *must* hear the end of this story?"

"There is not much more to tell.—The hour of strife was come for Ebba Dohna. Love raised itself against love, earth against heaven.

"Countess Märta told her of the wonderful journey which the young man had made for her sake, and she said to her that she, as a reward, had given him her hand.

"Ebba was so much better that she lay dressed on a sofa. She was weak and pale, and even more silent than usual.

"When she heard those words she lifted her brown eyes reproachfully to her mother, and said to her:—

"'Mamma, have you given me to a dismissed priest, to one who has forfeited his right to serve God, to a man who has been a thief, a beggar?'

"'But, child, who has told you that? I thought you knew nothing of it.'

"'I heard your guests speaking of him the day I was taken ill.'

"'But, child, remember that he has saved your life!'

"'I remember that he has deceived me. He should have told me who he was.'

"'He says that you love him.'

"'I have done so. I cannot love one who has deceived me.'

"'How has he deceived you?'

"'You would not understand, mamma.'

"She did not wish to speak to her mother of the kingdom of her dreams, which her beloved should have helped her to realize.

"'Ebba,' said the countess, 'if you love him you shall not ask what he has been, but marry him. The husband of a Countess Dohna will be rich enough, powerful enough, to excuse all the follies of his youth.'

"'I care nothing for his youthful follies, mamma; it is because he can never be what I want him to be that I cannot marry him.'

"'Ebba, remember that I have given him my promise!'

"The girl became as pale as death.

"'Mamma, I tell you that if you marry me to him you part me from God.'

"'I have decided to act for your happiness,' says the countess. 'I am certain that you will be happy with this man. You have already succeeded in making a saint of him. I have decided to overlook the claims of birth and to forget that he is poor and despised, in order to give you a chance to raise him. I feel that I am doing right. You know that I scorn all old prejudices.'

"The young girl lay quiet on her sofa for a while after the countess had left her. She was fighting her battle. Earth raised itself against heaven, love against love; but her childhood's love won the victory. As she lay there on the sofa, she saw the western sky glow in a magnificent sunset. She thought that it was a greeting from the good King; and as she could not be faithful to him if she lived, she decided to die. There was nothing else for her to do, since her mother wished her to belong to one who never could be the good King's servant.

"She went over to the window, opened it, and let the twilight's cold, damp air chill her poor, weak body.

"It was easily done. The illness was certain to begin again, and it did.

"No one but I knows that she sought death, Elizabeth. I found her at the window. I heard her delirium. She liked to have me at her side those last days.

"It was I who saw her die; who saw how she one evening stretched out her arms towards the glowing west, and died, smiling, as if she had seen some one advance from the sunset's glory to meet her. It was also I who had to take her last greeting to the man she loved. I was to ask him to forgive her, that she could not be his wife. The good King would not permit it.

"But I have never dared to say to that man that he was her murderer. I have not dared to lay the weight of such pain on his shoulders. And yet he, who won her love by lies, was he not her murderer? Was he not, Elizabeth?"

Countess Dohna long ago had stopped caressing the blue flowers. Now she rises, and the bouquet falls to the floor.

"Anna, you are deceiving me. You say that the story is old, and that the man has been dead a long time. But I know that it is scarcely five years since Ebba Dohna died, and you say that you yourself were there through it all. You are not old. Tell me who the man is!"

Anna Stjärnhök begins to laugh.

"You wanted a love-story. Now you have had one which has cost you both tears and pain."

"Do you mean that you have lied?"

"Nothing but romance and lies, the whole thing!"

"You are too bad, Anna."

"Maybe. I am not so happy, either.—But the ladies are awake, and the men are coming into the drawing-room. Let us join them!"

On the threshold she is stopped by Gösta Berling, who is looking for the young ladies.

"You must have patience with me," he says, laughing. "I shall only torment you for ten minutes; but you must hear my verses."

He tells them that in the night he had had a dream more vivid than ever before; he had dreamt that he had written verse. He, whom the world called "poet," although he had always been undeserving of the title, had got up in the middle of the night, and, half asleep, half awake, had begun to write. It was a whole poem, which he had found the next morning on his writing-table. He could never have believed it of himself. Now the ladies should hear it.

And he reads:—

"The moon rose, and with her came the sweetest hour of the day.
From the clear, pale-blue, lofty vault
She flooded the leafy veranda with her light.
On the broad steps we were sitting, both old and young,
Silent at first to let the emotions sing
The heart's old song in that tender hour.

"From the migponette rose a sweet perfume,
And from dark thickets shadows crept over the dewy grass.
Oh, who can be safe from emotion
When the night's shadows play, when the mignonette sheds its heavy perfume?

"The last faded petal dropped from the rose,
Although the offering was not sought by the wind.
So—we thought—will we give up our life,
Vanish into space like a sound,
Like autumn's yellowed leaf go without a moan.
Death is the reward of life; may we meet it quietly,
Just as a rose lets its last faded petal fall.

"On its fluttering wing a bat flew by us,
Flew and was seen, wherever the moon shone;
Then the question arose in our oppressed hearts,—

"The question which none can answer,
The question, heavy as sorrow, old as pain:
'Oh, whither go we, what paths shall we wander
When we no longer walk on earth's green pastures?'
Is there no one to show our spirits the way?
Easier were it to show a way to the bat who fluttered by us.

"She laid her head on my shoulder, her soft hair,
She, who loved me, and whispered softly:
'Think not that souls fly to far-distant places;
When I am dead, think not that I am far away.
Into my beloved's soul my homeless spirit will creep
And I will come and live in thee.'

"Oh what anguish! With sorrow my heart will break.
Was she to die, die soon? Was this night to be her last?
Did I press my last kiss on my beloved's waving hair?

'Years have gone by since then. I still sit many times
In the old place, when the night is dark and silent.
But I tremble when the moon shines on the leafy veranda,
For her who alone knows how often I kissed my darling there,
For her who blended her quivering light with my tears,
Which fell on my darling's hair.
Alas, for memory's pain! Oh, 't is the grief of my poor, sinful soul
That it should be her home! What punishment may he not await
Who has bound to himself a soul so pure, so innocent."

"Gösta," says Anna, jestingly, while her throat contracts with pain, "people say of you that you have lived through more poems than others have written, who have not done anything else all their lives; but do you know, you will do best to compose poems your own way. That was night work."

"You are not kind."

"To come and read such a thing, on death and suffering—you ought to be ashamed!"

Gösta is not listening to her. His eyes are fixed on the young countess. She sits quite stiff, motionless as a statue. He thinks she is going to faint.

But with infinite difficulty her lips form one word.

"Go!" she says.

"Who shall go? Shall *I* go?"

"The priest shall go," she stammers out.

"Elizabeth, be silent!"

"The drunken priest shall leave my house!"

"Anna, Anna," Gösta asks, "what does she mean?"

"You had better go, Gösta."

"Why shall I go? What does all this mean?"

"Anna," says Countess Elizabeth, "tell him, tell him!"

"No, countess, tell him yourself!"

The countess sets her teeth, and masters her emotion.

"Herr Berling," she says, and goes up to him, "you have a wonderful power of making people forget who you are. I did not know it till to-day. I have just heard the story of Ebba Dohna's death, and that it was the discovery that she loved one who was unworthy which killed her. Your poem has made me understand that you are that man. I cannot understand how any one with your antecedents can show himself in the presence of an honorable woman. I cannot understand it, Herr Berling. Do I speak plainly enough?"

"You do, Countess. I will only say one word in my defence. I was convinced, I thought the whole time that you knew everything about me. I have never tried to hide anything; but it is not so pleasant to cry out one's life's bitterest sorrow on the highways."

He goes.

And in the same instant Countess Dohna sets her little foot on the bunch of blue stars.

"You have now done what I wished," says Anna Stjärnhök sternly to the countess; "but it is also the end of our friendship. You need not think that I can forgive your having been cruel to him. You have turned him away, scorned, and wounded him, and I—I will follow him into captivity; to the scaffold if need be. I will watch over him, protect him. You have done what I wished, but I shall never forgive you."

"But, Anna, Anna!"

"Because I told you all that do you think that I did it with a glad spirit? Have I not sat here and bit by bit torn my heart out of my breast?"

"Why did you do it?"

"Why? Because I did not wish—that he should be a married woman's lover."

CHAPTER XIII. MAMSELLE MARIE

THERE is a buzzing over my head. It must be a bumblebee. And such a perfume! As true as I live, it is sweet marjoram and lavender and hawthorn and lilacs and Easter lilies. It is glorious to feel it on a gray autumn evening in the midst of the town. I only have to think of that little blessed corner of the earth to have it immediately begin to hum and smell fragrant about me, and I am transported to a little square rose-garden, filled with flowers and protected by a privet hedge. In the corners are lilac arbors with small wooden benches, and round about the flower-beds, which are in the shapes of hearts and stars, wind narrow paths strewed with white sea-sand. On three sides of the rose-garden stands the forest, silent and dark.

On the fourth side lies a little gray cottage.

The rose-garden of which I am thinking was owned sixty years ago by an old Madame Moreus in Svartsjö, who made her living by knitting blankets for the peasants and cooking their feasts.

Old Madame Moreus was in her day the possessor of many things. She had three lively and industrious daughters and a little cottage by the roadside. She had a store of pennies at the bottom of a chest, stiff silk shawls, straight-backed chairs, and could turn her hand to everything, which is useful for one who must earn her bread. But the best that she had was the rose-garden, which gave her joy as long as the summer lasted.

In Madame Moreus' little cottage there was a boarder, a little dry old maid, about forty years of age, who lived in a gable-room in the attic. Mamselle Marie, as she was always called, had her own ideas on many things, as one always does who sits much alone and lets her thoughts dwell on what her eyes have seen.

Mamselle Marie thought that love was the root and origin of all evil in this sorrowful world.

Every evening, before she fell asleep, she used to clasp her hands and say her evening prayers. After she had said "Our Father" and "The Lord bless us" she always ended by praying that God would preserve her from love.

"It causes only misery," she said. "I am old and ugly and poor. No, may I never be in love!"

She sat day after day in her attic room in Madame Moreus' little cottage, and knitted curtains and table-covers. All these she afterwards sold to the peasants and the gentry. She had almost knitted together a little cottage of her own.

For a little cottage on the side of the hill opposite Svartsjö church was what she wanted to have. But love she would never hear of.

When on summer evenings she heard the violin sounded from the cross roads, where the fiddler sat on the stile, and the young people swung in the polka till the dust whirled, she went a long way round through the wood to avoid hearing and seeing.

The day after Christmas, when the peasant brides came, five or six of them, to be dressed by Madame Moreus and her daughters, when they were adorned with wreaths of myrtle, and high crowns of silk, and glass beads, with gorgeous silk sashes and bunches of artificial roses, and skirts edged with garlands of taffeta flowers, she stayed up in her room to avoid seeing how they were being decked out in Love's honor.

But she knew Love's misdeeds, and of them she could tell. She wondered that he dared to show himself on earth, that he was not frightened away by the moans of the forsaken, by the curses of those of whom he had made criminals, by the lamentations of those whom he had thrown into hateful chains. She wondered that his wings could bear him so easily and lightly, that he did not, weighed down by pain and shame, sink into nameless depths.

No, of course she had been young, she like others, but she had never loved. She had never let herself be tempted by dancing and caresses. Her mother's guitar hung dusty and unstrung in the attic; she never struck it to sentimental love-ditties.

Her mother's rose bushes stood in her window. She gave them scarcely any water. She did not love flowers, those children of love. Spiders played among the branches, and the buds never opened.

There came a time when the Svartsjö congregation had an organ put into their church. It was the summer before the year when the pensioners reigned. A young organ-builder came there. He too became a boarder at Madame Moreus'.

That the young organ-builder was a master of his profession may be a matter of doubt. But he was a gay young blade, with sunshine in his eyes. He had a friendly word for every one, for rich and poor, for old and young.

When he came home from his work in the evening, he held Madame Moreus' skeins, and worked at the side of young girls in the rose-garden. Then he declaimed "Axel" and sang "Frithiof." He picked up Mamselle Marie's ball of thread as often as she dropped it, and put her clock to rights.

He never left any ball until he had danced with everybody, from the oldest woman to the youngest girl, and if an adversity befell him, he sat himself down by the side of the first woman he met and made her his *confidante*. He was such a man as women create in their dreams! It could not be said of him that he spoke of love to any one. But when he had lived a few weeks in Madame Moreus' gable-room, all the girls were in love with him, and poor Mamselle Marie knew that she had prayed her prayers in vain.

That was a time of sorrow and a time of joy. In the evening a pale dreamer often sat in the lilac arbor, and up in Mamselle Marie's little room the newly strung guitar twanged to old love-songs, which she had learned from her mother.

The young organ-builder was just as careless and gay as ever, and doled out smiles and services to all these languishing women, who quarrelled over him when he was away at his work. And at last the day came when he had to leave.

The carriage stood before the door. His bag had been tied on behind, and the young man said farewell. He kissed Madame Moreus' hand and took the weeping girls in his arms and kissed them on the cheek. He wept himself at being obliged to go, for he had had a pleasant summer in the little gray cottage. At the last he looked around for Mamselle Marie.

She came down the narrow attic-stairs in her best array. The guitar hung about her neck on a broad, green-silk ribbon, and in her hand she held a bunch of damask roses, for this year her mother's rosebushes had blossomed. She stood before the young man, struck the guitar and sang:—

> "Thou goest far from us. Ah! welcome again!
> Hear the voice of my friendship, which greets thee.
> Be happy: forget not a true, loving friend
> Who in Värmland's forests awaits thee!"

Thereupon she put the flowers in his buttonhole and kissed him square on the mouth. Yes, and then she vanished up the attic stairs again, the old apparition.

Love had revenged himself on her and made her a spectacle for all men. But she never again complained of him. She never laid away the guitar, and never forgot to water her mother's rose-bushes.

She had learned to cherish Love with all his pain, his tears, his longing.

"Better to be sorrowful with him than happy without him," she said.

The time passed. The major's wife at Ekeby was driven out, the pensioners came to power, and it so happened, as has been described, that Gösta Berling one Sunday evening read a poem aloud to the countess at Borg, and afterwards was forbidden by her to show himself in her house.

It is said that when Gösta shut the hall-door after him he saw several sledges driving up to Borg. He cast a glance on the little lady who sat in the first sledge. Gloomy as the hour was for him, it became still more gloomy at the sight. He hurried away not to be recognized, but forebodings of disaster filled his soul. Had the conversation in there conjured up this woman? One misfortune always brings another.

But the servants hurried out, the shawls and furs were thrown one side. Who had come? Who was the little lady who stood up in the sledge? Ah, it is really she herself, Märta Dohna, the far-famed countess!

She was the gayest and most foolish of women. Joy had lifted her on high on his throne and made her his queen. Games and laughter were her subjects. Music and dancing and adventure had been her share when the lottery of life was drawn.

She was not far now from her fiftieth year, but she was one of the wise, who do not count the years. "He whose foot is not ready to dance, or mouth to laugh," she said, "he is old. He knows the terrible weight of years, not I."

Pleasure had no undisturbed throne in the days of her youth, but change and uncertainty only increased the delight of his glad presence. His Majesty of the butterfly wings one day had afternoon tea in the court ladies' rooms at the palace in Stockholm, and danced the next in Paris. He visited Napoleon's camps, he went on board Nelson's fleet in the blue Mediterranean, he looked in on a congress at Vienna, he risked his life at Brussels at a ball the night before a famous battle.

And wherever Pleasure was, there too was Märta Dohna, his chosen queen. Dancing, playing, jesting, Countess Märta hurried the whole world round. What had she not seen, what had she not lived through? She had danced over thrones, played écarté on the fate of princes, caused devastating wars by her jests! Gayety and folly had filled her life and would always do so. Her body was not too old for dancing, nor her heart for love. When did she weary of masquerades and comedies, of merry stories and plaintive ballads?

When Pleasure sometimes could find no home out in the struggling world, she used to drive up to the old manor by Löfven's shores,—just as she had come there when the princes and their court had become too gloomy for her in the time of the Holy Alliance. It was then she had thought best to make Gösta Berling her son's tutor. She always enjoyed it there. Never had Pleasure a pleasanter kingdom. There song was to be found and card-playing, men who loved adventure, and gay, lovely women. She did not lack for dances and balls, nor boating-parties over moonlit seas, nor sledging through dark forests, nor appalling adventures and love's sorrow and pain.

But after her daughter's death she had ceased to come to Borg. She had not been there for five years. Now she had come to see how her daughter-in-law bore the life up among the pine forests, the bears, and the snow-drifts. She thought it her duty to come and see if the stupid Henrik had not bored her to death with his tediousness. She meant to be the gentle angel of domestic peace. Sunshine and happiness were packed in her forty leather trunks, Gayety was her waiting-maid, Jest her coachman, Play her companion.

And when she ran up the steps she was met with open arms. Her old rooms on the lower floor were in order for her. Her man-servant, her lady companion, and maid, her forty leather trunks, her thirty hat-boxes, her bags and shawls and furs, everything was brought by degrees into the house. There was bustle and noise everywhere. There was a slamming of doors and a running on the stairs. It was plain enough that Countess Märta had come.

It was a spring evening, a really beautiful spring evening, although it was only April and the ice had not broken up. Mamselle Marie had opened her window. She sat in her room, played on the guitar, and sang.

She was so engrossed in her guitar and her memories that she did not hear that a carriage came driving up the road and stopped at the cottage. In the carriage Countess Märta sat, and it amused her to see Mamselle Marie, who sat at the window with her guitar on her lap, and with eyes turned towards heaven sang old forgotten love-songs.

At last the countess got out of the carriage and went into the cottage, where the girls were sitting at their work. She was never haughty; the wind of revolution had whistled over her and blown fresh air into her lungs.

It was not her fault that she was a countess, she used to say; but she wanted at all events to live the life she liked best. She enjoyed herself just as much at peasant weddings as at court balls. She acted for her maids when there was no other spectator to be had, and she brought joy with her in all the places where she showed herself, with her beautiful little face and her overflowing love of life.

She ordered a blanket of Madame Moreus and praised the girls. She looked about the rose-garden and told of her adventures on the journey. She always was having adventures. And at the last she ventured up the attic stairs, which were dreadfully steep and narrow, and sought out Mamselle Marie in her gable-room.

She bought curtains of her. She could not live without having knitted curtains for all her windows, and on every table should she have Mamselle Marie's table-covers.

She borrowed her guitar and sang to her of pleasure and love. And she told her stories, so that Mamselle Marie found herself transported out into the gay, rushing world. And the countess's laughter made such music that the frozen birds in the rose-garden began to sing when they heard it, and her face, which was hardly pretty now,—for her complexion was ruined by paint, and there was such an expression of sensuality about the mouth,—seemed to Mamselle Marie so lovely that she wondered how the little mirror could let it vanish when it had once caught it on its shining surface.

When she left, she kissed Mamselle Marie and asked her to come to Borg.

Mamselle Marie's heart was as empty as the swallow's-nest at Christmas. She was free, but she sighed for chains like a slave freed in his old age.

Now there began again for Mamselle Marie a time of joy and a time of sorrow; but it did not last long,—only one short week.

The countess sent for her continually to come to Borg. She played her comedy for her and told about all her lovers, and Mamselle Marie laughed as she had never laughed before. They became the best of friends. The countess soon knew all about the young organ-builder and about the parting. And in the twilight she made Mamselle Marie sit on the window-seat in the little blue cabinet. Then she hung the guitar ribbon round her neck and got her to sing love-songs. And the countess sat and watched how the old maid's dry, thin figure and little plain head were outlined against the red evening sky, and she said that the poor old Mamselle was like a languishing maiden of the Middle Ages. All the songs were of tender shepherds and cruel shepherdesses, and Mamselle Marie's voice was the thinnest voice in the world, and it is easy to understand how the countess was amused at such a comedy.

There was a party at Borg, as was natural, when the count's mother had come home. And it was gay as always. There were not so many there, only the members of the parish being invited.

The dining-room was on the lower floor, and after supper it so happened that the guests did not go upstairs again, but sat in Countess Marta's room, which lay beyond. The countess got hold of Mamselle Marie's guitar and began to sing for the company. She was a merry person, Countess Märta, and she could mimic any one. She now had the idea to mimic Mamselle Marie. She turned up her eyes to heaven and sang in a thin, shrill, child's voice.

"Oh no, oh no, countess!" begged Mamselle Marie.

But the countess was enjoying herself, and no one could help laughing, although they all thought that it was hard on Mamselle Marie.

The countess took a handful of dried rose-leaves out of a pot-pourri jar, went with tragic gestures up to Mamselle Marie, and sang with deep emotion:—

> "Thou goest far from us. Ah! welcome again!
> Hear the voice of my friendship, which greets thee.
> Be happy: forget not a true, loving friend
> Who in Varmland's forests awaits thee!"

Then she strewed the rose-leaves over her head. Everybody laughed; but Mamselle Marie was wild with rage. She looked as if she could have torn out the countess's eyes.

"You are a bad woman, Märta Dohna," she said. "No decent woman ought to speak to you."

Countess Märta lost her temper too.

"Out with you, mamselle!" she said. "I have had enough of your folly."

"Yes, I shall go," said Mamselle Marie; "but first I will be paid for my covers and curtains which you have put up here."

"The old rags!" cried the countess. "Do you want to be paid for such rags? Take them away with you! I never want to see them again! Take them away immediately!"

Thereupon the countess threw the table-covers at her and tore down the curtains, for she was beside herself.

The next day the young countess begged her mother-in-law to make her peace with Mamselle Marie; but the countess would not She was tired of her.

Countess Elizabeth then bought of Mamselle Marie the whole set of curtains and put them up in the upper floor. Whereupon Mamselle Marie felt herself redressed.

Countess Märta made fun of her daughter-in-law for her love of knitted curtains. She too could conceal her anger—preserve it fresh and new for years. She was a richly gifted person.

PART II

CHAPTER I. COUSIN CHRISTOPHER

THEY had an old bird of prey up in the pensioners' wing. He always sat in the corner by the fire and saw that it did not go out. He was rough and gray. His little head with the big nose and the sunken eyes hung sorrowfully on the long, thin neck which stuck up out of a fluffy fur collar. For the bird of prey wore furs both winter and summer.

Once he had belonged to the swarm who in the great Emperor's train swept over Europe; but what name and title he bore no one now can say. In Värmland they only knew that he had taken part in the great wars, that he had risen to might and power in the thundering struggle, and that after 1815 he had taken flight from an ungrateful fatherland. He found a refuge with the Swedish Crown Prince, and the latter advised him to disappear in far away Värmland.

And so it happened that one whose name had caused the world to tremble was now glad that no one even knew that once dreaded name.

He had given the Crown Prince his word of honor not to leave Värmland and not to make known who he was. And he had been sent to Ekeby with a private letter to the major from the Crown Prince, who had given him the best of recommendations. It was then the pensioners' wing opened its doors to him.

In the beginning people wondered much who he was who concealed his identity under an assumed name. But gradually he was transformed into a pensioner. Everybody called him Cousin Christopher, without knowing exactly how he had acquired the name.

But it is not good for a bird of prey to live in a cage. One can understand that he is accustomed to something different than hopping from perch to perch and taking food from his keeper's hand. The excitement of the battle and of the danger of death had set his pulse on fire. Drowsy peace disgusts him.

It is true that none of the pensioners were exactly tame birds; but in none of them the blood burned so hot as in Cousin Christopher. A bear hunt was the only thing which could put life into him, a bear hunt or a woman, one single woman.

He had come to life when he, ten years ago, for the first time saw Countess Märta, who was already then a widow,—a woman as changeable as war, as inciting as danger, a startling, audacious creature; he loved her.

And now he sat there and grew old and gray without being able to ask her to be his wife. He had not seen her for five years. He was withering and dying by degrees, as caged eagles do. Every year he became more dried and frozen. He had to creep down deeper into his furs and move nearer the fire.

So there he is sitting, shivering, shaggy, and gray, the morning of the day, on the evening of which the Easter bullets should be shot off and the Easter witch burned. The pensioners have all gone out; but he sits in the corner by the fire.

Oh, Cousin Christopher, Cousin Christopher, do you not know?

Smiling she has come, the enchanting spring.

Nature up starts from drowsy sleep, and in the blue sky butterfly-winged spirits tumble in wild play. Close as roses on the sweet brier, their faces shine between the clouds.

Earth, the great mother, begins to live. Romping like a child she rises from her bath in the spring floods, from her douche in the spring rain.

But Cousin Christopher sits quiet and does not understand. He leans his head on his stiffened fingers and dreams of showers of bullets and of honors won on the field of battle.

One pities the lonely old warrior who sits there by the fire, without a people, without a country, he who never hears the sound of his native language, he who will have a nameless grave in the Bro churchyard. Is it his fault that he is an eagle, and was born to persecute and to kill?

Oh, Cousin Christopher, you have sat and dreamed long enough in the pensioners' wing! Up and drink the sparkling wine of life. You must know, Cousin Christopher, that a letter has come to the major this day, a royal letter adorned with the seal of Sweden. It is addressed to the major, but the contents concern you. It is strange to see you, when you read the letter, old eagle. Your eye regains its brightness, and you lift your head. You see the cage door open and free space for your longing wings.

Cousin Christopher is burrowing deep down to the bottom of his chest. He drags out the carefully laid away gold-laced uniform and dresses himself in it He presses the plumed hat on his head and he is soon hastening away from Ekeby, riding his excellent white horse.

This is another life than to sit shivering by the fire; he too now sees that spring has come.

He straightens himself up in his saddle and sets off at a gallop. The fur-lined dolman flutters. The plumes on his hat wave. The man has grown young like the earth itself. He has awaked from a long winter. The old gold can still shine. The bold warrior face under the cocked hat is a proud sight.

It is a wonderful ride. Brooks gush from the ground, and flowers shoot forth, as he rides by. The birds sing and warble about the freed prisoner. All nature shares in his joy.

He is like a victor. Spring rides before on a floating cloud. And round about Cousin Christopher rides a staff of old brothers-in-arms: there is Happiness, who stands on tiptoe in the saddle, and Honor on his stately charger, and Love on his fiery Arab. The ride is wonderful; wonderful is the rider. The thrush calls to him:—

"Cousin Christopher, Cousin Christopher, whither are you riding? Whither are you riding?"

"To Borg to offer myself, to Borg to offer myself," answers Cousin Christopher.

"Do not go to Borg, do not go to Borg! An unmarried man has no sorrow," screams the thrush after him.

But he does not listen to the warning. Up the hills and down the hills he rides, until at last he is there. He leaps from the saddle and is shown in to the countess.

Everything goes well. The countess is gracious to him. Cousin Christopher feels sure that she will not refuse to bear his glorious name or to reign in his palace. He sits and puts off the moment of rapture, when he shall show her the royal letter. He enjoys the waiting.

She talks and entertains him with a thousand stories. He laughs at everything, enjoys everything. But as they are sitting in one of the rooms where Countess Elizabeth has hung up Mamselle Marie's curtains, the countess begins to tell the story of them. And she makes it as funny as she can.

"See," she says at last, "see how bad I am. Here hang the curtains now, that I may think daily and hourly of my sin. It is a penance without equal. Oh, those dreadful knitted curtains!"

The great warrior, Cousin Christopher, looks at her with burning eyes.

"I, too, am old and poor," he says, "and I have sat for ten years by the fire and longed for my mistress. Do you laugh at that too, countess?"

"Oh, that is another matter," cries the countess.

"God has taken from me happiness and my fatherland, and forced me to eat the bread of others," says Cousin Christopher, earnestly. "I have learned to have respect for poverty."

"You, too," cries the countess, and holds up her hands. "How virtuous every one is getting!"

"Yes," he says, "and know, countess, that if God some day in the future should give me back riches and power, I would make a better use of them than to share them with such a worldly woman, such a painted, heartless monkey, who makes fun of poverty."

"You would do quite right, Cousin Christopher."

And then Cousin Christopher marches out of the room and rides home to Ekeby again; but the spirits do not follow him, the thrush does not call to him, and he no longer sees the smiling spring.

He came to Ekeby just as the Easter witch was tö be burned. She is a big doll of straw, with a rag face, on which eyes, nose, and mouth are drawn with charcoal. She is dressed in old cast-off clothes. The long-handled oven-rake and broom are placed beside her, and she has a horn of oil hung round her neck. She is quite ready for the journey to hell.

Major Fuchs loads his gun and shoots it off into the air time after time. A pile of dried branches is lighted, the witch is thrown on it and is soon burning gayly. The pensioners do all they can, according to the old, tried customs, to destroy the power of the evil one.

Cousin Christopher stands and looks on with gloomy mien. Suddenly he drags the great royal letter from his cuff and throws it on the fire. God alone knows what he thought. Perhaps he imagined that it was Countess Märta herself who was burning there on the pile. Perhaps he thought that, as that woman, when all was said, consisted only of rags and straw, there was nothing worth anything any more on earth.

He goes once more into the pensioners' wing, lights the fire, and puts away his uniform. Again he sits down at the fire, and every day he gets more rough and more gray. He is dying by degrees, as old eagles do in captivity.

He is no longer a prisoner; but he does not care to make use of his freedom. The world stands open to him. The battle-field, honor, life, await him. But he has not the strength to spread his wings in flight.

CHAPTER II. THE PATHS OF LIFE

WEARY are the ways which men have to follow here on earth.

Paths through the desert, paths through the marshes, paths over the mountains.

Why is so much sorrow allowed to go undisturbed, until it loses itself in the desert or sinks in the bog, or falls on the mountain? Where are the little flower-pickers, where are the little princesses of the fairy tale about whose feet roses grow, where are they who should strew flowers on the weary ways?

Gösta Berling has decided to get married. He is searching for a bride who is poor enough, humble enough for a mad priest.

Beautiful and high-born women have loved him, but they may not compete for his hand. The outcast chooses from among outcasts.

Whom shall he choose, whom shall he seek out?

To Ekeby a poor girl sometimes comes from a lonely forest hamlet far away among the mountains, and sells brooms. In that hamlet, where poverty and great misery exist, there are many who are not in possession of their full intellect, and the girl with the brooms is one of them.

But she is beautiful. Her masses of black hair make such thick braids that they scarcely find room on her head, her cheeks are delicately rounded, her nose straight and not too large, her eyes blue. She is of a melancholy, Madonna-like type, such as is still found among the lovely girls by the shores of Löfven's long lake.

Well, Gösta has found his sweetheart; a half-crazy broom-girl is just the wife for a mad priest. Nothing can be more suitable.

All he needs to do is to go to Karlstad for the rings, and then they can once more have a merry day by Löfven's shore. Let them laugh at Gösta Berling when he betroths himself to the broom-girl, when he celebrates his wedding with her! Let them laugh! Has he ever had a merrier idea?

Must not the outcast go the way of the outcasts,—the way of anger, the way of sorrow, the way of unhappiness? What does it matter if he falls, if he is ruined? Is there any one to stop him? Is there any one who would reach him a helping hand or offer him a cooling drink? Where are the little flower-pickers, where are the little princesses of the fairy-tale, where are they who should strew roses on the stony ways?

No, no, the gentle young countess at Borg will not interfere with Gösta Berling's plans. She must think of her reputation, she must think of her husband's anger and her mother-in-law's hate, she must not do anything to keep him back.

All through the long service in the Svartsjö church, she must bend her head, fold her hands, and only pray for him. During sleepless nights she can weep and grieve over him, but she has no flowers to strew on the way of the outcast, not a drop of water to give one who is thirsting. She does not stretch out her hand to lead him back from the edge of the precipice.

Gösta Berling does not care to clothe his chosen bride in silk and jewels. He lets her go from farm to farm with brooms, as her habit is, but when he has gathered together all the chief men and women of the place at a great feast at Ekeby, he will make his betrothal known. He will call her in from the kitchen, just as she has come from her long wanderings, with the dust and dirt of the road on her clothes, perhaps ragged, perhaps with dishevelled hair, with wild eyes, with an incoherent stream of words on her lips. And he will ask the guests if he has not chosen a suitable bride, if the mad priest ought not to be proud of such a lovely sweetheart, of that gentle Madonna face, of those blue, dreamy eyes.

He intended that no one should know anything beforehand, but he did not succeed in keeping the secret, and one of those who heard it was the young Countess Dohna.

But what can she do to stop him? It is the engagement day, the eleventh hour has come. The countess stands at the window in the blue cabinet and looks out towards the north. She almost thinks that she can see Ekeby, although her eyes are dim with tears. She can see how the great three-storied house shines with three rows of lighted windows; she thinks how the champagne flows in the glasses, how the toast resounds and how Gösta Berling proclaims his engagement to the broom-girl.

If she were only near him and quite gently could lay her hand on his arm, or only give him a friendly look, would he not turn back from the evil way? If a word from her had driven him to such a desperate deed, would not also a word from her check him?"

She shudders at the sin he is going to commit against that poor, half-witted child. She shudders at his sin against the unfortunate creature, who shall be won to love him, perhaps only for the jest of a single day. Perhaps too—and then she shudders even more at the sin he is committing against himself—to chain fast to his life such a galling burden, which would always take from his spirit the strength to reach the highest.

And the fault was chiefly hers. She had with a word of condemnation driven him on the evil way. She, who had come to bless, to alleviate, why had she twisted one more thorn into the sinner's crown?

Yes, now she knows what she will do. She will have the black horses harnessed into the sledge, hasten over the Löfven and to Ekeby, place herself opposite to Gösta Berling, and tell him that she does not despise him, that she did not know what she was saying when she drove him from her house. No, she could never do such a thing; she would be ashamed and would not dare to say a word. Now that she was married, she must take care. There would be such a scandal if she did such a thing. But if she did not do it, how would it go with him?

She must go.

Then she remembers that such a plan is impossible. No horse can go again this year over the ice. The ice is melting, it has already broken away from the land. It is broken, cracked, terrible to see. Water bubbles up through it, in some places it has gathered in black pools, in other places the ice is dazzlingly white. It is mostly gray, dirty with melting snow, and the roads look like long, black streaks on its surface.

How can she think of going? Old Countess Märta, her mother-in-law, would never permit such a thing. She must sit beside her the whole evening in the drawing-room and listen to those old stories which are the older woman's delight.

At last the night comes, and her husband is away; she is free.

She cannot drive, she does not dare to call the servants, but her anxiety drives her out of her home. There is nothing else for her to do.

Weary are the ways men wander on earth; but that way by night over melting ice, to what shall I compare it? Is it not the way which the little flower-pickers have to go, an uncertain, shaking, slippery way, the way of those who wish to make amends, the way of the light foot, the quick eye, and the brave, loving heart?

It was past midnight when the countess reached the shores of Ekeby. She had fallen on the ice, she had leaped over wide fissures, she had hurried across places where her footprints were filled with bubbling water, she had slipped, she had crept on all fours.

It had been a weary wandering; she had wept as she had walked. She was wet and tired, and out there on the ice, the darkness and the loneliness had given her terrible thoughts.

At the last she had had to wade in water over her ankles to reach land. And when she had come to the shore, she had not had the courage to do more than sit down on a rock and weep from fatigue and helplessness.

This young, high-born lady was, however, a brave little heroine. She had never gone such ways in her bright mother country. She may well sit by the edge of that terrible lake, wet, tired, unhappy as she is, and think of the fair, flowery paths of her Southern fatherland.

Ah, for her it is not a question of South or North. She is not weeping from homesickness. She is weeping because she is so tired, because she will not come in time. She thinks that she has come too late.

Then people come running along the shore. They hurry by her without seeing her, but she hears what they say.

"If the dam gives way, the smithy goes," one says. "And the mill and the work-shops and the smith's house," adds another.

Then she gets new courage, rises, and follows them.

Ekeby mill and smithy lay on a narrow point past which the Björksjö River rushes. It comes roaring down towards the point, whipped white in the mighty falls above, and to protect the land a great break-water was built before the point. But the dam was old now, and the pensioners were in power. In their day the dance filled all their thoughts, and no one took the trouble to see how the current and the cold and time had worn the old stone-dam.

Now with the spring-floods the dam begins to yield.

The falls at Ekeby are like mighty granite stairs, down which the waves come rushing. Giddy with the speed, they tumble over one another and rush together. They rise up in anger and dash in spray over one another, fall again, over a rock, over a log, and rise up again, again to fall, again and again, foaming, hissing, roaring.

And now these wild, raging waves, drunken with the spring air, dizzy with their newly won freedom, storm against the old stone-wall. They come, hissing and tearing, high up on to it and then fall back again, as if they had hit their white heads. They use logs as battering-rams, they strain, they beat, they rush against that poor wall, until suddenly, just as if some one had called to them, "Look out!" they rush backwards, and after them comes a big stone, which has broken away from the dam and sinks thundering down in the stream.

But why are these wild waves allowed to rage without meeting any resistance? Is every one dead at Ekeby?

No, there are people enough there,—a wild, perplexed, helpless crowd of people. The night is dark, they cannot see one another, nor see where they are going. Loud roars the falls, terrible is the din of the breaking ice and the pounding logs; they cannot hear their own voices. They have not a thought nor an idea. They feel that the end is coming. The dam is trembling, the smithy is in danger, the mill is in danger, and their own poor houses beloved in all their lowliness.

Message after message is sent up to the house to the pensioners.

Are they in a mood to think of smithy or mill? The hundred guests are gathered in the wide walls. The broom-girl is waiting in the kitchen. The hour has come. The champagne bubbles in the glasses.

Julius rises to make the speech. All the old adventurers at Ekeby are rejoicing at the petrifying amazement which will fall upon the assembly.

Out on the ice the young Countess Dohna is wandering a terrible, perilous way in order to whisper a word of warning to Gösta Berling. Down at the waterfall the waves are storming the honor and might of Ekeby, but in the wide halls only joy and eager expectation reign, wax-candles are shining, wine is flowing; no one thinks of what is happening in the dark, stormy spring night.

Now has the moment come. Gösta rises and goes out to bring in his sweetheart. He has to go through the hall, and its great doors are standing open; he stops, he looks out into the pitch dark night—and he hears, he hears!

He hears the bells ringing, the falls roaring. He hears the thunder of the breaking ice, the noise of the pounding logs, the rebellious waves' rushing and threatening voice.

He hastens out into the night, forgetting everything. Let them inside stand with lifted glasses till the world's last day; he cares nothing for them. The broom-girl can wait, Julius's speech may die on his lips. There would be no rings exchanged that night, no paralyzing amazement would fall upon the shining assembly.

Now the waves must in truth fight for their freedom, for Gösta Berling has come, the people have found a leader. Terrified hearts take courage, a terrible struggle begins.

Hear how he calls to the people; he commands, he sets all to work.

"We must have light, light first of all; the miller's horn-lantern is not enough. See all those piles of branches; carry them up on the cliff and set fire to them. That is work for the women and children. Only be quick; build up a great flaming brush-pile and set fire to it! That will light up our work; that will be seen far and wide and bring more to help us. And let it never go out! Bring straw, bring branches, let the flames stream up to the sky!"

"Look, look, you men, here is work for you. Here is timber, here are planks; make a temporary dam, which we can sink in front of this breaking wall. Quick, quick to work; make it firm and solid! Get ready stones and sand-bags to sink it with! Quick! Swing your axes! To work! to work!"

"And where are the boys? Get poles, get boat-hooks, and come out here in the midst of the struggle. Out on the dam with you, boys, right in the waves. Keep off, weaken, drive back their attacks, before which the walls are cracking. Push aside the logs and pieces of ice; throw yourselves down, if nothing else helps, and hold the loosening stones with your hands; bite into them, seize them with claws of iron. Out on the wall, boys! We shall fight for every inch of land."

Gösta himself takes his stand farthest out on the dam and stands there covered with spray; the ground shakes under him, the waves thunder and rage, but his wild heart rejoices at the danger, the anxiety, the struggle. He laughs. He jokes with the boys about him on the dam; he has never had a merrier night.

The work of rescue goes quickly forward, the fire flames, the axes resound, and the dam stands.

The other pensioners and the hundred guests have come down to the waterfall. People come running from near and far; all are working, at the fires, at the temporary dam, at the sand-bags, out on the tottering, trembling stone-wall.

Now the temporary dam is ready, and shall be sunk in front of the yielding break-water. Have the stones and sand-bags ready, and boat-hooks and rope, that it may not be carried away, that the victory may be for the people, and the cowed waves return to their bondage.

It so happens that just before the decisive moment Gösta catches sight of a woman who is sitting on a stone at the water's edge. The flames from the bonfire light her up where she sits staring out over the waves; he cannot see her clearly and distinctly through the mist and spray, but his eyes are continually drawn to her. Again and again he has to look at her. He feels as if that woman had a special errand to him.

Among all these hundreds who are working and busy, she is the only one who sits still, and to her his eyes keep turning, he can see nothing else.

She is sitting so far out that the waves break at her feet, and the spray dashes over her. She must be dripping wet. Her dress is dark, she has a black shawl over her head, she sits shrunk together, her chin on her hand, and stares persistently at him out on the dam. He feels as if those staring eyes were drawing and calling, although he cannot even distinguish her face; he thinks of nothing but the woman who sits on the shore by the white waves.

"It is the sea-nymph from the Löfven, who has come up the river to lure me to destruction," he thinks. "She sits there and calls and calls. I must go and drive her away."

All these waves with their white heads seem to him the black woman's hair; it was she who set them on, who led the attack against him.

"I really must drive her away," he says.

He seizes a boat-hook, runs to the shore, and hurries away to the woman.

He leaves his place on the end of the dam to drive the sea-nymph away. He felt, in that moment of excitement, as if the evil powers of the deep were fighting against him. He did not know what he thought, what he believed, but he must drive that black thing away from the stone by the river's edge.

Alas, Gösta, why is your place empty in the decisive moment? They are coming with the temporary dam, a long row of men station themselves on the break-water; they have ropes and stones and sand-bags ready to weight it down and hold it in place; they stand ready, they wait, they listen. Where is their leader? Is there no voice to command?

No, Gösta Berling is chasing the sea-nymph, his voice is silent, his commands lead no one.

So the temporary dam has to be sunk without him. The waves rush back, it sinks into the water and after it the stones and sand-bags. But how is the work carried out without a leader? No care, no order. The waves dash up again, they break with renewed rage against this new obstacle, they begin to roll the sand-bags over, tear the ropes, loosen the stones; and they succeed, they succeed. Threatening, rejoicing, they lift the whole dam on their strong shoulders, tear and drag on it, and then they have it in their power. Away with the miserable defence, down to the Löfven with it. And then on once more against the tottering, helpless stone-wall.

But Gösta is chasing the sea-nymph. She saw him as he came towards her swinging the boat-hook. She was frightened. It looked as if she was going to throw herself into the water, but she changed her mind and ran to the land.

"Sea-nymph!" cries Gösta, and brandishes the boat-hook. She runs in among the alder-bushes, gets entangled in their thick branches, and stops.

Then Gösta throws away the boat-hook, goes forward, and lays his hand on her shoulder.

"You are out late to-night, Countess Elizabeth," he says.

"Let me alone, Herr Berling, let me go home!"

He obeys instantly and turns away from her.

But since she is not only a high-born lady, but a really kind little woman, who cannot bear the thought that she has driven any one to despair; since she is a little flower-picker, who always has roses enough in her basket to adorn the barrenest way, she repents, goes after him and seizes his hand.

"I came," she says, and stammers, "I came to—Oh, Herr Berling, you have not done it? Say that you have not done it! I was so frightened when you came running after me, but it was you I wanted to meet I wanted to ask you not to think of what I said the other day, and to come to see me as usual."

"How have you come here, countess?"

She laughs nervously. "I knew that I should come too late, but I did not like to tell any one that I was going; and besides, you know, it is impossible to drive over the ice now."

"Have you walked across the lake, countess?"

"Yes, yes, of course; but, Herr Berling, tell me. Are you engaged? You understand; I wish so you were not. It is so wrong, you see, and I felt as if the whole thing was my fault. You should not have minded a word from me só much. I am a stranger, who does not know the customs of the country. It is so dull at Borg since you do not come any more, Herr Berling."

It seems to Gösta Berling, as he stands among the wet alder-bushes on the marshy ground, as if some one were throwing over him armfuls of roses. He wades in roses up to his knees, they shine before his eyes in the darkness, he eagerly drinks in their fragrance.

"Have you done that?" she repeats.

He must make up his mind to answer her and to put an end to her anxiety, although his joy is so great over it. It grows so warm in him and so bright when he thinks what a way she has wandered, how wet she is, how frozen, how frightened she must have been, how broken with weeping her voice sounds.

"No," he says, "I am not engaged."

Then she takes his hand again and strokes it "I am so glad, I am so glad," she says, and her voice is shaken with sobs.

There are flowers enough now on the poet's way, everything dark, evil, and hateful melts from his heart.

"How good you are, how good you are!" he says.

At their side the waves are rushing against all Ekeby's honor and glory. The people have no leader, no one to instil courage and hope into their hearts; the dam gives way, the waves close over it, and then rush triumphant forward to the point where the mill and smithy stand. No one tries any longer to resist the waves; no one thinks of anything but of saving life and property.

It seems quite natural to both the young people that Gösta should escort the countess home; he cannot leave her alone in this dark night, nor let her again wander alone over the melting ice. They never think that he is needed up at the smithy, they are so happy that they are friends again.

One might easily believe that these young people cherish a warm love for one another, but who can be sure? In broken fragments the glowing adventures of their lives have come to me. I know nothing, or next to nothing, of what was in their innermost souls. What can I say of the motives of their actions. I only know that that night a beautiful young woman risked her life, her honor, her reputation, her health, to bring back a poor wretch to the right way. I only know that that night Gösta Berling left the beloved

Ekeby fall to follow her who for his sake had conquered the fear of death, the fear of shame, the fear of punishment.

Often in my thoughts I have followed them over the ice that terrible night, which ended so well for them. I do not think that there was anything hidden or forbidden in their hearts, as they wandered over the ice, gay and chatting of everything which had happened during their separation.

He is once more her slave, her page, who lies at her feet, and she is his lady.

They are only happy, only joyous. Neither of them speaks a word which can denote love.

Laughing they splash through the water, they laugh when they find the path, when they lose it, when they slip, when they fall, when they are up again; they only laugh.

This blessed life is once more a merry play, and they are children who have been cross and have quarrelled. Oh, how good it is to make up and begin to play again.

Rumor came, and rumor went. In time the story of the countess's wanderings reached Anna Stjärnhök.

"I see," she said, "that God has not one string only to his bow. I can rest and stay where I am needed. He can make a man of Gösta Berling without my help."

CHAPTER III. PENITENCE

DEAR friends, if it should ever happen that you meet a pitiful wretch on your way, a little distressed creature, who lets his hat hang on his back and holds his shoes in his hand, so as not to have any protection from the heat of the sun and the stones of the road, one without defence, who of his own free will calls down destruction on his head,—well, pass him by in silent fear! It is a penitent, do you understand?—a penitent on his way to the holy sepulchre.

The penitent must wear a coarse cloak and live on water and dry bread, even if he were a king. He must walk and not ride. He must beg. He must sleep among thistles. He must wear the hard gravestones with kneeling. He must swing the thorny scourge over his back. He can know no sweetness except in suffering, no tenderness except in grief.

The young Countess Elizabeth was once one who wore the heavy cloak and trod the thorny paths. Her heart accused her of sin. It longed for pain as one wearied longs for a warm bath. Dire disaster she brought down on herself while she descended rejoicing into the night of suffering.

Her husband, the young count with the old-man's head, came home to Borg the morning after the night when the mill and smithy at Ekeby were destroyed by the spring flood. He had hardly arrived before Countess Märta had him summoned in to her and told him wonderful things.

"Your wife was out last night, Henrik. She was gone many hours. She came home with a man. I heard how he said good-night to her. I know too who he is. I heard both when she went and when she came. She is deceiving you, Henrik. She is deceiving you, the hypocritical creature, who hangs knitted curtains in all the windows only to cause me discomfort. She has never loved you, my poor boy. Her father only wanted to have her well married. She took you to be provided for."

She managed her affair so well that Count Henrik became furious. He wished to get a divorce. He wished to send his wife home to her father.

"No, my friend," said Countess Märta, "in that way she would be quite given over to evil. She is spoiled and badly brought up. But let me take her in hand, let me lead her to the path of duty."

And the count called in his countess to tell her that she now was to obey his mother in everything.

Many angry words the young man let the young woman hear. He stretched his hands to heaven and accused it of having let his name be dragged in the dirt by a shameless woman. He shook his clenched fist before her face and asked her what punishment she thought great enough for such a crime as hers.

She was not at all afraid. She thought that she had done right. She said that she had already caught a serious cold, and that might be punishment enough.

"Elizabeth," says Countess Märta, "this is not a matter to joke about."

"We two," answers the young woman, "have never been able to agree about the right time to joke and to be serious."

"But you ought to understand, Elizabeth, that no honorable woman leaves her home to roam about in the middle of the night with a known adventurer."

Then Elizabeth Dohna saw that her mother-in-law meant her ruin. She saw that she must fight to the last gasp, lest Countess Märta should succeed in drawing down upon her a terrible misfortune.

"Henrik," she begs, "do not let your mother come between us! Let me tell you how it all happened. You are just, you will not condemn me unheard. Let me tell you all, and you will see that I only acted as you have taught me."

The count nodded a silent consent, and Countess Elizabeth told how she had come to drive Gösta Ber-ling into the evil way. She told of everything which had happened in the little blue cabinet, and how she had felt herself driven by her conscience to go and save him she had wronged. "I had no right to judge him," she said, "and my husband has himself taught me that no sacrifice is too great when one will make amends for a wrong. Is it not so, Henrik?"

The count turned to his mother.

"What has my mother to say about this?" he asked. His little body was now quite stiff with dignity, and his high, narrow forehead lay in majestic folds.

"I," answered the countess,—"I say that Anna Stjärnhök is a clever girl, and she knew what she was doing when she told Elizabeth that story."

"You are pleased to misunderstand me," said the count. "I ask what you think of this story. Has

Countess Märta Dohna tried to persuade her daughter, my sister, to marry a dismissed priest?"

Countess Märta was silent an instant. Alas, that Henrik, so stupid, so stupid! Now he was quite on the wrong track. Her hound was pursuing the hunter himself and letting the hare get away. But if Märta Dohna was without an answer for an instant, it was not longer.

"Dear friend," she said with a shrug, "there is a reason for letting all those old stories about that unhappy man rest,—the same reason which makes me beg you to suppress all public scandal. It is most probable that he has perished in the night."

She spoke in a gentle, commiserating tone, but there was not a word of truth in what she said.

"Elizabeth has slept late to-day and therefore has not heard that people have already been sent out on to the lake to look for Herr Berling. He has not returned to Ekeby, and they fear that he has drowned. The ice broke up this morning. See, the storm has split it into a thousand pieces."

Countess Elizabeth looked out. The lake was almost open.

Then in despair she threw herself on her knees before her husband and confession rushed from her lips. She had wished to escape God's justice. She had lied and dissembled. She had thrown the white mantle of innocence over her.

"Condemn me, turn me out! I have loved him. Be in no doubt but that I have loved him! I tear my hair, I rend my clothes with grief. I do not care for anything when he is dead. I do not care to shield myself. You shall know the whole truth. My heart's love I have taken from my husband and given to a stranger. Oh, I am one of them whom a forbidden love has tempted."

You desperate young thing, lie there at your judges' feet and tell them all! Welcome, martyrdom! Welcome, disgrace! Welcome! Oh, how shall you bring the bolt of heaven down on your young head!

Tell your husband how frightened you were when the pain came over you, mighty and irresistible, how you shuddered for your heart's wretchedness. You would rather have met the ghosts of the graveyard than the demons in your own soul.

Tell them how you felt yourself unworthy to tread the earth. With prayers and tears you have struggled.

"O God, save me! O Son of God, caster out of devils, save me!" you have prayed.

Tell them how you thought it best to conceal it all. No one should know your wretchedness. You thought that it was God's pleasure to have it so. You thought, too, that you went in God's ways when you wished to save the man you loved. He knew nothing of your love. He must not be lost for your sake. Did you know what was right? Did you know what was wrong? God alone knew it, and he had passed sentence upon you. He had struck down your heart's idol. He had led you on to the great, healing way of penitence.

Tell them that you know that salvation is not to be found in concealment. Devils love darkness. Let your judges' hands close on the scourge! The punishment shall fall like soothing balm on the wounds of sin. Your heart longs for suffering.

Tell them all that, while you kneel on the floor and wring your hands in fierce sorrow, speaking in the wild accents of despair, with a shrill laugh greeting the thought of punishment and dishonor, until at last your husband seizes you and drags you up from the floor.

"Conduct yourself as it behooves a Countess Dohna, or I must ask my mother to chastise you like a child."

"Do with me what you will!"

Then the count pronounced his sentence:—

"My mother has interceded for you. Therefore you may stay in my house. But hereafter it is she who commands, and you who obey."

See the way of the penitent! The young countess has become the most humble of servants. How long? Oh, how long?

How long shall a proud heart be able to bend? How long can impatient lips keep silent; how long a passionate hand be held back?

Sweet is the misery of humiliation. When the back aches from the heavy work the heart is at peace. To one who sleeps a few short hours on a hard bed of straw, sleep comes uncalled.

Let the older woman change herself into an evil spirit to torture the younger. She thanks her benefactress. As yet the evil is not dead in her. Hunt her up at four o'clock every morning! Impose on the inexperienced workwoman an unreasonable day's work at the heavy weaving-loom! It is well. The penitent has perhaps not strength enough to swing the scourge with the required force.

When the time for the great spring washing comes,[3] Countess Märta has her stand at the tub in the wash-house. She comes herself to oversee her work. "The water is too cold in your tub," she says, and takes boiling water from a kettle and pours it over her bare arms.

The day is cold, the washerwomen have to stand by the lake and rinse out the clothes. Squalls rush by and drench them with sleet. Dripping wet and heavy as lead are the washerwomen's skirts.

Hard is the work with the wooden clapper. The blood bursts from the delicate nails.

But Countess Elizabeth does not complain. Praised be the goodness of God! The scourge's thorny knots fall softly, as if they were rose-leaves, on the penitent's back.

The young woman soon hears that Gösta Berling is alive. Her mother-in-law had only wanted to cheat her into a confession. Well, what of that? See the hand of God! He had won over the sinner to the path of atonement.

She grieves for only one thing. How shall it be with her mother-in-law, whose heart God for her sake has hardened? Ah, he will judge her mildly. She must show anger to help the sinner to win back God's love.

She did not know that often a soul that has tried all other pleasures turns to delight in cruelty. In the suffering of animals and men, weakened emotions find a source of joy.

The older woman is not conscious of any malice. She thinks she is only correcting a wanton wife. So she lies awake sometimes at night and broods over new methods of torture.

One evening she goes through the house and has the countess light her with a candle. She carries it in her hand without a candle-stick.

"The candle is burned out," says the young woman.

"When there is an end to the candle, the candlestick must burn," answers Countess Märta.

And they go on, until the reeking wick goes out in the scorched hand.

But that is childishness. There are tortures for the soul which are greater than any suffering of the body. Countess Märta invites guests and makes the mistress of the house herself wait on them at her own table.

That is the penitent's great day. Strangers shall see her in her humiliation. They shall see that she is no longer worthy to sit at her husband's table. Oh, with what scorn their cold eyes will rest on her!

Worse, much worse it is. Not an eye meets hers. Everybody at the table sits silent and depressed, men and women equally out of spirits.

But she gathers it all to lay it like coals of fire on her head. Is her sin so dreadful? Is it a disgrace to be near her?

Then temptation comes. Anna Stjärnhök, who has been her friend, and the judge at Munkerud, Anna's neighbor at the table, take hold of her when she comes, snatch the dish from her, push up a chair, and will not let her escape.

"Sit there, child, sit there!" says the judge. "You have done no wrong."

---

[3] In the country, in Sweden, they wash twice a year, in spring and autumn.

And with one voice all the guests declare that if she does not sit down at the table, they must all go. They are no executioners. They will not do Märta Dohna's bidding. They are not so easily deceived as that sheep-like count.

"Oh, good gentlemen! Oh, beloved friends! Do not be so charitable. You force me to cry out my sin. There is some one whom I have loved too dearly."

"Child, you do not know what sin is. You do not understand how guiltless you are. Gösta Berling did not even know that you liked him. Take your proper place in your home! You have done no wrong."

They keep up her courage for a while and are themselves suddenly gay as children. Laughter and jests ring about the board.

These impetuous, emotional people, they are so good; but still they are sent by the tempter. They want to make her think that she is a martyr, and openly scoff at Countess Märta as if she were a witch. But they do not understand. They do not know how the soul longs for purity, nor how the penitent is driven by his own heart to expose himself to the stones of the way and the heat of the sun.

Sometimes Countess Märta forces her to sit the whole day long quietly in the bay window, and then she tells her endless stories of Gösta Berling, priest and adventurer. If her memory does not hold out, she romances, only to contrive that his name the whole day shall sound in the young woman's ears. That is what she fears most. On those days she feels that her penance will never end. Her love will not die. She thinks that she herself will die before it. Her strength begins to give way. She is often very ill.

"But where is your hero tarrying?" asks the countess, spitefully. "From day to day I have expected him at the head of the pensioners. Why does he not take Borg by storm, set you up on a throne, and throw me and your husband, bound, into a dungeon cell? Are you already forgotten?"

She is almost ready to defend him and say that she herself had forbidden him to give her any help. But no, it is best to be silent, to be silent and to suffer.

Day by day she is more and more consumed by the fire of irritation. She has incessant fever and is so weak that she can scarcely hold herself up. She longs to die. Life's strongest forces are subdued. Love and joy do not dare to move. She no longer fears pain.

It is as if her husband no longer knew that she existed. He sits shut up in his room almost the whole day and studies indecipherable manuscripts and essays in old, stained print.

He reads charters of nobility on parchment, from which the seal of Sweden hangs, large and potent, stamped in red wax and kept in a turned wooden box. He examines old coats of arms with lilies on a white field and griffins on a blue. Such things he understands, and such he interprets with ease. And he reads over and over again speeches and obituary notices of the noble counts Dohna, where their exploits are compared to those of the heroes of Israel and the gods of Greece.

Those old things have always given him pleasure. But he does not trouble himself to think a second time of his young wife.

Countess Märta has said a word which killed the love in him: "She took you for your money." No man can bear to hear such a thing. It quenches all love. Now it was quite one to him what happened to the young woman. If his mother could bring her to the path of duty, so much the better. Count Henrik had much admiration for his mother.

This misery went on for a month. Still it was not such a stormy and agitated time as it may sound when it is all compressed into a few written pages. Countess Elizabeth was always outwardly calm. Once only, when she heard that Gösta Berling might be dead, emotion overcame her.

But her grief was so great that she had not been able to preserve her love for her husband that she would probably have let Countess Märta torture her to death, if her old housekeeper had not spoken to her one evening.

"You must speak to the count, countess," she said. "Good heavens, you are such a child! You do not perhaps know yourself, countess, what you have to expect; but I see well enough what the matter is."

But that was just what she could not say to her husband, while he cherished such a black suspicion of her.

That night she dressed herself quietly, and went out. She wore an ordinary peasant-girl's dress, and had a bundle in her hand. She meant to run away from her home and never come back.

She did not go to escape pain and suffering. But now she believed that God had given her a sign that she might go, that she must preserve her body's health and strength.

She did not turn to the west across the lake, for there lived one whom she loved very dearly; nor did she go to the north, for there many of her friends lived; nor towards the south, for, far, far to the south lay her father's home, and she did not wish to come a step nearer; but to the east she went, for there she knew she had no home, no beloved friend, no acquaintance, no help nor comfort.

She did not go with a light step, for she thought that she had not yet appeased God. But still she was glad that she hereafter might bear the burden of her sin among strangers. Their indifferent glances should rest on her, soothing as cold steel laid on a swollen limb.

She meant to continue her wandering until she found a lowly cottage at the edge of the wood, where no one should know her. "You can see what has happened to me, and my parents have turned me out," she meant to say. "Let me have food and a roof over my head here, until I can earn my bread. I am not without money."

So she went on in the bright June night, for the month of May had passed during her suffering. Alas, the month of May, that fair time when the birches mingle their pale green with the darkness of the pine forest, and when the south-wind comes again satiated with warmth.

Ah, May, you dear, bright month, have you ever seen a child who is sitting on its mother's knee listening to fairy stories? As long as the child is told of cruel giants and of the bitter suffering of beautiful princesses, it holds its head up and its eyes open; but if the mother begins to speak of happiness and sunshine, the little one closes its eyes and falls asleep with its head against her breast.

And see, fair month of May, such a child am I too. Others may listen to tales of flowers and sunshine; but for myself I choose the dark nights, full of visions and adventures, bitter destinies, sorrowful sufferings of wild hearts.

CHAPTER IV. THE IRON FROM EKEBY

SPRING had come, and the iron from all the mines in Värmland was to be sent to Gothenburg.

But at Ekeby they had no iron to send. In the autumn there had been a scarcity of water, in the spring the pensioners had been in power.

In their time strong, bitter ale foamed down the broad granite slope of Björksjö falls, and Löfven's long lake was filled not with water, but with brandy. In their time no iron was brought to the forge, the smiths stood in shirt-sleeves and clogs by the hearth and turned enormous roasts on long spits, while the boys on long tongs held larded capons over the coals. In those days they slept on the carpenter's bench and played cards on the anvil. In those days no iron was forged.

But the spring came and in the wholesale office in Gothenburg they began to expect the iron from Ekeby. They looked up the contract made with the major and his wife, where there were promises of the delivery of many hundreds of tons.

But what did the pensioners care for the contract? They thought of pleasure and fiddling and feasting.

Iron came from Stömne, iron from Sölje. From Uddeholm it came, and from Munkfors, and from all of the many mines. But where is the iron from Ekeby?

Is Ekeby no longer the chief of Varmland's iron works? Does no one watch over the honor of the old estate? Like ashes for the wind it is left in the hands of shiftless pensioners.

Well, but if the Ekeby hammers have rested, they must have worked at our six other estates. There must be there enough and more than enough iron.

So Gösta Berling sets out to talk with the managers of the six mines.

He travelled ten miles or so to the north, till he came to Lötafors. It is a pretty place, there can be no doubt of that. The upper Löfven lies spread out before it and close behind it has Gurlitta cliff, with steeply rising top and a look of wildness and romance which well suits an old mountain. But the smithy, that is not as it ought to be: the swing-wheel is broken, and has been so a whole year."

"Well, why has it not been mended?"

"The carpenter, my dear friend, the carpenter, the only one in the whole district who could mend it, has been busy somewhere else. We have not been able to forge a single ton."

"Why did you not send after the carpenter?"

"Send after! As if we had not sent after him every day, but he has not been able to come. He was busy building bowling-alleys and summer-houses at Ekeby."

He goes further to the north to Björnidet. Also a beautiful spot, but iron, is there any iron?

No, of course not. They had had no coal, and they had not been able to get any money from Ekeby to pay charcoal-burners and teamsters. There had been no work all winter.

Then Gösta turns to the south. He comes to Hån, and to Löfstafors, far in in the woods, but he fares no better there. Nowhere have they iron, and everywhere it seems to be the pensioners' own fault that such is the case.

So Gösta turns back to Ekeby, and the pensioners with gloomy looks take into consideration the fifty tons or so, which are in stock, and their heads are weighed down with grief, for they hear how all nature sneers at Ekeby, and they think that the ground shakes with sobs, that the trees threaten them with angry gestures, and that the grass and weeds lament that the honor of Ekeby is gone.

But why so many words and so much perplexity? There is the iron from Ekeby.

There it is, loaded on barges on the Klar River, ready to sail down the stream, ready to be weighed at Karlstad, ready to be conveyed to Gothenburg. So it is saved, the honor of Ekeby.

But how is it possible? At Ekeby there was not more than fifty tons of iron, at the six other mines there was no iron at all. How is it possible that full-loaded barges shall now carry such an enormous amount of iron to the scales at Karlstad? Yes, one may well ask the pensioners.

The pensioners are themselves on board the heavy, ugly vessels; they mean to escort the iron from Ekeby to Gothenburg. They are going to do everything for their dear iron and not forsake it until it is unloaded on the wharf in Gothenburg. They are going to load and unload, manage sails and rudder. They are the very ones for such an undertaking. Is there a shoal in the Klar River or a reef in the Vaner which they do not know?

If they love anything in the world, it is the iron on those barges. They treat it like the most delicate glass, they spread cloths over it. Not a bit may lie bare. It is those heavy, gray bars which are going to retrieve the honor of Ekeby. No stranger may cast indifferent glances on them.

None of the pensioners have remained at home. Uncle Eberhard has left his desk, and Cousin Christopher has come out of his corner. No one can hold back when it is a question of the honor of Ekeby.

Every one knows that often in life occur such coincidences as that which now followed. He who still can be surprised may wonder that the pensioners should be lying with their barges at the ferry over the Klar River just on the morning after when Countess Elizabeth had started on her wanderings towards the east. But it would certainly have been more wonderful if the young woman had found no help in her need. It now happened that she, who had walked the whole night, was coming along the highway which led down to the ferry, just as the pensioners intended to push off, and they stood and looked at her while she talked to the ferryman and he untied his boat. She was dressed like a peasant girl, and they never guessed who she was. But still they stood and stared at her, because there was something familiar about her. As she stood and talked to the ferryman, a cloud of dust appeared on the highway, and in that cloud of dust they could catch a glimpse of a big yellow coach. She knew that it was from Borg, that they were out to look for her, and that she would now be discovered. She could no longer hope to escape in the ferryman's boat, and the only hiding-place she saw was the pensioners' barges. She rushed down to them without seeing who it was on board. And well it was that she did not see, for otherwise she would rather have thrown herself under the horses' feet than have taken her flight thither.

When she came on board she only screamed, "Hide me, hide me!" And then she tripped and fell on the pile of iron. But the pensioners bade her be calm. They pushed off hurriedly from the land, so that the barge came out into the current and bore down towards Karlstad, just as the coach reached the ferry.

In the carriage sat Count Henrik and Countess Märta. The count ran forward to ask the ferryman if he had seen his countess. But as Count Henrik was a little embarrassed to have to ask about a runaway wife, he only said:—

"Something has been lost!"

"Really?" said the ferryman.

"Something has been lost. I ask if you have seen anything?"

"What are you asking about?"

"Yes, it makes no difference, but something has been lost. I ask if you have ferried anything over the river to-day?"

By these means he could find out nothing, and Countess Märta had to go and speak to the man. She knew in a minute, that she whom they sought was on board one of the heavily gliding barges.

"Who are the people on those barges?"

"Oh, they are the pensioners, as we call them."

"Ah," says the countess. "Yes, then your wife is in good keeping, Henrik. We might as well go straight home."

On the barge there was no such great joy as Countess Märta believed. As long as the yellow coach was in sight, the frightened young woman shrank together on the load motionless and silent, staring at the shore.

Probably she first recognized the pensioners when she had seen the yellow coach drive away. She started up. It was as if she wanted to escape again, but she was stopped by the one standing nearest, and she sank back on the load with a faint moan.

The pensioners dared not speak to her nor ask her any questions. She looked as if on the verge of madness.

Their careless heads began verily to be heavy with responsibility. This iron was already a heavy load for unaccustomed shoulders, and now they had to watch over a young, high-born lady, who had run away from her husband.

When they had met this young woman at the balls of the winter, one and another of them had thought of a little sister whom he had once loved. When he played and romped with that sister he needed to handle her carefully, and when he talked with her he had learned to be careful not to use bad words. If a strange boy had chased her too wildly in their play or had sung coarse songs for her, he had thrown himself on him with boundless fury and almost pounded the life out of him, for his little sister should never hear anything bad nor suffer any pain nor ever be met with anger and hate.

Countess Elizabeth had been like a joyous sister to them all. When she had laid her little hands in their hard fists, it had been as if she had said: "Feel how fragile I am, but you are my big brother; you shall protect me both from others and from yourself." And they had been courtly knights as long as they had been with her.

Now the pensioners looked upon her with terror, and did not quite recognize her. She was worn and thin, her neck was without roundness, her face transparent. She must have struck herself during her wanderings, for from a little wound on her temple blood was trickling, and her curly, light hair, which shaded her brow, was sticky with it. Her dress was soiled from her long walk on the wet paths, and her shoes were muddy. The pensioners had a dreadful feeling that this was a stranger. The Countess Elizabeth they knew never had such wild, glittering eyes. Their poor little sister had been hunted nearly to madness. It was as if a soul come down from other spaces was struggling with the right soul for the mastery of her tortured body.

But there was no need for them to worry over what they should do with her. The old thought soon waked in her. Temptation had come to her again. God wished to try her once more. See, she is among friends; does she intend to leave the path of the penitent?

She rises and cries that she must go.

The pensioners try to calm her. They told her that she was safe. They would protect her from all persecution.

She only begged to be allowed to get into the little boat, which was towed after the barge, and row to the land, to continue her wandering.

But they could not let her go. What would become of her? It was better to remain with them. They were only poor old men, but they would surely find some way to help her.

Then she wrung her hands and begged them to let her go. But they could not grant her prayer. She was so exhausted and weak that they thought that she would die by the roadside.

Gösta Berling stood a short distance away and looked down into the water. Perhaps the young woman would not wish to see him. He did not know it, but his thoughts played and smiled. "Nobody knows where she is," he thought; "we can take her with us to Ekeby. We will keep her hidden there, we pensioners, and we will be good to her. She shall be our queen, our mistress, but no one shall know that she is there. We will guard her so well, so well. She perhaps would be happy with us; she would be cherished like a daughter by all the old men."

He had never dared to ask himself if he loved her. She could not be his without sin, and he would not drag her down to anything low and wretched, that he knew. But to have her concealed at Ekeby and to be good to her after others had been cruel, and to let her enjoy everything pleasant in life, ah, what a dream, what a blissful dream!

But he wakened out of it, for the young countess was in dire distress, and her words had the piercing accents of despair. She had thrown herself upon her knees in the midst of the pensioners and begged them to be allowed to go.

"God has not yet pardoned me," she cried. "Let me go!"

Gösta saw that none of the others meant to obey her, and understood that he must do it. He, who loved her, must do it. He felt a difficulty in walking, as if his every limb resisted his will, but he dragged himself to her and said that he would take her on shore.

She rose instantly. He lifted her down into the boat and rowed her to the east shore. He landed at a little pathway and helped her out of the boat.

"What is to become of you, countess?" he said.

She lifted her finger solemnly and pointed towards heaven.

"If you are in need, countess—"

He could not speak, his voice failed him, but she understood him and answered:—

"I will send you word when I need you."

"I would have liked to protect you from all evil," he said.

She gave him her hand in farewell, and he was not able to say anything more. Her hand lay cold and limp in his.

She was not conscious of anything but those inward voices which forced her to go among strangers. She hardly knew that it was the man she loved whom she now left.

So he let her go and rowed out to the pensioners again. When he came up on the barge he was trembling with fatigue and seemed exhausted and faint He had done the hardest work of his life, it seemed to him.

For the few days he kept up his courage, until the honor of Ekeby was saved. He brought the iron to the weighing-office on Kanike point; then for a long time he lost all strength and love of life.

The pensioners noticed no change in him as long as they were on board. He strained every nerve to keep his hold on gayety and carelessness, for it was by gayety and carelessness that the honor of Ekeby was to be saved. How should their venture at the weighing-office succeed if they came with anxious faces and dejected hearts?

If what rumor says is true, that the pensioners that time had more sand than iron on their barges, if it is true that they kept bringing up and down the same bars to the weighing-office at Kanike point, until the many hundred tons were weighed; if it is true that all that could happen because the keeper of the public scales and his men were so well entertained out of the hampers and wine cases brought from Ekeby, one must know that they had to be gay on the iron barges.

Who can know the truth now? But if it was so, it is certain that Gösta Berling had no time to grieve. Of the joy of adventure and danger he felt nothing. As soon as he dared, he sank into a condition of despair.

As soon as the pensioners had got their certificate of weighing, they loaded their iron on a bark. It was generally the custom that the captain of the vessel took charge of the load to Gothenburg, and the Värmland mines had no more responsibility for their iron when they had got their certificate that the consignment was filled. But the pensioners would do nothing by halves, they were going to take the iron all the way to Gothenburg.

On the way they met with misfortune. A storm broke out in the night, the vessel was disabled, drove on a reef, and sank with all her precious load. But if one saw the matter rightly, what did it matter if the iron was lost? The honor of Ekeby was saved. The iron had been weighed at the weighing-office at Kanike point. And even if the major had to sit down and in a curt letter inform the merchants in the big town that he would not have their money, as they had not got his iron, that made no difference either. Ekeby was so rich, and its honor was saved.

But if the harbors and locks, if the mines and charcoal-kilns, if the schooners and barges begin to whisper of strange things? If a gentle murmur goes through the forests that the journey was a fraud? If it is asserted through the whole of Värmland that there were never more than fifty miserable tons on the barges and that the shipwreck was arranged intentionally? A bold exploit had been carried out, and a real pensioner prank accomplished. By such things the honor of the old estate is not blemished.

But it happened so long ago now. It is quite possible that the pensioners bought the iron or that they found it in some hitherto unknown storehouse. The truth will never be made clear in the matter. The keeper of the scales will never listen to any tales of fraud, and he ought to know.

When the pensioners reached home they heard news. Count Dohna's marriage was to be annulled. The count had sent his steward to Italy to get proofs that the marriage had not been legal. He had come back late in the summer with satisfactory reports. What these were,—well, that I do not know with certainty. One must treat old tales with care; they are like faded roses. They easily drop their petals if one comes too near to them. People say that the ceremony in Italy had not been performed by a real priest. I do not know, but it certainly is true that the marriage between Count Dohna and Elizabeth von Thurn was declared at the court at Borg never to have been any marriage.

Of this the young woman knew nothing. She lived among peasants in some out-of-the-way place, if she was living.

CHAPTER V. LILLIECRONA'S HOME

AMONG the pensioners was one whom I have often mentioned as a great musician. He was a tall, heavily built man, with a big head and bushy, black hair. He was certainly not more than forty years old at that time, but he had an ugly, large-featured face and a pompous manner. This made many think him old. He was a good man, but low-spirited.

One afternoon he took his violin under his arm and went away from Ekeby. He said no farewell to any one, although he never meant to return. He loathed the life there ever since he had seen Countess Elizabeth in her trouble. He walked without resting the whole evening and the whole night, until at early sunrise he came to a little farm, called Löfdala, which belonged to him.

It was so early that nobody was as yet awake. Lilliecrona sat down on the green bench outside the main building and looked at his estate. A more beautiful place did not exist The lawn in front of the house lay in a gentle slope and was covered with fine, light-green grass. There never was such a lawn. The sheep were allowed to graze there and the children to romp there in their games, but it was always just as even and green. The scythe never passed over it, but at least once a week the mistress of the house had all sticks and straws and dry leaves swept from the fresh grass. He looked at the gravel walk in front of the house and suddenly drew his feet back. The children had late in the evening raked it, and his big feet had done terrible harm to the fine work. Think how everything grew there. The six mountain-ashes which guarded the place were high as beeches and wide-spreading as oaks. Such trees had never been seen before. They were beautiful with their thick trunks covered with yellow lichens, and with big, white flower-clusters sticking out from the dark foliage. It made him think of the sky and its stars. It was indeed wonderful how the trees grew there. There stood an old willow, so thick that the arms of two men could not meet about it. It was now rotten and hollow, and the lightning had taken the top off it, but it would not die. Every spring a cluster of green shoots came up out of the shattered trunk to show that it was alive. That hawthorn by the east gable had become such a big tree that it overshadowed the whole house. The roof was white with its dropping petals, for the hawthorn had already blossomed. And the birches which stood in small clumps here and there in the pastures, they certainly had found their paradise on his farm. They developed there in so many different growths, as if they had meant to imitate all other trees. One was like a linden, thick and leafy with a wide-spreading arch, another stood close and tall like a poplar, and a third drooped its branches like a weeping-willow. No one was like another, and they were all beautiful.

Then he rose and went round the house. There lay the garden, so wonderfully beautiful that he had to stop and draw a long breath. The apple-trees were in bloom. Yes, of course he knew that He had seen it on all the other farms; but in no other place did they bloom as they did in that garden, where he had seen them blossom since he was a child. He walked with clasped hands and careful step up and down the gravel path. The ground was white, and the trees were white, here and there with a touch of pink. He had never seen anything so beautiful. He knew every tree, as one knows one's brothers and sisters and playmates. The astrachan trees were quite white, also the winter fruit-trees. But the russet blossoms were pink, and the crab-apple almost red. The most beautiful was the old wild apple-tree, whose little, bitter apples nobody could eat. It was not stingy with its blossoms; it looked like a great snow-drift in the morning light.

For remember that it was early in the morning! The dew made every leaf shine, all dust was washed away. Behind the forest-clad hills, close under which the farm lay, came the first rays of the sun. It was as if the tops of the pines had been set on fire by them. Over the clover meadows, over rye and corn fields, and over the sprouting oat-shoots, lay the lightest of mists, like a thin veil, and the shadows fell sharp as in moonlight.

He stood and looked at the big vegetable beds between the paths. He knows that mistress and maids have been at work here. They have dug, raked, pulled up weeds and turned the earth, until it has become fine and light. After they have made the beds even and the edges straight they have taken tapes and pegs and marked out rows and squares. Then they have sowed and set out, until all the rows and squares have been filled. And the children have been with them and have been so happy and eager to be allowed to help, although it has been hard work for them to stand bent and stretch their arms out over the broad beds. And of great assistance have they been, as any one can understand.

Now what they had sown began to come up.

God bless them! they stood there so bravely, both peas and beans with their two thick cotyledons; and how thick and nice had both carrots and beets come up! The funniest of all were the little crinkled parsley leaves, which lifted a little earth above them and played bopeep with life as yet.

And here was a little bed where the lines did not go so evenly and where the small squares seemed to be an experiment map of everything which could be set or sowed. That was the children's garden.

And Lilliecrona put his violin hastily up to his chin and began to play. The birds began to sing in the big shrubbery which protected the garden from the north wind. It was not possible for anything gifted with voice to be silent, so glorious was the morning. The fiddle-bow moved quite of itself.

Lilliecrona walked up and down the paths and played. "No," he thought, "there is no more beautiful place." What was Ekeby compared to Löfdala. His home had a thatched roof and was only one story high. It lay at the edge of the wood, with the mountain above it and the long valley below it. There was nothing wonderful about it; there was no lake there, no water-fall, no park, but it was beautiful just the same. It was beautiful because it was a good, peaceful home. Life was easy to live there. Every-thing which in other places caused bitterness and hate was there smoothed away with gentleness. So shall it be in a home.

Within, in the house, the mistress lies and sleeps in a room which opens on the garden. She wakes suddenly and listens, but she does not move. She lies smiling and listening. Then the musician comes nearer and nearer, and at last it sounds as if he had stopped under her window. It is indeed not the first time she has heard the violin under her window. He was in the habit of coming so, her husband, when they had done something unusually wild there at Ekeby.

He stands there and confesses and begs for forgiveness. He describes to her the dark powers which tempt him away from what he loves best,—from her and the children. But he loves them. Oh, of course he loves them!

While he plays she gets up and puts on her clothes without quite knowing what she is doing. She is so taken up with his playing.

"It is not luxury and good cheer, which tempt me away," he plays "not love for other women, nor glory, but life's seductive changes: its sweetness, its bitterness, its riches, I must feel about me. But now I have had enough of it, now I am tired and satisfied. I shall never again leave my home. Forgive me; have mercy upon me!"

Then she draws aside the curtain and opens the window, and he sees her beautiful, kind face.

She is good, and she is wise. Her glances bring blessings like the sun's on everything they meet. She directs and tends. Where she is, everything grows and flourishes. She bears happiness within her.

He swings himself up on to the window-sill to her, and is happy as a young lover.

Then he lifts her out into the garden and carries her down under the apple-trees. There he explains for her how beautiful everything is, and shows her the vegetable beds and the children's garden and the funny little parsley leaves.

When the children awake, there is joy and rapture that father has come. They take possession of him. He must see all that is new and wonderful: the little nail-manufactory which pounds away in the brook, the bird's-nest in the willow, and the little minnows in the pond, which swim in thousands near the surface of the water.

Then father, mother, and children take a long walk in the fields. He wants to see how close the rye stands, how the clover is growing, and how the potatoes are beginning to poke up their crumpled leaves.

He must see the cows when they come in from the pasture, visit the new-comers in the barn and sheep-house, look for eggs, and give all the horses sugar.

The children hang at his heels the whole day. No lessons, no work; only to wander about with their father!

In the evening he plays polkas for them, and all day he has been such a good comrade and playfellow that they fall asleep with a pious prayer that father may always stay with them.

He stays eight long days, and is joyous as a boy the whole time. He could stand it no longer, it was too much happiness for him. Ekeby was a thousand times worse, but Ekeby lay in the midst of the whirl of events. Oh, how much there was there to dream of and to play of! How could he live separated from the pensioners' deeds, and from Löfven's long lake, about which adventure's wild chase rushed onward?

On his own estate everything went on in its calm, wonted way. Everything flourished and grew under the gentle mistress's care. Every one was happy there. Everything which anywhere else could have caused discord and bitterness passed over there without complaints or pain. Everything was as it should be. If now the master of the house longed to live as pensioner at Ekeby, what then? Does it help to complain of heaven's sun because it disappears every evening in the west, and leaves the earth in darkness?

What is so unconquerable as submission? What is so certain of victory as patience?

CHAPTER VI. THE WITCH OF DOVRE

THE witch of Dovre walks on Löfven's shores. People have seen her there, little and bent, in a leather skirt and a belt of silver plates. Why has she come out of the wolf-holes to a human world? What does the old creature of the mountains want in the green of the valley?

She comes begging. She is mean, greedy for gifts, although she is so rich. In the clefts of the mountain she hides heavy bars of white silver; and in the rich meadows far away on the heights feed her great flocks of black cattle with golden horns. Still she wanders about in birch-bark shoes and greasy leather skirt soiled with the dirt of a hundred years. She smokes moss in her pipe and begs of the poorest. Shame on one who is never grateful, never gets enough!

She is old. When did the rosy glory of youth dwell in that broad face with its brown greasy skin, in the flat nose and the small eyes, which gleam in the surrounding dirt like coals of fire in gray ashes? When did she sit as a young girl on the mountainside and answer with her horn the shepherd-boy's love-songs? She has lived several hundred years. The oldest do not remember the time when she did not wander through the land. Their fathers had seen her old when they were young. Nor is she yet dead. I who write, myself have seen her.

She is powerful. She does not bend for any one. She can summon the hail, she can guide the lightning. She can lead the herds astray and set wolves on the sheep. Little good can she do, but much evil. It is best to be on good terms with her! If she should beg for your only goat and a whole pound of wool, give it to her; if you don't the horse will fall, or the cottage will burn, or the cow will sicken, or the child will die.

A welcome guest she never is. But it is best to meet her with smiling lips! Who knows for whose sake the bearer of disaster is roaming through the valley? She does not come only to fill her beggar's-pouch. Evil omens go with her; the army worm shows itself, foxes and owls howl and hoot in the twilight, red and black serpents, which spit venom, crawl out of the wood up to the very threshold.

Charms can she chant, philters can she brew. She knows all herbs. Everybody trembles with fear when they see her; but the strong daughter of the wilderness goes calmly on her way among them, protected by their dread. The exploits of her race are not forgotten, nor are her own. As the cat trusts in its claws, so does she trust in her wisdom and in the strength of her divinely inspired prophecies. No king is more sure of his might than she of the kingdom of fear in which she rules.

The witch of Dovre has wandered through many villages. Now she has come to Borg, and does not fear to wander up to the castle. She seldom goes to the kitchen door. Right up the terrace steps she comes. She plants her broad birch-bark shoes on the flower-bordered gravel-walks as calmly as if she were tramping up mountain paths.

Countess Märta has just come out on the steps to admire the beauty of the June day. Below her two maids have stopped on their way to the store-house. They have come from the smoke-house, where the bacon is being smoked, and are carrying newly cured hams on a pole between them. "Will our gracious Countess feel and smell?" say the maids. "Are the hams smoked enough?"

Countess Märta, mistress at Borg at that time, leans over the railing and looks at the hams, but in the same instant the old Finn woman lays her hand on one of them.

The daughter of the mountains is not accustomed to beg and pray! Is it not by her grace that flowers thrive and people live? Frost and storm and floods are all in her power to send. Therefore she does not need to pray and beg. She lays her hand on what she wants, and it is hers.

Countess Märta, however, knows nothing of the old woman's power.

"Away with you, beggar-woman!" she says.

"Give me the ham," says the witch.

"She is mad," cries the countess. And she orders the maids to go to the store-house with their burden.

The eyes of the old woman flame with rage and greed.

"Give me the brown ham," she repeats, "or it will go ill with you."

"I would rather give it to the magpies than to such as you."

Then the old woman is shaken by a storm of rage. She stretches towards heaven her runic-staff and waves it wildly. Her lips utter strange words. Her hair stands on end, her eyes shine, her face is distorted.

"You shall be eaten by magpies yourself," she screams at last.

Then she goes, mumbling curses, brandishing her stick. She turns towards home. Farther towards the south does she not go. She has accomplished her errand, for which she had travelled down from the mountains.

Countess Märta remains standing on the steps and laughs at her extravagant anger; but on her lips the laugh will soon die away, for there they come. She cannot believe her eyes. She thinks that she is dreaming, but there they come, the magpies who are going to eat her.

From the park and the garden they swoop down on her, magpies by scores, with claws ready to seize and bills stretched out to strike. They come with wild screams. Black and white wings gleam before her eyes. She sees as in delirium behind this swarm the magpies of the whole neighborhood approaching; the whole heaven is full of black and white wings. In the bright morning sun the metallic colors of the feathers glisten. In smaller and smaller circles the monsters fly about the countess, aiming with beaks and claws at her face and hands. She has to escape into the hall and shut the door. She leans against it, panting with terror, while the screaming magpies circle about outside.

From that time on she is shut in from the sweetness and green of the summer and from the joy of life. For her were only closed rooms and drawn curtains; for her, despair; for her, terror; for her, confusion, bordering on madness.

Mad this story too may seem, but it must also be true. Hundreds will recognize it and bear witness that such is the old tale.

The birds settled down on the railing and the roof. They sat as if they only waited till the countess should show herself, to throw themselves upon her. They took up their abode in the park and there they remained. It was impossible to drive them away. It was only worse if they shot them. For one that fell, ten came flying. Sometimes great flocks flew away to get food, but faithful sentries always remained behind. And if Countess Märta showed herself, if she looked out of a window or only drew aside the curtain for an instant, if she tried to go out on the steps,—they came directly. The whole terrible swarm whirled up to the house on thundering wings, and the countess fled into her inner room.

She lived in the bedroom beyond the red drawing-room. I have often heard the room described, as it was during that time of terror, when Borg was besieged by magpies. Heavy quilts before the doors and windows, thick carpets on the floor, softly treading, whispering people.

In the countess's heart dwelt wild terror. Her hair turned gray. Her face became wrinkled. She grew old in a month. She could not steel her heart to doubt of hateful magic. She started up from her dreams with wild cries that the magpies were eating her. She wept for days over this fate, which she could not escape. Shunning people, afraid that the swarm of birds should follow on the heels of any one

coming in, she sat mostly silent with her hands before her face, rocking backwards and forwards in her chair, low-spirited and depressed in the close air, sometimes starting up with cries of lamentation.

No one's life could be more bitter. Can any one help pitying her?

I have not much more to tell of her now, and what I have said has not been good. It is as if my conscience smote me. She was good-hearted and cheerful when she was young, and many merry stories about her have gladdened my heart, although there has been no space to tell them here.

But it is so, although that poor wayfarer did not know it, that the soul is ever hungry. On frivolity and play it cannot live. If it gets no other food, it will like a wild beast first tear others to pieces and then itself. That is the meaning of the story.

CHAPTER VII. MIDSUMMER

MIDSUMMER was hot then as now when I am writing. It was the most beautiful season of the year. It was the season when Sintram, the wicked ironmaster at Fors, fretted and grieved. He resented the sun's triumphal march through the hours of the day, and the overthrow of darkness. He raged at the leafy dress which clothed the trees, and at the many-colored carpet which covered the ground.

Everything arrayed itself in beauty. The road, gray and dusty as it was, had its border of flowers: yellow and purple midsummer blossoms, wild parsley, and asters.

When the glory of midsummer lay on the mountains and the sound of the bells from the church at Bro was borne on the quivering air even as far as Fors, when the unspeakable stillness of the Sabbath day reigned in the land, then he rose in wrath. It seemed to him as if God and men dared to forget that he existed, and he decided to go to church, he too. Those who rejoiced at the summer should see him, Sintram, lover of darkness without morning, of death without resurrection, of winter without spring.

He put on his wolf-skin coat and shaggy fur gloves. He had the red horse harnessed in a sledge, and fastened bells to the shining horse-collar. Equipped as if it were thirty degrees below zero, he drove to church. He believed that the grinding under the runners was from the severe cold. He believed that the white foam on the horse's back was hoarfrost. He felt no heat. Cold streamed from him as warmth from the sun.

He drove over the wide plain north of the Bro church. Large, rich villages lay near his way, and fields of grain, over which singing larks fluttered. Never have I heard larks sing as in those fields. Often have I wondered how he could shut his ears to those hundreds of songsters.

He had to drive by many things on the way which would have enraged him if he had given them a glance. He would have seen two bending birches at the door of every house, and through open windows he would have looked into rooms whose ceilings and walls were covered with flowers and green branches. The smallest beggar child went on the road with a bunch of lilacs in her hand, and every peasant woman had a little nosegay stuck in her neckerchief.

Maypoles with faded flowers and drooping wreaths stood in every yard. Round about them the grass was trodden down, for the merry dance had whirled there through the summer night.

Below on the Löfven crowded the floats of timber. The little white sails were hoisted in honor of the day, although no wind filled them, and every masthead bore a green wreath.

On the many roads which lead to Bro the congregation came walking. The women were especially magnificent in the light summer-dresses, which had been made ready just for that day. All were dressed in their best.

And the people could not help rejoicing at the peace of the day and the rest from daily work, at the delicious warmth, the promising harvest, and the wild strawberries which were beginning to redden at the edge of the road. They noticed the stillness of the air and the song of the larks, and said: "It is plain that this is the Lord's day."

Then Sintram drove up. He swore and swung his whip over the straining horse. The sand grated horribly under the runners, the sleigh-bells' shrill clang drowned the sound of the church bells. His brow lay in angry wrinkles under his fur cap.

The church-goers shuddered and thought they had seen the evil one himself. Not even to-day on the summer's festival might they forget evil and cold. Bitter is the lot of those who wander upon earth.

The people who stood in the shadow of the church or sat on the churchyard wall and waited for the beginning of the service, saw him with calm wonder when he came up to the church door. The glorious day had filled their hearts with joy that they were walking the paths of earth and enjoying the sweetness of existence. Now, when they saw Sintram, forebodings of strange disaster came over them.

Sintram entered the church and sat down in his seat, throwing his gloves on the bench, so that the rattle of the wolves' claws which were sewed into the skin was heard through the church. And several women who had already taken their places on the front benches fainted when they saw the shaggy form, and had to be carried out.

But no one dared to drive out Sintram. He disturbed the people's devotions, but he was too much feared for any one to venture to order him to leave the church.

In vain the old clergyman spoke of the summer's bright festival. Nobody listened to him. The people only thought of evil and cold and of the strange disaster which the wicked ironmaster announced to them.

When it was over, they saw him walk out on to the slope of the hill where the Bro church stands. He looked down on the Broby Sound and followed it with his eyes past the deanery and the three points of the west shore out into the Löfven. And they saw how he clenched his fist and shook it over the sound and its green banks. Then his glance turned further south over the lower Löfven to the misty shores which seemed to shut in the lake, and northward it flew miles beyond Gurlitta Cliff up to Björnidet, where the lake began. He looked to the west and east, where the long mountains border the valley, and he clenched his fist again. And every one felt that if he had held a bundle of thunderbolts in his right hand, he would have hurled them in wild joy out over the peaceful country and spread sorrow and death as far as he could. For now he had so accustomed his heart to evil that he knew no pleasure except in suffering. By degrees he had taught himself to love everything ugly and wretched. He was more insane than the most violent madman, but that no one understood.

Strange stories went about the land after that day. It was said that when the sexton came to shut up the church, the bit of the key broke, because a tightly folded paper had been stuck in the keyhole. He gave it to the dean. It was, as was to be expected, a letter meant for a being in the other world.

People whispered of what had stood there. The dean had burnt the paper, but the sexton had looked on while the devil's trash burned. The letters had shone bright red on a black ground. He could not help reading. He read, people said, that Sintram wished to lay the country waste as far as the Bro church tower was visible. He wished to see the forest grow up about the church. He wished to see bear and fox living in men's dwellings. The fields should lie uncultivated, and neither dog nor cock should be heard in the neighborhood. He wished to serve his master by causing every man's ruin. That was what he promised.

And the people looked to the future in silent despair, for they knew that his power was great, that he hated everything living, that he wished to see the wilderness spread through the valley, and that he would gladly take pestilence or famine or war into his service to drive away every one who loved good, joy-bringing work.

CHAPTER VIII. MADAME MUSICA

WHEN nothing could make Gösta Berling glad, after he had helped the young countess to escape, the pensioners decided to seek help of the good Madame Musica, who is a powerful fairy and consoles many who are unhappy.

So one evening in July they had the doors of the big drawing-room at Ekeby opened and the shutters taken down. The sun and air were let in, the late evening's big, red sun, the cool, mild, steaming air.

The striped covers were taken off the furniture, the piano was opened, and the net about the Venetian chandelier taken away. The golden griffins under the white-marble table-tops again reflected the light The white goddesses danced above the mirror. The variegated flowers on the silk damask glistened in the evening glow. Roses were picked and brought in. The whole room was filled with their fragrance. There were wonderful roses with unknown names, which had been brought to Ekeby from foreign lands. There were yellow ones in whose veins the blood shone red as in a human being's, and cream-white roses with curled edges, and pink roses with broad petals, which on their outside edge were as colorless as water, and dark red with black shadows. They carried in all Altringer's roses which had come from far distant lands to rejoice the eyes of lovely women.

The music and music-stands were brought in, and the brass instruments and bows and violins of all sizes; for good Madame Musica shall now reign at Ekeby and try to console Gösta Berling.

Madame Musica has chosen the Oxford Symphony of Hayden, and has had the pensioners practise it. Julius conducts, and each of the others attends to his own instrument. All the pensioners can play—they would not otherwise be pensioners.

When everything is ready Gösta is sent for. He is still weak and low-spirited, but he rejoices in the beautiful room and in the music he soon shall hear. For every one knows that for him who suffers and is in pain good Madame Musica is the best company. She is gay and playful like a child. She is fiery and captivating like a young woman. She is good and wise like the old who have lived a good life.

And then the pensioners began to play, so gently, so murmuringly soft.

It goes well, it goes brilliantly well. From the dead notes they charm Madame Musica herself. Spread out your magic cloak, dear Madame Musica, and take Gösta Berling to the land of gladness, where he used to live.

Alas that it is Gösta Berling who sits there pale and depressed, and whom the old men must amuse as if he were a child. There will be no more joy now in Värmland.

I know why the old people loved him. I know how long a winter evening can be, and how gloom can creep over the spirit in those lonely farm-houses. I understand how it felt when he came.

Ah, fancy a Sunday afternoon, when work is laid aside and the thoughts are dull! Fancy an obstinate north wind, whipping cold into the room,—a cold which no fire can relieve! Fancy the single tallow-candle, which has to be continually snuffed! Fancy the monotonous sound of psalms from the kitchen!

Well, and then bells come ringing, eager feet stamp off the snow in the hall, and Gösta Berling comes into the room. He laughs and jokes. He is life, he is warmth. He opens the piano, and he plays so that; they are surprised at the old strings. He can sing all songs, play any tune. He makes all the inmates of the house happy. He was never cold, he was never tired. The mourner forgot his sorrows when he saw him. Ah, what a good heart he had! How compassionate he was to the weak and poor! And what a genius he was! Yes, you ought to have heard the old people talk of him.

But now, just as they were playing, he burst into tears. He thinks life is so sad. He rests his head in his hands and weeps. The pensioners are dismayed. These are not mild, healing tears, such as Madame Musica generally calls forth. He is sobbing like one in despair. At their wits' end they put their instruments away.

And the good Madame Musica, who loves Gösta Berling, she too almost loses courage; but then she remembers that she has still a mighty champion among the pensioners.

It is the gentle Löwenborg, he who had lost his fiancée in the muddy river, and who is more Gösta Berling's slave than any of the others. He steals away to the piano.

In the pensioners' wing Löwenborg has a great wooden table, on which he has painted a keyboard and set up a music-stand. There he can sit for hours at a time and let his fingers fly over the black and white keys. There he practises both scales and studies, and there he plays his Beethoven. He never plays anything but Beethoven.

But the old man never ventures on any other instrument than the wooden table. For the piano he has a respectful awe. It tempts him, but it frightens him even more. The clashing instrument, on which so many polkas have been drummed, is a sacred thing to him. He has never dared to touch it. Think of that wonderful thing with its many strings, which could give life to the great master's works! He only needs to put his ear to it, to hear andantes and scherzos murmuring there. But he has never played on such a thing. He will never be rich enough to buy one of his own, and on this he has never dared to play. The major's wife was not so willing either to open it for him.

He has heard how polkas and waltzes have been played on it. But in such profane music the noble instrument could only clash and complain. No, if Beethoven should come, then it would let its true, clear sound be heard.

Now he thinks that the moment is come for him and Beethoven. He will take courage and touch the holy thing, and let his young lord and master be gladdened by the sleeping harmonies.

He sits down and begins to play. He is uncertain and nervous, but he gropes through a couple of bars, tries to bring out the right ring, frowns, tries again, and puts his hands before his face and begins to weep.

Yes, it is a bitter thing. The sacred thing is not sacred. There are no clear, pure tones hidden and dreaming in it; there are no mighty thunders, no rushing hurricanes. None of the endless harmonies direct from heaven had remained there. It is an old, worn-out piano, and nothing more.

But then Madame Musica gives the colonel a hint. He takes Ruster with him and they go to the pensioners' wing and get Löwenborg's table, where the keys are painted.

"See here, Löwenborg," says Beerencreutz, when they come back, "here is your piano. Play for Gösta!"

Then Löwenborg stops crying and sits down to play Beethoven for his sorrowful young friend. Now he would certainly be glad again.

In the old man's head sound the most heavenly tones. He cannot think but that Gösta hears how beautifully he is playing. He meets with no more difficulties. He plays his runs and trills with the greatest ease. He would have liked that the master himself could have heard him.

The longer he plays, the more he is carried away. He hears every note with unearthly clearness. He sits there glowing with enthusiasm and emotion, hearing the most wonderful tones, certain that Gösta must hear them too and be comforted.

Gösta sat and looked at him. At first he was angry at this foolery, but gradually he became of milder mood. He was irresistible, the old man, as he sat and enjoyed his Beethoven.

And Gösta began to think how this man too, who now was so gentle and so careless, had been sunk in suffering, how he too had lost her whom he loved. And now he sat beamingly happy at his wooden table. Nothing more was needed to add to his bliss.

He felt humbled. "What, Gösta," he said to himself, "can you no longer bear and suffer? You who have been hardened by poverty all your life, you who have heard every tree in the forest, every tuft in the meadow preach of resignation and patience, you who have been brought up in a land where the winter is severe and the summer short,—have you forgotten how to endure?"

Ah Gösta, a man must bear all that life offers with a brave heart and smiling lip, or he is no man. Regret as much as you like if you have lost what you hold dearest, let remorse tear at your vitals, but show yourself a man. Let your glance shine with gladness, and meet your friends with cheerful words!

Life is hard, nature is hard. But they both give courage and cheerfulness as compensations for their hardness, or no one could hold out.

Courage and cheerfulness! It is as if they were the first duties of life. You have never failed in them before, and shall not now.

Are you worse than Löwenborg, who sits there at his wooden piano, than all the other pensioners? You know well enough that none of them have escaped suffering!

And then Gösta looks at them. Oh, such a performance! They all are sitting there so seriously and listening to this music which nobody hears.

Suddenly Löwenborg is waked from his dreams by a merry laugh. He lifts his hands from the keys and listens as if in rapture. It is Gösta Berling's old laugh, his good, kind, infectious laugh. It is the sweetest music the old man has heard in all his life.

"Did I not say that Beethoven would help you, Gösta," he cries. "Now you are yourself again."

So did the good Madame Musica cure Gösta Bering's hypochondria.

CHAPTER IX. THE BROBY CLERGYMAN

EROS, all-powerful god, you know well that it often seems as if a man should have freed himself from your might. All the tender feelings which unite mankind seem dead in his heart. Madness stretches its claws after the unhappy one, but then you come in all your power, and like the great saint's staff the dried-up heart bursts into bloom.

No one is so mean as the Broby clergyman, no one more divided by malice and uncharitableness from his fellow-men. His rooms are unheated in the winter, he sits on an unpainted wooden seat, he dresses in rags, lives on dry bread, and is furious if a beggar enters his door. He lets the horse starve in the stable and sells the hay, his cows nibble the dry grass at the roadside and the moss on the wall. The bleating of the hungry sheep can be heard far along the highway. The peasants throw him presents of food which their dogs will not eat, of clothes which their poor disdain. His hand is stretched out to beg, his back bent to thank. He begs of the rich, lends to the poor. If he sees a piece of money his heart aches with longing till he gets it into his pocket. Unhappy is he who has not his affairs in order on the day of payment!

He was married late in life, but it had been better if he had never been. Exhausted and overworked, his wife died. His daughter serves with strangers. He is old, but age grants him no relief in his struggling. The madness of avarice never leaves him.

But one fine day in the beginning of August a heavy coach, drawn by four horses, drives up Broby hill. A delicate old lady comes driving in great state, with coachman and footman and lady's-maid. She comes to meet the Broby clergyman. She had loved him in the days of her youth.

He had been tutor at her father's house, and they had loved one another, although her proud family had separated them. And now she is journeying up Broby hill to see him before she dies. All that is left to her in life is to see once again the beloved of her youth.

She sits in the great carriage and dreams. She is not driving up Broby hill to a poor little pastorage. She is on her way to the cool leafy arbor down in the park, where her lover is waiting. She sees him; he is young, he can kiss, he can love. Now, when she knows that she soon shall meet him his image rises before her with singular clearness. He is so handsome, so handsome! He can adore, he can burn, he fills her whole being with rapture.

Now she is sallow, withered, and old. Perhaps he will not recognize her with her sixty years, but she has not come to be seen, but to see, to see the beloved of her youth, who has gone through life untouched by time, who is ever young, beautiful, glowing.

She has come from so far away that she has not heard a word of the Broby clergyman.

The coach clatters up the hill, and at the summit the pastorage is visible.

"For the love of God," whines a beggar at the wayside, "a copper for a poor man!"

The noble lady gives him a piece of silver and asks where the Broby pastorage is.

"The pastorage is in front of you," he says, "but the clergyman is not at home, there is no one at the pastorage."

The little lady seems to fade away. The cool arbor vanishes, her lover is not there. How could she expect, after forty years, to find him there?

What had the gracious lady to do at the vicarage?

She had come to meet the minister. She had known him in the old days.

Forty years and four hundred miles have separated them. And for each ten miles she has come nearer she has left behind her a year with its burden of sorrows and memories, so that when she now comes to the vicarage she is a girl of twenty again, without a care or a regret.

The beggar stands and looks at her, sees her change under his eyes from twenty to sixty, and from sixty back again to twenty.

"The minister is coming home this afternoon," he says. The gracious lady would do best to drive down to the Broby inn and come again later. In the afternoon, the beggar can answer for it, the minister will be at home.

A moment after, the heavy coach with the little faded lady rolls down the hill to the inn, but the beggar stands trembling and looks after her. He feels that he ought to fall on his knees and kiss the wheel tracks.

Elegant, newly shaven, and washed, in shoes with shining buckles, with silk stockings, with ruffles and frills, the Broby clergyman stands at noon that same day before the dean's wife at Bro.

"A fine lady," he says, "a count's daughter. Do you think that I, poor man, can ask her to come into my house? My floors are black, my drawing-room without furniture, the dining-room ceiling is green with mildew and damp. Help me! Remember that she is a noble count's daughter!"

"Say that you have gone away!"

"My dear lady, she has come four hundred miles to see me, poor man. She does not know how it is. I have not a bed to offer her. I have not a bed for her servants!"

"Well, let her go again."

"Dear heart! Do you not understand what I mean? I would rather give everything I possess, everything that I have gathered together by industry and striving, than that she should go without my having received her under my roof. She was twenty when I saw her last, and it is now forty years ago! Help me, that I may see her in my house! Here is money, if money can help, but here more than money is needed."

Oh, Eros, women love you. They would rather go a hundred steps for you than one for other gods.

In the deanery at Bro the rooms are emptied, the kitchen is emptied, the larder is emptied. Wagons are piled up and driven to the vicarage. When the dean comes home from the communion service, he will find empty rooms, look in through the kitchen door to ask after his dinner and find no one there. No dinner, no wife, no maids! What was to be done?

Eros has so wished it.

A little later in the afternoon the heavy coach comes clattering up Broby hill. And the little lady sits and wonders if any new mischance shall happen, if it is really true that she is now going to meet her life's only joy.

Then the coach swings into the vicarage, there comes some one, there he comes. He lifts her out of the carriage, he takes her on his arm, strong as ever, she is clasped in an embrace as warm as of old, forty years ago. She looks into his eyes; which glow as they did when they had only seen five and twenty summers.

A storm of emotion comes over her—warmer than ever. She remembers that he once carried her up the steps to the terrace. She, who believed that her love had lived all these years, had forgotten what it was to be clasped in strong arms, to look into young, glowing eyes.

She does not see that he is old. She only sees his eyes.

She does not see the black floors, the mildewed ceilings, she only sees his glowing eyes. The Broby clergyman is a stately man, a handsome man in that hour. He grows handsome when he looks at her.

She hears his voice, his clear, strong voice; caressingly it sounds. He only speaks so to her. Why did he need furniture from the deanery for his empty rooms; why food, why servants? The old lady would never have missed anything. She hears his voice and sees his eyes.

Never, never before has she been so happy.

She knows that he has been married, but she does not remember it. How could she remember such a thing? She is twenty, he twenty-five. Shall he become the mean Broby clergyman, that smiling youth? The wailing of the poor, the curses of the defrauded, the scornful gibes, the caricatures, the sneers, all that as yet does not exist for him. His heart burns only with a pure and innocent love. Never shall that proud youth love gold so that he will creep after it in the dirt, beg it from the wayfarer, suffer humiliation, suffer disgrace, suffer cold, suffer hunger to get it. Shall he starve his child, torture his wife, for that same miserable gold? It is impossible. Such he can never be. He is a good man like all others. He is not a monster.

The beloved of his youth does not walk by the side of a despised wretch, unworthy of the profession he has dared to undertake!

Oh, Eros, not that evening! That evening he is not the Broby clergyman, nor the next day either, nor the day after.

The day after that she goes.

What a dream, what a beautiful dream 1 For these three days not a cloud!

She journeyed smiling home to her castle and her memories. She never heard his name again, she never asked after him. She wanted to dream that dream as long as she lived.

The Broby clergyman sat in his lonely home and wept. She had made him young. Must he now be old again? Should the evil spirit return and he be despicable, contemptible, as he had been?

CHAPTER X. PATRON JULIUS

PATRON Julius carried down his red-painted wooden chest from the pensioners' wing. He filled with fragrant brandy a green keg, which had followed him on many journeys, and in the big carved luncheon-box he put butter, bread, and seasoned cheese, deliciously shading in green and brown, fat ham, and pan-cakes swimming in raspberry jam.

Then Patron Julius went about and said farewell, with tears in his eyes, to all the glory of Ekeby. He caressed for the last time the worn balls in the bowling-alley and the round-cheeked youngsters on the estate. He went about to the arbors in the garden and the grottos in the park. He was in stable and cow-house, patted the horses' necks, shook the angry bull's horns, and let the calves lick his bare hand. Finally he went with weeping eyes to the main building, where the farewell breakfast awaited him.

Woe to our existence! How can it be full of so much darkness? There was poison in the food, gall in the wine.

The pensioners' throats were compressed by emotion as well as his own. A mist of tears dimmed the eyes. The farewell speech was broken by sobs. Woe to our existence! His life would be, from now on, one long desire. He would never smile again; the ballads should die from his memory as flowers die in the autumn ground. He should grow pale and thin, wither like a frost-bitten rose, like a thirsting lily. Never more should the pensioners see poor Julius. Heavy forebodings traversed his soul, just as shadows of wind-swept clouds traverse our newly tilled fields. He would go home to die.

Blooming with health and well-being, he now stood before them. Never again should they see him so. Never more should they jestingly ask him when he last saw his feet; never more should they wish for his cheeks for bowls. In liver and lungs the disease had already settled. It was gnawing and consuming. He had felt it long. His days were numbered.

Oh, will the Ekeby pensioners but remember death? Oh, may they never forget him!

Duty called him. There in his home sat his mother and waited for him. For seventeen years she had waited for him to come home from Ekeby. Now she had written a summoning letter, and he would obey. He knew that it would be his death; but he would obey like a good son.

Oh, the glorious feasts! Oh, the fair shores, the proud falls! Oh, the wild adventures, the white, smooth floors, the beloved pensioners' wing! Oh, violins and horns, oh, life of happiness and pleasure! It was death to be parted from all that.

Then Patron Julius went out into the kitchen and said farewell to the servants of the house. Each and all, from the housekeeper to kitchen-girl, he embraced and kissed in overflowing emotion. The maids wept and lamented over his fate: that such a kind and merry gentleman should die, that they should never see him again.

Patron Julius gave command that his chaise should be dragged out of the carriage-house and his horse taken out of the stable.

His voice almost failed him when he gave that order. So the chaise might not mould in peace at Ekeby, so old Kajsa must be parted from the well-known manger. He did not wish to say anything hard about his mother; but she ought to have thought of the chaise and Kajsa, if she did not think of him. How would they bear the long journey?

The most bitter of all was to take leave of the pensioners.

Little, round Patron Julius, more built to roll than to walk, felt himself tragic to his very fingertips. He felt himself the great Athenian, who calmly emptied the poison cup in the circle of weeping students. He felt himself the old King Gösta, who prophesied to Sweden's people that they some day should wish to tear him up from the dust.

Finally he sang his best ballad for them. He thought of the swan, who dies in singing. It was so, he hoped, that they would remember him,—a kingly spirit, which does not lower itself to complaining, but goes its way, borne on melody.

At last the last cup was emptied, the last song sung, the last embrace given. He had his coat on, and he held the whip in his hand. There was not a dry eye about him; his own were so filled by sorrow's rising mist that he could not see anything.

Then the pensioners seized him and lifted him up. Cheers thundered about him. They put him down somewhere, he did not see where. A whip cracked, the carriage seemed to move under him. He was carried away. When he recovered the use of his eyes he was out on the highway.

The pensioners had really wept and been overcome by deep regret; still their grief had not stifled all the heart's glad emotions. One of them—was it Gösta Berling, the poet, or Beerencreutz, the card-playing old warrior, or the life-weary Cousin Christopher?— had arranged it so that old Kajsa did not have to be taken from her stall, nor the mouldering chaise from the coach-house. Instead, a big spotted ox had been harnessed to a hay-wagon, and after the red chest, the green keg, and the carved luncheon-box had been put in there, Patron Julius himself, whose eyes were dim with tears, was lifted up, not on to the luncheon-box, nor on to the chest, but on to the spotted ox's back.

For so is man, too weak to meet sorrow in all its bitterness! The pensioners honestly mourned for their friend, who was going away to die,—that withered lily, that mortally wounded singing swan; yet the oppression of their hearts was relieved when they saw him depart riding on the big ox's back, while his fat body was shaken with sobs, his arms, outspread for the last embrace, sank down in despair, and his eyes sought sympathy in an unkind heaven.

Out on the highway the mists began to clear for Patron Julius, and he perceived that he was sitting on the shaking back of an animal. And then people say that he began to ponder on what can happen in seventeen long years. Old Kajsa was visibly changed. Could the oats and clover of Ekeby cause so much? And he cried—I do not know if the stones in the road or the birds in the bushes heard it, but true it is that he cried—"The devil may torture me, if you have not got horns, Kajsa!"

After another period of consideration he let him-self slide gently down from the back of the ox, climbed up into the wagon, sat down on the luncheon-box, and drove on, deep in his thoughts.

After a while, when he has almost reached Broby, he hears singing.

It was the merry young ladies from Berga, and some of the judge's pretty daughters, who were walking along the road. They had fastened their lunch-baskets on long sticks, which rested on their shoulders like guns, and they were marching bravely on in the summer's heat, singing in good time.

"Whither away, Patron Julius?" they cried, when they met him, without noticing the cloud of grief which obscured his brow.

"I am departing from the home of sin and vanity," answered Patron Julius. "I will dwell no longer among idlers and malefactors. I am going home to my mother."

"Oh," they cried, "it is not true; you do not want to leave Ekeby, Patron Julius!"

"Yes," he said, and struck his wooden chest with his fist. "As Lot fled from Sodom and Gomorrah, so do I flee from Ekeby. There is not a righteous man there. But when the earth crumbles away under them, and the sulphur rain patters down from the sky, I shall rejoice in God's just judgment. Farewell, girls; beware of Ekeby!"

Whereupon he wished to continue on his way; but that was not at all their plan. They meant to walk up to Dunder Cliff, to climb it; but the road was long, and they felt inclined to ride in Julius' wagon to the foot of the mountain. Inside of two minutes the girls had got their way. Patron Julius turned back and directed his course towards Dunder Cliff. Smiling, he sat on his chest, while the wagon was filled with girls. Along the road grew daisies and buttercups. The ox had to rest every now and then for a while. Then the girls climbed out and picked flowers. Soon gaudy wreaths hung on Julius' head and the ox's horns.

Further on they came upon bright young birches and dark alder-bushes. They got out and broke branches to adorn the wagon. It looked, soon, like a moving grove. It was fun and play the whole day.

Patron Julius became milder and brighter as the day went on. He divided his provisions among the girls, and sang ballads for them. When they stood on the top of Dunder Cliff, with the wide panorama lying below, so proud and beautiful that tears came into their eyes at its loveliness, Julius felt his heart beat violently; words poured from his lips, and he spoke of his beloved land.

"Ah, Värmland," he said, "ever beautiful, ever glorious! Often, when I have seen thee before me on a map, I have wondered what thou might represent; but now I understand what thou art. Thou art an old, pious hermit, who sits quiet and dreams, with crossed legs and hands resting in his lap. Thou hast a pointed cap drawn down over thy half-shut eyes. Thou art a muser, a holy dreamer, and thou art very beautiful. Wide forests are thy dress. Long bands of blue water and parallel chains of blue hills border it. Thou art so simple that strangers do not see how beautiful thou art. Thou art poor, as the devout desire to be. Thou sittest still, while Vänern's waves wash thy feet and thy crossed legs. To the left thou hast thy fields of ore and thy iron-works. There is thy beating heart. To the north thou hast the dark, beautiful regions of the wilderness, of mystery. There is thy dreaming head.

"When I see thee, gigantic, serious, my eyes are filled with tears. Thou art stern in thy beauty. Thou art meditation, poverty, resignation; and yet I see in thy sternness the tender features of kindness. I see thee and worship. If I only look into the deep forest, if only the hem of thy garment touches me, my spirit is healed. Hour after hour, year after year, I have gazed into thy holy countenance. What mystery are you hiding under lowered eyelids, thou spirit of resignation? Hast thou solved the enigma of life and death, or art thou wondering still, thou holy, thou giant-like? For me thou art the keeper of great, serious thoughts. But I see people crawl on thee and about thee, creatures who never seem to see the majesty of earnestness on thy brow. They only see the beauty of thy face and thy limbs, and are so charmed by it that they forget all else.

"Woe is me, woe to us all, children of Värmland! Beauty, beauty and nothing else, we demand of life. We, children of renunciation, of seriousness, of poverty, raise our hands in one long prayer, and ask the one good: beauty. May life be like a rose-bush, with blossoms of love, wine, and pleasure, and may its roses be within every man's reach! Yes, that is what we wish, and our land wears the features of sternness, earnestness, renunciation. Our land is the eternal symbol of meditation, but we have no thoughts.

"Oh, Värmland, beautiful and glorious!"

So he spoke, with tears in his eyes, and with voice vibrating with inspiration. The young girls heard him with wonder and not without emotion. They had little guessed the depth of feeling which was hidden under that surface, glittering with jests and laughter.

When it drew towards evening, and they once more climbed into the hay-wagon, the girls hardly knew whither Patron Julius drove them, until they stopped before the steps at Ekeby.

"Now we will go in here and have a dance, girls," said Patron Julius.

What did the pensioners say when they saw Patron Julius come with a withered wreath round his hat, and the hay-cart full of girls?

"We might have known that the girls had carried him off," they said; "otherwise we should have had him back here several hours earlier." For the pensioners remembered that this was exactly the seventeenth time Patron Julius had tried to leave Ekeby, once for every departing year. Now Patron Julius had already forgotten both this attempt and all the others. His conscience slept once more its yearlong sleep.

He was a doughty man, Patron Julius. He was light in the dance, gay at the card-table. Pen, pencil, and fiddle-bow lay equally well in his hand. He had an easily moved heart, fair words on his tongue, a throat full of songs. But what would have been the good of all that if he had not possessed a conscience, which made itself be felt only once a year, like the dragon-flies, which free themselves from the gloomy depths and take wings to live only a few hours in the light of day and in the glory of the sun?

CHAPTER XI. THE PLASTER SAINTS

SVARTSJO church is white both outside and in: the walls are white, the pulpit, the seats, the galleries, the roof, the window-sashes, the altar-cloth,—everything is white. In Svartsjö church are no decorations, no pictures, no coats of arms. Over the altar stands only a wooden cross with a white linen cloth. But it was not always so. Once the roof was covered with paintings, and many colored images of stone and plaster stood in that house of God.

Once, many years ago, an artist in Svartsjö had stood and watched the summer sky and the path of the clouds across the sun. He had seen those white, shining clouds, which in the morning float low on the horizon, pile themselves up higher and higher and raise themselves to storm the heavens. They set up sails like ships. They raised standards like warriors. They encroached on the whole sky. They placed themselves before the sun, those growing monsters, and took on wonderful shapes. There was a devouring lion; it changed into a powdered lady. There was a giant with outstretched arms; he laid himself down as a dreaming sphinx. Some adorned their white nakedness with gold-bordered mantles; others spread rouge over snowy cheeks.

There were plains. There were forests. There were walled castles with high towers. The white clouds were lords of the summer sky. They filled the whole blue arch. They reached up to the sun and hid it.

"Oh, how beautiful," thought the gentle artist, "if the longing spirits could climb up on those towering mountains and be carried on those rocking ships ever higher and higher upwards!"

And all at once he understood that the white clouds were the vessels on which the souls of the blessed were carried.

He saw them there. They stood on the gliding masses with lilies in their hands and golden crowns on their heads. Space echoed with their song. Angels circled down on broad, strong wings to meet them. Oh, what a host there were! As the clouds spread out, more and more were visible. They lay on the cloud-beds like water-lilies on a pond; they adorned them, as lilies adorn the meadow. Cloud after cloud rolled up. And all were filled with heavenly hosts in armor of silver, of immortal singers in purple-bordered mantles.

That artist had afterwards painted the roof in the Svartsjö church. He had wished to reproduce there the mounting clouds of the summer day, which bore the blessed to the kingdom of heaven. The hand which had guided the pencil had been strong, but also rather stiff, so that the clouds resembled more the curling locks of a full-bottomed wig than mountains of soft mist. And the form the holy ones had taken for the painter's fancy he was not able to give them again, but instead clothed them in long, red cloaks, and stiff bishops' mitres, or in black robes with stiff ruffles. He had given them big heads and small bodies, and he had provided them with handkerchiefs and prayer-books. Latin sentences flew out of their mouths; and for them whom he meant to be the greatest, he had constructed solid wooden chairs on the backs of the clouds, so that they could be carried sitting comfortably to the everlasting life.

But every one knew that spirits and angels had never shown themselves to the poor artist, and so they were not much surprised that he had not been able to give them celestial beauty. The good master's pious work had seemed to many wonderfully fine, and much holy emotion had it wakened. It would have been worthy to have been looked at by our eyes as well.

But during the pensioners' year, Count Dohna had the whole church whitewashed. Then the paintings on the roof were destroyed. And all the plaster saints were also taken away.

Alas! the plaster saints!

There was a Saint Olof with crown on helm, an axe in his hand, and a kneeling giant under his feet; on the pulpit was a Judith in a red jacket and blue skirt, with a sword in one hand and an hour-glass in the other,—instead of the Assyrian general's head; there was a mysterious Queen of Sheba in a blue jacket and red skirt, with a web-foot on one leg and her hands full of Sibylline books; there was a gray Saint Göran lying alone on a bench in the choir, for both horse and dragon had been broken away; there was Saint Christopher with the flowering staff, and Saint Erik with sceptre and axe, dressed in a flowing brocaded cloak.

These saints were always losing their sceptres or their ears or hands and had to be mended and cleaned. The congregation wearied of it, and longed to be rid of them. But the peasants would never have done the saints any injury if Count Henrik Dohna had not existed. It was he who had them taken away.

When Count Dohna had caused his marriage to be declared null and void, instead of seeking out his wife and having it made legal, much indignation had arisen; for every one knew that his wife had left his house only not to be tortured to death. It seemed now as if he wanted to win back God's grace and men's respect by a good work, and so he had Svartsjö church repaired. He had the whole church whitewashed and the paintings torn down. He and his men carried the images out in a boat and sank them in the depths of the Löfven.

How could he dare to lay his hand on those mighty ones of the Lord?

Did the hand which struck off Holofernes' head no longer hold a sword? Had Sheba's queen forgotten all secret knowledge, which wounds more deeply than a poisoned arrow? Saint Olof, Saint Olof, old viking, Saint Göran, old dragon-killer, the noise of your deeds is, then, dead! But it was best that the saints did not wish to use force against their destroyers. Since the Svartsjö peasants would not pay for paint for their robes and gilding for their crowns, they allowed Count Dohna to carry them out and sink them in Löfven's bottomless depths. They would not stand there and disfigure God's house.

I thought of that boat with its load of saints gliding over Löfven's surface on a quiet summer evening in August. The man who rowed took slow strokes, and threw timorous glances at the strange passengers which lay in the bow and stern; but Count Dohna, who was also there, was not afraid. He took them one by one and threw them into the water. His brow was clear and he breathed deep. He felt like a defender of the pure Evangelical religion. And no miracle was performed in the old saints' honor. Silent and dejected they sank down into annihilation.

But the next Sunday morning Svartsjö church stood gleamingly white. No images disturbed the peace of meditation. Only with the eyes of the soul could the virtuous contemplate the glory of heaven and the faces of the blessed.

But the earth, men's beloved dwelling, is green, the sky is blue. The world glows with colors. Why should the church be white? White as winter, naked as poverty, pale as grief! It does not glitter with hoar-frost like a wintry wood; it does not shine in pearls and lace like a white bride. The church stands in white, cold whitewash, without an image, without a picture.

That Sunday Count Dohna sat in a flower-trimmed arm-chair in the choir, to be seen and to be praised by all men. He who had had the old benches mended, destroyed the disfiguring images, had set new glass in all the broken windows, and had the whole church whitewashed, should now be honored. If he wished to soften the Almighty's anger, it was right that he had adorned His temple as well as he knew how. But why did he take praise for it?

He, who came with implacable sternness on his conscience, ought to have fallen on his knees and begged his brothers and sisters in the church to implore God to suffer him to come into his sanctuary. It would have been better for him if he had stood there like a miserable culprit than that he should sit honored and blessed in the choir, and receive praise because he had wished to make his peace with God.

When the service was over and the last psalm sung, no one left the church, for the clergyman was to make a speech of thanks to the count. But it never went so far.

For the doors were thrown open, back into the church came the old saints, dripping with Löfven's water, stained with green slime and brown mud. They must have heard that here the praise of him who had destroyed them, who had driven them out of God's holy house and sunk them in the cold, dissolving waves, should be sung. The old saints wanted to have their share in the entertainment.

They do not love the waves' monotonous ripple. They are used to psalms and prayers. They held their peace and let it all happen, as long as they believed that it would be to the honor of God. But it was not so. Here sits Count Dohna in honor and glory in the choir and wishes to be worshipped and praised in the house of God. They cannot suffer such a thing. Therefore they have risen from their watery grave and march into the church, easily recognizable to all. There is Saint Olof, with crown on hat, and Saint Erik, with gold-brocaded cloak, and the gray Saint Göran and Saint Christopher; no more; the Queen of Sheba and Judith had not come.

But when the people have recovered a little from their amazement, an audible whisper goes through the church,—

"The pensioners!"

Yes, of course it is the pensioners. And they go up to the count without a word, and lift his chair to their shoulders and carry him from the church and set him down on the slope outside.

They say nothing, and look neither to the right nor to the left. They merely carry Count Dohna out of the house of God, and when that is done, they go away again, the nearest way to the lake.

They used no violence, nor did they waste much time in explanations. It was plain enough: "We the Ekeby pensioners have our own opinion. Count Dohna is not worthy to be praised in God's house. Therefore we carry him out. Let him who will carry him in again."

But he was not carried in. The clergyman's speech of thanks was never made. The people streamed out of the church. There was no one who did not think the pensioners had acted rightly.

They thought of the fair young countess who had been so cruelly tortured at Borg. They remembered her who had been so kind to the poor, who had been so sweet to look upon that it had been a consolation for them to see her.

It was a pity to come with wild pranks into the church; but both the clergyman and the congregation knew that they had been about to play a greater trick on the Omniscient. And they stood ashamed before the misguided old madmen.

"When man is silent, the stones must speak," they said.

But after that day Count Henrik was not happy at Borg. One dark night in the beginning of August a closed carriage drove close up to the big steps. All the servants stationed themselves about it, and Countess Märta came out wrapped in shawls with a thick veil over her face. The count led her, but she trembled and shuddered. It was with the greatest difficulty that they could persuade her to go through the hall and down the steps.

At last she reached the carriage, the count sprang in after her, the doors were slammed to, and the coachman started the horses off at a gallop. The next morning, when the magpies awoke, she was gone.

The count lived from that time on far away in the South of Sweden. Borg was sold and has changed owners many times. No one can help loving it. But few have been happy in its possession.

CHAPTER XII. GOD'S WAYFARER

GOD'S wayfarer, Captain Lennart, came one afternoon in August wandering up to the Broby inn and walked into the kitchen there. He was on his way to his home, Helgesäter, which lies a couple of miles northwest of Broby, close to the edge of the wood.

Captain Lennart did not then know that he was to be one of God's wanderers on the earth. His heart was full of joy that he should see his home again. He had suffered a hard fate; but now he was at home, and all would be well. He did not know that he was to be one of those who may not rest under their own roof, nor warm themselves at their own fires.

God's wayfarer, Captain Lennart, had a cheerful spirit. As he found no one in the kitchen, he poked about like a wild boy. He threw the cat at the dog's head, and laughed till it rang through the house when the two comrades let the heat of the moment break through old friendship, and fought with tooth and nail and fiery eyes.

The innkeeper's wife came in, attracted by the noise. She stopped on the threshold and looked at the man, who was laughing at the struggling animals. She knew him well; but when she saw him last, he had been sitting in the prison-van with handcuffs on his wrists. She remembered it well. Five years and a half ago, during the winter fair in Karlstad, thieves had stolen the jewels of the governor's wife. Many rings, bracelets, and buckles, much prized by the noble lady,—for most of them were heirlooms and presents,—had then been lost. They had never been found. But a rumor spread through the land that Captain Lennart at Helgesäter was the thief.

She had never been able to understand how such a rumor had started. He was such a good and honorable man. He lived happily with his wife, whom he had only a few years before brought home, for he had not been able to afford to marry before. Had he not a good income from his pay and his estate? What could tempt such a man to steal old bracelets and rings? And still more strange it seemed to her that such a rumor could be so believed, so proven, that Captain Lennart was discharged from the army, lost his order of the Sword, and was condemned to five years' hard labor.

He himself had said that he had been at the market, but had left before he heard anything of the theft. On the highway he had found an ugly old buckle, which he had taken home and given to the children. The buckle, however, was of gold, and belonged to the stolen things; that was the cause of his misfortune. It had all been Sintram's work. He had accused him, and given the condemning testimony. It seemed as if he wanted to get rid of Captain Lennart, for a short time after a law-suit was opened against himself, because it had been discovered that he had sold powder to the Norwegians during the war of 1814. People believed that he was afraid of Captain Lennart's testimony. As it was, he was acquitted on the ground of not proven.

She could not stare at him enough. His hair had grown gray and his back bent; he must have suffered. But he still had his friendly face and his cheerful spirit. He was still the same Captain Lennart who had led her forward to the altar, as a bride, and danced at her wedding. She felt sure he would still stop and chat with everybody he met on the road and throw a copper to every child; he would still say to every wrinkled old woman that she grew younger and prettier ever day; and he would still sometimes place himself on a barrel and play the fiddle for those who danced about the Maypole.

"Well, Mother Karin," he began, "are you afraid to look at me?"

He had come especially to hear how it was in his home, and whether they expected him. They must know that he had worked out his time.

The innkeeper's wife gave him the best of news. His wife had worked like a man. She had leased the estate from the new owner, and everything had succeeded for her. The children were healthy, and it was a pleasure to see them. And of course they expected him. His wife was a hard woman, who never spoke of what she thought, but she knew that no one was allowed to eat with Captain Lennart's spoon or to sit in his chair while he was away. This spring, no day had passed without her coming out to the stone at the top of Broby hill and looking down the road. And she had put in order new clothes for him, home-woven clothes, on which she herself had done nearly all the work. By that one could see that he was expected, even if she said nothing.

"They don't believe it, then?" said Captain Lennart.

"No, captain," answered the peasant woman. "Nobody believes it."

Then Captain Lennart would stop no longer; then he wished to go home.

It happened that outside the door he met some dear old friends. The pensioners at Ekeby had just come to the inn. Sintram had invited them thither to celebrate his birthday. And the pensioners did not hesitate a minute before shaking the convict's hand and welcoming him home. Even Sintram did it.

"Dear Lennart," he said, "were you certain that God had any meaning in it all?"

"Do you not think I know," cried Captain Lennart, "that it was not our Lord who saved you from the block?"

The others laughed. But Sintram was not at all angry. He was pleased when people spoke of his compact with the devil.

Yes, then they took Captain Lennart in with them again to empty a glass of welcome; after, he could go his way. But it went badly for him. He had not drunk such treacherous things for five years. Perhaps he had eaten nothing the whole day, and was exhausted by his long journey on foot. The result was that he was quite confused after a couple of glasses.

When the pensioners had got him into a state when he no longer knew what he was doing, they forced on him glass after glass, and they meant no harm by it; it was with good intention towards him, who had not tasted anything good for five years.

Otherwise he was one of the most sober of men. It is also easy to understand that he had no intention to get drunk; he was to have gone home to wife and children. But instead he was lying on the bench in the bar-room, and was sleeping there.

While he lay there, temptingly unconscious, Gösta took a piece of charcoal and a little cranberry-juice and painted him. He gave him the face of a criminal; he thought that most suitable for one who came direct from jail. He painted a black eye, drew a red scar across his nose, plastered his hair down on his forehead in matted tangles, and smeared his whole face.

They laughed at it for a while, then Gösta wished to wash it off.

"Let it be," said Sintram, "so that he can see it when he wakes. It will amuse him."

So they left it as it was, and thought no more of the captain. The feasting lasted the whole night. They broke up at daybreak. There was more wine than sense in their heads.

The question was what they should do with Captain Lennart. "We will go home with him," said Sintram. "Think how glad his wife will be! It will be a pleasure to see her joy. I am moved when I think of it. Let us go home with him!"

They were all moved at the thought. Heavens, how glad she would be!

They shook life into Captain Lennart and lifted him into one of the carriages which the sleepy grooms had long since driven up. And so the whole mob drove up to Helgesäter; some of them, half asleep, nearly fell out of the carriage, others sang to keep awake. They looked little better than a company of tramps, with dull eyes and swollen faces.

They arrived at last, left the horses in the backyard and marched with a certain solemnity up to the steps. Beerencreutz and Julius supported Captain Lennart between them.

"Pull yourself together, Lennart," they said to him, "you are at home. Don't you see that you 're at home?"

He got his eyes open and was almost sober. He was touched that they had accompanied him home.

"Friends," he said, and stopped to speak to them all, "have asked God, friends, why so much evil has passed over me."

"Shut up, Lennart, don't preach!" cries Beerencreutz.

"Let him go on," says Sintram. "He speaks well."

"Have asked Him and not understood; understand now. He wanted to show me what friends I had; friends who follow me home to see mine and my wife's joy. For my wife is expecting me. What are five years of misery compared to that?"

Now hard fists pounded on the door. The pensioners had no time to hear more.

Within there was commotion. The maids awoke and looked out. They threw on their clothes, but did not dare to open for that crowd of men. At last the bolt was drawn. The captain's wife herself came out.

"What do you want?" she asked.

It was Beerencreutz who answered:—

"We are here with your husband."

They pushed forward Captain Lennart, and she saw him reel towards her, drunk, with a prize-fighter's face; and behind him she saw the crowd of drunken, reeling men.

She took a step back; he followed with outstretched arms. "You left me as a thief," she cried, "and come home as a vagabond." Whereupon she turned to go in.

He did not understand. He wished to follow her, but she struck him a blow on the breast.

"Do you think that I will receive such a man as you as master in my house and over my children?"

The door slammed and the key turned in the lock.

Captain Lennart threw himself against the door and began to shake it.

The pensioners could not help it, they began to laugh. He had been so sure of his wife, and now she would have nothing to do with him. It was absurd, they thought.

When Captain Lennart heard them laughing, he rushed after them and wished to beat them. They ran away and leaped into their carriages, he after them; but in his eagerness he stumbled over a stone and fell. He got up again, but pursued them no farther. A thought struck him in his confusion. In this world nothing happens without God's will, nothing.

"Where wilt thou lead me?" he said. "I am a feather, driven by thy breath. I am thy plaything. Whither wilt thou send me? Why dost thou shut the doors of my home to me?"

He turned away from his home, believing that it was God's will.

When the sun rose he stood at the top of Broby hill and looked out over the valley. Ah, little did the poor people in the valley know that their rescuer was near. No mothers as yet lifted their children on their arms that they might see him as he came. The cottages were not clean and in order, with the black hearth hidden by fragrant juniper. As yet the men did not work with eager industry in the fields that his eyes might be gladdened by the sight of cared-for crops and well-dug ditches.

Alas, where he stood his sorrowful eyes saw the ravages of the drought, how the crops were burned up, and how the people scarcely seemed to trouble themselves to prepare the earth for the coming year. He looked up at the blue mountains, and the sharp morning sun showed him the blackened stretches where the forest-fires had passed. He understood by many small signs, by the tumble-down fences, by the small amount of wood which had been carted home and sawed, that the people were not looking after their affairs, that want had come, and that they sought consolation in indifference and brandy.

Captain Lennart stood there on Broby hill and began to think that God perhaps needed him. He was not called home by his wife.

The pensioners could not at all understand what their fault had been; Sintram held his tongue. His wife was much blamed through all the neighborhood, because she had been too proud to receive such a good husband. People said that any one who tried to talk to her of him was instantly interrupted. She could not bear to hear his name spoken. Captain Lennart did nothing to give her other thoughts.

It was a day later.

An old peasant is lying on his death-bed. He has taken the sacrament, and his strength is gone; he must die.

Restless as one who is to set off on a long journey, he has his bed moved from the kitchen to the bedroom and from the bedroom back to the kitchen. By that they understand, more than by the heavy rattling and the failing eyes, that his time has come.

Round about him stand his wife, his children, and servants. He has been fortunate, rich, esteemed. He is not forsaken on his death-bed. The old man speaks of himself as if he stood in the presence of God, and with sighs and confirming words those about him bear witness that he speaks the truth.

"I have been an industrious worker and a kind master," he says. "I have loved my wife like my right hand. I have not let my children grow up without discipline and care. I have not drunk. I have not moved my boundary line. I have not hurried my horse up the hills. I have not let the cows starve in winter. I have not let the sheep be tortured by their wool in summer."

And round about him the weeping servants repeat like an echo: "He has been a kind master. He has not hurried the horse up the hills, nor let the sheep sweat in their wool in summer."

But through the door unnoticed a poor man has come in to ask for a little food. He also hears the words of the dying man from where he stands silent by the door.

And the sick man resumes: "I have opened up the forest, I have drained the meadows. I drove the plough in straight furrows. I built three times as big a barn for three times as big a harvest as in my

father's time. Of shining money I had three silver goblets made; my father only made one. God shall give me a good place in his heaven."

"Our Lord will receive our master well," say the servants.

The man by the door hears the words, and terror fills him who for five long years has been God's plaything.

He goes up to the sick man and takes his hand.

"Friend, friend," he says, and his voice trembles, "have you considered who the Lord is before whose face you soon must appear? He is a great God, a terrible God. The earth is his pasture. The storm his horse. Wide heavens shake under the weight of his foot. And you stand before him and say: 'I have ploughed straight furrows, I have sowed rye, I have chopped wood.' Will you praise yourself to him and compare yourself to him? You do not know how mighty the Lord is to whose kingdom you are going.

"Do not come before your God with big words!" continues the wayfarer. "The mighty on the earth are like threshed-out straw in his barn. His day's work is to make suns. He has dug out oceans and raised up mountains. Bend before him! Lie low in the dust before your Lord, your God! Catch like a child at the hem of his garment and beg for protection! Humble yourself before your Creator!"

The sick man's eyes stand wide-open, his hands are clasped, but his face lights up and the rattling ceases.

"Soul, soul," cries the man, "as surely as you now in your last hour humble yourself before your God, will he take you like a child on his arm and carry you into the glory of his heaven."

The old man gives a last sigh, and all is over. Captain Lennart bends his head and prays. Every one in the room prays with heavy sighs.

When they look up the old peasant lies in quiet peace. His eyes seem still to shine with the reflection of glorious visions, his mouth smiles, his face is beautiful. He has seen God.

"He has seen God," says the son, and closes the dead man's eyes.

"He saw heaven opening," sob the children and servants.

The old wife lays her shaking hand on Captain Lennart's.

"You helped him over the worst, captain."

It was that hour which drove Captain Lennart out among the people. Else he would have gone home and let his wife see his real face, but from that time he believed that God needed him. He became God's wayfarer, who came with help to the poor. Distress was great, and there was much suffering which good sense and kindness could help better than gold and power.

Captain Lennart came one day to the poor peasants who lived in the neighborhood of Gurlitta Cliff. Among them there was great want; there were no more potatoes, and the rye could not be sown, as they had no seed.

Then Captain Lennart took a little boat and rowed across the lake to Fors and asked Sintram to give them rye and potatoes. Sintram received him well: he took him to the big, well-stocked grain-houses and down into the cellar, where the potatoes of last year's crop were, and let him fill all the bags and sacks he had with him.

But when Sintram saw the little boat, he thought that it was too small for such a load. He had the sacks carried to one of his big boats, and his servant, big Mons, row it across the lake. Captain Lennart had only his empty boat to attend to.

He came however after Mons, for the latter was a master of rowing and a giant in strength. Captain Lennart sits and dreams, while he rows across the beautiful lake, and thinks of the little seed-corns' wonderful fate. They were to be thrown out on the black earth among stones and stubble, but they would sprout and take root in the wilderness. He thinks how the soft, light-green shoots will cover the earth, and how, finally, when the ears are filled with soft, sweet kernels, the scythe will pass, and the straws fall, and the flail thunder over them, and the mill crush the kernels to meal, and the meal be baked into bread,—ah, how much hunger will be satisfied by the grain in the boat in front of him!

Sintram's servant landed at the pier of the Gurlitta people, and many hungry men came down to the boat.

Then the man said, as his master had ordered:—

"The master sends you malt and grain, peasants. He has heard that you have no brandy."

Then the people became as mad. They rushed down to the boat and ran out into the water to seize on bags and sacks, but that had never been Captain Lennart's meaning. He had now come, and he was furious when he saw what they were doing. He wanted to have the potatoes for food, and the rye for seed; he had never asked for malt.

He called to the people to leave the sacks alone, but they did not obey.

"May the rye turn to sand in your mouths, and the potatoes to stone in your throats!" he cried, for he was very angry because they had taken the grain.

It looked as if Captain Lennart had worked a miracle. Two women, who were fighting for a bag, tore a hole in it and found only sand; the men who lifted up the potato-sacks, felt how heavy they were, as if filled with stones.

It was all sand and stones, only sand and stones. The people stood in silent terror of God's miracle-worker who had come to them. Captain Lennart was himself for a moment seized with astonishment. Only Mons laughed.

"Go home, fellow," said Captain Lennart, "before the peasants understand that there has never been anything but sand in these sacks; otherwise I am afraid they will sink your boat."

"I am not afraid," said the man.

"Go," said Captain Lennart, with such an imperious voice that he went.

Then Captain Lennart let the people knew that Sintram had fooled them, but they would not believe anything but that a miracle had happened. The story of it spread soon, and as the people's love of the supernatural is great, it was generally believed that Captain Lennart could work wonders. He won great power among the peasants, and they called him God's wayfarer.

CHAPTER XIII. THE CHURCHYARD

IT was a beautiful evening in August. The Löfven lay like a mirror, haze veiled the mountains, it was the cool of the evening.

There came Beerencreutz, the colonel with the white moustaches, short, strong as a wrestler, and with a pack of cards in his coat pocket, to the shore of the lake, and sat down in a flat-bottomed boat. With him were Major Anders Fuchs, his old brother-at-arms, and little Ruster, the flute-player, who had been drummer in the Värmland *chasseurs,* and during many years had followed the colonel as his friend and servant.

On the other shore of the lake lies the churchyard, the neglected churchyard, of the Svartsjö parish, sparsely set with crooked, rattling iron crosses, full of hillocks like an unploughed meadow, overgrown with sedges and striped grasses, which had been sowed there as a reminder that no man's life is like another's, but changes like the leaf of the grass. There are no gravel walks there, no shading trees except the big linden on the forgotten grave of some old priest. A stone wall, rough and high, encloses the miserable field. Miserable and desolate is the churchyard, ugly as the face of a miser, which has withered at the laments of those whose happiness he has stolen. And yet they who rest there are blessed, they who have been sunk into consecrated earth to the sound of psalms and prayers. Acquilon, the gambler, he who died last year at Ekeby, had had to be buried outside the wall. That man, who once had been so proud and courtly, the brave warrior, the bold hunter, the gambler who held fortune in his hand, he had ended by squandering his children's inheritance, all that he had gained himself, all that his wife had saved. Wife and children he had forsaken many years before, to lead the life of a pensioner at Ekeby. One evening in the past summer he had played away the farm which gave them their means of subsistence. Rather than to pay his debt he had shot himself. But the suicide's body was buried outside the moss-grown wall of the miserable churchyard.

Since he died the pensioners had only been twelve; since he died no one had come to take the place of the thirteenth,—no one but the devil, who on Christmas Eve had crept out of the furnace.

The pensioners had found his fate more bitter than that of his predecessors. Of course they knew that one of them must die each year. What harm was there in that? Pensioners may not be old. Can their dim eyes no longer distinguish the cards, can their trembling hands no longer lift the glass, what is life for them, and what are they for life? But to lie like a dog by the churchyard wall, where the protecting sods may not rest in peace, but are trodden by grazing sheep, wounded by spade and plough, where the wanderer goes by without slackening his pace, and where the children play without subduing their laughter and jests,—to rest there, where the stone wall prevents the sound from coming when the angel of the day of doom wakes with his trumpet the dead within,—oh, to lie there!

Beerencreutz rows his boat over the Löfven. He passes in the evening over the lake of my dreams, about whose shores I have seen gods wander, and from whose depths my magic palace rises. He rows by Lagön's lagoons, where the pines stand right up from the water, growing on low, circular shoals, and where the ruin of the tumble-down Viking castle still remains on the steep summit of the island; he rows under the pine grove on Borg's point, where one old tree still hangs on thick roots over the cleft, where a mighty bear had been caught and where old mounds and graves bear witness of the age of the place.

He rows to the other side of the point, gets out below the churchyard, and then walks over mowed fields, which belong to the count at Borg, to Acquilon's grave.

Arrived there, he bends down and pats the turf, as one lightly caresses the blanket under which a sick friend is lying. Then he takes out a pack of cards and sits down beside the grave.

"He is so lonely outside here, Johan Fredrik. He must long sometimes for a game."

"It is a sin and a shame that such a man shall lie here," says the great bear-hunter, Anders Fuchs, and sits down at his side.

But little Ruster, the flute-player, speaks with broken voice, while the tears run from his small red eyes.

"Next to you, colonel, next to you he was the finest man I have ever known."

These three worthy men sit round the grave and deal the cards seriously and with zeal.

I look out over the world, I see many graves. There rest the mighty ones of the earth, weighed down by marble. Funeral marches thunder over them. Standards are sunk over those graves. I see the graves of those who have been much loved. Flowers, wet with tears, caressed with kisses, rest lightly on their green sods. I see forgotten graves, arrogant graves, lying resting-places, and others which say nothing, but never before did I see the right-bower and the joker with the bells in his cap offered as entertainment to a grave's occupant.

"Johan Fredrik has won," says the colonel, proudly. "Did I not know it? I taught him to play. Yes, now we are dead, we three, and he alone alive."

Thereupon he gathers together the cards, rises, and goes, followed by the others, back to Ekeby.

May the dead man have known and felt that not every one has forgotten him or his forsaken grave.

Strange homage wild hearts bring to them they love; but he who lies outside the wall, he whose dead body was not allowed to rest in consecrated ground, he ought to be glad that not every one has rejected him.

Friends, children of men, when I die I shall surely rest in the middle of the churchyard, in the tomb of my ancestors. I shall not have robbed my family of their means of subsistence, nor lifted my hand against my own life, but certainly I have not won such a love, surely will no one do as much for me as the pensioners did for that culprit. It is certain that no one will come in the evening, when the sun sets and it is lonely and dreary in the gardens of the dead, to place between my bony fingers the many-colored cards.

Not even will any one come, which would please me more,—for cards tempt me little,—with fiddle and bow to the grave, that my spirit, which wanders about the mouldering dust, may rock in the flow of melody like a swan on glittering waves.

CHAPTER XIV. OLD SONGS

MARIANNE SINCLAIR sat one quiet afternoon at the end of August in her room and arranged her old letters and other papers.

Round about her was disorder. Great leather trunks and iron bound boxes had been dragged into the room. Her clothes covered the chairs and sofas. From attics and wardrobes and from the stained chests of drawers everything had been taken out, glistening silk and linen, jewels spread out to be polished, shawls and furs to be selected and inspected.

Marianne was making herself ready for a long journey. She was not certain if she should ever return to her home. She was at a turning-point in her life and therefore burned a mass of old letters and diaries. She did not wish to be weighed down with records of the past.

As she sits there, she finds a bundle of old verses. They were copies of old ballads, which her mother used to sing to her when she was little. She untied the string which held them together, and began to read.

She smiled sadly when she had read for a while; the old songs spoke strange wisdom.

Have no faith in happiness, have no faith in the appearance of happiness, have no faith in roses.

"Trust not laughter," they said. "See, the lovely maiden Valborg drives in a golden coach, and her lips smile, but she is as sorrowful as if hoofs and wheels were passing over her life's happiness."

"Trust not the dance," they said. "Many a foot whirls lightly over polished floor, while the heart is heavy as lead."

"Trust not the jest," they said. "Many a one goes to the feast with jesting lips, while she longs to die for pain."

In what shall one believe? In tears and sorrow!

He who is sorrowful can force himself to smile, but he who is glad cannot weep.

But joy is only sorrow disguised. There is nothing real on earth but sorrow.

She went to the window and looked out into the garden, where her parents were walking. They went up and down the broad paths and talked of everything which met their eyes, of the grass and the birds.

"See," said Marianne, "there goes a heart which sighs with sorrow, because it has never been so happy before."

And she thought suddenly that perhaps everything really depended on the person himself, that sorrow and joy depended upon the different ways of looking at things. She asked herself if it were joy or sorrow which had passed over her that year. She hardly knew herself.

She had lived through a bitter time. Her soul had been sick. She had been bowed down to the earth by her deep humiliation. For when she returned to her home she had said to herself, "I will remember no evil of my father."But her heart did not agree. "He has caused me such mortal pain," it said; "he has parted me from him I loved; he made me desperate when he struck my mother. I wish him no harm, but I am afraid of him." And then she noticed how she had to force herself to sit still when her father sat down beside her; she longed to flee from him. She tried to control herself; she talked with him as usual and was almost always with him. She could conquer herself, but she suffered beyond endurance. She ended by detesting everything about him: his coarse loud voice, his heavy tread, his big hands. She wished him no harm, but she could no longer be near him without a feeling of fear and repulsion. Her repressed heart revenged itself. "You would not let me love," it said, "but I am nevertheless your master; you shall end by hating."

Accustomed as she was to observe everything which stirred within her, she saw too well how this repulsion became stronger, how it grew each day. At the same time she seemed to be tied forever to her home. She knew that it would be best for her to go away among people, but she could not bring herself to it since her illness. It would never be any better. She would only be more and more tortured, and some day her self-control would give way, and she would burst out before her father and show him the bitterness of her heart, and then there would be strife and unhappiness.

So had the spring and early summer passed. In July she had become engaged to Baron Adrian, in order to have her own home.

One fine forenoon Baron Adrian had galloped up to the house, riding a magnificent horse. His hussar jacket had shone in the sun, his spurs and sword and belt had glittered and flashed, to say nothing of his own fresh face and smiling eyes.

Melchior Sinclair had stood on the steps and welcomed him when he came. Marianne had sat at the window and sewed. She had seen him come, and now heard every word he said to her father.

"Good-day, Sir Sunshine!" cried Melchior. "How fine you are! You are not out to woo?"

"Yes, yes, uncle, that is just what I am," he answered, and laughed.

"Is there no shame in you, boy? What have you to maintain a wife with?"

"Nothing, uncle. Had I anything, I would never get married."

"Do you say that, do you say that, Sir Sunshine? But that fine jacket,—you have had money enough to get you that?"

"On credit, uncle."

"And the horse you are riding, that is worth a lot of money, I can tell you. Where did you get that?"

"The horse is not mine, uncle."

This was more than Melchior could withstand.

"God be with you, boy," he said. "You do indeed need a wife who has something. If you can win Marianne, take her."

So everything had been made clear between them before Baron Adrian had even dismounted. But Melchior Sinclair knew very well what he was about, for Baron Adrian was a fine fellow.

Then the suitor had come in to Marianne and immediately burst out with his errand.

"Oh, Marianne, dear Marianne. I have already spoken to uncle. I would like so much to have you for my wife. Say that you will, Marianne."

She had got at the truth. The old baron, his father, had let himself be cheated into buying some used-up mines again. The old baron had been buying mines all his life, and never had anything been found in them. His mother was anxious, he himself was in debt, and now he was proposing to her in order to thereby save the home of his ancestors and his hussar jacket.

His home was Hedeby; it lay on the other side of the lake, almost opposite Björne. She knew him well; they were of the same age and playmates.

"You might marry me, Marianne. I lead such a wretched life. I have to ride on borrowed horses and cannot pay my tailor's bills. It can't go on. I shall have to resign, and then I shall shoot myself."

"But, Adrian, what kind of a marriage would it be? We are not in the least in love with one another."

"Oh, as for love, I care nothing for all that nonsense" he had then explained. "I like to ride a good horse and to hunt, but I am no pensioner, I am a worker. If I only could get some money, so that I could take charge of the estate at home and give my mother some peace in her old age, I should be happy. I should both plough and sow, for I like work."

Then he had looked at her with his honest eyes, and she knew that he spoke the truth and that he was a man to depend upon. She engaged herself to him, chiefly to get away from her home, but also because she had always liked him.

But never would she forget that month which followed the August evening when her engagement was announced,—all that time of madness.

Baron Adrian became each day sadder and more silent. He came very often to Björne, sometimes several times a day, but she could not help noticing how depressed he was. With others he could still jest, but with her he was impossible, silent and bored, She understood what was the matter: it was not so easy as he had believed to marry an ugly woman. No one knew better than she how ugly she was. She had shown him that she did not want any caresses or love-making, but he was nevertheless tortured by the thought of her as his wife, and it seemed worse to him day by day. Why did he care? Why did he not break it off? She had given hints which were plain enough. She could do nothing. Her father had told her that her reputation would not bear any more ventures in being engaged. Then she had despised them both, and any way seemed good enough to get away from them. But only a couple of days after the great engagement feast a sudden and wonderful change had come.

In the path in front of the steps at Björne lay a big stone, which caused much trouble and vexation. Carriages rolled over it, horses and people tripped on it, the maids who came with heavy milk cans ran against it and spilled the milk; but the stone remained, because it had already lain there so many years. It had been there in the time of Sinclair's parents, long before any one had thought of building at Björne. He did not see why he should take it up.

But one day at the end of August, two maids, who were carrying a heavy tub, tripped over the stone; they fell, hurt themselves badly, and the feeling against the stone grew strong.

It was early in the morning. Melchior was out on his morning walk, but as the workmen were about the house between eight and nine, Madame Gustava had several of them come and dig up the big stone.

They came with iron levers and spades, dug and strained, and at last got the old disturber of the peace up out of his hole. Then they carried him away to the back yard. It was work for six men.

The stone was hardly taken up before Melchior came home. You can believe that he was angry. It was no longer the same place, he thought. Who had dared to move the stone? Madame Gustava had given the order. Those women had no heart in their bodies. Did not his wife know that he loved that stone?

And then he went direct to the stone, lifted it, and carried it across the yard to the place where it had lain, and there he flung it down. And it was a stone which six men could scarcely lift. That deed was mightily admired through the whole of Värmland.

While he carried the stone across the yard, Marianne had stood at the dining-room window and looked at him. He was her master, that terrible man with his boundless strength,—an unreasonable, capricious master, who thought of nothing but his own pleasure.

They were in the midst of breakfast, and she had a carving-knife in her hand. Involuntarily she lifted the knife.

Madame Gustava seized her by the wrist.

"Marianne!"

"What is the matter, mother?"

"Oh, Marianne, you looked so strange! I was frightened."

Marianne looked at her. She was a little, dry woman, gray and wrinkled already at fifty. She loved like a dog, without remembering knocks and blows. She was generally good-humored, and yet she made a melancholy impression. She was like a storm-whipped tree by the sea; she had never had quiet to grow. She had learned to use mean shifts, to lie when needed, and often made herself out more stupid than she was to escape taunts. In everything she was the tool of her husband.

"Would you grieve much if father died?" asked Marianne.

"Marianne, you are angry with your father. You are always angry with him. Why cannot everything be forgotten, since you have got a new fiancé?"

"Oh, mother, it is not my fault. Can I help shuddering at him? Do you not see what he is? Why should I care for him? He is violent, he is uncouth, he has tortured you till you are prematurely old. Why is he our master? He behaves like a madman. Why shall I honor and respect him? He is not good, he is not charitable. I know that he is strong. He is capable of beating us to death at any moment. He can turn us out of the house when he will. Is that why I should love him?"

But then Madame Gustava had been as never before. She had found strength and courage and had spoken weighty words.

"You must take care, Marianne. It almost seems to me as if your father was right when he shut you out last winter. You shall see that you will be punished for this. You must teach yourself to bear without hating, Marianne, to suffer without revenge."

"Oh, mother, I am so unhappy."

Immediately after, they heard in the hall the sound of a heavy fall.

They never knew if Melchior Sinclair had stood on the steps and through the open dining-room door had heard Marianne's words, or if it was only over-exertion which had been the cause of the stroke. When they came out he lay unconscious. They never dared to ask him the cause. He himself never made any sign that he had heard anything. Marianne never dared to think the thought out that she had involuntarily revenged herself. But the sight of her father lying on the very steps where she had learnt to hate him took all bitterness from her heart.

He soon returned to consciousness, and when he had kept quiet a few days, he was like himself—and yet not at all like.

Marianne saw her parents walking together in the garden. It was always so now. He never went out alone, grumbled at guests and at everything which separated him from his wife. Old age had come upon him. He could not bring himself to write a letter; his wife had to do it. He never decided anything by himself, but asked her about everything and let it be as she decided. And he was always gentle and kind. He noticed the change which had come over him, and how happy his wife was. "She is well off now," he said one day to Marianne, and pointed to Madame Gustava.

"Oh, dear Melchior," she cried, "you know very well that I would rather have you strong again."

And she really meant it. It was her joy to speak of him as he was in the days of his strength. She told how he held his own in riot and revel as well as any of the Ekeby pensioners, how he had done good business and earned much money, just when she thought that he in his madness would lose house and lands. But Marianne knew that she was happy in spite of all her complaints. To be everything to her husband was enough for her. They both looked old, prematurely broken. Marianne thought that she could see their future life. He would get gradually weaker and weaker; other strokes would make him more helpless, and she would watch over him until death parted them. But the end might be far distant. Madame Gustava could enjoy her happiness in peace still for a time. It must be so, Marianne thought. Life owed her some compensation.

For her too it was better. No fretting despair forced her to marry to get another master. Her wounded heart had found peace. She had to acknowledge that she was a truer, richer, nobler person than before; what could she wish undone of what had happened? Was it true that all suffering was good? Could everything be turned to happiness? She had begun to consider everything good which could help to develop her to a higher degree of humanity. The old songs were not right. Sorrow was not the only lasting thing. She would now go out into the world and look about for some place where she was needed. If her father had been in his old mood, he would never have allowed her to break her engagement. Now Madame Gustava had arranged the matter. Marianne had even been allowed to give Baron Adrian the money he needed.

She could think of him too with pleasure, she would be free from him. With his bravery and love of life he had always reminded her of Gösta; now she should see him glad again. He would again be that sunny knight who had come in his glory to her father's house. She would get him lands where he could plough and dig as much as his heart desired, and she would see him lead a beautiful bride to the altar.

With such thoughts she sits down and writes to give him back his freedom. She writes gentle, persuasive words, sense wrapped up in jests, and yet so that he must understand how seriously she means it.

While she writes she hears hoof-beats on the road.

"My dear Sir Sunshine," she thinks, "it is the last time."

Baron Adrian immediately after comes into her room.

"What, Adrian, are you coming in here?" and she looks dismayed at all her packing.

He is shy and embarrassed and stammers out an excuse.

"I was just writing to you," she says. "Look, you might as well read it now."

He takes the letter and she sits and watches him while he reads. She longs to see his face light up with joy.

But he has not read far before he grows fiery red, throws the letter on the floor, stamps on it, and swears terrible oaths.

Marianne trembles slightly. She is no novice in the study of love; still she has not before understood this inexperienced boy, this great child.

"Adrian, dear Adrian," she says, "what kind of a comedy have you played with me? Come and tell me the truth."

He came and almost suffocated her with caresses. Poor boy, so he had cared and longed.

After a while she looked out. There walked Madame Gustava and talked with her husband of flowers and birds, and here she sat and chatted of love. "Life has let us both feel its serious side," she thought, and smiled sadly. "It wants to comfort us; we have each got her big child to play with."

However, it was good to be loved. It was sweet to hear him whisper of the magical power which she possessed, of how he had been ashamed of what he had said at their first conversation. He had not then known what charm she had. Oh, no man could be near her without loving her, but she had frightened him; he had felt so strangely subdued.

It was not happiness, nor unhappiness, but she would try to live with this man.

She began to understand herself, and thought of the words of the old songs about the turtle-dove. It never drinks clear water, but first muddies it with its foot so that it may better suit its sorrowful spirit. So too should she never go to the spring of life and drink pure, unmixed happiness. Troubled with sorrow, life pleased her best.

CHAPTER XV. DEATH, THE DELIVERER

MY pale friend, Death the deliverer, came in August, when the nights were white with moonlight, to the house of Captain Uggla. But he did not dare to go direct into that hospitable home, for they are few who love him, and he does not wish to be greeted with weeping, rather with quiet joy,—he who comes to set free the soul from the fetters of pain, he who delivers the soul from the burden of the body and lets it enjoy the beautiful life of the spheres.

Into the old grove behind the house, crept Death. In the grove, which then was young and full of green, my pale friend hid himself by day, but at night he stood at the edge of the wood, white and pale, with his scythe glittering in the moonlight.

Death stood there, and the creatures of the night saw him. Evening after evening the people at Berga heard how the fox howled to foretell his coming. The snake crawled up the sandy path to the very house. He could not speak, but they well understood that he came as a presage. And in the apple-tree outside the window of the captain's wife the owl hooted. For everything in nature feels Death and trembles.

It happened that the judge from Munkerud, who had been at a festival at the Bro deanery, drove by Berga at two o'clock in the night and saw a candle burning in the window of the guest-room. He plainly saw the yellow flame and the white candle, and, wondering, he afterwards told of the candle which had burned in the summer night.

The gay daughters at Berga laughed and said that the judge had the gift of second sight, for there were no candles in the house, they were already burned up in March; and the captain swore that no one had slept in the guest-room for days and weeks; but his wife was silent and grew pale, for that white candle with the clear flame used to show itself when one of her family should be set free by Death.

A short time after, Ferdinand came home from a surveying journey in the northern forests. He came, pale and ill with an incurable disease of the lungs, and as soon as his mother saw him, she knew that her son must die.

He must go, that good son who had never given his parents a sorrow. He must leave earth's pleasures and happiness, and the beautiful, beloved bride who awaited him, and the rich estates which should have been his.

At last, when my pale friend had waited a month, he took heart and went one night up to the house. He thought how hunger and privation had there been met by glad faces, so why should not he too be received with joy?

That night the captain's wife, who lay awake, heard a knocking on the window-pane, and she sat up in bed and asked: "Who is it who knocks?"

And the old people tell that Death answered her:

"It is Death who knocks."

Then she rose up, opened her window, and saw bats and owls fluttering in the moonlight, but Death she did not see.

"Come," she said half aloud, "friend and deliverer! Why have you lingered so long? I have been waiting. I have called. Come and set my son free!"

The next day, she sat by her son's sick-bed and spoke to him of the blissfulness of the liberated spirit and of its glorious life.

So Ferdinand died, enchanted by bright visions, smiling at the glory to come.

Death had never seen anything so beautiful. For of course there were some who wept by Ferdinand Uggla's deathbed; but the sick man himself smiled at the man with the scythe, when he took his place on the edge of the bed, and his mother listened to the death-rattle as if to sweet music. She trembled lest Death should not finish his work; and when the end came, tears fell from her eyes, but they were tears of joy which wet her son's stiffened face.

Never had Death been so fêted as at Ferdinand Uggla's burial.

It was a wonderful funeral procession which passed under the lindens. In front of the flower-decked coffin beautiful children walked and strewed flowers. There was no mourning-dress, no crape; for his mother had wished that he who died with joy should not be followed to the good refuge by a gloomy funeral procession, but by a shining wedding train.

Following the coffin, went Anna Stjärnhök, the dead man's beautiful, glowing bride. She had set a bridal wreath on her head, hung a bridal veil over her, and arrayed herself in a bridal dress of white, shimmering satin. So adorned, she went to be wedded at the grave to a mouldering bridegroom.

Behind her they came, two by two, dignified old ladies and stately men. The ladies came in shining buckles and brooches, with strings of milk-white pearls and bracelets of gold. Ostrich feathers nodded in their bonnets of silk and lace, and from their shoulders floated thin silken shawls over dresses of many-colored satin. And their husbands came in their best array, in high-collared coats with gilded buttons, with swelling ruffles, and in vests of stiff brocade or richly-embroidered velvet. It was a wedding procession; the captain's wife had wished it so.

She herself walked next after Anna Stjärnhök, led by her husband. If she had possessed a dress of shining brocade, she would have worn it; if she had possessed jewels and a gay bonnet, she would have worn them too to do honor to her son on his festival day. But she only had the black silk dress and the yellowed laces which had adorned so many feasts, and she wore them here too.

Although all the guests came in their best array, there was not a dry eye when they walked forward to the grave. Men and women wept, not so much for the dead, as for themselves. There walked the bride; there the bridegroom was carried; there they themselves wandered, decked out for a feast, and yet—who is there who walks earth's green pathways and does not know that his lot is affliction, sorrow, un-happiness, and death. They wept at the thought that nothing on earth could save them.

The captain's wife did not weep; but she was the only one whose eyes were dry.

When the prayers were read, and the grave filled in, all went away to the carriages. Only the mother and Anna Stjärnhök lingered by the grave to bid their dead a last good-bye. The older woman sat down on the grave-mound, and Anna placed herself at her side.

"Anna," said the captain's wife, "I have said to God: 'Let Death come and take away my son, let him take away him I love most, and only tears of joy shall come to my eyes; with nuptial pomp I will follow him to his grave, and my red rose-bush, which stands outside my chamber-window, will I move to him in the grave-yard.' And now it has come to pass my son is dead. I have greeted Death like a friend, called him by the tenderest names; I have wept tears of joy over my son's dead face, and in the autumn, when the leaves are fallen, I shall plant my red rosebush here. But do you know, you who sit here at my side, why I have sent such prayers to God?"

She looked questioningly at Anna Stjärnhök; but the girl sat silent and pale beside her. Perhaps she was struggling to silence inward voices which already there, on the grave of the dead, began to whisper to her that now at last she was free.

"The fault is yours," said the captain's wife. The girl sank down as from a blow. She did not answer a word.

"Anna Stjärnhök, you were once proud and self-willed: you played with my son, took him and cast him off. But what of that? He had to accept it, as well as another. Perhaps too he and we all loved your money as much as you. But you came back, you came with a blessing to our home; you were gentle and mild, strong and kind, when you came again. You cherished us with love; you made us so happy, Anna Stjärnhök; and we poor people lay at your feet.

"And yet, and yet I have wished that you had not come. Then had I not needed to pray to God to shorten my son's life. At Christmas he could have borne to lose you, but after he had learnt to know you, such as you now are, he would not have had the strength.

"You know, Anna Stjärnhök, who to-day have put on your bridal dress to follow my son, that if he had lived you would never have followed him in that attire to the Bro church, for you did not love him.

"I saw that you only came out of pity, for you wanted to relieve our hard lot. You did not love him. Do you not think that I know love, that I see it, when it is there, and understand when it is lacking. Then I thought: 'May God take my son's life before he has his eyes opened!'

"Oh, if you had loved him! Oh, if you had never come to us and sweetened our lives, when you did not love him! I knew my duty: if he had not died, I should have been forced to tell him that you did not love him, that you were marrying him out of pity. I must have made him set you free, and then his life's happiness would have been gone. That is why I prayed to God that he might die, that I should not need to disturb the peace of his heart. And I have rejoiced over his sunken cheeks, exulted over his rattling breath, trembled lest Death should not complete his work."

She stopped speaking, and waited for an answer; but Anna Stjärnhök could not speak, she was still listening to the many voices in her soul.

Then the mother cried out in despair:—

"Oh, how happy are they who may mourn for their dead, they who may weep streams of tears! I must stand with dry eyes by my son's grave, I must rejoice over his death! How unhappy I am!"

Then Anna Stjärnhök pressed her hands against her breast. She remembered that winter night when she had sworn by her love to be these poor people's support and comfort, and she trembled. Had it all been in vain; was not her sacrifice one of those which God accepts? Should it all be turned to a curse?

But if she sacrificed everything would not God then give His blessing to the work, and let her bring happiness, be a support, a help, to these people?

"What is required for you to be able to mourn for your son?" she asked.

"That I shall not believe the testimony of my old eyes. If I believed that you loved my son, then I would grieve for his death."

The girl rose up, her eyes burning. She tore off her veil and spread it over the grave, she tore off her wreath and laid it beside it.

"See how I love him!" she cried. "I give him my wreath and veil. I consecrate myself to him. I will never belong to another."

Then the captain's wife rose too. She stood silent for a while; her whole body was shaking, and her face twitched, but at last the tears came,—tears of grief.

CHAPTER XVI. THE DROUGHT

IF dead things love, if earth and water distinguish friends from enemies, I should like to possess their love. I should like the green earth not to feel my step as a heavy burden. I should like her to forgive that she for my sake is wounded by plough and harrow, and willingly to open for my dead body. And I should like the waves, whose shining mirror is broken by my oars, to have the same patience with me as a mother has with an eager child when it climbs up on her knee, careless of the uncrumpled silk of her dress.

The spirit of life still dwells in dead things. Have you not seen it? When strife and hate fill the earth, dead things must suffer too. Then the waves are wild and ravenous; then the fields are niggardly as a miser. But woe to him for whose sake the woods sigh and the mountains weep.

Memorable was the year when the pensioners were in power. If one could tell of everything which happened that year to the people by Löfven's shores a world would be surprised. For then old love wakened, then new was kindled. Old hate blazed up, and long cherished revenge seized its prey.

From Ekeby this restless infection went forth; it spread first through the manors and estates, and drove men to ruin and to crime. It ran from village to village, from cottage to cottage. Everywhere hearts became wild, and brains confused. Never did the dance whirl so merrily at the cross-roads; never was the beer-barrel so quickly emptied; never was so much grain turned into brandy. Never were there so many balls; never was the way shorter from the angry word to the knife-thrust. But the uneasiness was not only among men. It spread through all living things. Never had wolf and bear ravaged so fiercely; never had fox and owl howled so terribly, and plundered so boldly; never did the sheep go so often astray in the wood; never did so much sickness rage among the cattle.

He who will see how everything hangs together must leave the towns and live in a lonely hut at the edge of the forest; then he will learn to notice nature's every sign and to understand how the dead things depend on the living. He will see that when there is restlessness on the earth, the peace of the dead things is disturbed. The people know it. It is in such times that the wood-nymph puts out the charcoal-kiln, the sea-nymph breaks the boat to pieces, the river-sprite sends illness, the goblin starves the cow. And it was so that year. Never had the spring freshets done so much damage. The mill and smithy at Ekeby were not the only offerings. Never had the lightning laid waste so much already before midsummer—after midsummer came the drought.

As long as the long days lasted, no rain came. From the middle of June till the beginning of September, the country was bathed in continual sunshine.

The rain refused to fall, the earth to nourish, the winds to blow. Sunshine only streamed down on the earth. The grass was not yet high and could not grow; the rye was without nourishment, just when it should have collected food in its ears; the wheat, from which most of the bread was baked, never came up more than a few inches; the late sowed turnips never sprouted; not even the potatoes could draw sustenance from that petrified earth.

At such times they begin to be frightened far away in the forest huts, and from the mountains the terror comes down to the calmer people on the plain.

"There is some one whom God's hand is seeking!" say the people.

And each one beats his breast and says: "Is it I? Is it from horror of me that the rain holds back? Is it in wrath against me that the stern earth dries up and hardens?—and the perpetual sunshine,—is it to heap coals of fire on my head? Or if it is not I, who is it whom God's hand is seeking?"

It was a Sunday in August. The service was over. The people wandered in groups along the sunny roads. On all sides they saw burned woods and ruined crops. There had been many forest fires; and what they had spared, insects had taken.

The gloomy people did not lack for subjects of conversation. There were many who could tell how hard it had been in the years of famine of eighteen hundred and eight and nine, and in the cold winter of eighteen hundred and twelve, when the sparrows froze to death. They knew how to make bread out of bark, and how the cows could be taught to eat moss.

There was one woman who had tried a new kind of bread of cranberries and corn-meal. She had a sample with her, and let the people taste it She was proud of her invention.

But over them all floated the same question. It stared from every eye, was whispered by every lip: "Who is it, O Lord, whom Thy hand seeks?"

A man in the gloomy crowd which had gone westward, and struggled up Broby hill, stopped a minute before the path which led up to the house of the mean Broby clergyman. He picked up a dry stick from the ground and threw it upon the path.

"Dry as that stick have the prayers been which he has given our Lord," said the man.

He who walked next to him also stopped. He took up a dry branch and threw it where the stick had fallen.

"That is the proper offering to that priest," he said.

The third in the crowd followed the others' example.

"He has been like the drought; sticks and straw are all that he has let us keep."

The fourth said: "We give him back what he has given us."

And the fifth: "For a perpetual disgrace I throw this to him. May he dry up and wither away like this branch!"

"Dry food to the dry priest," said the sixth.

The people who came after see what they are doing and hear what they say. Now they get the answer to their long questioning.

"Give him what belongs to him! He has brought the drought on us."

And each one stops, each one says his word and throws his branch before he goes on.

In the corner by the path there soon lies a pile of sticks and straw,—a pile of shame for the Broby clergyman.

That was their only revenge. No one lifted his hand against the clergyman or said an angry word to him. Desperate hearts cast off part of their burden by throwing a dry branch on the pile. They did not revenge themselves. They only pointed out the guilty one to the God of retribution.

"If we have not worshipped you rightly, it is that man's fault. Be pitiful, Lord, and let him alone suffer! We mark him with shame and dishonor. We are not with him."

It soon became the custom for every one who passed the vicarage to throw a dry branch on the pile of shame.

The old miser soon noticed the pile by the roadside. He had it carried away,—some said that he heated his stove with it The next day a new pile had collected on the same spot, and as soon as he had that taken away a new one was begun.

The dry branches lay there and said: "Shame, shame to the Broby clergyman!"

Soon the people's meaning became clear to him. He understood that they pointed to him as the origin of their misfortune. It was in wrath at him God let the earth languish. He tried to laugh at them and their branches; but when it had gone on a week, he laughed no more. Oh, what childishness! How can those dry sticks injure him? He understood that the hate of years sought an opportunity of expressing itself. What of that?—he was not used to love.

For all this he did not become more gentle. He had perhaps wished to improve after the old lady had visited him; now he could not. He would not be forced to it.

But gradually the pile grew too strong for him. He thought of it continually, and the feeling which every one cherished took root also in him. He watched the pile, counted the branches which had been added each day. The thought of it encroached upon all other thoughts. The pile was destroying him.

Every day he felt more and more the people were right. He grew thin and very old in a couple of weeks. He suffered from remorse and indisposition. But it was as if everything depended on that pile. It was as if his remorse would grow silent, and the weight of years be lifted off him, if only the pile would stop growing.

Finally he sat there the whole day and watched; but the people were without mercy. At night there were always new branches thrown on.

One day Gösta Berling passed along the road. The Broby clergyman sat at the roadside, old and haggard. He sat and picked out the dry sticks and laid them together in rows and piles, playing with them as if he were a child again. Gösta was grieved at his misery.

"What are you doing, pastor?" he says, and leaps out of the carriage.

"Oh, I am sitting here and picking. I am not doing anything."

"You had better go home, and not sit here in the dust."

"It is best that I sit here."

Then Gösta Berling sits down beside him.

"It is not so easy to be a priest," he says after a while.

"It is all very well down here where there are people," answers the clergyman. "It is worse up there."

Gösta understands what he means. He knows those parishes in Northern Värmland where sometimes there is not even a house for the clergyman, where there are not more than a couple of people in ten miles of country, where the clergyman is the only educated man. The Broby minister had been in such a parish for over twenty years.

"That is where we are sent when we are young," says Gösta. "It is impossible to hold out with such a life; and so one is ruined forever. There are many who have gone under up there."

"Yes," says the Broby clergyman; "a man is destroyed by loneliness."

"A man comes," says Gösta, "eager and ardent, exhorts and admonishes, and thinks that all will be well, that the people will soon turn to better ways."

"Yes, yes."

"But soon he sees that words do not help. Poverty stands in the way. Poverty prevents all improvement."

"Poverty," repeats the clergyman,—"poverty has ruined my life."

"The young minister comes up there," continues Gösta, "poor as all the others. He says to the drunkard: Stop drinking!"

"Then the drunkard answers," interrupts the clergyman: "Give me something which is better than brandy! Brandy is furs in winter, coolness in summer. Brandy is a warm house and a soft bed. Give me those, and I will drink no more."

"And then," resumes Gösta, "the minister says to the thief: You shall not steal; and to the cruel husband: You shall not beat your wife; and to the superstitious: You shall believe in God and not in devils and goblins. But the thief answers: Give me bread; and the cruel husband says: Make us rich, and we will not quarrel; and the superstitious say: Teach us better. But who can help them without money?"

"It is true, true every word," cried the clergyman. "They believed in God, but more in the devil, and most in the mountain goblin. The crops were all turned into the still. There seemed to be no end to the misery. In most of the gray cottages there was want. Hidden sorrow made the women's tongues bitter. Discomfort drove their husbands to drink. They could not look after their fields or their cattle. They made a fool of their minister. What could a man do with them? They did not understand what I said to them from the pulpit. They did not believe what I wanted to teach them. And no one to consult, no one who could help me to keep up my courage."

"There are those who have stood out," says Gösta. "God's grace has been so great to some that they have not returned from such a life broken men. They have had strength;

they have borne the loneliness, the poverty, the hopelessness. They have done what little good they could and have not despaired. Such men have always been and still are. I greet them as heroes. I will honor them as long as I live. I was not able to stand out."

"I could not," added the clergyman.

"The minister up there thinks," says Gösta, musingly, "that he will be a rich man, an exceedingly rich man. No one who is poor can struggle against evil. And so he begins to hoard."

"If he had not hoarded he would have drunk," answers the old man; "he sees so much misery."

"Or he would become dull and lazy, and lose all strength. It is dangerous for him who is not born there to come thither."

"He has to harden himself to hoard. He pretends at first; then it becomes a habit."

"He has to be hard both to himself and to others," continues Gösta; "it is hard to amass. He must endure hate and scorn; he must go cold and hungry and harden his heart: it almost seems as if he had forgotten why he began to hoard."

The Broby clergyman looked startled at him. He wondered if Gösta sat there and made a fool of him. But Gösta was only eager and earnest. It was as if he was speaking of his own life.

"It was so with me," says the old man quietly.

"But God watches over him," interrupts Gösta. "He wakes in him the thoughts of his youth when he has amassed enough. He gives the minister a sign when His people need him."

"But if the minister does not obey the sign, Gösta Berling?"

"He cannot withstand it," says Gösta, and smiles. "He is so moved by the thought of the warm cottages which he will help the poor to build."

The clergyman looks down on the little heaps he had raised from the sticks of the pile of shame. The longer he talks with Gösta, the more he is convinced that the latter is right. He had always had the thought of doing good some day, when he had enough,—of course he had had that thought.

"Why does he never build the cottages?" he asks shyly.

"He is ashamed. Many would think that he did what he always had meant to do through fear of the people."

"He cannot bear to be forced, is that it?"

"He can however do much good secretly. Much help is needed this year. He can find some one who will dispense his gifts. I understand what it all means," cries Gösta, and his eyes shone. "Thousands shall get bread this year from one whom they load with curses."

"It shall be so, Gösta."

A feeling of transport came over the two who had so failed in the vocation they had chosen. The desire of their youthful days to serve God and man filled them. They gloated over the good deeds they would do. Gösta would help the minister.

"We will get bread to begin with," says the clergyman.

"We will get teachers. We will have a surveyor come, and divide up the land. Then the people shall learn how to till their fields and tend their cattle."

"We will build roads and open new districts."

"We will make locks at the falls at Berg, so that there will be an open way between Löfven and Väner."

"All the riches of the forest will be of double blessing when the way to the sea is opened."

"Your head shall be weighed down by blessings," cries Gösta.

The clergyman looks up. They read in one another's eyes the same burning enthusiasm.

But at the same moment the eyes of both fall on the pile of shame.

"Gösta," says the old man, "all that needs a young man's strength, but I am dying. You see what is killing me."

"Get rid of it!"

"How, Gösta Berling?"

Gösta moves close up to him and looks sharply into his eyes. "Pray to God for rain," he says. "You are going to preach next Sunday. Pray for rain."

The old clergyman sinks down in terror.

"If you are in earnest, if you are not he who has brought the drought to the land, if you had meant to serve the Most High with your hardness, pray God for rain. That shall be the token; by that we shall know if God wishes what we wish."

When Gösta drove down Broby hill, he was astonished at himself and at the enthusiasm which had taken hold of him. But it could be a beautiful life—yes, but not for him. Up there they would have none of his services.

In the Broby church the sermon was over and the usual prayers read. The minister was just going to step down from the pulpit, but he hesitated, finally he fell on his knees and prayed for rain.

He prayed as a desperate man prays, with few words, without coherency.

"If it is my sin which has called down Thy wrath, let me alone suffer! If there is any pity in Thee, Thou God of mercy, let it rain! Take the shame from me! Let it rain in answer to my prayer! Let the rain fall on the fields of the poor! Give Thy people bread!"

The day was hot; the sultriness was intolerable.

The congregation sat as if in a torpor; but at these broken words, this hoarse despair, every one had awakened.

"If there is a way of expiation for me, give rain—"

He stopped speaking. The doors stood open. There came a violent gust of wind. It rushed along the ground, whirled into the church, in a cloud of dust, full of sticks and straw. The clergyman could not continue; he staggered down from the pulpit.

The people trembled. Could that be an answer?

But the gust was only the forerunner of the thunderstorm. It came rushing with an unheard-of violence. When the psalm was sung, and the clergyman stood by the altar, the lightning was already flashing, and the thunder crashing, drowning the sound of his voice. As the sexton struck up the final march, the first drops were already pattering against the green window-panes, and the people hurried out to see the rain. But they were not content with that: some wept, others laughed, while they let the torrents stream over them. Ah, how great had been their need! How unhappy they had been! But God is good! God let it rain. What joy, what joy!

The Broby clergyman was the only one who did not come out into the rain. He lay on his knees before the altar and did not rise. The joy had been too violent for him. He died of happiness.

CHAPTER XVII. THE CHILD'S MOTHER

THE child was born in a peasant's house east of the Klar river. The child's mother had come seeking employment one day in early June.

She had been unfortunate, she had said to the master and mistress, and her mother had been so hard to her that she had had to run away from home. She called herself Elizabeth Karlsdotter; but she would not say from whence she came, for then perhaps they would tell her parents that she was there, and if they should find her, she would be tortured to death, she knew it. She asked for no pay, only food and a roof over her head. She could work, weave or spin, and take care of the cows,—whatever they wanted. If they wished, she could also pay for herself.

She had been clever enough to come to the farmhouse bare-foot, with her shoes under her arm; she had coarse hands; she spoke the country dialect; and she wore a peasant woman's clothes. She was believed.

The master thought she looked sickly, and did not count much on her fitness for work. But somewhere the poor thing must be. And so she was allowed to stop.

There was something about her which made every one on the farm kind to her. She had come to "a good place. The people were serious and reticent Her mistress liked her; when she discovered that she could weave, they borrowed a loom from the vicarage, and the child's mother worked at it the whole summer.

It never occurred to any one that she needed to be spared; she had to work like a peasant girl the whole time. She liked too to have much work. She was not unhappy. Life among the peasants pleased her, although she lacked all her accustomed conveniences. But everything was taken so simply and quietly there. Every one's thoughts were on his or her work; the days passed so uniform and monotonous that one mistook the day and thought it was the middle of the week when Sunday came.

One day at the end of August there had been haste with the oat crop, and the child's mother had gone out with the others to bind the sheaves. She had strained herself, and the child had been born, but too soon. She had expected it in October. Now the farmer's wife stood with the child in the living room to warm it by the fire, for the poor little thing was shivering in the August heat. The child's mother lay in a room beyond and listened to what they said of the little one. She could imagine how the men and maids came up and looked at him.

"Such a poor little thing," they all said, and then followed always, without fail:—

"Poor little thing, with no father!"

They did not complain of the child's crying: they thought a child needed to cry; and, when everything was considered, the child was strong for its age; had it but a father, all would have been well.

The mother lay and listened and wondered. The matter suddenly seemed to her incredibly important. How would he get through life, the poor little thing?

She had made her plans before. She would remain at the farm-house the first year. Then she would hire a room and earn her bread at the loom. She meant to earn enough to feed and clothe the child. Her husband could continue to believe that she was unworthy. She had thought that the child perhaps would be a better man if she alone brought it up, than if a stupid and conceited father should guide it.

But now, since the child was born, she could not see the matter in the same way. Now she thought that she had been selfish. "The child must have a father," she said to herself.

If he had not been such a pitiful little thing, if he had been able to eat and sleep like other children, if his head had not always sunk down on one shoulder, and if he had not so nearly died when the attack of cramp came, it would not have been so important.

It was not so easy to decide, but decide she must immediately. The child was three days old, and the peasants in Värmland seldom wait longer to have the child baptized. Under what name should the baby be entered in the church-register, and what would the clergyman want to know about the child's mother?

It was an injustice to the child to let him be entered as fatherless. If he should be a weak and sickly man, how could she take the responsibility of depriving him of the advantages of birth and riches?

The child's mother had noticed that there is generally great joy and excitement when a child comes into the world. Now it seemed to her that it must be hard for this baby to live, whom every one pitied. She wanted to see him sleeping on silk and lace, as it behoves a count's son. She wanted to see him encompassed with joy and pride.

The child's mother began to think that she had done its father too great an injustice. Had she the right to keep him for herself? That she could not have. Such a precious little thing, whose worth it is not in the power of man to calculate, should she take that for her own? That would not be honest.

But she did not wish to go back to her husband. She feared that it would be her death. But the child was in greater danger than she. He might die any minute, and he was not baptized.

That which had driven her from her home, the grievous sin which had dwelt in her heart, was gone. She had now no love for any other than the child.

It was not too heavy a duty to try to get him his right place in life.

The child's mother had the farmer and his wife called and told them everything. The husband journeyed to Borg to tell Count Dohna that his countess was alive, and that there was a child.

The peasant came home late in the evening; he had not met the count, for he had gone away, but he had been to the minister at Svartsjö, and talked with him of the matter.

Then the countess heard that her marriage had been declared invalid, and that she no longer had a husband.

The minister wrote a friendly letter to her, and offered her a home in his house.

A letter from her own father to Count Henrik, which must have reached Borg a few days after her flight, was also sent to her. It was just that letter in which the old man had begged the count to hasten to make his marriage legal, which had indicated to the count the easiest way to be rid of his wife.

It is easy to imagine that the child's mother was seized with anger more than sorrow, when she heard the peasant's story.

She lay awake the whole night. The child must have a father, she thought over and over again.

The next morning the peasant had to drive to Ekeby for her, and go for Gösta Berling.

Gösta asked the silent man many questions, but could find out nothing. Yes, the countess had been in his house the whole summer. She had been well and had worked. Now a child was born. The child was weak; but the mother would soon be strong again.

Gösta asked if the countess knew that the marriage had been annulled.

Yes, she knew it now. She had heard it yesterday,

And as long as the drive lasted Gösta had alternately fever and chills.

What did she want of him? Why did she send for him?

He thought of the life that summer on Löfven's shores. They had let the days go by with jests and laughter and pleasure parties, while she had worked and suffered.

He had never thought of the possibility of ever seeing her again. Ah, if he had dared to hope! He would have then come into her presence a better man. What had he now to look back on but the usual follies!

About eight o'clock in the evening he arrived, and was immediately taken to the child's mother. It was dark in the room. He could scarcely see her where she lay. The farmer and his wife came in also.

Now you must know that she whose white face shone in the dimness was always the noblest and the purest he knew, the most beautiful soul which had ever arrayed itself in earthly dust. When he once again felt the bliss of being near her, he longed to throw himself on his knees and thank her for having again appeared to him; but he was so overpowered by emotion that he could neither speak nor act.

"Dear Countess Elizabeth!" he only cried.

"Good-evening, Gösta."

She gave him her hand, which seemed once more to have become soft and transparent. She lay silent, while he struggled with his emotion.

The child's mother was not shaken by any violently raging feelings when she saw Gösta. It surprised her only that he seemed to consider her of chief importance, when he ought to understand that it now only concerned the child.

"Gösta," she said gently, "you must help me now, as you once promised. You know that my husband has abandoned me, so that my child has no father."

"Yes, countess; but that can certainly be changed. Now that there is a child, the count can be forced to make the marriage legal. You may be certain that I shall help you!"

The countess smiled. "Do you think that I will force myself upon Count Dohna?"

The blood surged up to Gösta's head. What did she wish then? What did she want of him?

"Come here, Gösta," she said, and again stretched out her hand. "You must not be angry with me for what I am going to say; but I thought that you who are—who are—"

"A dismissed priest, a drunkard, a pensioner, Ebba Dohna's murderer; I know the whole list—"

"Are you already angry, Gösta?"

"I would rather that you did not say anything more."

But the child's mother continued:—

"There are many, Gösta, who would have liked to be your wife out of love; but it is not so with me. If I loved you I should not dare to speak as I am speaking now. For myself I would never ask such a thing, Gösta; but do you see, I can do it for the sake of the child. You must understand what I mean to beg of you. Of course it is a great degradation for you, since I am an unmarried woman who has a child. I did not think that you would be willing to do it because you are worse than others; although, yes, I did think of that too. But first I thought that you could be willing, because you are kind, Gösta, because you are a hero and can sacrifice yourself. But it is perhaps too much to ask. Perhaps such a thing would be impossible for a man. If you despise me too much, if it is too loathsome for you to give your name to another man's child, say so! I shall not be angry. I understand that it is too much to ask; but the child is sick, Gösta. It is cruel at his baptism not to be able to give the name of his mother's husband."

He, hearing her, experienced the same feeling as when that spring day he had put her on land and left her to her fate. Now he had to help her to ruin her life, her whole future life. He who loved her had to do it.

"I will do everything you wish, countess," he said.

The next day he spoke to the dean at Bro, for there the banns were to be called.

The good old dean was much moved by his story, and promised to take all the responsibility of giving her away.

"Yes," he said, "you must help her, Gösta, otherwise she might become insane. She thinks that she has injured the child by depriving it of its position in life. She has a most sensitive conscience, that woman."

"But I know that I shall make her unhappy," cried Gösta.

"That you must not do, Gösta. You must be a sensible man now, with wife and child to care for."

The dean had to journey down to Svartsjö and speak to both the minister there and the judge. The end of it all was that the next Sunday, the first of September, the banns were called in Svartsjö between Gösta Berling and Elizabeth von Thurn.

Then the child's mother was carried with the greatest care to Ekeby, and there the child was baptized.

The dean talked to her, and told her that she could still recall her decision to marry such a man as Gösta Berling. She ought to first write to her father.

"I cannot repent," she said; "think if my child should die before it had a father."

When the banns had been thrice asked, the child's mother had been well and up several days. In the afternoon the dean came to Ekeby and married her to Gösta Berling. But no one thought of it as a wedding. No guests were invited. They only gave the child a father, nothing more.

The child's mother shone with a quiet joy, as if she had attained a great end in life. The bridegroom was in despair. He thought how she had thrown away her life by a marriage with him. He saw with dismay how he scarcely existed for her. All her thoughts were with her child.

A few days after the father and mother were mourning. The child had died.

Many thought that the child's mother did not mourn so violently nor so deeply as they had expected; she had a look of triumph. It was as if she rejoiced that she had thrown away her life for the sake of the child. When he joined the angels, he would still remember that a mother on earth had loved him.

All this happened quietly and unnoticed. When the banns were published for Gösta Berling and Elizabeth von Thurn in the Svartsjö church, most of the congregation did not even know who the bride was. The clergyman and the gentry who knew the story said little about it. It was as if they were afraid that some one who had lost faith in the power of conscience should wrongly interpret the young woman's action. They were so afraid, so afraid lest some one should come and say: "See now, she could not conquer her love for Gösta; she has married him under a plausible pretext." Ah, the old people were always so careful of that young woman! Never could they bear to hear anything evil of her. They would scarcely acknowledge that she had sinned. They would not agree that any fault stained that soul which was so afraid of evil.

Another great event happened just then, which also caused Gösta's marriage to be little discussed.

Major Samzelius had met with an accident. He had become more and more strange and misanthropic. His chief intercourse was with animals, and he had collected a small menagerie at Sjö.

He was dangerous too; for he always carried a loaded gun, and shot it off time after time without paying much attention to his aim. One day he was bitten by a tame bear which he had shot without intending it. The wounded animal threw itself on him, and succeeded in giving him a terrible bite in the arm. The beast broke away and took refuge in the forest.

The major was put to bed and died of the wound, but not till just before Christmas. Had his wife known that he lay ill, she could have resumed her sway over Ekeby. But the pensioners knew that she would not come before their year was out.

CHAPTER XVIII. AMOR VINCIT OMNIA

UNDER the stairs to the gallery in the Svartsjö church is a lumber-room filled with the grave-diggers' worn-out shovels, with broken benches, with rejected tin labels and other rubbish.

There, where the dust lies thickest and seems to hide it from every human eye, stands a chest, inlaid with mother-of-pearl in the most perfect mosaic. If one scrapes the dust away, it seems to shine and glitter like a mountain-wall in a fairy-tale. The chest is locked, and the key is in good keeping; it may not be used. No mortal man may cast a glance into that chest. No one knows what is in it. First, when the nineteenth century has reached its close, may the key be placed in the lock, the cover be lifted, and the treasures which it guarded be seen by men.

So has he who owned the chest ordained.

On the brass-plate of the cover stands an inscription: "Labor vincit omnia." But another inscription would be more appropriate. "Amor vincit omnia" ought to stand there. For the chest in the rubbish room under the gallery stairs is a testimony of the omnipotence of love.

O Eros, all-conquering god!

Thou, O Love, art indeed eternal! Old are people on the earth, but thou hast followed them through the ages.

Where are the gods of the East, the strong heroes who carried weapons of thunderbolts,—they who on the shores of holy rivers took offerings of honey and milk? They are dead. Dead is Bel, the mighty warrior, and Thot, the hawk-headed champion. The glorious ones are dead who rested on the cloud banks of Olympus; so too the mighty who dwelt in the turreted Valhalla. All the old gods are dead except Eros, Eros, the all-powerful!

His work is in everything you see. He supports the race. See him everywhere! Whither can you go without finding the print of his foot? What has your ear perceived, where the humming of his wings has not been the key-note? He lives in the hearts of men and in the sleeping germ. See with trembling his presence in inanimate things!

What is there which does not long and desire? What is there which escapes his dominion? All the gods of revenge will fall, all the powers of strength and might. Thou, O Love, art eternal!

Old Uncle Eberhard is sitting at his writing-desk,—a splendid piece of furniture with a hundred drawers, with marble top and ornaments of blackened brass. He works with eagerness and diligence, alone in the pensioners' wing.

Oh, Eberhard, why do you not wander about wood and field in these last days of the departing summer like the other pensioners? No one, you know, worships unpunished the goddess of wisdom. Your back is bent with sixty and some years; the hair which covers your head is not your own; the wrinkles crowd one another on your brow, which arches over hollow eyes; and the decay of old age is drawn in the thousand lines about your empty mouth.

Oh, Eberhard, why do you not wander about wood and field? Death parts you just so much the sooner from your desk, because you have not let life tempt you from it.

Uncle Eberhard draws a thick stroke under his last line. From the desk's innumerable drawers he drags out yellowed, closely scribbled manuscripts, all the different' parts of his great work,—that work which is to carry on Eberhard Berggren's name through all time. But just as he has piled up manuscript on manuscript, and is staring at them in silent rapture, the door opens, and in walks the young countess.

There she is, the old men's young mistress,—she whom they wait on and adore more than grandparents wait on and adore the first grandson. There she is whom they had found in poverty and in sickness, and to whom they had now given all the glory of the world, just as the king in the fairy tale did to the beautiful beggar girl he found in the forest. It is for her that the horn and violin now sound at Ekeby,—for her everything moves, breathes, works on the great estate.

She is well again, although still very weak. Time goes slowly for her alone in the big house, and, as she knows that the pensioners are away, she wishes to see what it looks like in the pensioners' wing, that notorious room.

So she comes softly in and looks up at the whitewashed walls and the yellow striped bed-curtains, but she is embarrassed when she sees that the room is not empty.

Uncle Eberhard goes solemnly towards her, and leads her forward to the great pile of paper.

"Look, countess," he says; "now my work is ready. Now shall what I have written go out into the world. Now great things are going to happen."

"What is going to happen, Uncle Eberhard?"

"Oh, countess, it is going to strike like a thunderbolt, a bolt which enlightens and kills. Ever since Moses dragged him out of Sinai's thunder-cloud and put him on the throne of grace in the innermost sanctuary of the temple, ever since then he has sat secure, the old Jehovah; but now men shall see what he is: Imagination, emptiness, exhalation, the stillborn child of our own brain. He shall sink into nothingness," said the old man, and laid his wrinkled hand on the pile of manuscript. "It stands here; and when people read this, they will have to believe. They will rise up and acknowledge their own stupidity; they will use crosses for kindling-wood, churches for storehouses, and clergymen will plough the earth."

"Oh, Uncle Eberhard," says the countess, with a slight shudder, "are you such a dreadful person? Do such dreadful things stand there?"

"Dreadful!" repeated the old man, "it is only the truth. But we are like little boys who hide their faces in a woman's skirt as soon as they meet a stranger: we have accustomed ourselves to hide from the truth, from the eternal stranger. But now he shall come and dwell among us, now he shall be known by all."

"By all?"

"Not only by philosophers, but by everybody; do you understand, countess, by everybody."

"And so Jehovah shall die?"

"He and all angels, all saints, all devils, all lies."

"Who shall then rule the world?"

"Do you believe that any one has ruled it before?

Do you believe in that Providence which looks after sparrows and the hair of your head? No one has ruled it, no one shall rule it."

"But we, we people, what will we become—"

"The same which we have been—dust. That which is burned out can burn no longer; it is dead. We about whom the fire of life flickers are only fuel. Life's sparks fly from one to another. We are lighted, flame up, and die out. That is life."

"Oh, Eberhard, is there no life of the spirit?"

"None."

"No life beyond the grave?"

"None."

"No good, no evil, no aim, no hope?"

"None."

The young woman walks over to the window. She looks out at the autumn's yellowed leaves, at dahlias and asters which hang their heavy heads on broken stalks. She sees the Löfven's black waves, the autumn's dark storm-clouds, and for a moment she inclines towards repudiation.

"Uncle Eberhard," she says, "how ugly and gray the world is; how profitless everything is! I should like to lie down and die."

But then she hears a murmur in her soul. The vigor of life and its strong emotions cry out for the happiness of living.

"Is there nothing," she breaks out, "which can give life beauty, since you have taken from me God and immortality?"

"Work," answers the old man.

But she looks out again, and a feeling of scorn for that poor wisdom creeps over her. The unfathomable rises before her; she feels the spirit dwelling in every-thing; she is sensible of the power which lies bound in seemingly dead material, but which can develop into a thousand forms of shifting life. Dizzily she seeks for a name for the presence of God's spirit in nature.

"Oh, Eberhard," she says, "what is work? Is it a god? Has it any meaning in itself? Name another!"

"I know no other," answered the old man. Then she finds the name which she is seeking,—a poor, often sullied name.

"Uncle Eberhard, why do you not speak of love?" A smile glides over the empty mouth where the thousand wrinkles cross.

"Here," says the philosopher, and strikes the heavy packet with his clenched hand, "here all the gods are slain, and I have not forgotten Eros. What is love but a longing of the flesh? In what does he stand higher than the other requirements of the body? Make hunger a god! Make fatigue a god! They are just as worthy. Let there be an end to such absurdities! Let the truth live!"

The young countess sinks her head. It is not so, all that is not true; but she cannot contest it.

"Your words have wounded my soul," she says; "but still I do not believe you. The gods of revenge and violence you may be able to kill, no others."

But the old man takes her hand, lays it on the book, and swears in the fanaticism of unbelief. "When you have read this, you must believe."

"May it never come before my eyes," she says, "for if I believe that, I cannot live."

And she goes sadly from the philosopher. But he sits for a long time and thinks, when she has gone.

Those old manuscripts, scribbled over with heathenish confessions, have not yet been tested before the world. Uncle Eberhard's name has not yet reached the heights of fame.

His great work lies hidden in a chest in the lumber-room under the gallery stairs in the Svartsjö church; it shall first see the light of day at the end of the century.

But why has he done this? Was he afraid not to have proved his point? Did he fear persecutions? You little know Uncle Eberhard.

Understand it now; he has loved the truth, not his own glory. So he has sacrificed the latter, not the former, in order that a deeply loved child might die in the belief in that she has most cared for.

O Love, thou art indeed eternal!

CHAPTER XIX. THE BROOM-GIRL

NO one knows the place in the lee of the mountain where the pines grow thickest and deep layers of moss cover the ground. How should any one know it? No man's foot has ever trodden it before; no man's tongue has given it a name. No path leads to that hidden spot. It is the most solitary tract in the forest, and now thousands of people are looking for it.

What an endless procession of seekers! They would fill the Bro church,—not only Bro, but Löfviks and Svartsjö.

All who live near the road rush out and ask, "Has anything happened? Is the enemy upon us? Where are you going? Tell us where."

"We are searching," they answer. "We have been searching for two days. We shall go on today; but afterwards we can do no more. We are going to look through the Björne wood and the firclad heights west of Ekeby.

It was from Nygård, a poor district far away among the eastern mountains, the procession had first started. The beautiful girl with the heavy, black hair and the red cheeks had disappeared a week before. The broom-girl, to whom Gösta Ber-ling had wished to engage himself, had been lost in the great forests. No one had seen her for a week.

So the people started from Nygård to search through the wood. And everybody they met joined in the search.

Sometimes one of the new-comers asks,—

"You men from Nygård, how has it all happened? Why do you let that beautiful girl go alone in strange paths? The forest is deep, and God has taken away her reason."

"No one disturbs her," they answer; "she disturbs no one. She goes as safely as a child. Who is safer than one God himself must care for? She has always come back before."

So have the searching crowd gone through the eastern woods, which shut in Nygård from the plain. Now on the third day it passes by the Bro church towards the woods west of Ekeby.

But wherever they go, a storm of wondering rages; constantly a man from the crowd has to stop to answer questions: "What do you want? What are you looking for?"

"We are looking for the blue-eyed, dark-haired girl. She has laid herself down to die in the forest. She has been gone a week."

"Why has she laid herself down to die in the forest? Was she hungry? Was she unhappy?"

"She has not suffered want, but she had a misfortune last spring. She has seen that mad priest, Gösta Berling, and loved him for many years. She knew no better. God had taken away her wits."

"Last spring the misfortune happened,—before that, he had never looked at her. Then he said to her that she should be his sweetheart. It was only in jest; he let her go again, but she could not be consoled. She kept coming to Ekeby. She went after him wherever he went. He wearied of her. When she was there last, they set their dogs on her. Since then no one has seen her."

To the rescue, to the rescue! A human life is concerned! A human being has laid herself down to die in the wood! Perhaps she is already dead. Perhaps, too, she is still wandering there without finding the right way. The forest is wide, and her reason is with God.

Come everybody, men and women and children! Who can dare to stay at home? Who knows if God does not intend to use just him? Come all of you, that your soul may not some day wander helpless in dry places, seek rest and find none! Come! God has taken her reason, and the forest is wide.

It is wonderful to see people unite for some great object. But it is not hunger, nor the fear of God, nor war which has driven these out. Their trouble is without profit, their striving without reward; they are only going to find a fool. So many steps, so much anxiety, so many prayers it all costs, and yet it will only be rewarded by the recovery of a poor, misguided girl, whose reason is with God.

Those anxious searchers fill the highway. With earnest eyes they gauge the forest; they go forward sadly, for they know that they are more probably searching for the dead than the living.

Ah, that black thing at the foot of the cliff, it is not an ant-hill after all, but a fallen tree. Praised be Heaven, only a fallen tree! But they cannot see distinctly, the pines grow so thick.

It is the third day of the search; they are used to the work. They search under the sloping rock, on which the foot can slide, under fallen trees, where arm or leg easily could have been broken, under the thick growing pines' branches, trailing over soft moss, inviting to rest.

The bear's den, the fox's hole, the badger's deep home, the red cranberry slope, the silver fir, the mountain, which the forest fire laid waste a month ago, the stone which the giant threw,—all that have they found, but not the place under the rock where the black thing is lying. No one has been there to see if it is an ant-hill, or a tree-trunk, or a human being. Alas! it is indeed a human being, but no one has been there to see her.

The evening sun is shining on the other side of the wood, but the young woman is not found. What should they do now? Should they search through the wood once more? The wood is dangerous in the dark; there are bottomless bogs and deep clefts. And what could they, who had found nothing when the sun was shining, find when it was gone?

"Let us go to Ekeby!" cries one in the crowd.

"Let us go to Ekeby!" they all cry together.

"Let us ask those pensioners why they let loose the dogs on one whose reason God had taken, why they drove a fool to despair. Our poor, hungry children weep; our clothes are torn; the potatoes rot in the ground; our horses are running loose; our cows get no care; we are nearly dead with fatigue—and the fault is theirs. Let us go to Ekeby and ask about this.

"During this cursed year we have had to suffer everything. The winter will bring us starvation. Whom does God's hand seek? It was not the Broby clergyman. His prayers could reach God's ear. Who, then, if not these pensioners? Let us go to Ekeby!

"They have ruined the estate, they have driven the major's wife to beg on the highway. It is their fault that we have no work. The famine is their doing. Let us go to Ekeby!"

So the dark, embittered men crowd down to Ekeby; hungry women with weeping children in their arms follow them; and last come the cripples and the old men. And the bitterness spreads like an ever-increasing storm from the old men to the women, from the women to the strong men at the head of the train.

It is the autumn-flood which is coming. Pensioners, do you remember the spring-flood?

A cottager who is ploughing in a pasture at the edge of the wood hears the people's mad cries. He throws himself on one of his horses and gallops down to Ekeby.

"Disaster is coming!" he cries; "the bears are coming, the wolves are coming, the goblins are coming to take Ekeby!"

He rides about the whole estate, wild with terror.

"All the devils in the forest are let loose!" he cries. "They are coming to take Ekeby! Save yourselves who can! The devils are coming to burn the house and to kill the pensioners!"

And behind him can be heard the din and cries of the rushing horde. Does it know what it wants, that storming stream of bitterness? Does it want fire, or murder, or plunder?

They are not human beings; they are wild beasts. Death to Ekeby, death to the pensioners!

Here brandy flows in streams. Here gold lies piled in the vaults. Here the storehouses are filled with grain and meat. Why should the honest starve, and the guilty have plenty?

But now your time is out, the measure is overflowing, pensioners. In the wood lies one who condemns you; we are her deputies.

The pensioners stand in the big building and see the people coming. They know already why they are denounced. For once they are innocent. If that poor girl has lain down to die in the wood, it is not because they have set the dogs on her,—that they have never done,—but because Gösta Berling, a week ago, was married to Countess Elizabeth.

But what good is it to speak to that mob? They are tired, they are hungry; revenge drives them on, plunder tempts them. They rush down with wild cries, and before them rides the cottager, whom fear has driven mad.

The pensioners have hidden the young countess in their innermost room. Löwenborg and Eberhard are to sit there and guard her; the others go out to meet the people. They are standing on the steps before the main building, unarmed, smiling, as the first of the noisy crowd reach the house.

And the people stop before that little group of quiet men. They had wanted to throw them down on the ground and trample them under their iron-shod heels, as the people at the Lund ironworks used to do with the manager and overseer fifty years ago; but they had expected closed doors, raised weapons; they had expected resistance and fighting.

"Dear friends," say the pensioners; "dear friends, you are tired and hungry; let us give you a little food and first a glass of Ekeby's own home-brewed brandy."

The people will not listen; they scream and threaten. But the pensioners are not discouraged.

"Only wait," they say; "only wait a second. See, Ekeby stands open. The cellar doors are open; the store-rooms are open; the dairy is open. Your women are dropping with fatigue; the children are crying. Let us get them food first! Then you can kill us. We will not run away. The attic is full of apples. Let us go after apples for the children!"

An hour later the feasting is in full swing at Ekeby. The biggest feast the big house has ever seen is celebrated there that autumn night under the shining full moon.

Woodpiles have been lighted; the whole estate flames with bonfires. The people sit about in groups, enjoying warmth and rest, while all the good things of the earth are scattered over them.

Resolute men have gone to the farmyard and taken what was needed. Calves and sheep have been killed, and even one or two oxen. The animals have been cut up and roasted in a trice. Those starving hundreds are devouring the food. Animal after animal is led out and slaughtered. It looks as if the whole barn would be emptied in one night.

They had just baked that day. Since the young Countess Elizabeth had come, there had once more been industry in-doors. It seemed as if the young woman never for an instant remembered that she was Gösta Berling's wife. Neither he nor she acted as if it were so; but on the other hand she made herself the mistress of Ekeby. As a good and capable woman always must do, she tried with burning zeal to remedy the waste and the shiftlessness which reigned in the house. And she was obeyed. The servants felt a certain pleasure in again having a mistress over them.

But what did it matter that she had filled the rafters with bread, that she had made cheeses and churned and brewed during the month of September?

Out to the people with everything there is, so that they may not burn down Ekeby and kill the pensioners! Out with bread, butter, cheese! Out with the beer-barrels, out with the hams from the storehouse, out with the brandy-kegs, out with the apples!

How can all the riches of Ekeby suffice to diminish the people's anger? If we get them away before any dark deed is done, we may be glad.

It is all done for the sake of her who is now mistress at Ekeby. The pensioners are brave men; they would have defended themselves if they had followed their own will. They would rather have driven away the marauders with a few sharp shots, but for her, who is gentle and mild and begs for the people.

As the night advances, the crowds become gentler. The warmth and the rest and the food and the brandy assuage their terrible madness. They begin to jest and laugh.

As it draws towards midnight, it looks as if they were preparing to leave. The pensioners stop bringing food and wine, drawing corks and pouring ale. They draw a sigh of relief, in the feeling that the danger is over.

But just then a light is seen in one of the windows of the big house. All who see it utter a cry. It is a young woman who is carrying the light.

It had only been for a second. The vision disappeared; but the people think they have recognized the woman.

"She had thick black hair and red cheeks!" they cry. "She is here! They have hidden her here!"

"Oh, pensioners, have you her here? Have you got our child, whose reason God has taken, here at Ekeby? What are you doing with her? You let us grieve for her a whole week, search for three whole days. Away with wine and food! Shame to us, that we accepted anything from your hands! First, out with her! Then we shall know what we have to do to you."

The people are quick; quicker still are the pensioners. They rush in and bar the door. But how could they resist such a mass? Door after door is broken down. The pensioners are thrown one side; they are unarmed. They are wedged in the crowd, so that they cannot move. The people will come in to find the broom-girl.

In the innermost room they find her. No one has time to see whether she is light or dark. They lift her up and carry her out. She must not be afraid, they say. They are here to save her.

But they who now stream from the building are met by another procession.

In the most lonely spot in the forest the body of a woman, who had fallen over a high cliff and died in the fall, no longer rests. A child had found her. Searchers who had remained in the wood had lifted her on their shoulders. Here they come.

In death she is more beautiful than in life. Lovely she lies, with her long, black hair. Fair is the form since the eternal peace rests upon it.

Lifted high on the men's shoulders, she is carried through the crowd. With bent heads all do homage to the majesty of death.

"She has not been dead long," the men whisper. "She must have wandered in the woods till to-day. We think that she wanted to escape from us who were looking for her, and so fell over the cliff."

But if this is the broom-girl, who is the one who has been carried out of Ekeby?

The procession from the wood meets the procession from the house. Bonfires are burning all over the yard. The people can see both the women and recognize them. The other is the young countess at Borg.

"Oh! what is the meaning of this? Is this a new crime? Why is the young countess here at Ekeby? Why have they told us that she was far away or dead? In the name of justice, ought we not to throw ourselves on the pensioners and trample them to dust under iron-shod heels?"

Then a ringing voice is heard. Gösta Berling has climbed up on the balustrade and is speaking. "Listen to me, you monsters, you devils! Do you think there are no guns and powder at Ekeby, you madmen? Do you think that I have not wanted to shoot you like mad dogs, if she had not begged for you? Oh, if I had known that you would have touched her, not one of you should have been left alive!

"Why are you raging here to-night and threatening us with murder and fire? What have I to do with your crazy girls? Do I know where they run? I have been too kind to that one; that is the matter. I ought to have set the dogs on her,—it would have been better for us both,—but I did not. Nor have I ever promised to marry her; that I have never done. Remember that!

"But now I tell you that you must let her whom you have dragged out of the house go. Let her go, I say; and may the hands who' have touched her burn in everlasting fire! Do you not understand that she is as much above you as heaven is above the earth? She is as delicate as you are coarse; as good as you are bad.

"Now I will tell you who she is. First, she is an angel from heaven,—secondly, she has been married to the count at Borg. But her mother-in-law tortured her night and day; she had to stand at the lake and wash clothes like an ordinary maid; she was beaten and tormented as none of your women have ever been. Yes, she was almost ready to throw herself into the river, as we all know, because they were torturing the life out of her. I wonder which one of you was there then to save her life. Not one of you was there; but we pensioners, we did it.

"And when she afterwards gave birth to a child off in a farm-house, and the count sent her the message: 'We were married in a foreign land; we did not follow law and order. You are not my wife; I am not your husband. I care nothing for your child!'—yes, when that was so, and she did not want the child to stand fatherless in the church register, then you would have been proud enough if she had said to one of you: 'Come and marry me! I must have a father for the child!' But she chose none of you. She took Gösta Berling, the penniless priest, who may never speak the word of God. Yes, I tell you, peasants, that I have never done anything harder; for I was so unworthy of her that I did not dare to look her in the eyes, nor did I dare say no, for she was in despair.

"And now you may believe what evil you like of us pensioners; but to her we have done what good we could. And it is thanks to her that you have not all been killed to-night. But now I tell you: let her go, and go yourselves, or I think the earth will open and swallow you up. And as you go, pray God to forgive you for having frightened and grieved one who is so good and innocent. And now be off! We have had enough of you!"

Long before he had finished speaking, those who had carried out the countess had put her down on one of the stone steps; and now a big peasant came thoughtfully up to her and stretched out his great hand.

"Thank you, and good-night," he said. "We wish you no harm, countess."

After him came another and shook her hand. "Thanks, and good-night. You must not be angry with us!"

Gösta sprang down and placed himself beside her. Then they took his hand too.

So they came forward slowly, one after another, to bid them good-night before they went. They were once more subdued; again were they human beings, as they were when they left their homes that morning, before hunger and revenge had made them wild beasts.

They looked in the countess's face, and Gösta saw that the innocence and gentleness they saw there brought tears into the eyes of many. There was in them all a silent adoration of the noblest they had ever seen.

They could not all shake her hand. There were so many, and the young woman was tired and weak. But they all came and looked at her, and could take Gösta's hand,—his arm could stand a shaking.

Gösta stood as if in a dream. That evening a new love sprang up in his heart.

"Oh, my people," he thought, "oh, my people, how I love you!" He felt how he loved all that crowd who were disappearing into the darkness with the dead girl at the head of the procession, with their coarse clothes and evil-smelling shoes; those who lived in the gray huts at the edge of the wood; those who could not write and often not read; those who had never known the fulness and richness of life, only the struggle for their daily bread.

He loved them with a painful, burning tenderness which forced the tears from his eyes. He did not know what he wanted to do for them, but he loved them, each and all, with their faults, their vices and their weaknesses. Oh, Lord God, if the day could come when he too should be loved by them!

He awoke from his dream; his wife laid her hand on his arm. The people were gone. They were alone on the steps.

"Oh, Gösta, Gösta, how could you!" She put her hands before her face and wept. "It is true what I said," he cried. "I have never promised the broom-girl to marry her. 'Come here next Friday, and you shall see something funny!' was all I ever said to her. It is not my fault that she cared for me."

"Oh, it was not that; but how could you say to the people that I was good and pure? Gösta, Gösta! Do you not know that I loved you when I had no right to do it? I was ashamed, Gösta! I was ready to die of shame!"

And she was shaken by sobs.

He stood and looked at her.

"Oh, my friend, my beloved!" he said quietly. "How happy you are, who are so good! How happy to have such a beautiful soul!"

CHAPTER XX. KEVENHÜLLER

IN the year 1770, in Germany, the afterwards learned and accomplished Kevenhüller was born. He was the son of a count, and could have lived in lofty palaces and ridden at the Emperor's side if he had so wished; but he had not.

He could have liked to fasten windmill sails on the castle's highest tower, turn the hall into a locksmith's workshop, and the boudoir into a watch-maker's. He would have liked to fill the castle with whirling wheels and working levers. But when he could not do it he left all the pomp and apprenticed himself to a watch-maker. There he learned everything there was to learn about cog wheels, springs, and pendulums. He learned to make sun-dials and star-dials, clocks with singing canary-birds and horn-blowing shepherds, chimes which filled a whole church-tower with their wonderful machinery, and watch-works so small that they could be set in a locket.

When he had got his patent of mastership, he bound his knapsack on his back, took his stick in his hand, and wandered from place to place to study everything that went with rollers and wheels. Kevenhüller was no ordinary watch-maker; he wished to be a great inventor and to improve the world.

When he had so wandered through many lands, he turned his steps towards Värmland, to there study mill-wheels and mining. One beautiful summer morning it so happened that he was crossing the market-place of Karlstad. But that same beautiful summer morning it had pleased the wood-nymph to extend her walk as far as the town. The noble lady came also across the market-place from the opposite direction, and so met Kevenhüller.

That was a meeting for a watch-maker's apprentice. She had shining, green eyes, and a mass of light hair, which almost reached the ground, and she was dressed in green, changeable silk. She was the most beautiful woman Kevenhüller had ever seen.

He stood as if he had lost his wits, and stared at her as she came towards him.

She came direct from the deepest thicket of the wood, where the ferns are as high as trees, where the giant firs shut out the sun, so that it can only fall in golden drops on the yellow moss.

I should like to have been in Kevenhüller's place, to see her as she came with ferns and pine-needles tangled in her yellow, hair and a little black snake about her neck.

How the people must have stared at her! Horses bolted, frightened by her long, floating hair. The street boys ran after her. The men dropped their meat-axes to gape at her.

She herself went calm and majestic, only smiling a little at the excitement, so that Kevenhüller saw her small, pointed teeth shine between her red lips.

She had hung a cloak over her shoulders so that none should see who she was; but as ill-luck would have it, she had forgotten to cover her tail. It dragged along the paving-stones.

Kevenhüller saw the tail; he was sorry that a noble lady should make herself the laughing-stock of the town; so he bowed and said courteously:—

"Would it not please your Grace to lift your train?"

The wood-nymph was touched, not only by his kindness, but by his politeness. She stopped before him and looked at him, so that he thought that shining sparks passed from her eyes into his brain. "Kevenhüller," she said, "hereafter you shall be able with your two hands to execute whatever work you will, but only one of each kind."

She said it and she could keep her word. For who does not know that the wood-nymph has the power to give genius and wonderful powers to those who win her favor?

Kevenhüller remained in Karlstad and hired a workshop there. He hammered and worked night and day. In a week he had made a wonder. It was a carriage, which went by itself. It went up hill and down hill, went fast or slow, could be steered and turned, be stopped and started, as one wished.

Kevenhüller became famous. He was so proud of his carriage that he journeyed up to Stockholm to show it to the king. He did not need to wait for post-horses nor to scold ostlers. He proudly rode in his own carriage and was there in a few hours.

He rode right up to the palace, and the king came out with his court ladies and gentlemen and looked at him. They could not praise him enough.

The king then said: "You might give me that carriage, Kevenhüller." And although he answered no, the king persisted and wished to have the carriage.

Then Kevenhüller saw that in the king's train stood a court lady with light hair and a green dress. He recognized her, and he understood that it was she who had advised the king to ask him for his carriage. He was in despair. He could not bear that another should have his carriage, nor did he dare to say no to the king. Therefore he drove it with such speed against the palace wall that it was broken into a thousand pieces.

When he came home to Karlstad he tried to make another carriage. But he could not. Then he was dismayed at the gift the wood-nymph had given him. He had left the life of ease at his father's castle to be a benefactor to many, not to make wonders which only one could use. What good was it to him to be a great master, yes, the greatest of all masters, if he could not duplicate his marvels so that they were of use to thousands.

And he so longed for quiet, sensible work that he became a stone-cutter and mason. It was then he built the great stone tower down by the west bridge, and he meant to build walls and portals and courtyards, ramparts and turrets, so that a veritable castle should stand by the Klar River.

And there he should realize his childhood's dream. Everything which had to do with industry and handicraft should have a place in the castle halls. White millers and blacksmiths, watchmakers with green shades before their strained eyes, dyers with dark hands, weavers, turners, filers,—all should have their workshops in his castle.

And everything went well. Of the stones he himself had hewn he had with his own hand built the tower. He had fastened windmill sails on it,—for the tower was to be a mill,—and now he wanted to begin on the smithy.

But one day he stood and watched how the light, strong wings turned before the wind. Then his old longing came over him.

He shut himself in in his workshop, tasted no food, took no rest, and worked unceasingly. At the end of a week he had made a new marvel.

One day he climbed up on the roof of his tower and began to fasten wings to his shoulders.

Two street boys saw him, and they gave a cry which was heard through the whole town. They started off; panting, they ran up the streets and down the streets, knocking on all the doors, and screaming as they ran:—

"Kevenhüller is going to fly! Kevenhüller is going to fly!"

He stood calmly on the tower-roof and fastened on his wings, and in the meantime crowds of people came running through the narrow streets of old Karlstad. Soon the bridge was black with them. The market-place was packed, and the banks of the river swarmed with people.

Kevenhüller at last got his wings on and set out. He gave a couple of flaps with them, and then he was out in the air. He lay and floated high above the earth.

He drew in the air with long breaths; it was strong and pure. His breast expanded, and the old knights' blood began to seethe in him. He tumbled like a pigeon, he hovered like a hawk, his flight was as swift as the swallow's, as sure as the falcon's. If he had only been able to make such a pair of wings for every one of them! If he had only been able to give them all the power to raise themselves in this pure air! He could not enjoy it alone. Ah, that wood-nymph,—if he could only meet her!

Then he saw, with eyes which were almost blinded by the dazzling sunlight, how some one came flying towards him. Great wings like his own, and between the wings floated a human body. He saw floating yellow hair, billowy green silk, wild shining eyes. It was she, it was she!

Kevenhüller did not stop to consider. With furious speed he threw himself upon her to kiss her or to strike her,—he was not sure which,—but at any rate to force her to remove the curse from his existence. He did not look where he was going; he saw only the flying hair and the wild eyes. He came close up to her and stretched out his arms to seize her. But his wings caught in hers, and hers were the stronger. His wings were torn and destroyed; he himself was swung round and hurled down, he knew not whither.

When he returned to consciousness he lay on the roof of his own tower, with the broken flying-machine by his side. He had flown right against his own mill; the sails had caught him, whirled him round a couple of times, and then thrown him down on the tower roof.

So that was the end.

Kevenhüller was again a desperate man. He could not bear the thought of honest work, and he did not dare to use his magic power. If he should make another wonder and should then destroy it, his heart would break with sorrow. And if he did not destroy it, he would certainly go mad at the thought that he could not do good to others with it.

He looked up his knapsack and stick, let the mill stand as it was, and decided to go out and search for the wood-nymph.

In the course of his journeyings he came to Ekeby, a few years before the major's wife was driven out. There he was well received, and there he remained. The memories of his childhood came back to him, and he allowed them to call him count. His hair grew gray and his brain slept. He was so old that he could no longer believe in the feats of his youth. He was not the man who could work wonders. It was not he who had made the automatic carriage and the flying-machine. Oh, no,—tales, tales!

But then it happened that the major's wife was driven from Ekeby, and the pensioners were masters of the great estate. Then a life began there which had never been worse. A storm passed over the land; men warred on earth, and souls in heaven. Wolves came from Dovre with witches on their backs, and the wood-nymph came to Ekeby.

The pensioners did not recognize her. They thought that she was a poor and distressed woman whom a cruel mother-in-law had hunted to despair. So they gave her shelter, revered her like a queen, and loved her like a child.

Kevenhüller alone saw who she was. At first he was dazzled like the others. But one day she wore a dress of green, shimmering silk, and when she had that on, Kevenhüller recognized her.

There she sat on silken cushions, and all the old men made themselves ridiculous to serve her. One was cook and another footman; one reader, one court-musician, one shoemaker; they all had their occupations.

They said she was ill, the odious witch; but Kevenhüller knew what that illness meant. She was laughing at them all.

He warned the pensioners against her. "Look at her small, pointed teeth," he said, "and her wild, shining eyes. She is the wood-nymph,—all evil is about in these terrible times. I tell you she is the wood-nymph, come hither for our ruin. I have seen her before."

But when Kevenhüller saw the wood-nymph and had recognized her, the desire for work came over him. It began to burn and seethe in his brain; his fingers ached with longing to bend themselves about hammer and file; he could hold out no longer. With a bitter heart he put on his working-blouse and shut himself in in an old smithy, which was to be his workshop.

A cry went out from Ekeby over the whole of Värmland:—

"Kevenhüller has begun to work!"

A new wonder was to see the light. What should it be? Will he teach us to walk on the water, or to raise a ladder to the stars?

One night, the first or second of October, he had the wonder ready. He came out of the workshop and had it in his hand. It was a wheel which turned incessantly; as it turned, the spokes glowed like fire, and it gave out warmth and light. Kevenhüller had made a sun. When he came out of the workshop with it, the night grew so light that the sparrows began to chirp and the clouds to burn as if at dawn.

There should never again be darkness or cold on earth. His head whirled when he thought of it. The sun would continue to rise and set, but when it disappeared, thousands and thousands of his fire-wheels should flame through the land, and the air would quiver with warmth, as on the hottest summer-day. Harvests should ripen in midwinter; wild strawberries should cover the hillsides the whole year round; the ice should never bind the water.

His fire-wheel should create a new world. It should be furs to the poor and a sun to the miners. It should give power to the mills, life to nature, a new, rich, and happy existence to mankind. But at the same time he knew that it was all a dream and that the wood-nymph would never let him duplicate his wheel. And in his anger and longing for revenge, he thought that he would kill her, and then he no longer knew what he was doing.

He went to the main building, and in the hall under the stairs he put down his fire-wheel. It was his intention to set fire to the house and burn up the witch in it.

Then he went back to his workshop and sat there silently listening.

There was shouting and crying outside. Now they could see that a great deed was done.

Yes, run, scream, ring the alarm! But she is burning in there, the wood-nymph whom you laid on silken cushions.

May she writhe in torment, may she flee before the flames from room to room! Ah, how the green silk will blaze, and how the flames will play in her torrents of hair! Courage, flames! courage! Catch her, set fire to her! Witches burn! Fear not her magic, flames! Let her burn! There is one who for her sake must burn his whole life through.

Bells rang, wagons came rattling, pumps were brought out, water was carried up from the lake, people came running from all the neighboring villages. There were cries and waitings and commands; that was the roof, which had fallen in; there was the terrible crackling and roaring of a fire. But nothing disturbed Kevenhüller. He sat on the chopping-block and rubbed his hands.

Then he heard a crash, as if the heavens had fallen, and he started up in triumph. "Now it is done!" he cried. "Now she cannot escape; now she is crushed by the beams or burned up by the flames. Now it is done."

And he thought of the honor and glory of Ekeby which had had to be sacrificed to get her out of the world,—the magnificent halls, where so much happiness had dwelt, the tables which had groaned under dainty dishes, the precious old furniture, silver and china, which could never be replaced—

And then he sprang up with a cry. His fire-wheel, his sun, the model on which everything depended, had he not put it under the stairs to cause the fire?

Kevenhüller looked down on himself, paralyzed with dismay.

"Am I going mad?" he said. "How could I do such a thing?"

At the same moment the door of the workshop opened and the wood-nymph walked in.

She stood on the threshold, smiling and fair. Her green dress had neither hole nor stain, no smoke darkened her yellow hair. She was just as he had seen her in the market-place at Karlstad in his young days; her tail hung between her feet, and she had all the wildness and fragrance of the wood about her.

"Ekeby is burning," she said, and laughed.

Kevenhüller had the sledge-hammer lifted and meant to throw it at her head, but then he saw that she had his fire-wheel in her hand.

"See what I have saved for you," she said.

Kevenhüller threw himself on his knees before her.

"You have broken my carriage, you have rent my wings, and you have ruined my life. Have grace, have pity on me!"

She climbed up on the bench and sat there, just as young and mischievous as when he saw her first.

"I see that you know who I am," she said.

"I know you, I have always known you," said the unfortunate man; "you are genius. But set me free! Take back your gift! Let me be an ordinary person! Why do you persecute me? Why do you destroy me?"

"Madman," said the wood-nymph, "I have never wished you any harm. I gave you a great reward; but I can also take it from you if you wish. But consider well. You will repent it."

"No, no!" he cried; "take from me the power of working wonders!"

"First, you must destroy this," she said, and threw the fire-wheel on the ground in front of him.

He did not hesitate. He swung the sledgehammer over the shining sun; sparks flew about the room, splinters and flames danced about him, and then his last wonder lay in fragments.

"Yes, so I take my gift from you," said the wood-nymph. As she stood in the door and the glare from the fire streamed over her, he looked at her for the last time. More beautiful than ever before, she seemed to him, and no longer malicious, only stern and proud.

"Madman," she said, "did I ever forbid you to let others copy your works? I only wished to protect the man of genius from a mechanic's labor."

Whereupon she went. Kevenhüller was insane for a couple of days. Then he was as usual again.

But in his madness he had burned down Ekeby. No one was hurt. Still, it was a great sorrow to the pensioners that the hospitable home, where they had enjoyed so many good things, should suffer such injury in their time.

CHAPTER XXI. BROBY FAIR

ON the first Friday in October the big Broby Fair begins, and lasts one week. It is the festival of the autumn. There is slaughtering and baking in every house; the new winter clothes are then worn for the first time; the brandy rations are doubled; work rests. There is feasting on all the estates. The servants and laborers draw their pay and hold long conferences over what they shall buy at the Fair. People from a distance come in small companies with knapsacks on their backs and staffs in their hands. Many are driving their cattle before them to the market. Small, obstinate young bulls and goats stand still and plant their forefeet, causing much vexation to their owners and much amusement to the by-standers. The guest-rooms at the manors are filled with guests, bits of news are exchanged, and the prices of cattle discussed.

And on the first Fair day what crowds swarm up Broby hill and over the wide market-place! Booths are set up, where the tradespeople spread out their wares. Rope-dancers, organ-grinders, and blind violin-players are everywhere, as well as fortunetellers, sellers of sweetmeats and of brandy. Beyond the rows of booths, vegetables and fruit are offered for sale by the gardeners from the big estates. Wide stretches are taken up by ruddy copper-kettles. It is plain, however, by the movement in the Fair, that there is want in Svartsjö and Bro and Löfvik and the other provinces about the Löfven: trade is poor at the booths. There is most bustle in the cattle-market, for many have to sell both cow and horse to be able to live through the winter.

It is a gay scene. If one only has money for a glass or two, one can keep up one's courage. And it is not only the brandy which is the cause of the merriment; when the people from the lonely wood-huts come down to the market-place with its seething masses, and hear the din of the screaming, laughing crowd, they become as if delirious with excitement.

Everybody who does not have to stay at home to look after the house and cattle has come to this Broby Fair. There are the pensioners from Ekeby and the peasants from Nygård, horse-dealers from Norway, Finns from the Northern forests, vagrants from the highways.

Sometimes the roaring sea gathers in a whirlpool, which turns about a middle point. No one knows what is at the centre, until a couple of policemen break a way through the crowd to put an end to a fight or to lift up an overturned cart.

Towards noon the great fight began. The peasants had got it into their heads that the tradespeople were using too short yardsticks, and it began with quarrelling and disturbance about the booths; then it turned to violence.

Every one knows that for many of those who for days had not seen anything but want and suffering, it was a pleasure to strike, it made no difference whom or what. And as soon as they see that a fight is going on they come rushing from all sides. The pensioners mean to break through to make peace after their fashion, and the tradesmen run to help one another.

Big Mons from Fors is the most eager in the game. He is drunk, and he is angry; he has thrown down a tradesman and has begun to beat him, but at his calls for help his comrades hurry to him and try to make Mons let him go. Then Mons sweeps the rolls of cloth from one of the counters, and seizes the top, which is a yard broad and five yards long and made of thick planks, and begins to brandish it as a weapon.

He is a terrible man, big Mons. It was he who kicked out a wall in the Filipstad-jail, he who could lift a boat out of the water and carry it on his shoulders. When he begins to strike about him with the heavy counter, every one flies before him. But he follows, striking right and left. For him it is no longer a question of friends or enemies: he only wants some one to hit, since he has got a weapon.

The people scatter in terror. Men and women scream and run. But how can the women escape when many of them have their children by the hand? Booths and carts stand in their way; oxen and cows, maddened by the noise, prevent their escape.

In a corner between the booths a group of women are wedged, and towards them the giant rages. Does he not see a tradesman in the midst of the crowd? He raises the plank and lets it fall. In pale, shuddering terror the women receive the attack, sinking under the deadly blow.

But as the board falls whistling down over them, its force is broken against a man's upstretched arms. One man has not sunk down, but raised himself above the crowd, one man has voluntarily taken the blow to save the many. The women and children are uninjured. One man has broken the force of the blow, but he lies now unconscious on the ground.

Big Mons does not lift up his board. He has met the man's eye, just as the counter struck his head, and it has paralyzed him. He lets himself be bound and taken away without resistance.

But the report flies about the Fair that big Mons has killed Captain Lennart. They say that he who had been the people's friend died to save the women and defenceless children.

And a silence falls on the great square, where life had lately roared at fever pitch: trade ceases, the fighting stops, the people leave their dinners.

Their friend is dead. The silent throngs stream towards the place where he has fallen. He lies stretched out on the ground quite unconscious; no wound is visible, but his skull seems to be flattened.

Some of the men lift him carefully up on to the counter which the giant has let fall. They think they perceive that he still lives.

"Where shall we carry him?" they ask one another.

"Home," answers a harsh voice in the crowd.

Yes, good men, carry him home! Lift him up on your shoulders and carry him home! He has been God's plaything, he has been driven like a feather before his breath. Carry him home!

That wounded head has rested on the hard barrack-bed in the prison, on sheaves of straw in the barn.

Let it now come home and rest on a soft pillow! He has suffered undeserved shame and torment, he has been hunted from his own door. He has been a wandering fugitive, following the paths of God where he could find them; but his promised land was that home whose gates God had closed to him. Perhaps his house stands open for one who has died to save women and children.

Now he does not come as a malefactor, escorted by reeling boon-companions; he is followed by a sorrowing people, in whose cottages he has lived while he helped their sufferings. Carry him home!

And so they do. Six men lift the board on which he lies on their shoulders and carry him away from the fair-grounds. Wherever they pass, the people move to one side and stand quiet; the men uncover their heads, the women courtesy as they do in church when God's name is spoken. Many weep and dry their eyes; others begin to tell what a man he had been,—so kind, so gay, so full of counsel and so religious. It is wonderful to see, too, how, as soon as one of his bearers gives out, another quietly comes and puts his shoulder under the board.

So Captain Lennart comes by the place where the pensioners are standing.

"I must go and see that he comes home safely," says Beerencreutz, and leaves his place at the roadside to follow the procession to Helgesäter. Many follow his example.

The fair-grounds are deserted. Everybody has to follow to see that Captain Lennart comes home.

When the procession reaches Helgesäter, the house is silent and deserted. Again the colonel's fist beats on the closed door. All the servants are at the Fair; the captain's wife is alone at home. It is she again who opens the door.

And she asks, as she asked once before,—

"What do you want?"

Whereupon the colonel answers, as he answered once before,—

"We are here with your husband."

She looks at him, where he stands stiff and calm as usual. She looks at the bearers behind him, who are weeping, and at all that mass of people. She stands there on the steps and looks into hundreds of weeping eyes, who stare sadly up at her. Last she looks at her husband, who lies stretched out on the bier, and she presses her hand to her heart. "That is his right face," she murmurs.

Without asking more, she bends down, draws back a bolt, opens the hall-doors wide, and then goes before the others into the bedroom.

The colonel helps her to drag out the big bed and shake up the pillows, and so Captain Lennart is once more laid on soft down and white linen.

"Is he alive?" she asks.

"Yes," answers the colonel.

"Is there any hope?"

"No. Nothing can be done."

There was silence for a while; then a sudden thought comes over her.

"Are they weeping for his sake, all those people?"

"Yes."

"What has he done?"

"The last thing he did was to let big Mons kill him to save women and children from death."

Again she sits silent for a while and thinks.

"What kind of a face did he have, colonel, when he came home two months ago?"

The colonel started. Now he understands; now at last he understands.

"Gösta had painted him."

"So it was on account of one of your pranks that I shut him out from his home? How will you answer for that, colonel?"

Beerencreutz shrugged his broad shoulders.

"I have much to answer for."

"But I think that this must be the worst thing you have done."

"Nor have I ever gone a heavier way than that to-day up to Helgesäter. Moreover, there are two others who are guilty in this matter."

"Who?"

"Sintram is one, you yourself are the other. You are a hard woman. I know that many have tried to speak to you of your husband."

"It is true," she answers.

Then she begs him to tell her all about that evening at Broby.

He tells her all he can remember, and she listens silently. Captain Lennart lies still unconscious on the bed. The room is full of weeping people; no one thinks of shutting out that mourning crowd. All the doors stand open, the stairs and the halls are filled with silent, grieving people; far out in the yard they stand in close masses.

When the colonel has finished, she raises her voice and says,—

"If there are any pensioners here, I ask them to go. It is hard for me to see them when I am sitting by my husband's death-bed."

Without another word the colonel rises and goes out. So do Gösta Berling and several of the other pensioners who had followed Captain Lennart. The people move aside for the little group of humiliated men.

When they are gone the captain's wife says: "Will some of them who have seen my husband during this time tell me where he has lived, and what he has done?" Then they begin to give testimony of Captain Lennart to his wife, who has misjudged him and sternly hardened her heart against him.

It lasted a long time before they all were done. All through the twilight and the evening they stand and speak; one after another steps forward and tells of him to his wife, who would not hear his name mentioned.

Some tell how he found them on a sick-bed and cured them. There are wild brawlers whom he has tamed. There are mourners whom he has cheered, drunkards whom he had led to sobriety. Every one who had been in unbearable distress had sent a message to God's wayfarer, and he had helped them, or at least he had waked hope and faith.

Out in the yard the crowd stands and waits. They know what is going on inside: that which is said aloud by the death-bed is whispered from man to man outside. He who has something to say pushes gently forward. "Here is one who can bear witness," they say, and let him pass. And they step forward out of the darkness, give their testimony, and disappear again into the darkness.

"What does she say now?" those standing outside ask when some one comes out "What does she say?"

"She shines like a queen. She smiles like a bride. She has moved his arm-chair up to the bed and laid on it the clothes which she herself had woven for him."

But then a silence falls on the people. No one says it, all know it at the same time: "He is dying."

Captain Lennart opens his eyes and sees everything.

He sees his home, the people, his wife, his children, the clothes; and he smiles. But he has only waked to die. He draws a rattling breath and gives up the ghost.

Then the stories cease, but a voice takes up a death-hymn. All join in, and, borne on hundreds of strong voices, the song rises on high.

It is earth's farewell greeting to the departing soul.

CHAPTER XXII. THE FOREST COTTAGE

IT was many years before the pensioners' reign at Ekeby.

The shepherd's boy and girl played together in the wood, built houses with flat stones, and picked cloud-berries. They were both born in the wood. The wood was their home and mansion. They lived in peace with everything there.

The children looked upon the lynx and the fox as their watch-dogs, the weasel was their cat, hares and squirrels their cattle, owls and grouse sat in their bird-cage, the pines were their servants, and the young birch-trees guests at their feasts. They knew the hole where the viper lay curled up in his winter rest; and when they had bathed they had seen the water-snake come swimming through the clear water; but they feared neither snake nor wild creature; they belonged to the wood and it was their home. There nothing could frighten them.

Deep in the wood lay the cottage where the boy lived. A hilly wood-path led to it; mountains closed it in and shut out the sun; a bottomless swamp lay nearby and gave out the whole year round an icy mist Such a dwelling seemed far from attractive to the people on the plain.

The shepherd's boy and girl were some day to be married, live there in the forest cottage, and support themselves by the work of their hands. But before they were married, war passed over the land, and the boy enlisted. He came home again without wound or injured limb; but he had been changed for life by the campaign. He had seen too much of the world's wickedness and man's cruel activity against man. He could no longer see the good.

At first no one saw any change in him. With the love of his childhood he went to the clergyman and had the banns published. The forest cottage above Ekeby was their home, as they had planned long before; but it was not a happy home.

The wife looked at her husband as at a stranger. Since he had come from the wars, she could not recognize him. His laugh was hard, and he spoke but little. She was afraid of him.

He did no harm, and worked hard. Still he was not liked, for he thought evil of everybody. He felt himself like a hated stranger. Now the forest animals were his enemies. The mountain, which shut out the sun, and the swamp, which sent up the mist, were his foes. The forest is a terrible place for one who has evil thoughts.

He who will live in the wilderness should have bright memories. Otherwise he sees only murder and oppression among plants and animals, just as he had seen it before among men. He expects evil from everything he meets.

The soldier, Jan Hök, could not explain what was the matter with him; but he felt that nothing went well with him. There was little peace in his home. His sons who grew up there were strong, but wild. They were hardy and brave men, but they too lived at enmity with all men.

His wife was tempted by her sorrow to seek out the secrets of the wilderness. In swamp and thicket she gathered healing herbs. She could cure sickness, and give advice to those who were crossed in love. She won fame as a witch, and was shunned, although she did much good.

One day the wife tried to speak to her husband of his trouble.

"Ever since you went to the war," she said, "you have been so changed. What did they do to you there?"

Then he rose up, and was ready to strike her; and so it was every time she spoke of the war, he became mad with rage. From no one could he bear to hear the word war, and it soon became known. So people were careful of that subject.

But none of his brothers in arms could say that he had done more harm than others. He had fought like a good soldier. It was only all the dreadful things he had seen which had frightened him so that since then he saw nothing but evil. All his trouble came from the war. He thought that all nature hated him, because he had had a share in such things. They who knew more could console themselves that they had fought for fatherland and honor. What did he know of such things? He only felt that everything hated him because he had shed blood and done much injury.

When the major's wife was driven from Ekeby, he lived alone in his cottage. His wife was dead and his sons away. During the fairs his house was always full of guests. Black-haired, swarthy gypsies put up there. They like those best whom others avoid. Small, long-haired horses climbed up the wood path, dragging carts loaded with children and bundles of rags. Women, prematurely old, with features swollen by smoking and drinking, and men with pale, sharp faces and sinewy bodies followed the carts. When the gypsies came to the forest cottage, there was a merry life there. Brandy and cards and loud talking followed with them. They had much to tell of thefts and horse-dealing and bloody fights.

The Broby Fair began on a Friday, and then Captain Lennart was killed. Big Mons, who gave the death-blow, was son to the old man in the forest cottage. When the gypsies on Sunday afternoon sat together there, they handed old Jan Hök the brandy bottle oftener than usual, and talked to him of prison life and prison fare and trials; for they had often tried such things.

The old man sat on the chopping-block in the corner and said little. His big lack-lustre eyes stared at the crowd which filled the room. It was dusk, but the wood-fire lighted the room.

The door was softly opened and two women entered. It was the young Countess Elizabeth followed by the daughter of the Broby clergyman. Lovely and glowing, she came into the circle of light. She told them that Gösta Berling had not been seen at Ekeby since Captain Lennart died. She and her servant had searched for him in the wood the whole afternoon. Now she saw that there were men here who had much wandered, and knew all the paths. Had they seen him? She had come in to rest, and to ask if they had seen him.

It was a useless question. None of them had seen him.

They gave her a chair. She sank down on it and sat silent for a while. There was no sound in the room. All looked at her and wondered at her. At last she grew frightened at the silence, started, and tried to speak of indifferent things. She turned to the old man in the corner, "I think I have heard that you have been a soldier," she said. "Tell me something of the war!"

The silence grew still deeper. The old man sat as if he had not heard.

"It would be very interesting to hear about the war from some one who had been there himself," continued the countess; but she stopped short, for the Broby clergyman's daughter shook her head at her. She must have said something forbidden. Everybody was looking at her as if she had offended against the simplest rule of propriety. Suddenly a gypsy woman raised her sharp voice and asked: "Are you not she who has been countess at Borg?"

"Yes, I am."

"That was another thing than running about the wood after a mad priest."

The countess rose and said farewell. She was quite rested. The woman who had spoken followed her out through the door.

"You understand, countess," she said, "I had to say something; for it does not do to speak to the old man of war. He can't bear to hear the word. I meant well."

Countess Elizabeth hurried away, but she soon stopped. She saw the threatening wood, the dark mountain, and the reeking swamp. It must be terrible to live here for one whose soul is filled with evil memories. She felt compassion for the old man who had sat there with the dark gypsies for company.

"Anna Lisa," she said, "let us turn back! They were kind to us, but I behaved badly. I want to talk to the old man about pleasanter things."

And happy to have found some one to comfort, she went back to the cottage.

"I think," she said, "that Gösta Berling is wandering here in the wood, and means to take his own life. It is therefore important that he be soon found and prevented. I and my maid, Anna Lisa, thought we saw him sometimes, but then he disappeared. He keeps to that part of the mountain where the broom-girl was killed. I happened to think that I do not need to go way down to Ekeby to get help. Here sit many active men who easily could catch him."

"Go along, boys!" cried the gypsy woman. "When the countess does not hold herself too good to ask a service of the forest people, you must go at once."

The men rose immediately and went out to search.

Old Jan Hök sat still and stared before him with lustreless eyes. Terrifyingly gloomy and hard, he sat there. The young woman could think of nothing to say to him. Then she saw that a child lay sick on a sheaf of straw, and noticed that a woman had hurt her hand. Instantly she began to care for the sick. She was soon friends with the gossiping women, and had them show her the smallest children.

In an hour the men came back. They carried Gösta Berling bound into the room. They laid him down on the floor before the fire. His clothes were torn and dirty, his cheeks sunken, and his eyes wild. Terrible had been his ways during those days; he had lain on the damp ground; he had burrowed with his hands and face in bogs, dragged himself over rocks, forced his way through the thickest underbrush. Of his own will he had never come with the men; but they had overpowered and bound him.

When his wife saw him so, she was angry. She did not free his bound limbs; she let him lie where he was on the floor. With scorn she turned from him.

"How you look!" she said.

"I had never meant to come again before your eyes," he answered.

"Am I not your wife? Is it not my right to expect you to come to me with your troubles? In bitter sorrow I have waited for you these two days."

"I was the cause of Captain Lennart's misfortunes. How could I dare to show myself to you?"

"You are not often afraid, Gösta."

"The only service I can do you, Elizabeth, is to rid you of myself."

Unspeakable contempt flashed from under her frowning brows at him.

"You wish to make me a suicide's wife!"

His face was distorted.

"Elizabeth, let us go out into the silent forest and talk."

"Why should not these people hear us?" she cried, speaking in a shrill voice. "Are we better than any of them? Has anyone of them caused more sorrow and injury than we? They are the children of the forest, and of the highway; they are hated by every man. Let them hear how sin and sorrow also follows the lord of Ekeby, the beloved of all, Gösta Berling! Do you think your wife considers herself better than any one of them—or do you?"

He raised himself with difficulty onto his elbow, and looked at her with sudden defiance. "I am not such a wretch as you think."

Then she heard the story of those two days. The first day Gösta wandered about in the wood, driven by remorse. He could not bear to meet any one's eye. But he did not think of dying. He meant to journey to far distant lands. On Sunday, however, he came down from the hills and went to the Bro church. Once more he wished to see the people: the poor, hungry people whom he had dreamed of serving when he had sat by the Broby clergyman's pile of shame, and whom he had learned to love when he saw them disappear into the night with the dead broom-girl.

The service had begun when he came to the church. He crept up to the gallery, and looked down on the people. He had felt bitter agony. He had wanted to speak to them, to comfort them in their poverty and hopelessness. If he had only been allowed to speak in God's house, hopeless as he was, he would have found words of hope and salvation for them all.

Then he left the church, went into the sacristy, and wrote the message which his wife already knew. He had promised that work should be renewed at Ekeby, and grain distributed to those in greatest need. He had hoped that his wife and the pensioners would fulfil his promises when he was gone.

As he came out, he saw a coffin standing before the parish-hall. It was plain, put together in haste, but covered with black crape and wreaths. He knew that it was Captain Lennart's. The people had begged the captain's wife to hasten the funeral, so that all those who had come to the Fair could be at the burial.

He was standing and looking at the coffin, when a heavy hand was laid on his shoulder. Sintram had come up to him.

"Gösta," he said, "if you want to play a regular trick on a person, lie down and die. There is nothing more clever than to die, nothing which so deceives an honest man who suspects no harm. Lie you down and die, I tell you!"

Gösta listened with horror to what he said. Sin-tram complained of the failure of well-laid plans. He had wanted to see a waste about the shores of the Löfven. He had made the pensioners lords of the place; he had let the Broby clergyman impoverish the people; he had called forth the drought and the famine. At the Broby Fair the decisive blow was to have fallen. Excited by their misfortunes, the people should have turned to murder and robbery. Then there should have been lawsuits to beggar them. Famine, riot, and every kind of misfortune should have ravaged them. Finally, the country would have become so odious and detestable that no one could have lived there, and it would all have been Sintram's doing. It would have been his joy and pride, for he was evil-minded. He loved desert wastes and uncultivated fields. But this man who had known how to die at the right moment had spoiled it all for him.

Then Gösta asked him what would have been the good of it all.

"It would have pleased me, Gösta, for I am bad. I am the grizzly bear on the mountain; I am the snowstorm on the plain; I like to kill and to persecute. Away, I say, with people and their works! I don't like them. I can let them slip from between my

claws and cut their capers,—that is amusing too for a while; but now I am tired of play, Gösta, now I want to strike, now I want to kill and to destroy."

He was mad, quite mad. He began a long time ago as a joke with those devilish tricks, and now his maliciousness had taken the upper hand; now he thought he really was a spirit from the lower regions. He had fed and fostered the evil in him until it had taken possession of his soul. For wickedness can drive people mad, as well as love and brooding.

He was furious, and in his anger he began to tear the wreaths from off the coffin; but then Gösta Ber-ling cried: "Let the coffin be!"

"Well, well, well, so I shall not touch it! Yes; I shall throw my friend Lennart out on the ground and trample on his: wreaths. Do you not see what he has done to me? Do you not see in what a fine gray coach I am riding?"

And Gösta then saw that a couple of prison-vans with the sheriff and constables of the district stood and waited outside the church-yard wall.

"I ought to send Captain Lennart's wife thanks that she yesterday sat herself down to read through old papers in order to find proof against me in that matter of the powder, you know? Shall I not let her know that she would have done better to occupy herself with brewing and baking, than in sending the sheriff and his men after me? Shall I have nothing for the tears I have wept to induce Scharling to let me come here and read a prayer by my good friend's coffin?"

And he began again to drag on the crape,

Then Gösta Berling came close up to him and seized his arms.

"I will give anything to make you let the coffin alone," he said.

"Do what you like," said the madman. "Call if you like. I can always do something before the sheriff gets here. Fight with me, if you like. That will be a pleasing sight here by the church. Let us fight among the wreaths and palls."

"I will buy rest for the dead at any price. Take my life, take everything!"

"You promise much."

"You can prove it."

"Well, then, kill yourself!"

"I will do it; but first the coffin shall be safely under earth."

And so it was. Sintram took Gösta's oath that he would not be alive twelve hours after Captain Lennart was buried. "Then I know that you can never be good for anything," he said.

It was easy for Gösta Berling to promise. He was glad to be able to give his wife her liberty. Remorse had made him long for death. The only thing which troubled him was, that he had promised the major's wife not to-die as long as the Broby clergyman's daughter was a servant at Ekeby. But Sintram said that she could no longer be considered as servant, since she had inherited her father's fortune. Gösta objected that the Broby clergyman had hidden his treasures so well that no one had been able to find them. Then Sintram laughed and said that they were hidden up among the pigeons' nests in the church tower. Thereupon he went away. And Gösta went back to the wood again. It seemed best to him to die at the place where the broom-girl had been killed. He had wandered there the whole after-noon. He had seen his wife in the wood; and then he had not had the strength to kill himself.

All this he told his wife, while he lay bound on the floor of the cottage.

"Oh," she said sadly, when he had finished, "how familiar it all is! Always ready to thrust your hands into the fire, Gösta, always ready to throw yourself away! How noble such things seemed to me once! How I now value calmness and good sense! What good did you do the dead by such a promise? What did it matter if Sintram had overturned the coffin and torn off the crape? It would have been picked up again; there would have been found new crape, new wreaths. If you had laid your hand on that good man's coffin, there before Sintram's eyes, and sworn to live to help those poor people whom he wished to ruin, that I should have commended. If you had thought, when you saw the people in the church: 'I will help them; I will make use of all my strength to help them,' and not laid that burden on your weak wife, and on old men with failing strength, I should also have commended that."

Gösta Berling lay silent for a while.

"We pensioners are not free men," he said at last "We have promised one another to live for pleasure, and only for pleasure. Woe to us all if one breaks his word!"

"Woe to you," said the countess, indignantly, "if you shall be the most cowardly of the pensioners, and slower to improve than any of them. Yesterday afternoon the whole eleven sat in the pensioners' wing, and they were very sad. You were gone; Captain Lennart was gone. The glory and honor of Ekeby were gone. They left the toddy tray untouched; they would not let me see them. Then the maid, Anna Lisa, who stands here, went up to them. You know she is an energetic little woman who for years has struggled despairingly against neglect and waste.

"'To-day I have again been at home and looked for father's money,' she said to the pensioners; 'but I have not found anything. All the debts are paid, and the drawers and closets are empty.'

"'We are sorry for you, Anna Lisa,' said Beerencreutz.

"'When the major's wife left Ekeby,' continued Anna Lisa, 'she told me to see after her house. And if I had found father's money, I would have built up Ekeby. But as I did not find anything else to take away with me, I took father's shame heap; for great shame awaits me when my mistress comes again and asks me what I have done with Ekeby.'

"'Don't take so much to heart what is not your fault, Anna Lisa,' said Beerencreutz again.

"'But I did not take the shame heap for myself alone,' said Anna Lisa. 'I took it also for your reckoning, good gentlemen. Father is not the only one who has been the cause of shame and injury in this world.'

"And she went from one to the other of them, and laid down some of the dry sticks before each. Some of them swore, but most of them let her go on. At last Beerencreutz said, calmly:—

"'It is well. We thank you. You may go now.' When she had gone, he struck the table with his clenched hand till the glasses rang.

"'From this hour,' he said, 'absolutely sober. Brandy shall never again cause me such shame.' Thereupon he rose and went out.

"They followed him by degrees, all the others. Do you know where they went, Gösta? Well, down to the river, to the point where the mill and the forge had stood, and there they began to work. They began to drag away the logs and stones and clear the place. The old men have had a hard time. Many of them have had sorrow. Now they can no longer bear the disgrace of having ruined Ekeby. I know too well that you pensioners are ashamed to work; but now the others have taken that shame on them. Moreover, Gösta, they mean to send Anna Lisa up to the major's wife to bring her home. But you, what are you doing?"

He found still an answer to give her.

"What do you want of me, of a dismissed priest? Cast off by men, hateful to God?"

"I too have been in the Bro church to-day, Gösta. I have a message to you from two women. 'Tell Gösta,' said Marianne Sinclair, 'that a woman does not like to be ashamed of him she has loved.' 'Tell Gösta,' said Anna Stjärnhök, 'that all is now well with me. I manage my own estates. I do not think of love, only of work. At Berga too they have conquered the first bitterness of their sorrow. But we all grieve for Gösta. We believe in him and pray for him; but when, when will he be a man?'

"Do you hear? Are you cast off by men?" continued the countess. "Your misfortune is that you have been met with too much love. Women and men have loved you. If you only jested and laughed, if you only sang and played, they have forgiven you everything. Whatever it has pleased you to do has seemed right to them. And you dare to call yourself an outcast! Or are you hateful to God?

Why did you not stay and see Captain Lennart's burial?

"As he had died on a Fair day, his fame had gone far and wide. After the service, thousands of people came up to the church. The funeral procession was formed by the town hall. They were only waiting for the old dean. He was ill and had not preached; but he had promised to come to Captain Lennart's funeral. And at last he came, with head sunk on his breast, and dreaming his dreams, as he is wont to do now in his old age, and placed himself at the head of the procession. He noticed nothing unusual He walked on the familiar path and did not look up. He read the prayers, and threw the earth on the coffin, and still noticed nothing. But then the sexton began a hymn. Hundreds and hundreds of voices joined in. Men, women, and children sang. Then the dean awoke from his dreams. He passed his hand over his eyes and stepped up on the mound of earth to look. Never had he seen such a crowd of mourners. All were singing; all had tears in their eyes,—all were mourning.

"Then the old dean began to tremble. What should he say to these people? He must say a word to comfort them.

"When the song ceased, he stretched out his arms over the people.

"'I see that you are mourning,' he said; 'and sorrow is heavier to bear for one who has long to live than for me who will soon be gone.'

"He stopped dismayed. His voice was too weak, and words failed him.

"But he soon began again. His voice had regained its youthful strength, and his eyes glowed.

"First, he told all he knew of God's wayfarer. Then he reminded us that no outward polish nor great ability had made that man so honored as he now was, but only that he had always followed God's ways. And now he asked us to do the same. Each should love the other, and help him. Each should think well of the other. And he explained everything which had happened this year. He said it was a preparation for the time of love and happiness which now was to be expected.

"And we all felt as if we had heard a prophet speak. All wished to love one another; all wished to be good.

"He lifted his eyes and hands and proclaimed peace in the neighborhood. Then he called on a helper for the people. 'Some one will come,' he said. 'It is not God's will that you shall perish. God will find some one who will feed the hungry and lead you in His ways.'

"Then we all thought of you, Gösta. We knew that the dean spoke of you. The people who had heard your message went home talking of you. And you wandered here in the wood and wanted to die! The people are waiting for you, Gösta. In all the cottages they are sitting and saying that, as the mad priest at Ekeby is going to help them, all will be well. You are their hero, Gösta.

"Yes, Gösta, it is certain that the old man meant you, and that ought to make you want to live. But I, Gösta, who am your wife, I say to you that you shall go and do your duty. You shall not dream of being sent by God,—any one can be that. You shall work without any heroics; you shall not shine and astonish; you shall so manage that your name is not too often heard on the people's lips. But think well before you take back your promise to Sintram. You have now got a certain right to die, and life ought not to offer you many attractions. There was a time when my wish was to go home to Italy, Gösta. It seemed too much happiness for me, a sinner, to be your wife, and be with you through life. But now I shall stay. If you dare to live, I shall stop; but do not await any joy from that. I shall force you to follow the weary path of duty. You need never expect words of joy or hope from me. Can a heart which has suffered like mine love again? Tearless and joyless I shall walk beside you. Think well, Gösta, before you choose to live. We shall go the way of penance."

She did not wait for his answer. She nodded to Anna Lisa and went. When she came out into the wood, she began to weep bitterly, and wept until she reached Ekeby. Arrived there, she remembered that she had forgotten to talk of gladder things than war to Jan Hök, the soldier.

In the cottage there was silence when she was gone.

"Glory and honor be to the Lord God!" said the old soldier, suddenly.

They looked at him. He had risen and was looking eagerly about him.

"Wicked, wicked has everything been," he said. "Everything T have seen since I got my eyes opened has been wicked. Bad men, bad women! Hate and anger in forest and plain! But she is good. A good woman has stood in my house. When I am sitting here alone, I shall remember her. She shall be with me in the wood."

He bent down over Gösta, untied his fetters, and lifted him up. Then he solemnly took his hand.

"Hateful to God," he said and nodded. "That is just it. But now you are not any more; nor I either, since she has been in my house. She is good."

The next day old Jan Hök came to the bailiff Scharling. "I will carry my cross," he said. "I have been a bad man, therefore I have had bad sons."And he asked to be allowed to go to prison instead of his son; but that could not be.

The best of old stories is the one which tells of how he followed his son, walking beside the prison van; how he slept outside his cell; how he did not forsake him until he had suffered his punishment.

CHAPTER XXIII. MARGARETA CELSING

A FEW days before Christmas the major's wife started on her journey down to the Löfsjö district; but it was not till Christmas Eve that she came to Ekeby. During the whole journey she was ill. Yet, in spite of cold and fever, people had never seen her in better spirits nor heard her speak more friendly words.

The Broby clergyman's daughter, who had been with her in the Älfdal forests ever since October, sat by her side in the sledge and wished to hasten the journey; but she could not prevent the old woman from stopping the horses and calling every wayfarer up to her to ask for news.

"How is it with you all here in Löfsjö?" she asked.

"All is well," was the answer. "Better times are coming. The mad priest there at Ekeby and his wife help us all."

"A good time has come," answered another. "Sintram is gone. The Ekeby pensioners are working. The Broby clergyman's money is found in the Bro church-tower. There is so much that the glory and power of Ekeby can be restored with it. There is enough too to get bread for the hungry."

"Our old dean has waked to new life and strength," said a third. "Every Sunday he speaks to us of the coming of the Kingdom of God."

And the major's wife drove slowly on, asking every one she met: "How is it here? Do you not suffer from want here?"

And the fever and the stabbing pain in her breast were assuaged, when they answered her: "There are two good and rich women here, Marianne Sinclair and Anna Stjärnhök. They help Gösta Berling to go from house to house and see that no one is starving. And no more brandy is made now."

It was as if the major's wife had sat in the sledge and listened to a long divine service. She had come to a blessed land. She saw old, furrowed faces brighten, when they spoke of the time which had come. The sick forgot their pains to tell of the day of joy.

"We all want to be like the good Captain Lennart," they said. "We all want to be good. We want to believe good of every one. We will not injure any one. It shall hasten the coming of God's Kingdom."

She found them all filled with the same spirit. On the larger estates free dinners were given to those who were in greatest need. All who had work to be done had it done now.

She had never felt in better health than when she sat there and let the cold air stream into her aching breast. She could not drive by a single house without stopping and asking.

"Everything is well," they all said. "There was great distress, but the good gentlemen from Ekeby help us. You will be surprised at everything which has been done there. The mill is almost ready, and the smithy is at work, and the burned-down house ready for the roof."

Ah, it would only last a short time! But still it was good to return to a land where they all helped one another and all wished to do good. The major's wife felt that she could now forgive the pensioners, and she thanked God for it.

"Anna Lisa," she said, "I feel as if I had already come into the heaven of the blessed."

When she at last reached Ekeby, and the pensioners hurried to help her out of the sledge, they could hardly recognize her, for she was as kind and gentle as their own young countess. The older ones, who had seen her as a young girl, whispered to one another: "It is not the major's wife at Ekeby; it is Margareta Celsing who has come back."

Great was the pensioners' joy to see her come so kind and so free from all thoughts of revenge; but it was soon changed to grief when they found how ill she was. She had to be carried immediately into the guest-room in the wing, and put to bed. But on the threshold she turned and spoke to them.

"It has been God's storm," she said,—"God's storm. I know now that it has all been for the best!"

Then the door to the sick-room closed, and they never saw her again.

There is so much to say to one who is dying. The words throng to the lips when one knows that in the next room lies one whose ears will soon be closed for always. "Ah, my friend, my friend," one wants to say, "can you forgive? Can you believe that I have loved you in spite of everything! Ah, my friend, thanks for all the joy you have given me!"

That will one say and so much, much more.

But the major's wife lay in a burning fever, and the voices of the pensioners could not reach her. Would she never know how they had worked, how they had taken up her work?

After a little while the pensioners went down to the smithy. There all work was stopped; but they threw new coal and new ore into the furnace, and made ready to smelt. They did not call the smith, who had gone home to celebrate Christmas, but worked themselves at the forge. If the major's wife could only live until the hammer got going, it would tell her their story.

Evening came and then night, while they worked. Several of them thought, how strange it was that they should again celebrate the night before Christmas in the smithy.

Kevenhüller, who had been the architect of the mill and the smithy, and Christian Bergh stood by the forge and attended to the melting iron. Gösta and Julius were the stokers. Some of the others sat on the anvil under the raised hammer, and others sat on coal-carts and piles of pig-iron. Löwenborg was talking to Eberhard, the philosopher, who sat beside him on the anvil.

"Sintram dies to-night," he said.

"Why just to-night?" asked Eberhard.

"You know that we made an agreement last year. Now we have done nothing which has been ungentle-manly, and therefore he has lost."

"You who believe in such things know very well that we have done a great deal which has been un-gentlemanly. First, we did not help the major's wife; second, we began to work; third, it was not quite right that Gösta Berling did not kill himself, when he had promised."

"I have thought of that too," answered Löwen-borg; "but my opinion is, that you do not rightly comprehend the matter. To act with the thought of our own mean advantage was forbidden us; but not to act as love or honor or our own salvation demanded. I think that Sintram has lost."

"Perhaps you are right."

"I tell you that I know it. I have heard his sleigh-bells the whole evening, but they are not real bells. We shall soon have him here."

And the little old man sat and stared through the smithy door, which stood open, out at the bit of blue sky studded with stars which showed through it.

After a little while he started up.

"Do you see him?" he whispered. "There he comes creeping. Do you not see him in the doorway?"

"I see nothing," replied Eberhard. "You are sleepy, that is the whole story."

"I saw him so distinctly against the sky. He had on his long wolfskin coat and fur cap. Now he is over there in the dark, and I cannot see him. Look, now he is up by the furnace. He is standing close to Christian Bergh; but Christian seems not to see him. Now he is bending down and is throwing something into the fire. Oh, how wicked he looks! Take care, friends, take care!"

As he spoke, a tongue of flame burst out of the furnace, and covered the smiths and their assistants with cinders and sparks. No one, however, was injured.

"He wants to be revenged," whispered Löwenborg.

"You too are mad!" cried Eberhard. "You ought to have had enough of such things."

"Do you not see how he is standing there by the prop and grinning at us? But, verily, I believe that he has unfastened the hammer."

He started up and dragged Eberhard with him. The second after the hammer fell thundering down onto the anvil. It was only a clamp which had given way; but Eberhard and Löwenborg had narrowly escaped death.

"You see that he has no power over us," said Löwenborg, triumphantly. "But it is plain that he wants to be revenged."

And he called Gösta Berling to him.

"Go up to the women, Gösta. Perhaps he will show himself to them too. They are not so used as I to seeing such things. They may be frightened. And take care of yourself, Gösta, for he has a special grudge against you, and perhaps he has power over you on account of that promise."

Afterwards they heard that Löwenborg had been right, and that Sintram had died that night. Some said that he had hanged himself in his cell. Others believed that the servants of justice secretly had him killed, for the trial seemed to be going well for him, and it would never do to let him out again among the people in Löfsjö. Still others thought that a dark visitor had driven up in a black carriage, drawn by black horses, and had taken him out of prison. And Löwenborg was not the only one who saw him that night. He was also seen at Fors and in Ulrika Dillner's dreams. Many told how he had shown himself to them, until Ulrika Dillner moved his body to the Bro churchyard. She also had the evil servants sent away from Fors and introduced there good order. After that it was no longer haunted.

It is said that before Gösta Berling reached the house, a stranger had come to the wing and had left a letter for the major's wife. No one knew the messenger, but the letter was carried in and laid on the table beside the sick woman. Soon after she became unexpectedly better; the fever decreased, the pain abated, and she was able to read the letter.

The old people believe that her improvement depended on the influence of the powers of darkness. Sintram and his friends would profit by the reading of that letter.

It was a contract written in blood on black paper. The pensioners would have recognized it. It was composed on the last Christmas Eve in the smithy at Ekeby.

And the major's wife lay there now and read that since she had been a witch, and had sent pensioners' souls to hell, she was condemned to lose Ekeby. That and other similar absurdities she read. She examined the date and signatures, and found the following note beside Gösta's name: "Because the major's wife has taken advantage of my weakness to tempt me away from honest work, and to keep me as pensioner at Ekeby, because she has made me Ebba Dohna's murderer by betraying to her that I am a dismissed priest, I sign my name."

The major's wife slowly folded the paper and put it in its envelope. Then she lay still and thought over what she had learned. She understood with bitter pain that such was the people's thought of her. She was a witch and a sorceress to all those whom she had served, to whom she had given work and bread. This was her reward. They could not believe anything better of an adulteress.

Her thoughts flew. Wild anger and a longing for revenge flamed up in her fever-burning brain. She had Anna Lisa, who with Countess Elizabeth tended her, send a message to Högfors to the manager and overseer. She wished to make her will.

Again she lay thinking. Her eyebrows were drawn together, her features were terribly distorted by suffering.

"You are very ill," said the countess, softly.

"Yes, more ill than ever before."

There was silence again, but then the major's wife spoke in a hard, harsh voice:—

"It is strange to think that you, too, countess, you whom every one loves, are an adulteress."

The young woman started.

"Yes, if not in deed, yet in thoughts and desire, and that makes no difference. I who lie here feel that it makes no difference."

"I know it!"

"And yet you are happy now. You may possess him you loved without sin. That black spectre does not stand between you when you meet. You may belong to one another before the world, love one another, go side by side through life."

"Oh, madame, madame!"

"How can you dare to stay with him?" cried the old woman, with increasing violence. "Repent, repent in time! Go home to your father and mother, before they come and curse you. Do you dare to consider Gösta Berling your husband? Leave him! I shall give him Ekeby. I shall give him power and glory. Do you dare to share that with him? Do you dare to accept happiness and honor? I did not dare to. Do you remember what happened to me? Do you remember the Christmas dinner at Ekeby? Do you remember the cell in the bailiff's house?"

"Oh, madame, we sinners go here side by side without happiness. I am here to see that no joy shall find a home by our hearth. Do you think I do not long for my home? Oh, bitterly do I long for the protection and support of home; but I shall never again enjoy them. Here I shall live in fear and trembling, knowing that everything I do leads to sin and sorrow, knowing that if I help one, I ruin another. Too weak and foolish for the life here, and yet forced to live it, bound by an everlasting penance."

"With such thoughts we deceive our hearts," cried the major's wife; "but it is weakness. You will not leave him, that is the only reason."

Before the countess could answer, Gösta Berling came into the room.

"Come here, Gösta," said the major's wife instantly, and her voice grew still sharper and harder. "Come here, you whom everybody praises. You shall now hear what has happened to your old friend whom you allowed to wander about the country, despised and forsaken.

"I will first tell you what happened last spring, when I came home to my mother, for you ought to know the end of that story.

"In March I reached the iron-works in the Alfdal forest, Gösta. Little better than a beggar I looked. They told me that my mother was in the dairy. So I went there, and stood for a long while silent at the door. There were long shelves round about the room, and on them stood shining copper pans filled with milk. And my mother, who was over ninety years old, took down pan after pan and skimmed off the cream. She was active enough, the old woman; but I saw well enough how hard it was for her to straighten up her back to reach the pans. I did not know if she had seen me; but after a while she spoke to me in a curious, shrill voice.

"'So everything has happened to you as I wished,' she said. I wanted to speak and to ask her to forgive me, but it was a waste of trouble. She did not hear a word of it,—she was stone-deaf. But after a while she spoke again: 'You can come and help me,' she said.

"Then I went in and skimmed the milk. I took the pans in order, and put everything in its place, and skimmed just deep enough, and she was pleased. She had never been able to trust any of the maids to skim the milk; but I knew of old how she liked to have it.

"'Now you can take charge of this work,' she said. And then I knew that she had forgiven me.

"And afterwards all at once it seemed as if she could not work any more. She sat in her arm-chair and slept almost all day. She died two weeks before Christmas. I should have liked to have come before, Gösta, but I could not leave her."

She stopped. She began to find breathing difficult; but she made an effort and went on:—

"It is true, Gösta, that I wished to keep you near me at Ekeby. There is something about you which makes every one rejoice to be with you. If you had shown a wish to be a settled man, I would have given you much power. I always hoped that you would find a good wife. First, I thought that it would be Marianne Sinclair, for I saw that she loved you already, when you lived as wood-cutter in the wood. Then I thought that it would be Ebba Dohna, and one day I drove over to Borg and told her that if she would have you for husband, I would leave you Ekeby in my will. If I did wrong in that, you must forgive me."

Gösta was kneeling by the bed with his face hidden in the blankets, and was moaning bitterly.

"Tell me, Gösta, how you mean to live? How shall you support your wife? Tell me that You know that I have always wished you well." And Gösta answered her smiling, while his heart almost burst with pain.

"In the old days, when I tried to be a laborer here at Ekeby, you gave me a cottage to live in, and it is still mine. This autumn I have put it quite in order. Löwenborg has helped me, and we have whitewashed the ceilings and hung the walls with paper and painted them. The inner little room Löwenborg calls the countess's boudoir, and he has gone through all the farm-houses round about for furniture, which has come there from manor-house auctions. He has bought them, so that there we have now high-backed armchairs and chests of drawers with shining mountings. But in the outer big room stands the young wife's weaving-loom and my lathe. Household utensils and all kinds of things are there, and there Löwenborg and I have already sat many evenings and talked of how the young countess and I will have it in the cottage. But my wife did not know it till now. We wanted to tell her when we should leave Ekeby."

"Go on, Gösta."

"Löwenborg was always saying that a maid was needed in the house. 'In the summer it is lovely here in the birch grove,' he used to say; 'but in winter it will be too lonely for the young wife. You will have to have a maid, Gösta.'

"And I agreed with him, but I did not know how I could afford to keep one. Then he came one day and carried down his music, and his table with the painted keyboard, and put it in the cottage. 'It is you, Löwenborg, who are going to be the maid,' I said to him. He answered that he would be needed. Did I mean the young countess to cook the food, and to carry wood and water? No, I had not meant her to do anything at all, as long as I had a pair of arms to work with. But he still thought that it would be best if there were two of us, so that she might sit the whole day on her sofa and embroider. I could never know how much waiting upon such a little woman needed, he said."

"Go on," said the major's wife. "It eases my pain. Did you think that your young countess would be willing to live in a cottage?"

He wondered at her scornful tone, but continued:

"No, I did not dare to think it; but it would have been so perfect if she had been willing. It is thirty miles from any doctor. She, who has a light hand and a tender heart, would have had work enough to tend wounds and allay fevers. And I thought that everybody in trouble would find the way to the lady mistress in the forest cottage. There is so much distress among the poor which kind words and a gentle heart can help."

"But you yourself, Gösta Berling?"

"I shall have my work at the carpenter's bench and lathe. I shall hereafter live my own life. If my wife will not follow me, I cannot help it. If some one should offer me all the riches of the universe, it would not tempt me. I want to live my own life. Now I shall be and remain a poor man among the peasants, and help them with whatever I can. They need some one to play the polka for them at weddings and at Christmas; they need some one to write letters to their distant sons,—and that some one I will be. But I must be poor."

"It will be a gloomy life for you, Gösta."

"Oh, no, it would not be if we were but two who kept together. The rich and happy would come to us as well as the poor. It would be gay enough in our cottage. Our guests would not care if the food was cooked right before their eyes, or be shocked that two must eat from the same plate."

"And what would be the good of it all, Gösta? What praise would you win?"

"Great would be my reward if the poor would remember me for a year or two after my death. I should have done some good if I had planted a couple of apple-trees at the house-corners, if I had taught the country fiddlers some of the old tunes, and if the shepherd children could have learnt a few good songs to sing in the wood-paths.

"You can believe me, I am the same mad Gösta Berling that I was before. A country fiddler is all I can be, but that is enough. I have many sins to atone for. To weep and to repent is not for me. I shall give the poor pleasure, that is my penance."

"Gösta," said the major's wife, "it is too humble a life for a man with your powers. I will give you Ekeby."

"Oh," he cried in terror, "do not make me rich! Do not put such duties upon me! Do not part me from the poor!"

"I will give Ekeby to you and the pensioners," repeated the major's wife. "You are a capable man, Gösta, whom the people bless. I say like my mother, 'You shall take charge of this work!'"

"No, we could not accept it,—we who have misjudged you and caused you such pain!"

"I will give you Ekeby, do you hear?"

She spoke bitterly and harshly, without kindness. He was filled with dismay.

"Do not tempt the old men! It would only make them idlers and drunkards again. God in Heaven, rich pensioners! What would become of us!"

"I will give you Ekeby, Gösta; but then you must promise to set your wife free. Such a delicate little woman is not for you. She has had to suffer too much here in the land of the bear. She is longing for her bright native country. You shall let her go. That is why I give you Ekeby."

But then Countess Elizabeth came forward to the major's wife and knelt by the bed.

"I do not long any more. He who is my husband has solved the problem, and found the life I can live. No longer shall I need to go stern and cold beside him, and remind him of repentance and atonement. Poverty and want and hard work will do that. The paths which lead to the poor and sick I can follow without sin. I am no longer afraid of the life here in the north. But do not make him rich; then I do not dare to stay."

The major's wife raised herself in the bed.

"You demand happiness for yourselves," she cried, and threatened them with clenched fists,—"happiness and blessing. No, let Ekeby be the pensioners', that they may be ruined. Let man and wife be parted, that they may be ruined! I am a witch, I am a sorceress, I shall incite you to evil-doing. I shall be what my reputation is."

She seized the letter and flung it in Gösta's face. The black paper fluttered out and fell on the floor. Gösta knew it too well.

"You have sinned against me, Gösta. You have misjudged one who has been a second mother to you. Do you dare to refuse your punishment? You shall accept Ekeby, and it shall ruin you, for you are weak. You shall send home your wife, so that there will be no one to save you. You shall die with a name as hated as mine. Margareta Celsing's obituary is that of a witch. Yours shall be that of a spendthrift and an oppressor of the poor."

She sank back on the pillows, and all was still. Through the silence rang a muffled blow, now one and then another. The sledge-hammer had begun its far-echoing work.

"Listen," said Gösta Berling, "so sounds Margareta Celsing's obituary! That is not a prank of drunken pensioners; that is the song of the victory of labor, raised in honor of a good, old worker. Do you hear what the hammer says? 'Thanks,' it says; 'thanks for good work; thanks for bread, which you have given the poor; thanks for roads, which you have opened; thanks for districts, which you have cultivated! Thanks for pleasure, with which you have filled your halls!'—'Thanks,' it says, 'and sleep in peace! Your work shall live and continue. Your house shall always be a home for happy labor.'—'Thanks,' it says, 'and do not judge us who have sinned! You who are now starting on the journey to the regions of peace, think gentle thoughts of us who still live.'"

Gösta ceased, but the sledge-hammer went on speaking. All the voices which had ever spoken kindly to the major's wife were mingled with the ring of the hammer. Gradually her features relaxed, as if the shadow of death had fallen over her.

Anna Lisa came in and announced that the gentlemen from Högfors had come. The major's wife let them go. She would not make any will.

"Oh, Gösta Berling, man of many deeds," she said, "so you have conquered once more. Bend down and let me bless you!"

The fever returned with redoubled strength. The death-rattle began. The body toiled through dreary suffering; but the spirit soon knew nothing of it. It began to gaze into the heaven which is opened for the dying.

So an hour passed, and the short death-struggle was over. She lay there so peaceful and beautiful that those about her were deeply moved.

"My dear old mistress," said Gösta, "so have I seen you once before. Now has Margareta Celsing come back to life. Now she will never again yield to the major's wife at Ekeby."

When the pensioners came in from the forge, they were met by the news of Margareta Celsing's death.

"Did she hear the hammer?" they asked.

She had done so, and they could be satisfied.

They heard, too, that she had meant to give Ekeby to them; but that the will had never been drawn. That they considered a great honor, and rejoiced over it as long as they lived. But no one ever heard them lament over the riches they had lost.

It is also said that on that Christmas night Gösta Berling stood by his young wife's side and made his last speech to the pensioners. He was grieved at their fate when they now must all leave Ekeby. The ailments of old age awaited them. The old and worn-out find a cold welcome.

And so he spoke to them. Once more he called them old gods and knights who had risen up to bring pleasure into the land of iron. But he lamented that the pleasure garden where the butterfly-winged pleasure roves is filled with destructive caterpillars, and that its fruits are withered.

Well he knew that pleasure was a good to the children of the earth, and it must exist. But, like a heavy riddle, the question always lay upon the world, how a man could be both gay and good. The easiest thing and yet the hardest, he called it. Hitherto they had not been able to solve the problem. Now he wanted to believe that they had learned it, that they had all learned it during that year of joy and sorrow, of happiness and despair.

You dear old people! In the old days you gave me precious gifts. But what have I given you?

Perhaps it may gladden you that your names sound again in connection with the dear old places? May all the brightness which belonged to your life fall again over the tracts where you have lived! Borg still stands; Björne still stands; Ekeby still lies by lake Löfven, surrounded by falls and lake, by park and smiling meadows; and when one stands on the broad terraces, legends swarm about one like the bees of summer.

But, speaking of bees, let me tell one more old story. The little Ruster, who went as a drummer at the head of the Swedish army, when in 1813 it marched into Germany, could never weary of telling stories of that wonderful land in the south. The people there were as tall as church towers, the swallows were as big as eagles, the bees as geese.

"Well, but the bee-hives?"

"The bee-hives were like our ordinary bee-hives."

"How did the bees get in?"

"Well, that they had to look out for," said the little Ruster.

Dear reader, must I say the same? The giant bees of fancy have now swarmed about us for a year and a day; but how they are going to come into the bee-hive of fact, that they really must find out for themselves.

THE END

www.ingramcontent.com/pod-product-compliance
Lightning Source LLC
Chambersburg PA
CBHW030315180626
46810CB00003B/1092